BANDMANCE

Marci Viola

Bandmance
The Complete Series In One Volume

ISBN 979-8-218-94479-7
Ebook ISBN 979-8-218-94480-3

For film, TV, publishing, and foreign language rights, address Cindy Bullard:
cindy@birchliterary.com
Author Photo: Darrell Nutt

Misty Morn Publishing

Bandmance is dedicated to every musician with whom I've shared the stage. Thank you, thank you, thank you. Let's do it again tonight!

THEO

MILLIONS OF MEMES AGREE; MUSIC heals. And we need each other to make music. That's why we have the tough talks before we start rehearsal. This way, if it gets heated, no one can walk out. Afterward, we play, which reminds us that we're good together. Other full-time, working bands have meetings to resolve conflicts, but we're brutally honest and don't pull punches, so we call ours Band Beatings.

"Bands and chicks do not mix." Max accompanies his statement with brooding minor chords from his keyboard.

Our guitar player, Nico, focuses on tuning as he nods in agreement. "It's bandmageddon, man. Each of us can name a dozen bands that broke up within a year after adding a girl."

I warm up by playing a paradiddle sticking pattern on the drum pad that temporarily covers my snare. The exercise has the added benefit of releasing frustration. It sucks that Jimmy left before we had a replacement, but his departure provides an opportunity to reimagine our musicality and general appeal. I know what I'm proposing is the right move, regardless of the pushback. And I know convincing Nico and Max will be an uphill battle.

"What we really need is a dedicated sound man," Max says. "Emphasis on *man*."

"Nico does a great job running sound," I say calmly.

Max scoffs and rolls his eyes. "Yeah, that's why I can never hear myself."

"For fuck's sake. Buy the fucking in-ear monitors. You're the only one who doesn't have them and the only one who constantly bitches about not being able to hear yourself," Nico says sharply. "And I swear to God if you say the word *tinnitus*, I'll shove one of Theo's drumsticks into your ringing ear and pull it out the other side."

"Okay." I make a show of gripping my drumsticks more tightly. "Let's get back to the matter at hand. We've been told by numerous clubs that they would book us more if we had a girl. We have the chance to add a chick who sings her ass off and is also a working bass player. We loved Jimmy as a band brother, but he didn't sing lead. And, let's be honest, he wasn't exactly Jaco Pastorius. Maris brings her musicianship and experience while giving us the capability of expanding our originals."

"How long before one of us sleeps with her and makes it weird for everyone else? Or, worse yet, she breaks off with one of us and starts sleeping with someone else in the band?" Max asks.

"I love that you're comfortable talking about me like I'm not here. Makes me feel like one of the guys already." Maris plugs in her bass. "For the record, I have a boyfriend, and I don't date musicians. We band chicks know too much." Maris tilts her head and smiles. "Let's just play some of the songs Theo sent me and see how it goes. I'm auditioning you guys, too. If I'm leaving my band, I have to feel like it's a step up."

I let my hair fall forward to curtain the amusement on my face. Maris isn't going to take any shit from these guys. She earned her confidence, and she can hold her own among the best. After Jimmy eloped and quit, I started scoping out local bass players. When I went to see Maris play with Backyard Breeder, it was obvious that she's the powerhouse we need. It's true that females and bands are usually problematic, whether as groupies, girlfriends, wives, or band members. But when a chick has the music bug like we do, when she's a proven pro who understands the business and wants in anyway, she turns into a bro. It's rare, but it can work.

I blindsided Nico and Max by inviting her to audition, but that was the only way they were going to give her a listen. If temporarily pissing them off is the price of getting Maris in the band, so be it.

"Let's start with 'Coming Around'," I say in my gig voice. The bass line is pretty complicated, and I plan to let Maris solo instead of Nico to give her the chance to show off. I smack my sticks together as I count the intro and set the meter. "One, two, three ..."

MARIS

ARE THESE GUYS REVOLUTIONIZING THE Miami music scene? No. Are they better than the band I'm with now? Absolutely. More importantly, I see an opportunity to influence their music. I refuse to be a gimmick or a token female and that's what's happening with Backyard Breeder. They mostly play rock covers, which pays the bills, but it's not what I want to do. I like a funkier groove, and I want to collaborate on originals. Theo's band is *almost* awesome. They play ska, funk, and some mainstream stuff, but I'm here for the originals. I think I can help shape their sound. I want synergy. I want to build something from the ground up, and these guys are good enough to make some magic together.

When Theo approached me about auditioning, I wanted the lowdown from the dude I'd be replacing, so Theo gave me his number. Jimmy encouraged me to go for the job and assured me that Funkengroovin' was a great experience. He only moved on because he's entering a new phase of life. Playing with the guys now, I'm putting faces to names and seeing for myself what Jimmy was talking about.

Max, the keyboard player, is a little dorky, but he has mad skills. He's wearing a Berklee College of Music T-shirt, so that's probably where he got so good. I'd say he's technically better than ninety percent of the working piano players in South Florida. He should be playing for the Philharmonic or in a jazz ensemble, but those types of musicians don't have the female following that Nico and Theo do. Almost every dude I've ever played with has confessed to joining a band to get laid.

Nico sings lead and plays guitar. He's an intimidating presence and is dedicated to his craft. He's at least 6' 5" and muscular, with sandy colored hair and blue eyes that haven't settled on me since I walked in. Nico has a reputation for pulling chicks but shows zero interest in me as a female or as Funkengroovin's new bass player. Is that a terrible band name? We might have to change it. As I play "Coming Around", I try to lay down some hits for Nico to follow, and he falls in after hearing the pattern once. Maybe if he and I can have some fun together, he'll see the benefit of having me around.

Theo gives me the solo. I stretch it. I show off. Then, I call on Nico, and he takes over. He unleashes. Raises the bar. I hold the bottom down and stay out of the way while he shines. He closes his eyes while he plays, unlike Theo who stays focused on me and smiles encouragingly when our lines of sight cross.

Theo is a solid drummer and Jimmy said he's a good leader. He keeps the band running the same way he lays down its heartbeat … steadily. He books the gigs and handles the business side, which must be in his blood. Jimmy told me that Theo's father has businesses in Greece and Miami, which is why Theo has a two-story house on a canal to himself most of the time.

I don't want to seem nosy, but I can't help surveying my surroundings. We're in the first-floor master bedroom, which has been converted into a rehearsal and recording studio. Sunlight pours through two sets of triple sliders that lead to the pool, but the A/C must be set to freezing because, even with all the gear plugged in, it's cold in here. The walls are covered with acoustic foam, and the closet has been converted to a vocal booth. It's a sophisticated set up compared to the rehearsal spaces I'm used to, namely garages and storage units. I started playing gigs as a teenager and the smell of lawn fertilizer, car tires, and gasoline still makes me nostalgic for the early days.

I catch Theo's eyes again and he grins as he signals for us to play the final measure of the song. When he stretches his arms over his head between songs, I notice his T-shirt is a little too short, exposing V-shredded abs and a trail of dark hair that tracks down from his belly button. I divert my eyes to his kit. His high hat sits much higher on its stand than my drummer's, and his throne wobbles because it's extended as high as it goes to accommodate Theo's height. I'm five-seven, and he's easily six inches taller than I am.

He calls a new song and counts us in. I'm on the opening root without having to ask anyone to refresh my memory with the key. I'm very low maintenance. Experience has taught me that dudes will happily help a brother out, but if the chick isn't flawless, they exchange eye rolls.

NICO

MARIS DOESN'T SUCK. I'VE HEARD her name around town, but I haven't heard her play until today. She's more than capable of doing the job, but I don't like change, and this chick will change everything.

Jimmy learned his basslines and didn't dare improvise. He played the gig the same way, note for note, every night. Maris is a seasoned musician, so she'll be creative, which could be great, but might be awful. Until now, I wrote the bass parts for our original music. If we hire Maris, I'm sure that'll change, too.

I can't believe Theo didn't talk to me before inviting her to practice. We started this band together five years ago, and we've become like brothers. He doesn't usually make decisions without my input. I don't know what he's thinking. Are we going to become her back-up band? How much of our song list is she going to sing? Why didn't Theo set up other musicians to audition? The fact that he only brought Maris in makes me think his mind is set.

Max complains about everything, so it's no surprise that he was against hiring a girl, but, this time, I agree with him. Not that Max would be the dude Maris would go for. It's hilarious that he seems to think he's in the running. I'm not a conceited guy, but I do get the most female attention. Maybe it's the guitar, maybe it's confidence, maybe it's just down to looks, but I play in a league that's out of Max's reach. I told him to cut his hair and get contacts, but he didn't want to. If he started lifting weights now, he could beef up within six or eight months. God forbid he'd go lay by the pool and get rid of his vampire pallor. My point is, he doesn't have to worry about being the guy who breaks up the band.

Anyway, I'm too pissed off right now to be polite, so I'm keeping my mouth shut.

MAX

JIMMY WASN'T A VERY SKILLED musician, but he was a sweet guy. He made sure to include me in the jokes and conversations that took place when we weren't playing or talking about music. I liked him a lot. Having a girl in the band is going to isolate me. I don't know how exactly; I just know it will. I don't click with the cool set of guys, and I really don't click with females.

The thing is, Theo hired me because he knows I'm a solid musician. I have a music degree for fuck's sake. I have a first-rate education in theory, performance, composition, and sound engineering. These guys should be listening to me and asking for my opinion, but they act like I'm lucky to be here. Sometimes, I get embarrassingly passive-aggressive during writing sessions and throw out suggestions for a *diminished triad with a seventh* as a transition chord, just to remind them that they play by ear.

I mean, Theo is a pocket drummer, for sure. He bought all the recording gear and gave me a place to live. Without him, I'd still be at my parents' house. He deals with the agents and club owners. I'm indebted to the guy. A little respect shouldn't be too much to ask, though. He respects Nico. I hate to admit it, but I do, too. Nico is self-taught. He has a gift. He can hear something once and play it flawlessly. His contributions to our writing seshes are pretty cool, too, because he isn't limited by convention. He plays guitar ten hours a day, so he's always discovering things.

Maris seems nice enough, even when she's putting us in our place. She's a good player and has great tone. I bet she's inventive when she's more comfortable. Maybe she has girlfriends, or a sister, who would come see the band. That could be good for me. I think Maris is around my age, early to mid-twenties. I look younger than everyone else in the band, but I'm actually older than Theo, who is twenty-three. Come to think of it, I don't know how old Nico is. Maybe if we ever have a mano y mano, I'll ask him. I'll probably die not knowing.

Maris is low-key hot. She would spice up our band photos. She isn't wearing make-up today and her long, wavy, dark blonde hair won't stay contained under her FSU baseball cap, but she doesn't try to fix it. As long tendrils escape, she tosses her head to trap them behind her shoulders. I wonder if her very short denim shorts are part of the audition. Her tan legs go forever, and she's taller than I am. Not great. She has a huge T-shirt on that hangs below her shorts when she stands up to tweak her bass amp. She smells good. I'm sure we've all noticed, and that's how shit goes sideways.

THEO

AFTER PLAYING THREE DIFFERENT COVERS, each a different style, I suggest that Maris pick a favorite song to sing. She goes old-school and calls an Aretha song, which causes Max to reach for his iPad. He calls the chords out to Nico, and they get through it as Maris and I lock in on bass and drums. She has a great feel and, together, we're a funky rhythm section. She's nailing the audition and giving me all the evidence I need to convince Nico and Max that she's the best "man" for the job. I'm proud that I found her and brought her in. She's making me look good.

When the song ends, Nico says, "Maris, you can saaang ... obviously. And you can play. But I thought we were having a Band Beating today to decide how we want to move forward." Nico shoots me a look. "The three of us need to do that before we seriously audition players. As good as you are, hiring you changes the trajectory of the band, and I don't know if I want to do that."

Maris nods. "I understand." Her voice is calm and confident, but she looks annoyed.

Max noodles on his keyboard. "You really are great," he says. "If you were a dude, I'd be begging you to join the band, but ..."

I stand up behind my drum throne and stretch my arms behind my back, loosening my shoulders. "I would like for all of us to be on the same page, but the reality is that I'm the leader, and I'm going to hire the person I think is best for the product."

"You're not a one-man show, Theo. As I told Maris, I think we need to discuss this privately." Nico unplugs the guitar and places it in the stand.

"Who is this mystery bass player that can walk onto the job tomorrow?" I ask Nico. "If we hire someone who's working five nights a week, our gig means a pay cut because we carve out time to record."

"So, we go back to playing five nights a week," Max says. "That gave us time to get tight on the gig before we recorded. Paid rehearsals."

"Sure, Max. You take over booking the band. Find us rooms looking for original music. You know damn well we're lucky to get away with playing one original per set before the club owner tells us to play what people know."

"Well, thanks for the opportunity." Maris stands, unplugs her bass, and slides it into a carrying case. "Please don't tell Backyard Breeder that I came to jam with you, because I can't be unemployed."

"Maris, please don't leave," I say. "I'm sorry that I didn't set this up better. I was sure that once the guys met you and heard you, they would feel like I do."

"It's one against two, and I don't want to come into a band that's conflicted about whether they want me."

"We'd be lucky as fuck to get you into the band," I tell her.

Maris removes her ballcap and lets her hair fall down her back. "You make a good point about the pay cut. I'm gigging five or six nights a week right now, but I don't want to get stuck doing that forever. I'm looking for a group to write and record with to chase that record deal. But I have bills, too."

"Well, that's why I have the band live here." I gesture outwardly. "You'd be welcome to move in to keep your expenses down."

"That's another thing we should discuss," Nico says. "Having a female in the band is one thing, but having a girl move into our house is a whole other conversation."

"It's my house!"

Max stops playing and the room gets uncomfortably quiet. When he swallows, the microphone he uses for background vocals amplifies the sound through speakers on each end of the room.

"It's too hostile," Maris says. "I'm out."

I blow air through my cheeks and shoot a look toward Nico who's standing in the doorway. Before heading to the kitchen, he waves dismissively. "Thanks for coming by Maris. Good luck to you."

I clear my throat. "I'll walk you out."

When we're alone Maris says, "Hey, thanks for giving me a shot. Sorry it didn't work out."

"Yeah, no, I'm sorry that was such a shit show." I open one side of the double front doors and walk through, holding it open for Maris. Her Jeep is parked in the circular driveway, and she gently wedges her bass case across the floor of the backseat.

"Don't worry about it." Maris wraps her hair and piles it on top of her head, securing it with her cap.

"As bad as it went in there, please don't totally write us off." I squint as the midmorning Miami sun blazes behind her. "We need you. Not just a bass player, we need *you*."

"Theo, I know you're the leader, but you have to keep your band members happy, or you'll have more positions to fill."

"Just don't block my number, okay?" I ask, opening the driver's side door of the open vehicle.

"I won't block you, but I'm not holding my breath, either."

I laugh as Maris climbs into the Jeep and starts it up. I wave as she drives away and then shove my hands into my jean pockets and walk with purpose back into the house. Nico and Max are in the kitchen, and I smell freshly brewed coffee. I grab a mug from the cabinet and pour a cup.

"You guys don't have anything to say?"

Max looks to Nico to respond, but Nico just scoffs as he scans the interior of the refrigerator.

"I mean, we don't have to hire the first person we audition, right?" Max asks. "Let's bring in some other people to weigh our options."

"Sure," I say, nodding. I lean back against the countertop and take a sip of coffee while Max settles into a chair on the other side of the kitchen island. "Who's your first call?"

Max looks toward Nico again, who makes no attempt to join the conversation.

"Um, well, I could post an ad on the Berklee jobs page."

I nod again. "Go right ahead. Make sure you're upfront about being Miami based."

"Yeah, of course." Max gets his phone out and starts typing.

"Nico, my guy? Who's your first call?"

Nico closes the fridge door with more force than necessary and meets my eyes. "What you did was bullshit, and you know it. You invited her to audition without asking me, or Max, what we thought about hiring her."

"And, if I had asked your opinion about bringing her in?"

"I would have said *no* because I don't want a chick in the band."

"Why can't you have a female as a counterpart?"

Nico sneers. "Don't make it something it isn't. I'm not a male chauvinist."

I shrug. "Sounds like you are."

"Dude." Nico shakes his head as he walks to where I'm standing. He stops in front of me for a moment before saying, "Excuse me. I made coffee because I wanted some." I step aside and Nico opens the cabinet door to retrieve a mug. "I would be pissed that you invited *anyone* to audition without consulting us. I'm not mad because it was Maris. I'm mad because I've invested a lot of years into this band, and we've always made the big decisions together. We hired Max together." Nico gestures toward him and the color leaves Max's cheeks, like he wants to disappear. Nico pours himself a cup of coffee as he continues. "Any new person is going to change our dynamic, so we have to choose the person who makes the smallest ripple. Adding Maris changes so much, it's like starting over from scratch."

I feel my mouth form into a frown. "How many followers did our YouTube channel gain over the last year?"

"I don't know." Nico drinks his coffee.

"Yeah, you do. When we first started it, we checked ten times a day. Our base is still with us, but we've gotten stagnant. As far as bookings go, we're not opening any new rooms. We're playing the same circuit on rotation."

"Okay." Nico runs his hand through his hair, and his eyes challenge me.

"We've been doing the same thing for five years, and we're no closer to getting a deal than we were two years ago."

"It's a matter of saturation and luck. We just keep doin' what we're doin'—"

"With who playing bass?" I raise my eyebrows.

"Guys, guys, let's not let a girl come between us," Max says.

I scrunch my face, and Nico's eyes open wide before we both bust out laughing.

"What?" Max asks, laughing along.

"Your mom," Nico says. "That's the only girl that would come between you and us."

"You guys are assholes," Max says without emotion.

"Thanks for cutting the tension, Max. Seriously. Let me know if you get any replies to your ad." I finish my coffee and place the mug in the dishwasher. Walking backwards on the way to the pool, I put it on Nico. "Get some feelers out, man."

I step through the sliding doors and get down to my boxers before jumping into

the pool, enjoying the freedom of doing so until a female moves into the house.

MARIS

ON THE DRIVE BACK TO my boyfriend's condo, I try to tell myself that I held my own during the audition and that they need me a lot more than I need them. I still feel lousy. I don't like being rejected any more than anyone else, but music has a way of humbling everyone who falls in love with it.

I park my Jeep in Damon's second parking spot beside his 7 series BMW. I'm glad he's home. He'll help me shake this funk.

"Hey, babe!" I call as I open the door with my key.

"How did it go?" His voice comes from his home office. Damon practices family law but works from home when he's not meeting with clients.

I walk down the short hallway and see my handsome man, seated behind an open laptop on his desk. He looks at me expectantly when I stick my head into the doorway.

"Meet the bass player for …" I make a drumroll sound with my tongue. "Backyard Breeder!"

Damon smiles and holds his arms out as a signal for me to go hug him, which I do eagerly.

"You can always go back to law school," he says, laughing.

"Geez, the audition wasn't *that* bad!" I say, planting myself in his lap. "They need a bass player, but don't want a chick and all the trouble that comes with boobs."

"Did you tell them you have a man?" Damon asks, tucking my hair behind my ear.

"I did, but I guess my undeniable sensuality bothered them, anyway."

Damon pulls on the T-shirt I borrowed from his drawer. "Well, you're just asking for attention when you wear sexy clothes like this."

I kiss him while I mumble, "I know."

"I have a Zoom call in a few minutes, but we can go for lunch afterward."

I smooth his dress shirt and tighten his tie as I study his face. Damon is what you would call traditionally good-looking. His features are so symmetrical that I like to take pictures of one side of his face, mirror it, and compare that to a full-face photo. It's a hobby. He has brown hair, cut with such precision that it never requires styling. His brown eyes project kindness. He doesn't have time to work out like he used to when we were in school, but I like cuddling his softer form.

It was Damon who encouraged me to drop out of law school. Best thing I ever did. But I'm still paying down my student debt. Thankfully, Damon got a good job right after graduation, and he doesn't ask me to contribute to his mortgage. I don't think of his place as mine, but I think of him as home.

I vacate his lap and ask if I have time for a bath before lunch. It was so cold in Theo's house that I'm still chilled, despite the eighty-degree temperature outside.

"Take all the time you need, baby. If you're not ready to go when my call ends, I'll just wait."

"You're the best," I say, before planting another kiss on his face.

As I predicted, I'm already over any negative feelings I had earlier. And, I still have a job with a band that plays five gigs a week. Life is good.

NICO

I HAD TO PARK MY TRUCK more than a block away from the field where the food trucks surround the stage, and I hear Backyard Breeder as soon as I open the door. I consider listening from here, but, with this many people hanging out, I'm sure I can get a view of the stage without anyone on the stage seeing me. Also, I'm hungry.

Maris is singing lead on a P!nk cover as I walk up. She sounds great. The song rolls into my favorite single from Paramore, and Maris nails that, too. Shit. I stand backwards to watch the band while waiting in line for some fish tacos. I know the guitar player and the drummer. We've crossed paths but never worked together. I like Brett's playing, but his sound is too crunchy for what we do. He relies on a lot of distortion and sustain, to cover for his lack of finger dexterity. I've been accused of overplaying, but I think I keep it tasteful. Glenn is probably a better drummer than Theo, technically, but Theo hits harder and his meter is flawless. More importantly, he's a great dude. He puts up with my moodiness. I have brotherly love for Theo, which is why I'm here tonight.

I put my taco order in and stand where the other hungry bastards are waiting for their names to be called. The food truck park is absolutely packed. In the middle, where the stage is, people of all ages are dancing, drinking, and having a great time under the canopy of string lights. It's a cool vibe, and Backyard Breeder handles the crowd well. They seem to be having as much fun as the Friday night partiers.

Maris is wearing jeans with more holes than denim and a tank top. Her hair is down and when she whips it around the crowd reacts with screams of approval. She is wireless and walks around the stage when she isn't singing lead. She engages the audience more than anyone else in the band. I hate doing that, and Theo is always on me to interact more with the crowd. She has a great smile and great stage presence.

It's been three weeks since Maris auditioned with us. Max's post got a lot of interest, but after watching videos of the guys who wanted the gig, we didn't see anyone we'd invite for an audition. There was one guy we were excited about, but he wanted us to fly him back and forth for jobs, which is ridiculous. We've been gigging as a three piece without Jimmy. Max is playing left hand bass on one of his keyboards. He's doing his best, but his jazz bass patch sounds like shit on our song list. I'm grateful that he's trying to keep us working, but it's a cheap substitute. So, that's why I'm here, trying to blend into the crowd. I didn't tell Theo or Max I planned to come. I don't expect to see anything that will change my mind. Or, maybe, I hope to see something that will change my mind.

My tacos are ready, and I find an open seat at a picnic table nearer to the stage than I want to be, but off to the side. I have to sit facing the band, but I keep my head down, eat, and listen.

After a couple tunes, the band breaks down to drums and bass. "Thanks so much, everybody!" Maris yells into her mic. "We are Backyard Breeder and we're going to pause for a short break, but the party rolls on, so hydrate while we're gone, and we'll see you back here in fifteen minutes." Canned break music blares through the speakers as soon as she finishes talking.

"Hey, are you the guitar player from Funkengroovin'?" a female voice yells into my right ear.

My hand instinctively goes to the side of my head as I turn to see two pretty girls holding two beers each. I hold up a finger while I swallow and nod.

"Oh, my God. I told you!" the one closest to me shouts to the other one.

"My friend is a little tipsy," the other girl says, "but we both love your band. Are you playing here tonight?"

"No. We played poolside at Hotel Brickell from 6-9. We're at Club Fish tomorrow from 9-1, though. You know it?"

"On the beach, right?" Drunk Girl asks.

"Yeah," I say, trying not to extend the conversation. These girls are both in their early twenties, and, since turning 25, I'm finished with girls younger than I am.

"Does the band have a list at the door?" Less Drunk Girl asks. "I think the cover there is, like, twenty bucks, right?"

I want them to go away. "Tell ya what. I'll put your names on our list if you promise to bring five more people."

"Cool of you, man. I'm Lisa and this is Lisa. Weird, right?"

"Makes it easier to remember," I say, turning back to my remaining tacos.

"Okay, Lisa and Lisa. Don't forget!" Drunk Girl sings loudly.

"How could I?" I sing back.

They leave me alone with my tacos, and I'm grateful.

"Nico! Hey, I thought that was you." Maris stops in her tracks on the way to the stage. I see her innate kindness dissolve when she remembers that I'm an asshole. Her smile disappears, and she waves as she takes an awkward step in the direction she was heading.

My mouth is full again and I hold a napkin over it as I yell, "Maris, wait."

She looks over her shoulder, and I motion for her to have a seat across from me. For a minute, I think she's going to decline, but then she smiles politely and sits down. "Did you guys have an early gig tonight?"

I nod.

"I love those. Have you ever played here? It's loose and fun, but it doesn't pay very well. None of these cheap asses are the tipping type either, so we treat it like a showcase."

"Hi." My mouth is finally vacant. "Yeah, these guys called Theo about booking some dates here, so I wanted to check it out. Shit money, huh?"

"They pay Tuesday money all week long." Maris taps her fingers on the tabletop. "So, who did you guys hire to replace Jimmy?"

I clear my throat. "No one yet. Still vetting prospects."

Maris nods her head and doesn't follow up. "Well, I stood in line for the bathroom for ten minutes, and now it's probably time to play again. You wanna sit in?"

I shake my head and make a face. "No."

"Aw, people love that. Your little fan club would be so excited."

I let out a genuine laugh. "You saw that, huh?"

"Lisa Lisa and the Cult Jam? Yeah, I saw them." Maris laughs along.

"See, this is where Max comes in handy. If he was here, I could have sicced him on them, and they'd probably form a meaningful and lasting friendzoneship."

Maris shakes her head. "Spoken like a big brother."

"Max plays the role of annoying little brother very well."

"You can be honest with me since I'm not joining the band. Do you guys fight like that all the time, or was it just over me?"

I choose my words carefully. "We get along well … musically. Theo and I are tight, and we'd be tight if we weren't in a band together. Max and I work well together on stage. But, to answer your question, we get along in the sense that we care more about serving the music than each other's feelings, and none of us is too sensitive. Except maybe Max."

"Interesting." Maris points her thumb behind her toward the stage. "We get along well enough to play and rehearse, but we don't hang on our off time. Let alone live together."

I perk up. "Maybe if we kicked Max out of the house, I'd like him more."

Maris laughs. "Poor Max."

"Nah, he's a good kid. He's just …" I study Maris's eyes and decide I can tell her the truth. "He's like a gnat that won't leave you alone. He's always there, wondering what you're doing, and if he can do it with you."

"So, being in the band is his whole personality?"

I feel my eyes go wide. "Exactly. And it's nice that he's so committed, but—"

"You don't want to be connected at the hip on stage and off?" Maris guesses.

"Right."

"I can see why you'd try to get him a girlfriend."

"Maris to the stage, please," Brett says over the mic, imitating the classic grocery store PA delivery. "Oh, shit. Hey, Nico! Ladies and gentlemen, Nico from Funkengroovin' is here. Maybe he'll grace our stage with his presence. You're always welcome, dude."

"Fuck," I mutter, while saluting in Brett's direction.

"You have to play now," Maris says, shrugging her shoulders and smiling. She gets up from the table and runs to the stairs leading to the stage. While she straps her bass on, she talks into the mic. "What's good, gang? If you're just walking in, we're Backyard Breeder, and we've got a special guest star coming to the stage in a bit. Nico from Funkengroovin' will be sitting in this set."

Lisa, Lisa, and other people who recognize the band name, clap and cheer, which, I have to admit, is nice to hear.

The band starts playing a song from Toto and, suddenly, I want to sit in. I don't get to play 80s rock in our band. I finish my tacos, throw away the wrapping they came in, and Maris notices. When the song ends, she calls me up. Brett has his guitar unstrapped and is holding it out to me as I climb the stairs to the stage.

As I adjust the strap, I say hello to the band. "Sweet Child O' Mine?" I ask.

Glenn yells, "Sweet Child!" Then, he bangs his sticks together and I open the song with the familiar lick as the crowd goes nuts. I look at Maris as I play and yell, "Do you sing this?"

She makes a face and shakes her head.

Well, shit. I make a panicked face, and she laughs. I shrug like, WTF, and start singing. I sing to Maris because the song is about a girl, and she plays along. When the first guitar solo hits, she matches my stance and holds the bassline. The audience loves it. Equal numbers of people are holding up their phone flashlights and recording videos. Maris throws her hair around and I am shredding on Brett's barely adequate guitar set up. Shit. The chemistry is great. This is what I came to try to judge. Shit. Theo's right.

When the song is over, I unstrap the guitar while the crowd screams and whistles. I hand the guitar back to Brett and thank him, along with the rest of the band.

Brett motions for me to lean in close and he yells in my ear. "I know Jimmy quit. Don't jack our bass-player, douchebag."

I smile at him and wave at the crowd as I run down the stage stairs. I call Theo on the way back to my truck. As soon as he answers I say, "You were right."

"I know. About what?"

"Maris. We have to get her if we still can."

THEO

I CALLED MARIS THE DAY AFTER Nico sat in with her band, but the conversation didn't go as well as I hoped. Maris didn't want to leave a job that was a sure thing to work with guys who, only three weeks earlier, had been adamant about not wanting to hire her. If she parted ways with Backyard Breeder, there would be no going back. She told me that the night Nico sat in, Brett lectured her the entire time they were breaking down about using their gigs to audition for another band. That made her feel guilty because, even though she hadn't known that Nico would show at her gig, she did audition for us.

I apologized for the role I played in setting her up to fail in her initial meeting with Nico and Max, and I tried to explain why I didn't warn them in advance of her audition. I think she understood, but she was still wary. I told her that I didn't blame her for feeling the way she did, and I left our offer with her to consider. She said she'd let me know, ASAP.

The three of us stayed at the house for the rest of the day, watching my phone screen. Maris didn't call. We did our gig and babysat the phone again the next day. Maris didn't call.

Finally, four days later, an M appears inside of a circle on my phone and all three of us reach for it.

"Put it on speaker," Nico demands.

"Hey, Maris, say hi to Nico and Max."

"Hey, guys," she says cheerily. "I have some conditions. One, I don't want to stay at the house. I'm living with my boyfriend, Damon, and we're only about twenty minutes from you, so I can come over for writing seshes, rehearsals, or whatever, but I'm not moving in."

Nico makes a celebratory gesture with his fist as I say, "That's totally understandable."

"Okay, good. Number two, I need to give Brett at least two weeks' notice. I don't want to leave him high and dry."

"Yeah, Jimmy kind of screwed us over, so I appreciate that you want to do this right," I say.

"Third, I have an equal say about what venues we play and our social media presence, along with an equal split on writing and publishing."

Max looks at me. "Should I have asked for that?"

I shake my head at him.

"I don't have an issue with that, Maris, but I'd put it more like this … if you ever have a problem with a job, or a post, or whatever, come straight to me, and I'll do whatever I can to appease you. As far as the writing goes, you'll always get credit and points if we're lucky enough to get that far. We're dysfunctional as fuck, but we're loyal to each other, and we watch each other's backs."

Maris's voice gets quieter. "That last part was from my boyfriend. He's a lawyer."

Nico and I raise our eyebrows at each other.

"If you want him to put together some kind of agreement, I'd be happy to—"

"No, no, no. I don't need a contract. Let's just verbally agree that I get writing credits and equal publishing to whatever you guys get."

I nod at Nico, and he speaks for us, "Agreed. I hope we have to hold up our end of that bargain someday."

"I'll be gigging every night for the next two weeks, but I can rehearse during the day," Maris offers.

"Get your ass over here," Max says enthusiastically. Then, he turns red. "I mean, like not your *ass*. I didn't mean that in a demeaning way because you're female …"

"Say less, Max." Maris laughs. "And don't worry so much. I'm not nearly as precious as you think I am."

"Honestly, though, if you can spare some time today, we can wood-shed material with you," I say.

"Give me an hour."

Sixty minutes later, I'm waiting by the front door to open the driveway gate for Maris's blue Jeep. I'll know that she's really one of us when I give her the five-digit code.

My face smiles without permission from my brain when I see her pull up and lean out the Jeep window to try to reach the call button. I buzz her in and go outside to carry any gear she might have brought. I'm still smiling as she parks in front of the doors like she did last time.

"I can honestly say I never thought I'd be back here," she says with a laugh as she steps down from the lifted Jeep.

"I hoped and maybe even prayed a little that you would be," I confess, reaching into the back and lifting her gig bag from the floor.

"Thanks for grabbing that. I figure I'll just use your Hartke rig for rehearsals, right? Like I did before?"

"Yeah, it's always set up in the studio." I open the door for her, and Max comes into the room like a puppy excited to greet company.

"Hey, Maris." He smiles and waves.

"What's up, Max? You cut your hair!"

Maris's observation prompts me to study Max.

"Yeah, I had it done Saturday."

"It looks good short. I like it," Maris says with a smile.

I live with the guy, and he went from long hair to short three days ago and I didn't notice. Females are different.

"Do you need a bottle of water or coffee or anything before we get started?" Max asks her.

"I'm good, thanks." Maris digs her Stanley out of the huge hobo bag she's carrying.

When we walk into the studio, Nico is there playing his guitar with headphones on. He's in the zone and we startle him.

"Fuck!" He says his favorite word louder than he would if he wasn't wearing headphones. Taking them off, he says, "Hey, Maris. How did it go with Brett? Is he going to try to kill me next time I see him?"

Maris chuckles and makes a *so-so* gesture with her hand.

"He one hundred percent thinks I was already committed to Funkengroovin' when you sat in with us, even though I told him that wasn't the case. He didn't believe me, and that pissed me off so much that I don't feel as badly about leaving. I'm not a liar and he's never known me to be, but he's casting me as one, and I bet he'll tell everyone in town that I played him and took this gig behind his back."

"I'll talk to him," Nico says.

Maris makes a face and shakes her head. "That's between me and him. Don't worry about it. But he knows I'm joining you guys if you want to start blasting social media." Maris laughs wickedly.

"I don't want to have bad blood with any other bands. Players move around, though. It's part of the business," I say.

Maris shrugs her shoulders and doesn't say anything more about Brett, so I hand out the set lists I made as soon as we'd hung up. "I don't usually make a set list," I explain. "But for our first few weeks of gigging together, I think it will be easier for you. After you settle in, I'll start calling audibles, and we'll go back to winging it."

"Okay." Maris looks at the papers I've handed her, and she nods frequently as she reads. "For most of these, I'll just need keys."

As I watch her, I can't help thinking how fucking pretty she is. Her long hair hangs halfway down her back, and the blonde highlights seem more prominent than I remember. She isn't wearing make-up, but her skin glows and she smells so good. My thoughts make me self-conscious, so I snap myself out of it. I've been living with dudes too long.

"Yeah, I know most of these already. I'll mark the songs I've never played before and listen to those on my own, so I don't waste your time. But let's run down the list for beginnings, arrangements, and endings. Good?"

I nod and take my seat on the drum throne.

"Watch me for keys, Mare," Max says, shortening her name in a way that I think is presumptive. "I can talk you through the changes, too."

"Cool, Max. Thanks. In fact, I'll come over there by you, so you don't have to yell over the music."

Max looks pleased. Nico looks annoyed. Truth be told, Max probably is the person Maris needs most to get up to speed with the material.

I'm aware of how happy I am as I look around the studio and see these musicians ready to play. I feel an excitement I haven't felt in a long time. I watch Maris secure her hair into a clip, and I'm still looking at her as she turns, expecting me to count us into the first song. Shit. I'm in trouble.

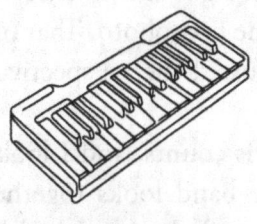

MAX

I TOOK NICO'S SIDE IN THIS whole *no chicks in the band thing* to form an alliance with him. Not that I want to team up against Theo, but Nico and I don't really have anything in common outside of playing music. I just don't understand him, but I went all in for him anyway, and then he changed his mind and went to sit in with Maris's band. Now, I feel like Maris thinks I'm a dick, and I'm determined to show her that I'm not. I need a friend in this band. Or I want one, anyway. Theo and Nico are both decent guys, but they click in a way that doesn't leave room for me.

Anyway, they let me take the lead during rehearsal and if Maris has any questions about chord progressions or anything, she asks me. She's a pro and needs very little direction. The only times she trips up, her mistake makes sense and that tells me a lot about her musicality. I'm glad she's here. I'm glad she's the one replacing Jimmy and I want her to know that, so I compliment her and encourage her all through rehearsal. When it's time for us to start getting ready for work, I suggest that we take a band selfie to use as a tease on our social media pages.

"Use my phone, it has the best camera," I say, handing Nico my Google.

He takes the phone, and we all squeeze together behind Theo's drum throne. Maris puts her arm around me, and my smile grows from a crescent to a toothy grin.

"You have to hold it above our eyeline for the best angle," Maris tells Nico.

He looks at her with eyebrows scrunched.

"Like this," she motions for the phone, and he hands it to her. Unfortunately, she uses her right arm, which was the one she had draped around my shoulders in the first photo. That one won't make it onto the socials now, since she adjusted the perspective, but at least I have it in my camera roll.

"Three, two ..." Maris counts, and I look at the screen and notice how good the rest of the band looks together. I like my haircut. It's better than the early Harry Styles 'do I had before. I took a photo of Christopher Briney to Supercuts and, I have to say, the girl did a good job. Too bad I don't have his face. Maybe Nico was right, and I should come to terms with poking myself in the eyes and having plastic discs float on my eyeballs instead of wearing glasses. Sounds terrible.

Nico hands the phone back to me after he snapped a few shots.

"Send those to me, Max," Theo says.

"I want them, too. Oh, do you have my number?" Maris asks.

"I'll forward them to you, Maris," Theo says as he studies the photos I just delivered. "This is the money shot," Theo says and laughs. "Check it out." He turns the phone to show: Maris's flirty expression with puckered lips, Nico's stone face looking like an action star on a movie poster, Theo's sticks entwined within the fingers of his left hand while throwing a shaka with his right, and then there's me, looking just below the camera lens while smiling like a Muppet.

"Dudes, I need a retake," I say.

"Oh, Max, you look cute," Maris says.

I cringe.

"No, I wasn't paying attention, sorry, can we just click one more so I can look into the camera like everyone else?"

"No one can see where you're looking cause you're wearing glasses," Nico says.

"Honestly, this photo is introducing Maris as a new band member, so no one is going to look at any of us, anyway." Theo is making an IG post using the photo I objected to.

It says: *Welcome, Maris! Funkengroovin' is so funkinlucky to add you to the lineup! Rehearsals are fire! Watch this space for debut dates!*

"Make sure you tag me. I have a lot of followers," Maris tells Theo.

"Can we bang some more material out tomorrow around the same time?" he asks.

Maris nods as she slips her bass into its bag. "Sure. I'll listen to those songs that I haven't heard before on breaks tonight. I don't think anyone in my band will want to hang with me, so I'll have the opportunity."

"If you have any questions about any of the material, feel free to reach out. Do you have my number?" This is my second attempt to get a direct line of communication with Maris in the same conversation.

"Oh, no, I don't." She tosses me her phone. "Go ahead and put it in there."

I make a new contact and provide my full name, Max Anthony Castellano, my number, email, and IG handle. Then, I text my phone from hers.

"All set," I say, handing the phone back as Maris makes her way to the great room.

"I'll get the gate for you," Theo offers.

"Hey, Maris, if Brett's a dick to you tonight, please shoot me a text. I know you can handle him, but I feel responsible for how things look to him, since I showed up at your gig that night. I'm happy to shut his shit down."

"Thanks, Nico. It's probably going to be a long two weeks, but I've got this. I'd like to finish things with BB on a happy note. Pun intended."

Nico presses his lips together and looks dejected, which makes me feel empowered for some reason.

"We get off at ten tonight, so if you need friendlies in the audience, you have my number," I tell Maris.

"Thanks, Max, but I think you guys better stay as far away from my band members as possible right now."

"Understood," I say, nodding like I've been in this situation a million times.

Maris turns toward the door, and Theo follows as Nico and I raid the refrigerator.

"I hate to admit it, but Maris is a far better player than Jimmy and she's gonna be a big draw," Nico says.

I look around to see if Theo came back in or if he's actually talking to me. He is.

"Yeah, I'm glad you went to see her band that night. It seems that was the tipping point to make this happen."

"It became clear she was the best choice." Nico places premade pulled pork in the microwave and hunts through the cabinet for the brioche buns he hides from Theo and me.

I fill a pot with water and place it on the stove, adding some boxed pasta. "She seems really cool, too. Easy to be around. I guess we'll see if she's low maintenance once we start gigging," I say.

"She isn't waving any red flags," Nico says.

"Well, that went great," Theo says, coming back inside. "How do you guys feel?"

"Same," I say.

"She's solid," Nico says.

Theo pulls his phone out of his pocket and laughs. "That post hasn't been up for five minutes, and it has over two hundred likes already." He scrolls. "Lots of comments about how hot Maris is."

"They haven't even seen her in gig attire and make-up yet," Nico says. "She's smokin' hot on stage."

The microwave beeps and Nico grabs the package of meat with his bare fingertips. I admire his guitar calluses and note that piano players can't do that.

"Smokin' hot in the way a sister would be smokin'," Theo says pointedly.

"Obviously," Nico says, spooning the fragrant mixture across three buns.

"You made one for each of us?" I ask.

Nico laughs. "As much as I advocate for you adding some protein to your diet, Max, no, I made three for me."

"I guess I could buy some meatballs for my spaghetti," I say thoughtfully. "Do they sell microwaveable meatballs at Publix?"

Theo replies instead of Nico. "They do. In the freezer section."

"I really miss my mom's cooking," I say, trying not to sound miserable.

"You can always eat with me at the club," Theo offers.

"You payin'?" I ask.

"We get an employee discount at most places."

I shake my head. "I can't get into the habit of doing that. Too rich for my blood."

Nico busts out laughing. "My grandfather used to say that. Max, you're like the grandfather of the band. I didn't realize it until this very second."

I watch my boiling pot as Nico chuckles to himself while filling his face.

"Someone around here has to be mature and responsible," I mutter.

Theo slaps me on the back. "He's just kidding, my man. And, for the record, we appreciate your maturity and responsibility. You're a very steady dude. Especially for a musician."

"You don't have to say that." I roll my eyes.

"Dude, really. I also appreciate how you took it upon yourself to lead the rehearsal today."

I retrieve a jar of sauce from the pantry. "No problem."

"We complement each other and fill each other's gaps. That's what makes Funkengroovin' so awesome," Theo says.

"I'd like to fill Maris's gaps," Nico blurts.

Theo lets his jaw drop dramatically. "In the way that you'd fill your sister's gaps, you mean."

"Sure," Nico says, shoving the last bit of the third sandwich in his mouth. "Hitting the shower. We play in ninety, so don't dawdle, boys."

I look at Theo. "I'm the grandpa?"

He lets out a genuine laugh, which makes me feel good. I decide to play my ass off later tonight, whether we have a good crowd or not. While I'm optimistic about going forward with Maris, I feel the need to stake my territory and remind these motherfuckers why they're lucky to have me. I may never be the coolest guy in the room, but I am the best damn musician, and I'm happy to remind them of that.

THEO

MARIS SPECIFICALLY ASKED US NOT to show up at her gig, so I'm not doing that. Not in the sense that I'll get out of my car and walk inside, but I'm parked in the employee parking lot a half hour before the gig ends to make sure Brett doesn't, I don't know, corner her or something. I can see her Jeep from where I'm parked, but I'm far enough away that she won't see me. I've been in bands long enough to know that tensions that percolate on stage tend to overflow after the last song of the night. I feel protective of Maris and a little responsible for the awkward situation in which she finds herself.

I drove through DQ on the way here to get myself an Oreo blizzard and fries. My favorite post-gig indulgence. I figure I might as well eat it here, rather than flashing it in front of Max at home. I'm starting to wonder what he spends his money on. He's always crying poverty, but he doesn't pay rent or utilities, and he doesn't have a car.

As I plow my flimsy plastic spoon into my Blizzard, I realize I'm going to get a little show with my snack. A girl in a super-short tight dress teeters on sky-high heels over to a BMW with its interior light on. She opens the door and climbs into the passenger side, and I'm not sure why I think this doesn't make sense, but it seems strange. I didn't see where she came from, so maybe that's throwing me off. If she was an employee getting a ride after work, she would have come out of the back door of the club and my eyes have been trained there looking for Maris, even though it's too early for her to appear.

The interior light of the Bimmer stays on and I empty my French fry container into the bottom of the brown DQ bag. The juxtaposition of the cold and sweet smashes with the hot and salty, and I'm so happy right now.

Oh, boy, here we go. The chick in the dress is leaning over the driver's lap, and the interior light gets switched off. Good for you, my man … I guess. I passed up a few opportunities myself tonight. I'm not full of myself, but it isn't hard for me to pick up women. I used to qualify contenders based on appearance alone and I had a lot, and I mean a lot, of fun nights having sex with beautiful girls. I've also dated one girl at a time, but girlfriends never understand the business. They freak out when I talk to girls at the clubs and interact on social media to generate a following. It always gets messy. Lately, I've been alone ten nights for every one I've spent at some rando's apartment.

Nico and I used to compare notes, but since he turned 25, he started acting superior and above the game. I'm not one to take advantage of girls, but if a gorgeous chick wants a roll with the drummer, who am I to deny her?

I'm halfway through my Blizzard when the girl's head appears again, and she straddles the driver. She's moving the whole car now. So much for discretion. I look around and there's no one else out here besides me. Maybe they know the dead and peak times of this particular lot.

Fifteen minutes later, the interior light of the car goes on again. I'm not sure I want a clearer view, so I raise the DQ bag to my mouth and Godzilla the remaining fries. As I crush the bag into a ball, the chick gets out of the car and walks toward the front of the building. That's why I didn't see her before; she came around the side of the club. Weird little tryst, but I've gotten down in some non-traditional places, so whatever.

I finish my Blizzard, disappointed that, once again, I failed to ration the portions equally to the last bite. Tomorrow night, I should order a smaller Blizzard. Or two large fries. Probably doubling the fries would— there's Maris. Someone is walking with her, and I strain to see if it's Brett. The dude looks too skinny, so it must be Glenn. He's a good drummer. Seems to be a decent guy, too, if he's walking Maris to her car at the end of the night. I make a note of that. I've never thought about what it would be like to be a female on stage in front of a club full of drunk dudes and then have to walk yourself through a dark parking lot behind the venue to the isolated area where they make the bands park and load in.

Glenn turns to go back inside, and Maris walks past her Jeep. Shit. Did she see me? No. My truck was in the garage both times she was at the house. There's no way she recognized it. She's going toward the BMW. I sit up and consider beeping my horn. I bet the guy called her over there. She's not naïve enough to fall for that, is she? Damn, it's a good thing I'm here. My left hand is on the door handle when Maris leans into the window of the BMW.

Shit. What if the guy's a drug dealer and Maris has a habit? I knew all of this was too good to be true. Maris goes back to her car less than a minute later, on the nose for the amount of time it takes to conduct business, and puts her bass in the back. The BMW backs out of its spot, leaving room for Maris to get ahead of him, and waits for her to maneuver. I get a better look at the guy. Super clean cut. Looks to be wearing a shirt and tie for fuck's sake.

Maris exits the lot with the Bimmer following behind. What the hell? I'm here, so I follow both of them. If the dude is a deranged drug dealer, Maris could be in danger. They stay together in traffic, and I try to make sense of all of this. I really don't know anything about off-stage Maris. I didn't even consider that she might indulge in drugs because none of our band members have. Sure, Nico, Max, Jimmy, and I down a few beers during the night, and I think Max smokes weed sometimes. I've smelled it on him, but he doesn't do it at the house, and it has never affected his performance, so I don't care. Maybe Maris was buying weed. The customer before her wasn't buying weed, though. Unless she was using a different form of payment than cash.

Maris pulls into a gated condo community and the BMW follows her. Fuck. I can't get through the gate. By now, she knows he's behind her though, right? She didn't blow any red lights trying to get rid of him. Should I call her? And say what? "I was stalking you tonight and I think someone else might also be stalking you, too."

All I know for sure is that I'm not going to sleep very well because our new bass player is either a drug addict or is about to get murdered.

MARIS

"What's good, Club Fish? We're Funkengroovin'!" I yell into the mic. I have to pause for a minute to let the cheers die down. I smile widely and turn around to look at the guys as we enjoy the warm welcome. "Thank you very much. Good night!" I joke. The crowd turns on us in the friendliest way possible. "Oh, okay. Sometimes it's better to quit while you're ahead, but you want us to play?" The crowd cheers enthusiastically as Theo smacks his sticks together to count us into the first song on the set list. And we're off.

I played my last gig with Backyard Breeder three weeks ago, and I feel very much at home with Theo, Nico, and Max. We've come a long way together. Woodshedding songs every day for five weeks will bond you. We decided, together, that working from a set list makes for a smoother show than having Theo call songs off the top of his head at gigs, and we've worked out some really cool transitions between tunes. I'd say we're a well-oiled machine already.

Nico and I are carrying the vocals, so we stand in front of Theo and Max, who are staggered behind us. From what Theo says, I've drawn Nico out of his shell a little bit when it comes to interacting with the audience. We even have a few bits here and there during the night. We've developed an effortless rhythm, but I knew that would happen after he sat in with BB.

The first set flies by and we pause for a break. The guys stick together on break, which is cool with me. Theo and I put our food orders in before we start playing each night and the kitchen has them ready for our first break. The bartender knows to pour Nico a Guinness and get something cold and on tap for Max, and we cram around a table or into a booth, like we do now, and give each other shit for twenty minutes. It might be my favorite part of the night.

"Did you see the hot brunette at the four top stage left?" I ask before taking the first bite of my grilled grouper sandwich.

"Yeah," Max answers first. "I'm trying to figure out if one of those guys is her boyfriend. She isn't wearing a ring. None of those dudes seem to notice she's even there."

I laugh with the napkin pressed to my lips. "Exactly what I was thinking. And she's just watching the band. Not drinking, not talking to anyone."

"So weird," Max confirms. "Maybe she's AI."

Nico steals one of my fries. "I got a request for 'Smokin' Out the Window' by Silk Sonic. You know it, Maris?"

I nod and swallow. "We played it when it came out."

"Let's open with it," Nico suggests.

"Mmm, we have to do 'Don't Stop Believin'' as the last song of the night because it's Bartender Barbie's birthday," Theo says.

Nico and I look at each other and say, "You can sing it," in perfect unison.

"Not it," I say.

"You're a chick. It's easier for you to hit the money note," Nico argues.

"Okay, Axl Rose," I tease.

Max takes his coaster from under his beer mug and balances it on his thumb and forefinger. "Heads is Heineken. Tails is blank."

"Heads," Nico calls aggressively, boxing me out with his body by smushing me into the corner of the booth.

"It's heads. Nico sings it," Max announces as the rest of us cheer and jeer.

"Heads means I DON'T have to sing it," Nico says as the rest of us laugh. "That's what you said."

Max laughs. "I didn't say shit, cuh."

"Flip again," Nico instructs.

"No, no, no," I say. "It's decided."

Theo is getting up to return his plate to the bar. "Anyone need another beer? Maris, do you want anything?"

"Me," Nico says.

I gasp, but then I realize he means he wants something from the bar. I thought he was flirting. "Another bottle of water will get me through the next set. Thanks," I say.

"You know it's okay if we drink at gigs, right? Did we tell you that?" Theo asks me.

I shrug. "I don't drink off the job, really, so … I know it's part of the whole vibe for some people, and I don't care, at all, if you guys have a few during the night, but I'd rather hydrate and wake up feeling good tomorrow."

Theo smiles at me and looks into my eyes as if he's thinking about what to say next. I hope I didn't offend him. I just like to stay sharp while I'm playing and not drive under the influence. I wonder if I should explain further, but I don't know what else to say. It seems like he's waiting for me to keep talking.

"That's good," he says, finally. "Nico, I got you. See you guys up there."

"I noticed you haven't had a drink at any of our gigs thus far," Max says.

"Yeah. I started playing in bars before I was old enough to drink. My parents would take me to gigs and stay all night. I started working at age 13, so drinking wasn't possible until I was eight years in, and by that time, it was almost like the novelty of it passed."

"And you saw too much from the stage," Nico guesses. "We have a bird's eye view of the drunk fucks in the club every night. That's good incentive to stay straight."

"Meh. If you can't beat 'em, join 'em," Max says, taking a swig of beer for emphasis.

I smile so that he knows I get where he's coming from. I think Max is sweet. He just needs to find himself. He's not like Theo and Nico, so he has to be what they can't. He has to be Max. I want to tell him that, but I don't know him well enough yet.

"Let's get ready to rumble," Nico said, standing up. "Oh, Maris, I almost forgot. When we were up there, I noticed that the heel on your right shoe is wobbly. Let me see if I can fix it."

"Really?" I reach down to slip off my right platform pump. "It doesn't feel wobbly." I hand it to Nico, who smiles wickedly the second he has it in his possession.

"Last one to the stage has to sing 'Don't Stop'!" He takes off running.

Max and I look at each other with shocked faces.

"That was fucking diabolical," he says.

"Mad respect," I reply.

"Want a piggy-back ride?" Max asks.

"Hell yes. I'm not walking across the bar floor barefoot."

Max stands at the edge of the booth and I climb on his back. Theo has been informed of the developing situation and is standing on stage next to Nico, laughing his ass off.

Nico gets on the mic. "Ladies and gentlemen, please welcome to the stage, Maris and her royal steed!"

The clubgoers laugh and cheer as Max places me on the stage, then takes a bow.

I hop on one foot until I reach Nico, who gets down on one knee to place my shoe back on my foot. The crowd goes nuts.

"My Prince Charming," I say into the mic as I slide my bass over my shoulder.

"We had a request for this one on the break. It's from a few years back, from a band called Silk Sonic." Nico nods at Theo, who counts us in.

I'm still laughing at Nico's shenanigans as we sing the background lyrics about how someone could do something to someone, and he smirks while singing along.

I'm so happy with how things are going with Funkengroovin'. I might even delete the list of alternate band names I have going on my phone. I like being one of them. So much so that I invited Damon out to see us tonight. I'm comfortable enough to play off the other band members, now, so it's time.

This night, like all of them since I started playing with these guys, flies. I am watching the time, though, because I expect Damon earlier than he shows up. We only have about three songs left when he finally comes in, but I see he's still in business attire, so he must have had a long day. Poor guy. He works so hard.

I smile and wink at him from the stage and he blows a kiss back. He takes a seat at the bar and orders, then turns his chair to watch us with a big smile on his face. He imitates my stink face when I play my solo on the AJR song we just learned. He's so supportive of me doing what I love. I wasn't flunking out of law school or anything, but I didn't love it. I was doing it because I thought it would make me a lot of money. Being rich and miserable is not a great life goal and Damon helped me see that.

Max starts playing the keyboard part to begin "Don't Stop", and Nico dedicates it to Bartender Barbie, who blows an alcohol-fueled fireball in celebration. Damon must have felt the heat because he whips around in his chair to see what the hell's going on. I can't help but laugh at how out-of-place he looks.

Nico backs away, slowly, slowly, from his mic so that he couldn't be heard if he started singing the first line. Fine, I'll show off for my boy-friend. I slay this song; it just hurts my throat to push out the big notes.

"Don't stop!" We sing in four-part harmony, and the night ends on a huge crescendo.

Nico says goodnight to the crowd as I place my bass in its stand and wave Damon over to the stage. "I want you guys to meet Damon," I tell them before they all disperse in different directions.

"Cool. Okay," Max says.

Damon walks over and climbs the stairs to the stage. I realize that he looks downright chubby as he shakes hands with Nico, Theo, and Max. I hate myself for thinking that about the man I love so much. So what if he isn't a starving musician or a starving law student anymore. That's a good thing.

Introductions go around and the band is anxious to leave, so I suggest we all walk out together. On the way to the door, Max pulls me aside and compliments me for dating a geek. I can't help but laugh. "Geeks rule the world," I say.

Barely out the front door, Damon points to a spot up front where he's parked. "Well, guys, this is me," he says, unlocking the BMW and triggering the interior lights.

Nico and Max smile and thank him for coming out, shaking his hand again while saying goodnight, but Theo is frozen.

"That's you?" he asks, pointing to the BMW.

Damon nods. "That's me." He looks a little confused, and I'm not sure why Theo is suddenly acting weird, either.

"Huh," Theo says.

Shit gets awkward.

"Okay, well, I'll see you guys tomorrow, and Damon, you'll follow me, right?" I ask.

"As per usual. Maris's personal security service is on duty." Damon chuckles, and Nico and Max join in.

"'Night," Theo says quietly on the way to his truck.

I wish I knew what just happened there. Theo's demeanor did a one-eighty when he saw Damon's car. I doubt it's jealousy. Theo has a pretty great standard of living, thanks to his father's success. I don't get it. Maybe he had more to drink tonight than I realized. Whatever. It was a great night.

NICO

I LAY BACK ON THE CHAISE lounge beside the pool and look at the night sky. "I can't believe he would take such a big risk of being caught. You're absolutely sure it was him?" I ask again.

"Dude, one hundred percent," Theo says from the chair next to mine. "I saw Damon doin' the nasty with some chick outside the club while he was waiting for Maris."

"Hmm." I bite the inside of my cheek as I think. "Either that guy has the biggest balls on the planet, or they have an open relationship."

Theo scoffs. "You've heard how she talks about him. In her mind, they're married. And, if she was in an open relationship, she would have hit on me by now." He looks over at me to see my reaction.

I turn my head to make eye contact with him and say, "Theo, you beautiful beast, take me. Take me now," in a high voice.

"Anyway, welcome to my dilemma, dude. I don't know what to do."

I run my hands through my hair and intertwine my fingers behind my head. "I can see why you didn't say anything before. The whole reason you were there is kinda fucked up after she asked us to let her handle things with Brett, but I know you well enough to understand what you were thinking."

"Thank you," Theo says adamantly.

"But now, five weeks have gone by—"

"I didn't know for sure that it was Damon until I met him tonight."

"I get that. But keeping the secret is as damning as exposing the secret."

Theo stands up and takes his shirt off.

"You're cute and everything, but I was just kidding before."

"Fuck off." Theo dips out of his jeans next. "I just don't know if I'm obligated to tell Maris."

"She's our bro, not Damon, so what's the bro code here? I think you have to tell her."

"I'm not the only one who knows. You know, too. WE would have to tell her," Theo says before diving into the pool.

When he surfaces, I'm laughing, and he swims to the side and asks what's funny. "We could solve the issue by telling Max. He would call her immediately. Like, wake her up and tell her to pack her shit and get out of there."

Theo chuckles. "Maybe Max should be the moral center of the band."

"Like he isn't already? The dude is practically a priest."

"Maybe that's our answer, then. Maybe we owe it to Maris to tell her."

Theo lets himself sink under water while I wait for the answer to surface. I hear him come up for air and I carry on the conversation. "I don't want her to hate us."

"Things are going so well right now," Theo agrees. "I'm turning down club dates, so we don't get too burned out to write. Our socials have picked up steam again. Maris's followers jumped on, so we're reaching new people. The cohesiveness of the band, RIP Jimmy, has never been better. Everything just feels really good right now."

"What if we tell her, and then she tells Damon we told her, and they work it out, but he insists she quits the band?"

"Fuck!" Theo exhales. "She wouldn't do that. She doesn't seem like the type to do what her guys tells her if she didn't want to."

I sit up and lean forward in the chaise. "We don't know that. We don't know her that well. If we do nothing, we have a better chance of keeping the band together and that has to be our priority right now."

Theo puffs air out of his cheeks as he treads water. "If they break up, we'll be there for her. Get her through it."

"Exactly. At this point, it's none of our business."

"Okay. Yeah, it's not our place."

I hold my hands out wide and repeat the obvious. "It's not our place."

"Good. Thanks for helping me think that through."

I stand up and groan as I stretch. "I'm hitting the sack, man. Don't drown."

"Don't lock the sliders and set the alarm again. That was a dick move, bruh."

I laugh at the memory of some of my best work. "That was classic. No promises." I close the slider behind me and climb the stairs to my room. After a hot shower, I throw on some loose boxers and flop onto my bed. My phone alerts and I check IG. Maris just tagged us in a post. Damon must have taken some photos of the band tonight. I expand the first photo until it's just me and Maris in the frame. I know exactly what moment was captured. We had just traded harmony parts based on a quick hand signal. I had no idea if Maris would pick up on what I meant, but she did, and it cracked us both up. The remaining photos were only of Maris. I expanded those, too. The girl has legs for days.

I'm a leg man. It's so cool that she can do what I do. I've never dated a female musician before. She's one of the bros, but not. I feel a song coming. I'm so tired, but I don't want it to get away. I stumble down to the studio to lay down my guitar part along with the first verse and the chorus before going back to bed. Too bad I'll never play it for anyone because it will be obvious that I wrote it about Maris.

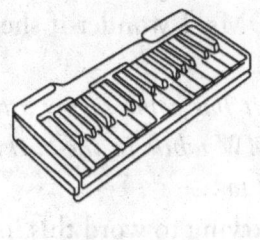

MAX

I DON'T THINK THEO AND NICO are stupid, but I would think they know sound carries over water, and that my bedroom is on the pool side of the house. I heard everything they said from my balcony, even the part about me being a priest. I think it was a compliment, though, and I'm feeling a lot more comfortable in the role I play in the band these days. I still regret rejecting the idea of Maris joining the band the first time I met her. My concerns, or the concerns I was echoing from Nico, couldn't have been more baseless. Maris has been a great addition musically, and she is already becoming the glue we needed as mates. Females have that magical effect. Anyway, I love her. I think she's a great person, and, the guys were right, I think Damon is a pig.

Theo and Nico made good points about the possibility of alienating Maris if we're the ones to drop the hammer on her boyfriend.

My phone alerts and I see that I've been tagged on Insta. It's a band photo from earlier. I'm a little surprised to see how good I look. I have a wide smile and look really happy as I play my lower board with my left hand and the horn sounds on my top keyboard with my right. I look as good as Nico and Theo. I think so, anyway. I share the post.

It's only been five weeks, but Maris has changed my life. I owe her a lot. I owe her the truth. How am I going to tell her something that will break her heart, though? I scroll through Instagram and let my mind wander. Then, I land on the answer. It isn't exactly brave, but it would get the job done without the band having to worry about blowback.

I sign out of my account and use a different browser to reopen the website. I don't know if this is necessary because I'm not used to having to cover my tracks, but it can't hurt. I make a new IG account using the name: A Friend. I hope that will get Maris's attention. I bet she has a lot of weirdos slip into her DMs. I wonder if she even bothers to read her messages. I guess we'll see.

I write: *Dear Maris, it has come to my attention that Damon entertained a woman in his BMW while in the parking lot of LIVE, five weeks ago, Tuesday. She appeared to …*

I stop and think. I'm trying to word this in a way that doesn't sound like me, but also is clinical enough to, maybe, make it hurt less.

… provide oral pleasure before engaging in intercourse with him. She was brunette and wore a short, tight dress and very high heels. When she left the car, she walked toward the front of the club. Minutes later, you exited the club through the back door and spoke with Damon, who remained inside his car, then you drove off with him following behind.

I see no need to freak her out further and tell her that the person informing her of this event followed them all the way home.

I'm only telling you this because I think you're great and deserve to know.

Satisfied with my wording, I hit send. That asshole doesn't deserve Maris. I was actually a fan when I saw that one of us dorks had landed a hot chick. For a minute, I looked up to the guy and he gave me hope. Turns out, he's a scumbag and I have no problem burning him. My loyalty is to Maris. No contest. I put my phone down and fall into a deep, sound sleep.

MARIS

I can't breathe. When I first read the message, I think it must be a cruel joke. None of the information included is private, apart from the sex bit. I've tagged Damon in posts and there have been photos of both the BMW and my Jeep. My gig schedule is public knowledge. Anyone could concoct this story. But, why? I don't think anyone hates me enough to try to hurt me this way.

Then, I remember the boxer brief incident. The night Damon got into the shower still wearing his boxers and I happened to interrupt him because I was out of bathroom tissue in my bathroom, so I barged into his while he was in the shower to steal some. I saw him through the glass and pointed out to him that he was still wearing his underwear, and we had a laugh about how tired he was after waiting for me after my gig that night. It had been my first gig with Brett after telling him that I was leaving the band, and Damon had been worried that shit might hit the fan after the job, so he insisted on waiting for me afterward and following me home. Brett had been an ass on the phone earlier that day but was okay at the gig. Barely talked to me, but that was fine. After that night, I told Damon he didn't need to worry. He was relieved because he isn't used to staying up so late.

Wearing his underwear into the shower suddenly didn't seem so innocent. Was the counselor getting rid of evidence? If he fucked someone in his car, it seemed likely. I shined my phone screen at his sleeping face as he lay beside me. Was Damon cheating on me? My Damon? After four years together and arriving at this place where we both have the jobs we want, he has a home, and we talk about marriage weekly ... he's cheating? The chick in a band is faithful, but he's cheating? I can't make it make sense. Should I wake him up and ask him? Maybe he would tell the truth in his sleepy state. Maybe his guard would be down. No. He's a lawyer; he wouldn't say the wrong thing. He's too well conditioned. I look at the bed stand on his side and see his phone on the wireless charger. I have never invaded his privacy before. Never looked at any of his devices. I'm going to now, though.

I get out of bed and grab the phone as I leave the room. Shit, I need his face. I go back into the room and try to scan his face, but it doesn't work. The phone wants me to unlock it with a code. I try the pin for our security system, and it opens. "Weak," I mutter. I open his Insta app and see that he has no DMs and hasn't posted anything for four months. Hmmm. How else would he communicate with a side piece? I can't believe he would be stupid enough to text with her. When I open his messages, he has someone named Ruthie muted. I read message after message and the tears start flowing. For the second time tonight, I feel like I can't breathe. I can't believe this motherfucker. After scrolling through messages that were generated over a year ago, my heartbreak turns to rage. I need to get the fuck out of here. Right now.

The next thing I know, I'm at Theo's gate with a Jeep full of band gear and clothes. I call his phone, since he isn't replying to texts.

"He-o?" he mutters.

"Theo, it's Maris. I'm at your gate. Can you buzz me in, please?"

THEO

I DIDN'T ASK MARIS ANY QUESTIONS last night. I opened the gate, met her in the driveway, and let her into the house. Her face was swollen and bright red. She was wearing a matching pajama set with pink silk shorts and a loose tank under a zip hoodie. She wore slipper socks with Birkenstocks. When she got out of her Jeep, we stood there looking at each other for a minute, neither of us knowing what to say. Words didn't come, so I held my arms wide, and she fell into me. I hugged her as a new wave of tears spilled over. I assumed that this had to do with Damon, but part of me didn't want to know.

I led her into the house and asked if she wanted anything to eat. She didn't. Maris squeaked out that she would be fine on the couch, but I wasn't going to let her sleep there when we had an empty bedroom upstairs. The upstairs master is where my father sleeps when he's in Miami, but he hasn't been here since last Christmas, so I coaxed Maris upstairs and peeled the covers back on the California King. She curled up in the fetal position. I covered her up and asked if she needed me to stay. She thanked me and told me I'd done enough. She thanked me again, and I closed the door behind me when I left to go back to my room.

This morning, I woke up earlier than everyone to go grocery shopping. I didn't know what Maris would want to eat, so I bought half the bakery and several frozen breakfast possibilities. I felt responsible for her. Again. I put the groceries away at home and made coffee, then waited for everyone to get up. I must have fallen asleep on the sofa because I'm shocked awake by a pillow hitting me in the face.

"Maris's Jeep is here," Nico says as he walks into the kitchen.

I adjust to being conscious. "Yeah, she came over around three, I think it was."

Nico's eyebrows reach for his hairline to ask what happened.

I shrug in reply.

Nico sees the bakery items on the counter. "Are all these for her, or?"

"Have whatever you want, man. I just noticed we didn't have much food in the house. I bought Max some Italian meatballs, too."

Nico laughs. "You're such a good mom."

I get up off the couch and join him in the kitchen where I open a box of croissants and shove half of one into my mouth. I talk around the flakey goodness. "*Bruhver.*"

Nico snags one and stuffs his face. "*Mhm.*"

"Good morning, men!" Maris appears in the kitchen, wearing denim shorts and a tank top.

I look at Nico, whose cheeks are turning pink, so I assume mine are as well. Nothing like getting caught being animals in front of our new roomie. Is Maris our new roomie?

I hold up a finger and Maris laughs.

"I like how you roll," she says, eyeing the breakfast buffet spread out across the island.

"I didn't know what you'd like …" I say, sounding more pathetic than I want to.

"You went to the store for me?"

"We didn't have much to offer," I explain.

Maris's face softens and she presses her palms together in front of her heart. "Thank you so much, Theo. You're the best."

I try to hide how proud I am of doing something nice for her, but I feel my cheeks lifting into an "aw shucks" smile.

"How do you like your coffee?" Nico asks, pouring three cups.

"Black is fine, thank you," Maris says, taking a seat on one of the barstool chairs. "Thank you for giving me a place to sleep last night. I didn't really have a plan when I left Damon's. I just kind of ended up here."

I get a stack of plates from the cabinet and set it next to the bakery boxes. Maris raises herself up on her chair to reach over the island to grab a plate and a Danish.

"You don't have to tell us what happened, but are you okay?" Nico asks softly.

Maris washes a bite of Danish down with some coffee. "I'm still processing, but my four-year relationship wasn't what I thought it was, and my boyfriend wasn't at all who I thought he was."

"Is it over?" Nico asks.

I flinch, but Maris doesn't.

She nods her head and then attempts a smile. "There's no going back. To him. I have to go back to his house to get my stuff, but I don't know where I'm going. Dude, one minute everything is fine, and the next, I'm single and homeless."

"You're not homeless," I say. "You're more than welcome to stay here. Just, if my dad comes for Christmas, you'll have to sleep with him."

Maris's mournful face breaks into a smile followed by a laugh and a snort. "Done," she says. "No, really, I appreciate the offer. I had no intention of moving in when I took the gig, but band house life would be really good for my spirit right now. And, I don't have enough savings for first, last, and security in the Miami rental market. This would give me some time to save up and get my feet back under me."

"I'm doing the same thing," Nico said. "I'm only nine hundred thousand short after three years of living here."

Maris laughs. "Inspiring!"

Max shuffles into the kitchen wearing his pajama pants and a Weather Report T-Shirt. "Shit. Did I oversleep? Am I late for practice?" He checks his iWatch.

"No, I'm early," Maris said. "I got here at like, three a.m.? Was it?"

I shrug and reach for another croissant. "Max, I got you some meatballs. They're in the freezer."

Max's eyes widen like I just told him he won the lottery. "Seriously?"

I chuckle. "It's just meatballs, my guy."

"I appreciate you, Theo."

Maris *awwwwwwed*. "I already like living with you guys. You're all so sweet to each other."

"We're on our best behavior for your sake," Nico says, smirking. "Wait until Theo takes a swim in his white boxers, and Max uses that nose vacuum thing over the kitchen sink when allergy season starts."

"Or when Nico brings home some rando from the club and she leaves glitter on his sheets and then everything that comes out of the washing machine for the next week has glitter on it," Max says.

Nico looks like he's going to kill him, but Max is oblivious. I look at Maris and make a face that, I hope, indicates how awkward I feel.

"You act like I bring girls home all the time," Nico says. Then to Maris, "I don't, by the way."

"Sometimes you stay at their house if they have a place," Max says.

Nico is getting a little worked up. "I guess hooking up every now and then seems like a lot when you hook up never."

Max looks hurt. "I have a girlfriend, remember?"

Nico and I both laugh harder than we should. "He has a girlfriend from Berklee," I say to Maris.

"Whom we've never seen or met," Nico explains.

"What guy would bring his girl around you two?" Max asks, sitting next to Maris at the island.

"Good point," Maris tells him. "He has a point."

I smile at her, and she returns my expression with conspiratorial kindness. She wants us to lay off Max, and I will. Now.

"When do you want to go get your stuff?" I ask. "I have a truck, and Nico has one, too, if there's furniture or anything."

Maris rolls her eyes. "Ugh. I don't even want to think about that, but it's probably better to do it sooner rather than later." She pulls her phone from her back pocket. "Let me find out when Dickhead won't be there today."

"Oh …" Max says. Then, he turns to Maris. "Sorry about that."

She shrugs. "I feel very fortunate that it happened when it did. Because of you guys, I have a job that I love and a place to live."

"And brothers," Max says, putting his arm around Maris and squeezing her shoulders briefly before letting go.

"Tomorrow morning, I'll make a frittata and my world-famous French toast," Maris says.

Max looks excited again. The way to that kid's heart is through his stomach.

Less than twelve hours ago, I was worried about how Maris might react if we exposed Damon. Not to mention the possible blowback on the band. Now, things are better than ever. I knock on the wooden cabinet. It seems fate is on my side.

MARIS

THEO CAME WITH ME TO the condo to pick up the rest of my stuff.

There wasn't much. I left things that were technically mine, like the Ugg bedding and the candle whose fragrance would always remind me of Damon. He can live with those reminders. Or throw them out. I don't care. I do, but I don't want to, so I'm faking it until it's true.

Theo was very respectful and sensitive as he helped me carry things down the stairwell to the truck. He asked if I wanted a few minutes alone in the condo when we were finished, and I told him I was glad he was there with me. Being there alone would have been too sad. Every time we walked by the Ring doorbell, I made sure to appear to be laughing or at least smiling. I could see the red lights indicating that Damon was watching. I want to hurt him back, like he hurt me. I know that isn't mature, or kind, but fuck that guy. I had so many opportunities to cheat and I was never tempted. I was faithful. At least I can hold my head up and live with myself knowing that I'm not deceitful.

Back at his house, Theo helped me carry my things up to the master suite, which I really didn't want to take. I told him that it made far better sense for him to be in that room, but he said I'm probably neater than he is and that I might actually use the soaking tub, whereas he wouldn't.

It's a ridiculous house and the master suite is amazing. There are two sets of French doors leading to a deck overlooking the pool. Max is my deck neighbor. He was lounging on his side reading a book when I went to check it out. The bed is bigger than anything I've ever slept in, and the nearly empty closet is bigger than Damon's living room. There are two sinks, toilets, and separate entrances to the huge shower in the bathroom. The soaking tub that Theo talked about could fit a family of four.

Theo said I was welcome to use the closet or the bureau for my clothes, whichever worked. The closet felt less invasive. I claimed a small section and hung my clothes after stacking my shoes and purses in designated places.

The other side of the closet holds some men's suits, pants, and shirts. I can't help but notice a photo of Theo and his parents, displayed on a shelf. He looks to be in his teen years. The girls must have already been going nuts for his budding sexy smile and gorgeous eyes. Theo looks a lot like his father. Dark hair and eyes. Classic Greek features. I stare at the woman in the photo and wonder what happened to her.

I guess it's possible that Theo's parents are still together, and she just doesn't keep things in this house, but I get the impression that it's just him and his father. The woman in the photo might not even be Theo's mom. What do I know? She's pretty, though. Dark hair and eyes like the boys. I notice her lips and decide that is definitely Theo's mother. *Nice job, ma'am.*

The guys called off getting into the studio today so we could all catch up on some sleep. I'm grateful. We're working tonight, but we can wake up and write together tomorrow. I take a long, hot bath in the tub and don't miss the tiny one at Damon's at all. I'm heartbroken and I hate that motherfucker, but I think I'm going to be okay here, with these guys. My new band brothers.

NICO

FUNKENGROOVIN' IS PLAYING THE SAME venue three nights in a row, so we get to leave our gear set up, which means we'll get home earlier tonight and can walk in fifteen minutes before hit time tomorrow. I love it when this happens. Setting up and breaking down is the work part of our job. The playing part is fun.

Maris found it weird that we drive separately to the venue and back home again, since we are going from the same place to the same place. Evidently, our reason for doing so, which is, *we just do*, wasn't satisfactory, so Max rode with Theo, and Maris came with me. The night was great, so we're feeling good on the way home. Maris rolls down the passenger side window in my truck and turns up the music. My playlist is a true mash-up and Fleetwood Mac's Silver Springs starts.

"Oh, my God. This song!" Maris's volume increases on the word song. "This is the perfect song for me to sing right now."

"We can do it tomorrow," I say, turning it up.

"Let's do it!" Maris's eyes are sparkly. I've noticed that happens when she gets excited about something. She starts singing along with Stevie Nicks. When she gets to the part about asking her partner if cheating was worth it and then admitting she doesn't want to know, Maris's eyes close.

I listen as she makes me feel the power of the lyrics from her perspective.

"Do you know the story behind this song?" she asks suddenly.

I laugh a little. "Oh, yeah. Stevie wrote the lyrics about Lindsey and sang it at him at their reunion concert in 1997. I was there."

"You lie." Maris spins sideways in her seat to look at me.

I chuckle again. "You're right, I wasn't born yet, but my mom and dad were there. My mom tells the story every time she hears the song."

"Stevie is so badass," Maris says wistfully. Then, she picks up the song again, singing with emotion.

I can't help myself, so I sing the harmony along with her and the blend is electric. We look into each other's eyes while I'm driving sixty in a forty-five and sing to each other.

When the song breaks down, Maris's voice rises over Stevie's with a quality that's different from the original. The clarity of Maris's voice makes her sound more vulnerable. The purity of the notes makes the hair on my arms stand up. When the song ends, I don't want to break the spell. Then, the moment is gone.

"Thank you for that," I say softly. "I feel so lucky to have witnessed what you just expressed. We definitely have to add it to the set list."

Maris exhales with sound. "On second thought, I'm not sure I want to pull my heart out of my chest every night and hold the beating mess in my hands in front of an audience."

I give her words the space and consideration they deserve.

"Let's record a cover of it. Tonight," I suggest.

"Capture lightning in a bottle," she says confidently.

"Text the boys. Tell them to give it a listen and tell Theo not to jump in the pool."

Maris laughs. "So, this is how it works, huh? We have everything we need to create at our fingertips."

"All we need is each other," I say. "Sorry, that was fucking cheesy. Sounds like something Max would say."

"I like Max," Maris says as she types into her phone.

"We all love Max," I concede. "That doesn't mean I want to *be* like him ..."

"They're in. Theo is stopping at DQ first. He wants to know if we want anything."

"No, thanks. I don't know how he stays in such good shape eating all the junk food he does after midnight."

Maris is narrating her message. "Nico says he doesn't want to get fat like Theo, and I'll have a lava brownie ice cream sundae thing."

"Oh, nice. Throw me under the bus."

Maris reads Theo's reply. "Tell Nico he's sexy. See you at home in ten."

I make a kissy face in the general direction of the passenger seat.

"Do you work out a lot?" Maris asks.

"Not nearly as much as I used to," I admit. "I played football at UM, but I blew my knee out freshman year and that was that. I had no plan B."

"Oh, wow, that's awful. I'm sorry that happened to you. Were you into music at that time?"

I shake my head. "Not at all. My roommate had a guitar, and I spent a lot of time sitting still while I was recuperating, so I grabbed it and looked up some stuff on YouTube. I became obsessed. And now, instead of being a wealthy Safety in the NFL, I'm a penniless musician."

"I dropped out of law school," Maris blurts.

My mouth falls open. "Okay, so that's where you met Damon."

"His new name is Dickhead, but yeah."

I stop the truck next to the gate at Theo's and punch the code into the keypad. "Sounds like music claimed both of us," I say. "What the hell is wrong with me tonight? I sound like a total sap."

"Maybe you're more sentimental than you'd like to admit," Maris says.

I laugh softly. "Let's go make a song that will make jilted lovers cry and gnash their teeth!" I growl.

Maris busts out laughing as we get out of the truck and enter the house through the garage.

"Seriously, I was very moved by your treatment of that song. I can't wait to record it."

Maris places her purse on the kitchen counter and stops quickly, not realizing I'm so close. I put my hands around her waist and hold her as I guide her forward, so I don't smash into her. The skin between the top of her jeans and her shirt is soft, warm, and firm. I feel something when I touch her.

"Sorry … sorry," I mutter.

Maris is laughing and turns to face me. She's several inches shorter than my six-foot, five-inch frame. As her chin tilts upward, my eyes devour her mouth. I want to kiss her so badly. For a moment, we're frozen in time.

"What's up, fuckers?" Max yells from the garage door, and we instinctively avert our eyes and put some physical distance between us.

"Maris, here's your brownie sundae and, Nico, we got you a Blizzard, even though you said you didn't want anything because Theo said you'd want one once you saw his." Max sets the DQ bag on the counter and sits at the island to unpack his own bag. "Do you wanna keep the same arrangement from the '97 show, or are we going to put our spin on it?"

"Do you have ideas?" Maris asks Max.

"I hadn't heard the song before tonight, but, yeah, when I was listening, I thought we could turn the heat up by modulating after the solo section. Give you the chance to really belt there."

My mouth is full of ice cream, so I wave my spoon at him and nod in agreement.

Max has a cheeseburger in one hand and is manipulating his phone with the other. He has a keyboard app up, and he plays a moody chord progression that increases intensity as it walks up the scale. "Something like that," he says.

"That's beautiful," Maris says.

"Yeah, man," I agree.

"Hey, losers." Theo finally appears in the kitchen holding a balled up DQ bag. "We ready to do this?"

"I love how an idea that was only born twenty minutes ago is already happening. I can't get over that," Maris says.

Theo smiles at her and shrugs as if making dreams come true is his specialty. Okay, maybe I'm reading too much into one expression, but it's because I'm starting to see Theo as an adversary. Which is … dangerous.

"I'll go get everything powered up in the studio," Theo says.

I watch Maris watch him leave. I don't like that she's watching him. Any girl in her right mind would choose Theo over me if she had the choice. He has family money. He's never had to struggle, so he has one gear, which is chill. Everything about Theo is easy. I know I'm more jaded than he is. More cynical. I can be a loose cannon, and Theo is more consistent. I'm a lot more fun, though. I have a bigger presence. Women are drawn to both of us, but the more adventurous ones like me best. *Dude, what the ever-loving mindfuck are you perpetrating on yourself right now?* I shake my head as if clearing my thoughts.

"Brain freeze?" Max guesses. "You're supposed to put your thumb on the roof of your mouth like this." He demonstrates. I kind of want to throw something at him.

"Thanks, Max. I'm gonna live." I pour the last quarter of the Blizzard down the garbage disposal side of the sink and rinse the paper cup before tossing it in the recycle bin.

"Would you mind terribly?" Maris asks, handing her empty container across the island.

I reach out with my left hand to take it from her, and my fingertips gently slide across her palm and pinky finger before I secure the plastic box. I feel something again, but I can tell she's not on the same page.

"I'm sorry," I say quickly.

She tilts her head. "For what?"

We both know what I mean.

I laugh it off and make a show of getting my hands tangled up as I pass the box from one to the other. Maris laughs and rolls her eyes.

Max's judgmental stare is burning into my profile. I can hear him mentally accusing me of being a hypocrite. He's not wrong.

Maris tells us that she's going to the bathroom and will see us in the studio. When I get there, Theo is already sitting on his drum throne and is zeroing out the mix on his iPad.

"What prompted the desire to do this song?" he asks me quietly.

"It's in my playlist." I strap on the studio guitar and find the sound I want on my pedal board. "It came on in the truck, and Maris started singing along with this hauntingly beautiful delivery. I suggested we add it to the playlist, but she said it would take too much out of her to sing it every night, so I told her we should record it." I find what I want and sit down on a stool.

"She was too cool today when we were moving her out. I don't think this has hit her yet."

"Hasn't even been twenty-four hours," I say, feeling shitty about how quickly I want her to move on … to me.

"Remember when I broke up with Shana?" Theo laughs.

I look him in the eye. "Shana broke up with you, my guy."

Theo laughs even harder. "True, but I like my version better. Anyway, it took me a week to shower. I was a fucking puddle, dude."

"You don't have to tell me. I was there."

"I'm just saying, we should keep an eye on Maris. We don't know her that well, but if anything seems off, we have to let her know we've got her."

"I'm sure she has family and friends for that," I say.

"Then, why isn't she with them?" Theo asks, raising his eyebrows.

I start playing the intro to the song, but I'm thinking about what Theo said. Maris has to have people in Miami she's known longer than she's known us. I just figured she came here because she knew we had the room. What if Damon was the only person she had here? I really can be a selfish prick sometimes. All I'm seeing is a clear runway, and I'm already configuring for landing.

Max slides onto the bench behind his keyboard set up and starts playing Silver Springs. "Who is the chick playing keys on this song?" he asks.

"Christine McVie," I say. "Don't you know Fleetwood Mac? You have to watch the Behind the Music episode on them. You know so much of their music already. It's in you via osmosis, maybe you just didn't know the band name."

Max shakes his head. "I think I'm a Fleetwood Mac virgin."

Theo and I look at each other as the jokes overwhelm our brains into a state of paralysis.

"Okay, guys, thanks for waiting so patiently." Maris appears holding four jars of different colors. "For the mood," she explains. "Can I kill the lights?"

We all offer versions of "Whatever makes you happy" and she makes a configuration of candles on the floor in the center of the room. Once burning, the glow casts shadows and drenches the room in ambiance.

"Wanna run it down a few times?" Theo asks. "Nico can get levels while we put it together."

Maris puts headphones on and whispers, "Let's see where it takes us, men."

When we have the magic take, I mix the track as everyone weighs in. No one is going to bed anytime soon. We stay with our creation, and each other. We play it back at unity through the studio speakers over and over again, complimenting each other as we focus on the nuance of each part. Of course, Maris receives most of the compliments. She bared her soul in this performance. It is lightning in a bottle, just as she promised. We know we have something remarkably special. While the rest of the east coast sleeps, we're the vessels that brought this gift into the world.

"Are we ready to put it out there?" I ask.

We look at each other, knowing that letting the song out of this room will change the intimacy of what happened between us. But it's too fucking good to keep to ourselves. We splash it across social media and drag our spent bodies up the stairs to bed.

THEO

WHEN I HEAR THE SOFT knock on my door, I know it's Maris. Nico or Max would walk right in. I'm just out of the shower and with a towel around my waist, so I whisper, "Just a minute," and slip into a pair of shorts.

"I'm sorry to bother you," she says when I open the door. "Did I wake you up?"

"No." I laugh. "As exhausted as I am, I think I have too much adrenaline pumping from that session to sleep."

"It was incredible, right?" Maris is beaming. "I just wanted to thank you again for giving me this job and a place to stay. I feel like the luckiest chick in the world right now."

"We should all be thanking you," I say sincerely. "You're what we needed to unlock what we did tonight, and I only wish we had found you years ago when Nico and I started this thing."

"Yeah," Maris whispers. "Finding you guys years ago might have saved me some heartache."

I'm hyper-aware that we're standing in the hallway not far from Nico and Max's doors. Maris is speaking softly, and I'm doing the same because neither of us wants to include them in this conversation.

She smells like vanilla. Her hair is wet, and she's wearing a long T-shirt without a bra underneath. I want to lift her up and pull her to me so she can wrap her legs around my waist. I want to carry her straight to my bed and make her feel the sensations I felt tonight listening to her sing. The unspoken question hangs between us. The woman decides. That's my rule. But this woman is in a vulnerable state. She seems to be wondering if she can trust her judgment. She certainly can't be wondering if I want her. I finally break the silence.

"It's been a crazy day for you. Moving out and everything."

Maris nods. "Yeah. But I'm okay. I'm better than okay."

Her breath smells like cinnamon.

"I went through a breakup a while back. You can ask Nico about it. I was a mess. It's okay if you aren't okay. It took me a long time to get my shit together."

Maris reaches for my hand. "I'm okay because I can see the path in front of me. I'm not spinning out wondering what's next."

I take a deep breath and squeeze Maris's hand. "The girl who dumped me was nowhere near as cool as you. Or as beautiful. Damon is a complete and total douche, but he's also an idiot."

Maris chuckles. "Thanks for saying that."

"I think … we should …" I trail off.

Maris looks up at me through her long eyelashes and raises her eyebrows. She smiles seductively and her voice deepens as she says, "I think we should … what?"

I clear my throat. "Get some sleep." I'm almost surprised to hear myself saying the opposite of what I'm thinking.

Maris searches my eyes for confirmation, and I smile.

She nods. "Goodnight, Theo."

"Goodnight, Superstar," I say.

She doesn't move. She stands in front of me looking into my eyes. I want to grab her and close the door behind us so badly that I have pain in my chest. The longing is fucking excruciating, and she's practically begging me. But it isn't the right time. Maris is worth more than this. I don't want to be the guy that takes advantage of her in a moment when she may be feeling weak. And I don't want to be a rebound.

Maris squeezes my hand again and then releases it, heading toward the second-floor master. I tell myself that if she looks back, I'm following her.

She doesn't.

MARIS

How much rejection can I take? I walk away from Theo's door, feeling humiliated. I'm sure he meant what he said and that he's trying to be a gentleman. But I don't need a gentleman right now. I need to feel wanted.

I close the door to the master bedroom behind me, grab my phone, and sit on the edge of the bed.

How do you feel about a no-strings bad decision to celebrate a successful night in the studio?

I hold my breath and press send.

> Nico: *My room or yours?*
> Me: *Mine. Be discreet.*
> Nico: *Ofc*

I'm suddenly very excited. Nico has a reputation. Brett made sure to tell me to watch myself around him as he's known to go through women like a gorilla goes through bananas. All I'm thinking now, is that practice must have made him an expert banana peeler.

Nico knocks softly on my door and, as I get up to answer it, he opens it and steps inside. He smells musky and sweet at the same time. It's the same fragrance I noticed earlier in the truck, so he must have reapplied after his shower. Loose, black boxers are the only thing covering his former football player's physique.

"I hope I didn't wake you," I said.

Nico silently closes the door behind him and walks over to me. "Who could sleep after a recording session like that? I feel like every nerve ending in my body is on fire."

We stand looking at one another until we simultaneously bust out laughing. He places his finger over his lips. "Max is a light sleeper."

I stifle my nervous giggle. "Oh, okay."

"I didn't take you for the booty-call type, but I'm pleasantly surprised," he whispers.

"Do you respect me less?" I ask.

Nico takes me in his arms and starts kissing my neck. "Sometimes, we humans need intimate human interaction."

His slow kisses are melting me. "I just …"

"No need to explain, Maris. We're consenting adults. Just be here with me." Nico presses himself against me and lifts my body off the ground until our lips are level, and then he kisses me as he carries me to the bed.

This was a snap decision, and one I might regret, but I regret nothing in the moment. Nico's kisses are seductive and so well coordinated that I feel tingling sensations beneath my skin as he concentrates first on my neck and then moves down to my thighs.

"I love your legs," he says as he expertly trails his tongue up the inside of my right leg.

I hold my breath as I anticipate whether he will focus between my legs next, but he doesn't. When he reaches my underwear, he briefly kisses the fabric pressing down just enough to tease what's coming. He uses his hands to move my shirt up my torso as he gently nuzzles the flesh between my belly button and the top of my underwear. Why did I put underwear on? It's only a wisp of fabric, but any barrier seems like a suit of armor right now.

Nico moves up my torso and raises his head to look at my face. "Is this okay?" he asks, as he starts to lift my shirt up. I want to strip the shirt from my body, but I also want to let him remove it.

"Yeah. If you don't finish what you've started, I'm afraid I'll explode."

Nico's rugged, handsome face twists into the smirk I admit I've always found sexy, and his eyes are filled with mischief. In this moment, he looks like a younger version of himself who is about to steal his dream car and get away with it.

He pushes my shirt up, revealing my breasts and says, "Maris, Maris, Maris. God gave you everything."

I can't help but giggle, but I lose my breath when he uses the palm of his hand to gently tease one nipple, while his mouth gives the other his full attention. I'm already lifting my hips to try to relieve an ache between my legs that needs his touch. I close my eyes as electricity emanates from multiple sensory points in my body at once. I feel a little guilty for receiving so much pleasure and worry for a second that I should be reciprocating more, but then Nico's mouth covers mine, and he's kissing me so urgently that I can't think of anything else. I hold the back of his head so when one kiss crests, there is no space between that one and the next.

Nico places a strong arm under my hips, indicating that he wants me to lift up, which I do, then he slides a pillow underneath me. He places a hand on my thigh, gently opening my legs. Then, he moves my underwear aside and enters me, building the intensity slowly, slowly, slowly until my body explodes and shudders with pure delight. I start to scream, and he covers my mouth with his own. When I'm spent, he whispers in my ear, "Can you come again?"

I chuckle. "I think it might kill me," I say.

"Are you sure?" he smirks.

"Yeah, let's take care of you."

Nico touches his nose to mine. "All you have to do is be here, Maris. I've been holding back since the first time we were on stage together."

I kiss him, feeling urgency again. "Let me on top," I command.

Nico rolls to the side while holding me tightly to him. He watches me and his hands cup my breasts as I move. Much to my surprise, I do have another climax in me, and we reach the peak together.

This is easily the best sex I've ever experienced. I feel like I should thank Nico, but that sounds super weird even in my head.

We lay next to each other on our backs as our breathing returns to normal and our heart rates come down. He massages my head with his strong fingers, and I realize musician hands are even different in bed.

"Since we were first on stage together, huh?" I ask.

He turns his face toward mine and his cheeks seem to flush. That could be from the sex, though. "Yes. Since then."

"Nico Van Asten, the most eligible bachelor on the music scene in Miami, has a crush on me?" I ask.

Nico laughs. "Come on, now," he says softly. "When you have that kind of chemistry on stage, you don't wonder if it would carry over to the bedroom?"

I try to maintain an innocent expression as I shrug, which makes Nico laugh so hard he has to stifle himself.

"Now we know that nitroglycerine and sodium nitrate do, indeed, make dynamite," he said.

"Indeed," I reply.

Nico leans over and kisses me tenderly, but it feels like a kiss goodbye.

"Are you leaving?" I ask, trying to sound totally nonchalant.

"We should probably both get some sleep. And I don't want to get caught in here," Nico says softly.

"That's probably smart," I agree. "Get home safe."

Nico chuckles again and I watch him search for his underwear without lifting a finger to help. It gives me the chance to see him naked, because I really haven't yet. He isn't modest and he has no reason to be. Once he finds what he's looking for, Nico holds the boxers triumphantly over his head and then steps into them. He raises his eyebrows at me and gives me a type of salute before he opens the door the tiniest bit to scan the hallway before he departs. He closes the door behind him as gently as he opened it, and I watch the lever on my side slowly return to the horizontal position.

MAX

THE SUN IS SETTING MY bed ablaze, so I know it's after ten a.m. This time of year, the sun invades my room mid-morning. I stretch and practice some deep breathing as my mind recalls the night before. I think about the extraordinary recording session, where the four of us

merged musical souls to make tangible evidence that Funkengroovin'
has sublime alchemy. And then, I remember what I told myself I'd talk
to Theo about first thing. Nico and Maris hooking up. Nico's a big guy.
When he moves around the quiet house, the house notices, and so do I.
I can't believe he didn't wait a night, not one night, before jumping in
Maris's pants. I'm kind of disappointed in Maris, too, but I'm mad at
Nico. Fucking hypocrite.

I reach for my phone to make sure the world is okay before getting
out of bed. I've always known I'll wake up to terrible news someday,
and the number of notifications and texts I have make me think my
premonition is coming true. I start to panic over who must have died,
but then I read the messages. My sleep-soaked brain tries to make sense
of the words *Silver Springs* and then it hits me. We're going viral.

I throw both legs over the side of my bed, and they crisscross on
landing, causing my first steps of the day to be desperate attempts to
avoid falling.

"Theo!" I yell before I open my bedroom door. "Theo!"

"Max?" I hear Theo's voice calling from the kitchen. "You okay?"

"We've gone viral!" I yell as I barely maintain an upright position
while descending the stairs. When I explode into the kitchen, I see my
three bandmates huddled around a MacBook on the kitchen island.

At seventy-five percent of my previous volume, I repeat, "We've
gone viral."

"Is two hundred thousand likes actually viral?" Maris asks calmly.

I feel my head jiggle on top of my neck, like a bobble head that
someone flicked in the forehead. "It's only been six hours since we
posted it, so yeah, it's got legs. That's what viral means."

"The likes are more than double the shares. Is that bad?" Nico asks.

"No. You're always going to get more likes than shares," I say,
owning my role of resident computer geek. "And not everyone who
views it leaves feedback, but if a user initiates play and watches for thirty
seconds, it counts. YouTube updates those numbers every 24-48 hours.
Why didn't you guys wake me up?"

"We didn't want to wake you up, but we couldn't wait to tell you, either," Theo said. "This is pretty cool, huh?" He smiles at me, and I can feel my face light up in reciprocation.

"Crazy, cool, brother."

Nico gets off his stool and carries his coffee cup to the sink, pausing to wrap his arm around my shoulders on the way. "The modulation makes it, man."

Getting praise from Nico feels like a drink of ice water on a scorching hot day.

"I mean, we all contributed," I say. "The feel you put on the guitar parts, your background vocals, Theo's tasteful swells and hushes … not to mention Maris's vocal. Shit, man, we should be going viral."

My bandmates laugh. Not at me, either.

"We have to ride this wave," Theo says. "We need to put out more content."

"You're right," Nico says. "There's a shitload of songs on our page, but they're all with Jimmy."

"Do we have any originals that could be finished in a couple hours?"

Nico opens his mouth to respond and then doesn't say anything.

"Nico? Do you have something?" I ask.

He shakes his head. "Theo's material is probably closer to finished than mine."

Theo finishes his breakfast and refreshes the web page. His eyes stay on the screen as he adds, "I have a couple I could play for you guys. Max, you have anything?"

I do, but don't want to risk the camaraderie I'm feeling right now. "Not really. Maris?"

She's next to Theo, pointing to a comment, and he laughs softly after reading it. He turns his face toward hers and something exchanges between them in a glance. Holy shit. Was Theo in Maris's room last night? Maybe it wasn't Nico, after all. Theo could make the floorboards squeak. I guess I figured Nico was the douchebag because Nico can be a douchebag sometimes.

"Sound good, Max?" Theo asks.

"Sorry, what?"

"He's daydreaming about all the single ladies listening to our song right now," Nico teases.

"Shut the fuck up, Van Asten."

"We were just wondering if you were cool with spending the day in the studio," Maris says softly.

"Yeah. Of course. I just have to eat something."

"Take your time, man," Theo tells me. "We don't have to roll for the gig until eight thirty."

This is exactly the kind of day I dreamed of when I attended Berklee. Wake up, record music, get paid to play music, sleep. This is my life. It might not be happening with the people I choose, but they choose me, which is more impressive in a way. They need me. Something has shifted in our dynamic since last night and it isn't just that two of us are having sex. There is a different level of respect this morning. We're more of a band than we've ever been before. Suddenly, I'm happy. Genuinely happy and optimistic. These are new feelings for me.

I select a couple pastries and pour myself a cup of coffee. Theo follows Nico into the studio, but Maris tells me that she doesn't want me to eat alone, so she stays. We don't talk, but it's nice that she stuck around to keep me company. I'm definitely not going to say anything to anyone about last night. Or own up to exposing Damon. I feel like my dreams are finally on track and self-sabotage isn't going to derail me. Plus, I owe it to the band to do my part to maintain cohesiveness.

"Okay, I'm finished." I spring up from my stool and rinse my plate and cup before dropping them haphazardly into the dishwasher.

Maris watches me with amusement, and she looks much happier than she did yesterday at this time.

"Let's do this!" she says as she links her arm through mine and steers us toward the studio.

"Let's do this," I repeat in a deep baritone, which makes Maris laugh. I love making Maris laugh.

THEO

NICO AND I ARE WAITING for Max and Maris to join us in the studio, so I take the opportunity to play some of the stuff I've been working on. I'm an adequate piano player, but Max adds flair to my basic ideas. Nico can hear beyond the skeleton of the songs I write. I record drums, piano, and add the vocal melody to my demos. In their current condition, they're far from hits, but Nico's ears hear the finished product. He noodles on his guitar as he listens.

"I like the vibe on this one. One part The Neighbourhood, one part The Beatles. Max can layer a lot of beachy chords on it. I like the melody, too."

"It's in a key that would be good for you, but we could change it for Maris," I suggest.

"Yeah, for sure." Nico transposes the key a step up and watches my face as he plays. I nod and advance to the next track I want him to hear.

"I like the four on the floor dance groove," he says a minute into the song, "but the hook isn't there yet."

I agree and stop the playback. The next song is the one I really want Nico to love. I press play and keep my head down as my eyes sweep up to watch him listen. He immediately starts playing along, which I know is a good sign. The time signature changes, and Nico starts laughing.

"Yes, man! That's the shit."

I clap my hands as Maris and Max join us.

"This hits," Maris says almost to herself.

"Okay, here's the hook," I say above the volume of the track. As the time signature of the song changes again to a slower groove the lyrics are *Slow it down, so I don't miss a heartbeat.*

"I like it," Maris says. "Can I sing it?" she asks Nico.

"We're looking for material for you," he says softly.

I'm glad Nico's delivery is less snarky than usual. The interest in Silver Springs seems to be making him giddy. I can relate.

"So, we like this one to work on first?" I ask.

"I dig it," Max confirms, taking his place behind the keyboards.

"Can we hear it from the beginning?" Maris asks as she picks up her bass and checks the tuning.

Nico slides her stool closer to him and she takes a seat. I think that's a little weird, but then he's calling out the changes. I glance at Max, who was walking her through material yesterday, and he doesn't seem to care that Nico is taking his place. This is our first time writing together, and I hope we will fall in line naturally.

When Nico lifts the fingers on Maris's left hand and places them in a different configuration on the neck of the bass, I cringe. Nico never did that to Jimmy.

"Just say diminished," Max tells Nico, who nods rather than giving him a death stare.

"No worries," Maris says. "That's a good idea, Nico."

"When I move here …" Nico strums a chord and Maris plays a cool run that ends with the configuration that Nico showed her. Max adds a unique part on top, and we all exclaim our approval.

"The song's already better than what I imagined," I say.

"Good bones, brother." Nico winks at me.

"Dude, you're all sunshine and positivity this morning," I joke. "I'm not sure if I trust it."

"I had a great night," he replies as Maris giggles.

"Two hundred thousand people agree that we all had a great night," Max says.

"Theo, go over the pre-chorus with me, please," Maris says as she starts playing it. "Is it this?" She phrases the bassline to sync with the groove and then switches to off-time. "Or that?"

"I think you have to stay with Theo there," Nico answers for me.

I shrug. "We can try it both ways and see how we feel."

"Okay." Maris nods. "I'd like to hear both versions."

As it turns out, the off-time bassline is cooler. Maris smiles with satisfaction when we all agree. Nico doesn't defend his opinion and rolls with the majority. If Jimmy were playing bass, Nico would have dictated what he played and drilled him until Jimmy was duplicating what Nico had in his head. I wonder if the change in his attitude is because he thinks Maris is a more competent player, and she is, or if it's because she's Maris.

We work through the arrangement and take the song from the top. This is where Nico and I usually lock in and communicate non-verbally, but his focus and attention are on Maris as we play. It feels weird. Like Max and I are playing together, and the guitar and bass are somehow disconnected from us.

"We're not syncing in the verse," I say into my mic, which carries my voice over the music.

Maris stops playing and bites her bottom lip as she listens. She circles her pointer finger in the air, which means to repeat what we just did, and she jumps back into the song with a simplified version of what she was playing before. Once we hit the pre-chorus, she makes her mark with the counter rhythm stuff and then slaps through the hook.

"Yes!" I say into the mic.

Nico nods his head and Max is howling. She fixed the problem.

"Yo ..." I say into the mic, which is my signal to stop playing.

"Less is more in that spot, Mare," Max says. "Good catch. Takes discipline to play less."

"Thank you, Max," she says sincerely. "It was getting muddled. And I think it helps the build later."

"Absolutely," Max agrees.

"Nico," I say into the mic. "What do you think?"

"Yeah, I'm with Maris on that."

I like this new Nico. I was worried about how he might react to having a bass player with her own ideas, but Nico seems to be content covering the guitar and background vocal parts on this one.

"Great. Let's run the music a few more times and then add vocals." I hit my sticks together to count us into the song.

We have the music recorded by two o'clock and take a lunch break before recording the vocals. Maris reworks some of the lyrics while we eat, and her tweaks make the song better. She sits beside me as she pencils in her ideas.

"Theo, we need some imagery here." She points to the lyrics in the pre-chorus. "We need to know exactly what shouldn't be rushed. What feeling are you trying to hold onto here? You don't want to miss a heartbeat, but what does that mean? Is that a lingering kiss or a prolonged touch?" Maris looks into my eyes as she talks, as if she will find the answer there. "You want to slow down ... what, exactly?"

I'm afraid to blink, but I'm afraid to maintain her gaze, because with her looking into my eyes like this, I'm reminded of last night when she came to my room, and what so easily could have happened between us.

I stutter. "Um, I ... well, first, it's just a song." I laugh uncomfortably. "But I guess what I was trying to say is not to bypass the sweet moments. The things that might seem inconsequential but can be huge if you let yourself fully feel. Like the first time you hold someone's hand, and you feel that spark. That can be hotter than sex on the beach if you pay attention."

A napkin hits me in the forehead.

"Theo's a girl," Nico announces, laughing. "Your pretty face makes sense now."

I smile and shake my head. "You should try it sometime. Touch a girl with something other than your penis."

"Fuck you," Nico shoots back angrily.

I can feel my face scrunch up, and I glance at Maris to check her reaction to Nico's outburst. Max continues to eat his lunch, but I watch his posture shift from relaxed to stiff.

"What the fuck, man?" I ask Nico. "Sorry if I struck a nerve. I thought we were just joking around. You know, the way we have for the last five years?"

Nico stands up and starts wrapping the rest of his sandwich. "I'm getting a little tired of being the butt of the man whore jokes, okay? I'm the oldest dude here, so, yeah, maybe I've had the most girlfriends, but I'm not an animal for fuck's sake."

"Nico," I say harshly. "Dude, you're overreacting. I'm sorry. I didn't mean anything."

"Whatever, just watch it from now on."

I look at Max, who is focusing on his lunch and trying to remain neutral.

"Brother, I'm sorry. I wish I had your rizz. That's never been a sore spot for you before, but if you've outgrown getting laid …"

Nico rolls his eyes and slams the refrigerator closed. "Leave it, Theo. Let's go get the vocals down. I want a nap before the gig." Nico leaves the kitchen, heading for the studio.

"What the fuck did I say?"

Max finally speaks up. "You didn't mean anything, Theo. Maybe Nico's just tired. None of us got much sleep last night." He looks at Maris, probably hoping she would reinforce his observation.

"Maybe there's another side to Nico and he wants us to acknowledge it," Maris says softly, which makes me scoff.

"Sure," I say sarcastically. "Whatever."

"I think I have the lyrics for the pre-chorus," Maris says, reading out loud.

Let my lips linger for a heartbeat more
Fingertips teasing what I have in store
Seduction too sweet to hurry
Baby, we'll get there, don't you worry"

I watch Maris's face as she reads the words, and her face flushes a little as emotions rise to the surface.

"That'll work," Max says as he heads to the studio.

"That's it?" I ask Maris.

"That's all you need to get the imagination flowing," she promises.

"That's what I was trying to convey. The whole idea was slowing down and enjoying the process of falling in love."

"But now I think you have to sing it, because a dude saying this stuff is hot."

I chuckle and lower my voice. "So, it's hot when a guy wants to slow things down? It's not taken as rejection? Because slowing down and not skipping the sweet steps, especially when the girl is really special, is how I would want to proceed." I hold my breath waiting for Maris to respond.

"You're a rare commodity, Theo."

I feel the heat rising in my cheeks. "I don't want you to think that we're all like Dickhead."

Maris laughs. "I like that you're honoring the name he earned."

"He shall be referred to as Dickhead forevermore," I promise.

Nico appears in the doorway. "You two joining us, or are you going to keep us waiting for the rest of the afternoon while you chat?"

Maris makes a face at him. "We're going over the lyrics," she says as she pushes her chair back. "We also decided that Theo is going to sing this one."

"Theo? We're supposed to be recording songs that feature you on lead vocals."

"Yeah, well, I fucked myself out of a song by writing words that should come from a guy."

"Well, then, should I sing it?" Nico asks.

"You can. You're obviously the Don Henley to my Glenn Fry."

"Who?" Maris asks. Her comment unites Nico and me again.

"Girl. Stop it right now," I say.

"The Eagles?" Nico says with his hands wide.

Maris's expression shows understanding. "Oh, you mean Linda Ronstadt's back-up band?"

Nico looks at me with disbelief painted all over his face, and he's my brother again.

"She did *not*!" I yell.

"She did."

"Oh, my God."

Maris cleans up after herself and sneaks to the studio through the patio door to avoid us.

"Chicks, man," I say.

Nico shakes his head. "Chicks, man."

73

NICO

MARIS RODE TO THE GIG tonight with Theo *to change things up*. I didn't say what I was thinking, which was that she started the trend of ride sharing to the gig exactly one night ago, and the musical epiphany she and I had together resulted in the band having half a million views across social media platforms less than twenty-four hours later, but whatever.

Theo's joke at lunch pissed me off royally. He made me sound like some kind of sexual deviant in front of Maris. She doesn't know me well enough to have formed her own opinion of me yet, and I don't want Theo and Max planting discord in her mind. I woke up in such a great mood after the recording session and my totally satisfying experience with Maris, but the day went to shit after lunch. We got the song recorded and it sounded good. I sang lead on it, and we recorded it in the key we transposed for Maris, so it gave me the chance to stretch, and I like my full-voice upper register. Every time we do a Panic at the Disco song, people tell me I sound just like Brendon Urie, which is a great compliment. I got to show off that part of my range on the song. I put some extra on it to impress Maris, and I think it worked. We'll see how well received it is. An original isn't going to pique the same interest the cover of Silver Springs did, and the whole idea was to put out another song with Maris singing lead. I was frustrated all afternoon, even after taking a forty-five-minute nap. Maris announcing that she was riding with Theo set me further on edge, and there's no way I could have tolerated Max riding with me, so I said I had an errand to run first and drove to the gig myself.

Now, on the way home, Max doesn't want to "squish" into the backseat of Theo's truck, so I'm stuck with him.

"Do you think we'll record another one of Theo's songs tomorrow?"

"Probably, Max."

"I think we should pick one for Maris to sing lead on."

"Me, too."

"The band sounded really good tonight; don't you think?"

Oh, my God, he isn't getting the hint that I don't wanna do small talk. "Yep." As soon as the light turns green, I send it and climb traffic to get us home as soon as possible.

"What's wrong?"

"Nothing."

"Did you sleep with Maris last night?"

I look at Max with murderous intensity. "What the fuck did you just ask me?"

"If it wasn't you, then it was Theo."

"Are you the band house Cock Block, Max?"

He tests a bro-y laugh. "Nah, man, I'm just worried. Shit got weird today, and I want to know if that's why. I was going to say something this morning, but then things were gelling so well, and we were all excited about the response to Silver Springs. Seemed things were better than ever, but this afternoon and tonight were kind of tense. You seem really tense. I mean, this is the whole reason we didn't want a girl in the band—"

"Max. We're not going to have this conversation because it's no one's business. Understood?"

"Nico, man, I'm just worried that our rising star is gonna get shot down before we get off the ground."

"Mind your business, do your job to the best of your ability, and don't talk about your fellow band members behind their backs. That's all you can control, Max."

He nods and makes a sound that indicates agreement. "I'm just worried," he says again.

"What song do you think we should record tomorrow?" I don't want to have this conversation with Max, but I want the previous topic of conversation squashed.

"Maris has a song idea that she was going to flush out and play for us tomorrow. It's kinda angsty, but funky from what she says."

"Good. It will be nice to have her musical perspective represented."

"I have some stuff, too, if anyone wants to hear it."

I close my eyes for longer than a person should when driving twenty miles over the speed limit. "What genre are you writing?"

"I mean, it's a departure from what we normally do, but we have the musicianship to pull it off."

"You should hire Theo and me as work-for-hire studio musicians and release your songs as your own project."

That quiets Max for a few minutes.

"I get where you're coming from, Nico, but I'd never charge you to play on your stuff."

"I'm suggesting that you get your rocks off doing your own music in a project where you have creative control, rather than in the band which has to be a collaboration. That way, you can record the stuff you like, and you don't have to share writing credits, or any subsequent licensing or sales that might come from it."

Max doesn't say anything else for the rest of the ride home, and I start to feel like a douche, but tonight is not the time for Max to pitch more of his "outside the box" ideas to me. I've never been less receptive to his proclivity to "change things up" than I am right now.

We pull up to the gate, and I punch the code in. The iron barrier has never retracted more slowly. Once parked, I tell Max that I'm hitting the sack and that I'll see him in the studio in the morning. I don't wait for Theo and Maris to get home before I go to my room.

I take a long, hot shower and then rinse with the lever on the coldest setting. Tomorrow will be better. I let Theo's innocent comment torpedo my mood today and I couldn't unfuck it. I'll feel better in the morning.

As I am toweling off, I hear my phone. It's a text from Maris.

Are you up for Round 2?

A smile spreads across my face, but my fingers hesitate. Certainly, everyone is still awake. I was sure the whole house was asleep last night, but somehow, Max knows. Even if he isn't entirely sure what he knows or about whom. But she wants me again. I can't turn Maris down. I want her, too. I feel my mood turning around already.

Ofc. Wait an hour after Max goes to bed and then come to me.

Maris "thumbs ups" the message, which is so dude-like that it turns me on.

I spray my chest with cologne and lie down, naked, on my bed. I must have fallen asleep because I regain consciousness balls deep in Maris's mouth. The realization, and sensation, makes me moan. She skillfully pleases me, but I don't want to finish, so I ask if I can return the favor. We compete with one another to see who can bring the other more pleasure until our bodies can't take any more and we explode in shudders.

Maris collapses on top of me, and I love feeling her weight fully melt into my body. It feels like we're fusing into one another. Her hips nestle perfectly under mine, and her head rests on my chest while I stroke her hair. Her breathing evens out and I feel the muscles in her legs release. She's asleep. I lift my head and press my lips to the top of her head. We barely spoke tonight. At the gig or in bed. "Sleep well, Sweet Maris," I whisper.

I should wake her up and send her back to her room, but Max already knows something's going on, and he'll have the same conversation with Theo that he had with me tonight, so there's no point hiding. I don't care who knows that Maris chose me. I'm happy she did.

But when I wake up in the morning, I'm alone.

MARIS

AFTER THEO TOLD ME THAT he didn't want to rush falling in love with a special girl, I figured we should talk. I told Max to ride with Nico, so we'd have some privacy. As soon as he started the engine for the trip home from the gig, I dove in.

"Can we talk about the last night?"

Theo turns to face me. His eyes are soft and curious. "Sure." He backs out of the parking spot and waits for an opportunity to get onto the ramp for I-95.

"I was feeling rejected, by Dickhead, and you were so kind to me when you helped me move out. You've been great since we first met. I was having a moment and wanted to feel desired, you know?" I look at Theo and he nods, but he doesn't interrupt while I'm verbalizing my thoughts. Geez, he does everything right, which makes this even harder. "I'm not ready for anything serious. Just some sexual healing, maybe." My nerves bubble over as laughter. "You're everything to me right now, Theo. You're my bandmate, my employer, my landlord, and the best friend I have, which is kind of sad, considering I've lived in Miami for almost three years."

Theo looks over at me and smiles, encouraging me to continue.

"I came here with Damon because he got hired by a law firm down here right out of law school, and we both figured the music scene in Miami had to be better than in Tallahassee."

Theo laughs politely.

"It's probably different for guys, but most bands only have one girl, so it's not like I meet a lot of potential girlfriends. Backyard Breeder played the same circuit, and I made the effort to get together with girls I'd meet out, but real friendships didn't develop." I inhale and exhale with exasperation at myself for dancing around the issue.

"I was wrong to put you on the spot last night, and it was a stupid move on my part because you hold my future in your hands. More importantly than that, you're a Grade A, Top Shelf, Next Level, One-In-A-Million dude. I, on the other hand, am a hot mess." I look down at my hands and start pinching the hard skin on my finger pads, as I've done since they formed years ago when I started playing an instrument with heavy gauge strings.

Theo takes the next exit and pulls the truck off the road. He parks and turns in his seat to face me. "For starters, I don't think you're a hot mess at all. You should have seen me when my relationship ended. I was the personification of a hot mess." He raises his eyebrows and nods for emphasis. "I'm glad you came to me last night. If you hadn't just been through a totally traumatizing event, I would have swept you up and shut the door behind us so fast, Maris. You're telling me what you needed, but last night I didn't know that, and I didn't want to take advantage of a vulnerable moment. If you aren't ready for a relationship, that's totally understandable. It took me a while to trust again. My heart was locked up tight. And, as much as I'd love to be your sexual healer ..." Theo gives me a wicked look, "... I can't. Because I have the feeling that if we ever got together, we could be incredible. But I don't want to wrap you up before you're ready, and I don't want to be your rebound."

"God, you're perfect," I growl. "How are you single?"

Theo laughs. "Nico says I'm too picky. He says my perfect match might be someone I'm not necessarily attracted to, so I should play the numbers game."

I don't like hearing that Nico likes the numbers game. Kind of makes my skin crawl, but I'll give him the benefit of the doubt that maybe he meant love should be based on more than looks.

"So, wrong time?" I summarize.

"I'd rather look at it this way; we're already important to each other and we're just getting started."

"I think my heart just swelled. Like, actually grew in size."

"Just know that I'm here for you, Maris. And, if you want to use me sexually and toss me by the wayside, I'll consent. I just want you to be sure that's what you want."

I bust out laughing. "You're the fucking best, Theo. Thank you for talking to me about this and for being so understanding."

He puts the car in drive again and starts toward home. "DQ?"

"Obviously."

By the time we get home, Nico's upstairs.

"Hey, Max. Got ya a burger." I toss the DQ bag onto the kitchen island and his face lights up.

"Thanks, Mare!"

"Theo paid, so—"

"Aw, thanks, Theo. I appreciate it, man."

Theo laughs. "No problem, my guy. I feel less guilty about my habit if I indulge with friends."

Theo and I sit at the island on either side of Max to crush our midnight snacks.

"Nico was asking what song we're going to record tomorrow. Did you guys decide?"

Theo's mouth is full, so he points to me.

I wipe hot fudge off my lip and reply, "I was thinking I'd like to have you listen to the one I was telling you about, Max."

"The angsty-slash-funky one?" Max asks.

"Yeah. It's called 'New Me, Who Dis?'."

Max and Theo both laugh.

"I like it already," Max says.

"The lyrics are pretty clever, and I think it could be an anthem for dissed chicks," I say, bouncing my eyebrows up and down.

"Sounds good," Theo says, crushing his DQ bag into a ball. "Studio at eleven?"

Max and I exchange looks and confirm that eleven works.

Theo yells over his shoulder as he takes the stairs two at a time, "Don't stay up too late, kids."

"Wanna watch a movie?" Max asks.

"I don't think I have two hours of gas left in the tank," I say. "Another time, though, for sure. I'm a movie buff."

"Me, too! What are some of your favorites?"

I like seeing Max so excited. The littlest things seem to make him happy. "I am obsessed with Humphrey Bogart and all the film noir from the 1940s, but I also like DC superhero movies. Hold your tongue if you're a Marvel guy, but I am obsessed with Chris Hemsworth."

"I think Nico kind of looks like a young Chris Hemsworth. Or at least a Hemsworth," Max says, watching for my reaction.

"Hmm. Maybe a little." I walk to the opposite side of the island to rinse my ice cream container in the sink before throwing it in the recycle bin.

"So, that's your type? More Thor than Dickhead?"

I let out a genuine laugh. "I honestly don't think I have a type, but

Dickhead was my first long-term relationship, so who knows? I was attracted to his nature more than anything, which turned out to be only one of his personalities." I don't want to talk about my situation, so I say, "What's your type? Do you have a photo of your girlfriend?"

Max takes the last bite of his burger and wipes his fingers on a napkin before he grabs his phone. I lean across the sink and see that his lock screen and home page are both new band photos with me in them. That warms my heart and makes me sad for him at the same time.

"Here she is," he announces, holding up a photo of a girl sitting on a bench by a lake. She has short, bobbed black hair, and her closed mouth smile looks awkward.

"She's pretty. The distance thing must be hard, huh?"

Max exhales with sound and then says, "Yeah. I mean, I don't know if she's telling anyone that she has a boyfriend at this point, to be honest. Don't tell Nico or Theo that, though. They'll give me endless shit about it because I kinda led them to believe we're a committed couple. Which might be cutting off my nose to spite my face, because I'm sure they could introduce me to girls."

I smile at Max and hold up my pinky, which he wraps with his own. "Pinky swear. And, if I ever run into a chick I think might be good enough for you, I'll hook a brutha up. I'm here now, so I'll give you the female perspective."

Max drums his fingertips on the island. "That, right there," he says.

"I'm going to hit the shower," I say. "See you in the morning, Max."

"Goodnight, Maris. Sleep well."

I mull over my conversation with Theo as I wash off the gig. My initial instinct was right. He's the man. Theo is going to make someone a great husband one day. Maybe sooner than later. He's young, but it seems like he's ready to find his forever person. A few days ago, I was someone's forever person, or so I thought. Finding myself single at twenty-six after expecting an engagement ring for every holiday for a few years running is like being plunged into a freezing lake from a warm bed. I'm still shocked by the recent turn of events, but Nico showed me what's possible. I've only been with a few guys, and there's only been Dickhead for the last several years. Sex with Damon was nice because I was in love with him, but sex with Nico is different. That thing he did where he lifted my hips before entering me. Holy shit. The man knows what he's doing. His body is incredible, he's charming in that bad-boy way, and I want him again.

When I get out of the shower, I text him and he tells me to come to his room after Max is asleep. I was a little nervous to reach out to him because he was moody tonight at the gig. I was worried that it had something to do with me, but I couldn't think what I might have done to upset him.

I take my time blow drying my hair and massaging body oil into my skin. I decide to change things up in the nether region and shave myself smooth. Much to my dismay, the skin there starts turning red, so I apply some aloe and am thankful that it will have time to calm the angry clam before Nico sees me. I really hope Max isn't watching a movie downstairs. I haven't heard him come up, but he could have done so while I was in the shower. I crack open my door and peek at the door between mine and Theo's. Max's door is closed, but there's a light coming from underneath. He's in there, but he's still awake. I wonder why Nico was so specific about Max being asleep before I sneak to his room.

Not gonna lie, sneaking is fun. It's spicy knowing that Nico and I have this secret.

I throw a silk robe on, tie it at the waist, and decide to paint my toenails. Thanks to Max, I have the time. As I paint, I try to imagine what Nico has in store for tonight. I try not to think about the other girls he's been with. Theo and Max make it sound like that's a big number. I bet he's been with a lot of experienced women who want to please him and make him come back for more. I stop painting, the small brush suspended mid-air when the thought pops into my head … what if Dickhead cheated because I wasn't pleasing him in bed? What if he wanted a different kind of sex than we were having, and he didn't want to ask me for it? Did he ever suggest anything different? I can't recall a time when he did. What if I suck in bed? What if Nico thinks I suck in bed? Did I *do* enough last night? I was incapacitated by his skills most of the time. He invited me back, so it couldn't have been terrible, but I feel like I need to step up my game tonight.

I make my way to Nico's room, after Max's light finally goes out. I find him sleeping in the nude, on his back; the perfect opportunity to blow his mind. When I close his bedroom door, I twist the lock to be safe. I go to the bed and take Nico into my mouth. His body responds and he wakes up happy.

I can see his body tonight, and every time he touches me, my skin tingles under his hands. God, he's sexy. We don't say much, but we become one effortlessly. Afterwards, I stay on top of him. I'm too exhausted to move. I close my eyes and I feel him playing with my hair. I feel so safe. My body and mind fully surrender, and I relax. As I enter that magical place between wakefulness and sleep, I hear Nico whisper, "Sleep well, Sweet Maris." His tender words surprise me, but I don't respond. I don't think he'd want me to. I fall asleep for a few hours and wake up to Nico tapping my back. I look at his eyes. They're closed. He's breathing steadily. I giggle because I know what's happening. I've been told I do the same thing … play bass in my sleep. Nico is fingering my back like it's the neck of his guitar. I gently lift myself off him and sneak back to my room for the rest of the night.

THEO

I MUST HAVE FORGOTTEN TO TURN my phone off before I fell asleep. I hear it in my dream and then I realize that it's ringing on my bed stand next to me.

"Whaaaaa?" I answer without opening my eyes or mouth.

"Son! Can you believe this? I'm watching Stevie Nicks talk about you! I can't believe this!"

"Dad?"

I hear my father whoop and laugh through the phone. "She called you guys the torch carriers! Holy shit!"

"What are you ... what?" I sit up and look at my phone screen as if it will help me figure out what my dad's talking about. "What time is it there, Dad?"

"Three in the afternoon. Are you sleeping through the biggest break you've ever had?"

I find the time. It's nine in the morning. I don't have to be up for another two hours. "I guess so. I don't know."

"Son, Stevie Nicks shared your cover of Silver Springs. She's introducing you to the world on her Insta page. She's on live right now. I'm going to share my screen with you."

My mind absorbs the words, and adrenaline starts rushing through my body. I drop the phone accidentally and pick it up again, fumbling to turn the volume up.

"This singer, Maris, makes this song her own with her gorgeous delivery. And the arrangement ..." Stevie Nicks chef's kisses toward the camera. "Check out Funkengroovin', guys. Tell 'em Stevie sent you. Love you all."

"Holy SHIT!" I hear my dad's voice booming through the phone. I forgot we were on a call for a second.

"Stevie Nicks is talking about my son!" He must have been shouting to everyone in his office because a big cheer rises in the background.

"How did this happen?" I ask.

"Who knows? Who cares? You're about to have your fifteen minutes, so strategize. Seize the day. If you want marketing advice, call my team. I'll give you all the resources you need."

"Um, thanks, Dad. I don't really know what's happening, so I don't know what to say right now, but let me catch up and I'll call you back, okay?"

"Opa!" my dad yells in celebration.

I can't help laughing at the image in my mind of my dad, in a three-piece suit in his high-rise office building in Athens, smashing whatever glassware is within reach while yelling *opa*.

"Love you, Dad. I'll call you back soon."

I hang up and see that Silver Springs, Stevie Nicks, and Funkengroovin' are trending. My shocked brain needs help interpreting information in this moment, so I run down the hall banging on doors, yelling, "Wake up! Wake up!"

Nico opens his door first, still wet from the shower with a towel around his waist. "Where's the fire, Theo?"

"Stevie Nicks shared our cover of Silver Springs, and she did an Insta live about us!"

Nico's face transforms from confusion to disbelief to shock in a matter of seconds. "Get the fuck out."

"I will not."

"Show me." Nico rewraps his towels and tucks the end more securely as he yells, "Wake up, everyone!"

I play the video of Stevie as Maris appears, hair sticking out in every direction, her palm shading her eyes, with a pink silk wrap tied too tightly on one side and too loosely on the other. "Somebody better be dead," she whispers.

"Stevie Nicks—"

"Oh, shit, NO!" she screams. "No, not her. We just did her song—"

Nico steadies her by touching her shoulder while I laugh and resume my explanation. "Stevie Nicks ... shared our version of Silver Springs on her IG page."

"What?" Maris screams.

"Dudes, we said eleven. What the ever-loving fuck?" Max comes out of his room wearing glasses and sweatpants.

"Okay. Listen to me," I say. "Listen."

Nico smirks while Maris and Max nod for me to continue.

"Stevie Nicks shared our version of Silver Springs on her IG page. Then," I raise my voice for the second part, so they won't start freaking out too soon, "she made a video where she talks about passing the torch to us, she compliments Maris, and she tells everyone to check out Funkengroovin'."

"Get the fuck out," Maris whispers.

"That's what I said but look." Nico replays the video.

Max leans against the wall and slides down to a seated position. Maris screams and jumps up and down, which she shouldn't do in a short robe, and Nico remains stoic, apart from a shit-eating grin, which is quite wider than his usual. I have a moment with Nico. This started with the two of us. He holds up his big paw, and I crash my open palm into it, producing a smack that makes Max flinch.

"Oh, my … I can't believe this," Maris says. "Stevie Nicks heard me sing one of her songs. And she liked it! I think I'm gonna pass out. I can die now."

Nico smiles at her and leans against his doorframe.

"This is a moment we'll never forget, guys," I say solemnly.

"I've left my body," Max drones.

I look at Nico again, and we shake our heads and laugh together.

"Now what?" he asks me.

"My dad said we can tap his marketing team."

"That's a great start, but they're not exactly music managers, and they're not on this continent," Nico points out.

"I'm so overwhelmed right now, and I feel like I have to take all the right steps in the next ten minutes," I admit. "I could use all the guidance I can get."

"Maybe we should wait for the industry to reach out to us," Nico says, shrugging his shoulders.

I bounce my fingertips off my chin to jumpstart my brain. It doesn't work.

"We need a lawyer," Maris says. We all look at her with suspicious eyes. "Not Dickhead. An entertainment attorney. Someone to help us navigate this and capitalize on the recognition Ms. Nicks just gave us."

"Do you know anyone?" Nico asked.

"I say we start at the top of the list and work down. Shoot for the moon."

"Or we wait for the industry to come calling like Nico said. Cut out the middleman," I say, unsure which idea to pursue. "My dad probably knows people who know people."

No one knows what to say. Maris's phone is ringing in her room, and then mine goes off in my hand, making me jump. Max's screen lights up, and Nico's crickets start chirping from his bed stand. The four of us search each other's faces and start laughing.

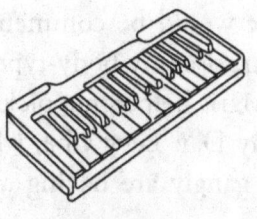

MAX

I'm having the greatest week of my life. I don't want to sleep at night because I'm afraid I'll miss something awesome. Since the Stevie Nicks thing, everyone I've ever met has reached out to congratulate me on my success. They don't know that I'm still making a hundred seventy-five bucks per gig and that we have a bunch of club dates on the calendar that we have to honor, or we'll get sued. It's not like the recognition turned into instant cash flow, but Theo's working on it. He got us signed with a management company that books tours and festivals. He says that we're "fielding offers." All I know is, our shows are standing room only and every video we post catches fire.

Poor Jimmy stopped by the house yesterday. It was great to see him, but I could smell regret all over him. It made me sad.

Today, we're recording another original and then syncing the recording with a video shoot that we'll do later. I don't hear anyone moving around the band house yet. The sun is crawling across my bedroom floor and hasn't reached where I'm prone on my bed reading YouTube comments on the video we posted yesterday.

The comments are mostly complimentary, but there are some landmines. Of course there are, it's the internet. I'm secretly thrilled that the mean comments are pretty evenly directed at all four us and not just me as I initially feared. I fully expected a plethora of *which of these things doesn't belong* takes, but the criticism ranges from the ridiculous to the constructive and no band member is unscathed.

Maris is generally criticized and complimented on her looks, which makes me realize that being a well-adjusted woman in present day society must be impossible. The comments should be about her voice and her playing, and some are, but the vast majority are about her appearance. I thought there would be comments about me being geeky and gangly, but, to my surprise, my body-type hasn't been compared to Nico's and Theo's at all. Maris helped me pick out new glasses last week and they give me a skinny Dan Levy vibe, which feels good. I've been noticing that geeky and gangly are having a moment, so I might be hittin' at the right time.

The girls are overwhelmingly crushin' on Theo and Nico, though. That's fine. It's what I expect. Nico used to play football, and he still has that physique that girls cream themselves over. He has all the moves and says all the right things. Theo is a *snack* according to Nole4Life315 and a few thousand others who *love* the comment. He is also described as a Zaddy, the meaning of which is not clear to me even after a trip to the Urban Dictionary page. I think they're saying he dresses like an older guy. Theo has money and taste, so I guess that makes sense.

The sun is climbing onto the bed now and I want to eat breakfast before we start. Also, I need to put some effort into how I look due to the video we're shooting later. Nico would bust my balls if I started the day in one 'fit and changed clothes before we shoot the vid. He's always making me feel self-conscious.

I pull a wildly colored Hawaiian shirt out of my closet and pair it with tan board shorts. The mirror says it's cool. I ask myself what Nico would say, then I remember that I have a trusted stylist right next door. Maris will help me. It's almost ten a.m., so she's probably awake and doing exactly what I'm doing.

I open my door and see Maris's opening at the same time. I feel my face break into a big smile, but then my eyes clock what I've stumbled onto. I was right. I called it weeks ago. A month? Longer? Nico locks eyes with me and his face is stern. He doesn't say a word, but I hear an echo of him telling me this is none of my business. He's right out of the shower and has a towel around his waist, which is pretty normal for Nico. I'd never walk around the house that way, but he often does. If he was coming out of his own room, I wouldn't think a thing of it, but he's not. He closes Maris's door behind him, and his expression changes to a look that seems to ask *Can I help you?*

"Does this look cool for the video?" I ask him. Fuck. The last thing I want to do is invite Nico to insult me, but here we are.

He considers the shirt for a second and says, "Yeah. It's kinda 70s. Especially with the glasses. Bruno Mars would approve."

I nod and close my bedroom door behind me. "Cool." I head downstairs to breakfast and try to collect my thoughts. I mean, I figured it was Nico. Now, I know for sure. So, what does that change? Nothing. I hope he and Maris know what the fuck they're doing so that when this little sneaky link blows up, and it will, it doesn't affect the continuity of the band. I wonder if Theo knows. Maybe they're just keeping it a secret from me because they think I won't be cool with it. I mean, I'm not, but it's not like they need my permission.

I microwave a bacon, egg, and cheese croissant and start the coffee maker.

"I like the 'fit, Maxer," Maris says as she strolls into the kitchen with a big smile on her face. Morning sex has that effect on faces.

I consider telling her that Nico liked it, too, but I feel like I should keep that in my back pocket. "Thanks. I want to do better than a T-shirt, you know?"

Maris is wearing her signature denim shorts with a crochet top. "I like that style. It feels authentic for you," she says, smiling. "You ready to go with the song for today?"

I play hot potato with my breakfast as I transfer it from the microwave to a plate. "Yeah. I have an idea for the bridge that elevates it quite a bit, I think."

"Cool. Can't wait to hear it." Maris retrieves cottage cheese and fruit from the fridge. It's the same breakfast she eats every day.

When the coffee is ready, I pour two cups, add almond milk and stevia to mine, and drop off her mug on my way to the island stools.

"Thanks, Maxer."

"Have you ever toured with a band, Maris? What are the accommodations like on the road?"

She shakes her head. "I've done fly gigs, but never a full tour. I imagine we'll have some say in our accommodations, but you should ask Theo. I bet he knows."

"I know, and I'm not telling you guys shit." Theo appears in the kitchen and begins draining the coffee pot. "What's the question? And good morning. I like the shirt, Magnum."

I look down at my shirt and feel my eyebrows display confusion. I don't know what Magnum means, but my mouth is full, so I let Maris speak.

"We were just talking about accommodations on the tour. Did they talk to you about any of that yet?"

"Our manager, Phil ... I love saying that ... said they shoved four-piece bands into one hotel room in the past, but I told him that's not going to work for us. A female needs privacy, so we'll get at least two." Theo adds sugar to his coffee and circles the spoon around the mug a few times before taking the stool next to mine.

"It's no big deal, I was just curious," I tell him.

"Phil says we'll get a look at the proposed contract, but he warned me that we won't be able to make many changes. We're getting some priceless PR right now, but we're lucky to be on the bottom of the ticket." Theo shrugs. "I'll take it."

"I'll take it, too," I add. "I'm excited. I hope we have dates in Boston eventually so I can play close to school."

"That would be cool," Maris says.

"Good morning, men!" Nico enters the kitchen like a general rousing his troops. I watch Maris to see how she reacts to him, but she just looks up from her plate and smiles.

"Nico, do you have my Bose spot in your truck? It wasn't in mine when I was unloading last night."

"Yeah, man. You left it on the stage."

Theo looks relieved. "Awesome. I thought I left it behind or it got ripped off. I wanted to ask you last night, but I couldn't find you, and you didn't answer my text."

Nico takes a long swig of coffee, and, beside me, Maris stiffens. He swallows and leans back against the counter. I notice that Nico is dressed better than he would be for normal rehearsal. He's wearing the current style of men's shorts that show off his muscular thighs with a long sleeve knit shirt pushed up to his elbows.

"I actually went back to the club for it," Nico says. "Bartender

Barbie called me to tell me we left it behind. I thought you guys were already asleep, all the doors were closed, so I just jumped in the truck and went back for it."

"Barbie has your number?" I ask.

Nico shoots me a look. "I've known Barbie for a long time, so yeah, she has my number."

Maris inhales sharply but doesn't say anything.

Theo laughs wickedly. "So, that's why you didn't answer my text." He finishes his coffee and slaps Nico on the shoulder on his way to the sink. "I'll go power up in the studio."

"Right behind you," Maris says as she finishes her fruit. She walks past Nico without glancing in his direction and rinses her dish in the sink. Nico looks up at me and tilts his head toward the door, so I leave. I really want to hang back and listen, but there isn't anywhere to stand in the great room where Nico wouldn't see me.

As I turn my keyboards on, I make conversation with Theo.

"Did you know the girls online call you a Zaddy?"

His face scrunches up as he tunes his snare drum. "A Zaddy? What's that?"

"I think it has to do with how you dress. Like you're sophisticated."

He scoffs and hits the snare to test the tuning. "This is sophisticated?" He gestures to his short sleeved, collared V-neck knit shirt with a vertical stripe of embellishment on either side. His shorts are the same length as Nico's. They both have the legs for shorter shorts. I, on the other hand, will stick with board shorts due to the size of my quads being only slightly larger than my calves.

"Chicks think so." I test all three keyboards. "Although, some say you're way too young to be a Zaddy. I'm not sure the definition is well defined."

"I haven't read anything that anyone is writing about us online." Theo admits. "Don't wanna know."

"Dude, you should. I mean, there are some assholes, but the vast majority of the comments and reviews are positive."

Theo has the tuning he wants. "Nice."

I'm not sure if he's still talking to me.

"I was pleasantly surprised that people weren't bullying me. I think I've been conditioned to expect that."

Theo stops hitting his snare. "You're an accomplished musician, Max. Why would you expect to be bullied?"

"Once a geek, always a geek." I laugh.

Theo points one of his sticks at me. "I don't have geeks in my band."

I smile and look down at my keys. I know I'm blushing. I wish I didn't love hearing that from him as much as I do. I wish I didn't need that reassurance. "Thanks, my guy."

"Really, dude. You gotta let that shit go. You know how many names I got called in school because of my last name? My whole third grade class pronounced Athanasiou, *Athens asshole*."

I laugh and then hold my hand up in apology.

"See? Miami is a melting pot, but there aren't a lot of Greeks here. I took a lot of shit. Kids looked up who my dad is and either wanted to be friends because my family was rich or wanted to put me in my place because my family was rich. Then my mom died ..." Theo inhales deeply and uses his hands to clear the space as he exhales. "You gotta let that shit go, man. Define yourself, don't let anyone else define you. You're an essential member of a band that's blowing up. You gotta decide which Max Anthony Castelano you're gonna present to the world. You tell the world who you are, not vice versa."

I clear my throat and swallow hard. "Thanks, Theo. I really needed to hear that."

"Where the fuck is the other half of the band?" Theo smacks his crash cymbal. "Let's GO, delinquents!"

Nico comes in looking bewildered. "We were cleaning up in the kitchen and starting the dishwasher. Do you guys think the dishes clean themselves?"

Theo rolls his eyes dramatically.

"Sorry. Sorry. I had to go to the bathroom." Maris tosses her bass strap over her shoulder. "Thanks for powering up my gear, Theo."

"No problem," he replies. "Okay, Nico, it's your song today, so you are the musical director for rehearsal."

I keep an eye on Nico and Maris. I'm curious about what's happening between them. I know it's none of my business, like Nico said, but I can't help wondering if Nico is in trouble for dropping Maris off at home after the gig and going back out again. It didn't seem like she knew he had done that. I'd like to be a fly on the wall in whichever room they discuss this later.

MARIS

WHEN MAX LEAVES THE KITCHEN, Nico takes my hand in his and turns me to him. "I'm sorry I didn't tell you that I went back to the club last night. I was afraid it looked bad, and now it looks worse."

I shrug. "You don't owe me an explanation," I say softly.

"Of course I do. I fucked up."

"Did you?" I tilt my chin upward to find Nico's eyes. He looks confused and that peaks my anger.

"By not telling you that I was going back out. Yeah. By not telling you that Barbie called me."

"Why is any of that fucked?"

"I could have told Theo to go get the speaker himself. It's his, after all."

I slow blink.

"Instead, I didn't tell you that I was leaving, and I went to the club myself to pick up a speaker from a girl I had a fling with last year. And I felt like a total shit the entire time and that's what made me realize that I used to do that kind of stuff routinely. I lied by omission, I lied outright, I kept secrets … I don't want to be that guy anymore."

"Yeah, well, it seems you wanted to be that guy last night. But it's really none of my business because it's not like we're together. We're not a couple."

Nico lets my hand go and I reach for the dishwasher detergent.

"I think I was testing myself. I hear how stupid and juvenile that sounds, by the way. Barbie and I didn't have an emotional connection, but we had fun together. On my way to the club, all I wanted to do was turn around and make my way back to your room—"

"Which you did, eventually." There's an accusatory tone in my voice.

Nico nods in acknowledgment and continues. "... But I already told her I was coming to get Theo's spot. So, when I got there, I texted her to send William out the back door with the speaker, he put it in the truck, and I came home. I didn't even see Barbie. You can ask her, Maris."

I press my lips together and start the dishwasher. "You know, I just got out of a long relationship. The last thing I'm looking for is a complicated situation. I don't want to have to think about this all day."

Nico takes my hand in his again. "I'm sorry."

"Nothing to be sorry about," I say.

"Okay," Nico says, but I can't tell if it's a statement or a question.

"Okay."

"I'm ..." He points toward the studio just as Theo smashes his crash cymbal as punctuation.

I try to laugh, but the result is weak.

I promise myself to focus only on music for the rest of the day, but I know I'm lying to myself. Why am I shocked that playing with fire burns?

NICO

I wish I had more time to talk to Maris, but I hope she'll hear the lyrics in the song I wrote and realize it's about her. I lucked out with the timing ... spending hours on this tune this morning might keep me in Maris's bed. When I wrote it, I didn't expect to offer it up as a band song, but I like it a lot, and I think Maris and Theo can give it a great groove. Max might not get the feel right away, but he'll get there. If there was anything I could magically bestow on Max, it would be feel.

Instead of playing the recording, I get out my acoustic and play the song while I sing it to the band live. I don't trust my voice to remain steady if I look at Maris while I sing, so I close my eyes before I start.

Once I'm through the first verse and the chorus, Theo jumps in and anticipates the bridge. He knows where I'm going before I go there. Maris and Max just listen as I sing:

> *I know I don't have a chance*
> *with a woman like you*
> *You're more than I deserve*
> *We both know that's true*
>
> *I'll never have your heart*
> *I'm not on your mind,*
> *But with one word from you*
> *I'd leave the others behind*

When I get to the part about becoming the man who protects the girl's heart, Maris says, "Awww." I'm glad she's listening. I sing through the first verse, the bridge, and the hook, and then stop abruptly. "Dig it?"

Theo's face makes me believe he's going to shoot it down, but he says, "Yeah, man. I like the acoustic vibe. We don't have much of that, so it gives us the chance to explore a little bit of a different sound."

"I'll layer electric guitar parts over the hook," I say.

"Do you have an idea for the bass line?" Maris asks. She's sitting equal distance between Theo and me, and she's noodling on her bass, eyes cast down as she speaks.

"I'd love to hear anything you came up with while you were listening."

Maris nods and starts playing a simple walking line that repeats the pattern after six notes. I join in with her, and Theo plays a soft rimshot to keep time. It works.

Smiling, I raise my eyebrows at Max. "Come on, man."

Max layers some strings on the song that completes the atmospheric vibe I didn't intend but am delighted to hear. "That's cool, Max."

The ideas start flowing and the mood in the studio lifts. When we're creating something and get a glimmer of potential greatness, it's a feeling like no other. Theo and Maris fall into a pattern that drops the beat every other time through and we all yell, "OH!" to show our approval.

"This is going to be cool, Nico," Theo says.

"That space is everything, man." I smile and pick up the electric studio guitar to add another layer of sound. It gets an immediate exclamation of approval. I'm glad the song is coming together, but I feel like the lyrics made Theo suspicious while going completely over Maris's head. Whatever. The song is finding itself, and I sing the panties off it, so it's a win, regardless.

***

The song took longer than the others we've recorded, but I think it's the best original we have to date. We filmed the video of us playing it, or playing along to the track, if I'm disclosing behind the scenes details. I'm making an effort to be very precise with my thoughts to train myself to be fully forthright with my words and actions. I don't want to make another mistake like the one I made last night.

Max and Maris made dinner while Theo and I mixed the song and produced the video. They brought our plates into the studio and had time to get ready for the gig, but Theo and I hit the road wearing the clothes we had on in the video, which wasn't a big deal. We looked good enough for the outdoor, waterfront one-off gig we had tonight. We arrived later than we like to and set up in record time. I barely got a sound check in before it was time to hit. On a three-hour gig like that, we only take one break, and Theo and I spent it in his truck with the AC on listening to the final product from the day's session through his car speakers. It's funny how car speakers are sometimes better than industry standard studio speakers for identifying separations in the mix.

All day long, I've been watching Maris for signs that she's either upset with me, or a signal that we're cool, but she's been utterly and completely normal. Usually when I piss a girl off, I know it. But with

Maris, I can't tell. Maybe that's partly because we hide what's going on between us. She's treating me exactly the same as Theo and Max. I don't like it. I want to be able to take her into my arms on the break and nuzzle her neck. I want to show the dudes that are eyeing her on stage that she's taken. I want to kiss her in front of everyone. I want to be her man.

We have the night off tomorrow, so when we get back to the band house, we all jump in the pool. Theo and I strip down to our boxers, and Max and Maris join us after changing into swim trunks and a bikini that sets my desire ablaze. Unfortunately, Theo and Max notice that fewer clothes do more for Maris than a sexy outfit does, and I catch both of them staring at her. I clear my throat when I feel Theo is being particularly obvious with his appreciation. *That's my girl, man.*

As usual, Max was the last one in the water and the first one out. "Can we agree to sleep in tomorrow?" He asks as he climbs the pool steps. "I feel like I haven't slept in a week."

"Fine with me," Theo says. "We can take the day off and hit the studio after dinner if we want to."

"I would love to get some sun!" Maris says excitedly. "I haven't been to the beach in forever."

Theo presses his hands on the edge of the pool and lifts himself to a seated position with his feet dangling in the water. "I could go for a beach day," he says.

"Right on." Maris paddles her pool float over for a high five.

"I could do a beach day," I say.

"You hate the beach, Nico." Theo keeps me real.

He's right. I absolutely, positively do. I don't understand the appeal of getting coated in sugar sand that has the staying power of glue mixed with salt, then sitting still as the sun bakes you for hours on end. I'll go for a swim in the ocean, but afterwards, I'm back in the truck heading home for a shower.

I roll my eyes dramatically. "You're right, I grew up on a lake, so I'm a lake dude. Just trying to support the family outing, my man."

"Oh, it won't be a family outing," Max says. "No way in hell I'm going to the beach. My paleness is glaring enough in the moonlight. I'm gonna sleep all day, like the vampire I am."

Theo laughs, and Maris tells Max to do what makes him happy.

"So, do you get up early to stake your claim on prime beach real estate, Maris?" Theo asks.

"I like to go at low tide to collect shells, but I haven't looked at a tide table in weeks. I have no idea what time that happens tomorrow."

Theo stands up to get his phone and I want Maris's attention, so I choose the most adult way to get it. I swim under her pool float and turn it over, spilling her into the water.

She lets out a satisfactory scream and when she resurfaces, I'm lying on the float with my hands behind my head.

"There are other floats that aren't being used, Nico," she says sassily.

"I like blue," I say, smirking.

Maris's eyes become slits and she dives underwater with purpose. I look at Theo. "Uh-oh."

I hear him say, "You brought it on—" before my ears are underwater. Her feet are on my shoulders, so I grab her ankles and get my feet underneath me. The shoulder stand falls apart and Maris slaps against the water hard.

"Oh!" I reach for her. "Are you okay, baby?" I lift her out of the water and hug her close to me. Then, I feel Theo and Max's eyes boring into my back, and everyone goes quiet.

Maris saves us. "I'm fine, *baby!*" She sweeps my feet from underneath me on *baby*, and I surrender to buoyancy.

"Simmer down, kids," Theo teases. "The first low tide is at noon, Maris, so what time do you want to head out?"

"About ten? We can take my Jeep. I have an in-vehicle parking permit." Maris looks excited about the day she's planning with Theo, and I'm both happy for her and jealous as hell.

She turns to me. "Do you really hate the beach?" It's like she's reading my mind.

"I really do. But I was willing to go. For the record. You'll have fun with Theo, though. He has a wide variety of frisbees. The soft kind, the hard plastic kind, your classic glow-in-the-dark flying saucer ..."

Maris lets out a genuine laugh and exits the pool. "Thanks for the fun and supremely creative day, men. I'm off to bed."

"Ditto, what Mare said." Max follows her into the house.

"I'm out, too." Theo starts toweling off and I'm the rotten egg in the pool.

Maris has texted me every night since that first night. This is the first time since we started sleeping together that I don't know if that text is coming. I can't tell if she's angry about last night. I'm angry at myself, though.

I grab the blue lounge float and straddle it like a surfboard. I glance up at Maris's balcony and see that her bedroom light is on. When her bathroom window illuminates, I wonder if I should be heading to the shower myself. I paddle to the side of the pool where I left my phone and make sure my ringer is on and my volume is up, and then I lay back and look at the stars. I admire the ones strong enough to break through the noise of Miami's bright skyline. I miss the sky in northern Wisconsin. I don't think I could stand the cold winters anymore, but I loved the summer sky at night. The northern lights reached us occasionally, and my parents always took us camping when the show was expected.

From my peripheral vision, I see Maris's bathroom light go out. Seconds later, her bedroom turns dark. I've floated to the shallow end, so I push myself off one side of the pool to propel myself closer to my phone. I consider texting Maris. Maybe I should call her. Ask her if I can come up to talk. I look up at the glass doors leading to her room and will her to think about me. Will her to want me.

As the minutes pass, I feel more and more tired. The next time I look at my phone, it's a half-hour later. Two-thirty in the morning here, but an hour earlier in Wisconsin. Still late, but Marcus will probably be closing the bar. I pick up the phone and call.

"What's wrong, little brother?" I hear his Northwoods accent and already feel better.

"Ayo, big brother," I say, rounding my Os. "I was just thinking about when mom and dad used to take us camping to see the northern lights and thought I'd call."

"You ready to come home from hurricane central?"

I laugh. "Dude, you'd love it here. You really need to come down to visit."

"Nah, I got everything I could want right here at home, but that isn't why you called. Tell me what's goin' on."

"Well, there's this chick—"

"Just one?" Marcus asks, laughing.

"Just one."

"I'm listening."

Talking to Marcus is helping cushion the realization that the text I'm waiting for isn't coming tonight.

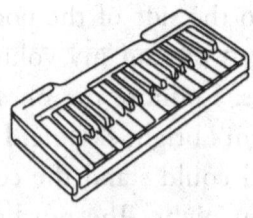

MAX

EVERYTHING SAID IN THE POOL is amplified onto my balcony as if I'm sitting right next to the person speaking and, man oh man, Nico has fallen hard for Maris. He's really baring his heart to his brother. I didn't think Nico had a heart.

MARIS

AS I DEBATE WHETHER TO text Nico to come to my room, I glance down at the pool through the French doors. I see Nico is still floating on the blue lounge and talking on the phone. I swear if he's talking to Barbie … I crack the door open and hear my name. Whoever is on the other end of the phone is getting a whole dissertation on how Nico feels about me and how shocked he is to find himself in this position. I should close the door and give Nico his privacy. He clearly isn't ready to share this with me. Instead, I sit on the floor on my side of the door and put my ear to the open balcony, which transmits sound waves like a speaker.

THEO

I SET MY ALARM FOR NINE o'clock and when it goes off, I can't remember why I'm getting up early. My mind goes to my first year, first semester college schedule and I try to work out which class I have. Then, I remember Maris and the beach.

I jump in the shower to fully wake up, then throw on swim shorts and a rash guard. I pack an insulated bag with two bottles of water, a couple bottles of Kombucha, ice, two sandwiches, and a bag of grapes. From the garage, I grab a beach umbrella, and a sand mat big enough for two. I remember Nico's crack about my frisbees and choose a soft one and a hard plastic variety. I leave the goods next to Maris's Jeep and hit the kitchen for coffee. I'm happy to see Maris is already there having her cottage cheese and fruit.

"Good morning, Beach Buddy," she says, smiling.

I pour myself a large mug of coffee and sing, "Beach Buddies!"

"I have plenty of sunscreen and two bags for shelling in case we get lucky," Maris says between bites.

"I put some essentials together, too. There's a bag by your Jeep."

"You're the best Beach Buddy, ever."

"I know." I savor my first sip of coffee. "I take beach very seriously."

"When I was at FSU, I missed being near the coast so much. It physically hurt to be so far inland."

I chuckle. "When I was young, we lived in Athens, right on the water, and my parents used to love to go to the Isles for holidays and weekends, so I grew up in the water. I know what you're saying."

"I can't imagine having Mykonos and Patmos at your disposal. I hope you appreciated that," Maris says.

"I was a kid. Of course I didn't."

Maris laughs. "I grew up on Fort Myers Beach and I loved every second."

"Girls are smarter than boys, and you grow up faster."

"You right." Maris winks at me as she finishes her breakfast. "I'll be ready to roll in five."

I swig the rest of my coffee and try to manage my expectations for the day. I'm looking forward to getting to know Maris better. I didn't know she grew up on FMB. I wonder if that's where she started playing out professionally. Before the big hurricane hit there, it had a thriving live music scene. That would have coincided with the timeframe Maris was there. I write a note to Max and Nico and leave it on the coffee maker. *Good morning, gents. Have a great day.* I guess I am a Zaddy. But a young one.

When Maris returns to the kitchen, I'm ready to go. We systematically remove the doors of her Jeep and hit the road. Her driving makes me nervous. She's very fast and climbs traffic like Nico does. I decide to distract myself from the fear of death with music. Maris and I sing along to the songs I choose from her phone's playlist. I fully enjoy the sun on my face and the wind in my hair. Once we cross the bridge to the beach, traffic slows our pace, making death less likely. I turn the music down and help Maris look for an open spot. Luck is on our side, and we find street parking, which will be impossible once the Snowbirds come back for the season. Summer in South Florida is sweltering, but it's the best time to be here. Our state is overpopulated year-round, but more pleasant during the months the Northerners vacate.

I follow Maris to a spot on the sand near the water and we set up camp. I hang my rash guard from the spokes of the beach umbrella, and Maris follows suit with the sundress she wore over her bikini. It's a different one than she was wearing last night. Bright pink today with light blue butterflies everywhere. It's cute and sexy at the same time. Maris has a bangin' body. Damon is such an idiot. How could he lose her?

"So, rewind to earlier when you were telling me about Ft. Myers Beach. How long did you live there?" I'm sitting on the mat, applying sunscreen, and Maris is beside me, laying on her back with her hat over her face.

"Until I left for college. Born and raised on the island. It was a pretty cool place to grow up. Small town feel, but plenty of opportunities to play music. My dad was the music teacher at Ft. Myers High for years."

"Dude, you're lucky you had someone to teach you. Or was it forced on you?" I ask the Seminoles football cap.

Maris laughs. "I think it was both. Honestly, playing music was the only way to spend time with my dad. He was a utility player. He was proficient on every instrument. One of those guys, you know? He kind of let me play with instruments like they were toys, and I picked the bass most often. How did you start playing?"

I groan. "I want to lie to you really bad right now."

Maris moves her hat and peeks at me from underneath it. "Must. Tell. Truth. Especially if it's embarrassing."

"If you tell anyone else, I'll … be angry with you." I warn sternly.

"Bro code," Maris promises.

"Okay. I started playing the drums because I thought I looked enough like one of the Jonas Brothers to get hired into their band because none of them play drums. I was filling a need."

Maris laughs so hard the hat falls off her face. "That's adorable, Theo."

"Am I turning red? I swear it's from the sun and not because I'm burning from humiliation."

"I watched Camp Rock too many times to count," Maris admits.

"Me, too!" I sit up and grab a bottle of water. "Want some agua?"

"Yes, please."

"Were you ever in a band with your dad?"

Maris returns the hat to her face and answers affirmatively. "At first, yeah. Then, we both got fired because the other band members didn't want to be in a *kid band*. So, Dad got me a job playing with some of his former students who already graduated. He booked us and drove me to gigs. It was a great, easy way to start out."

"I bet he's super proud of what you're doing now. Will he and your mom come see the band anytime soon?"

"Hmm." The hat took a deep breath. "No. They divorced the summer before my senior year, and dad took it really hard. He moved back up north, where he grew up, and was killed in a car accident just before Christmas."

"Oh, shit, Maris. I'm sorry."

She's quiet for a few minutes, and I wonder if I ruined the day.

"I lost my mom senior year of high school, too," I confide. "Cancer."

She removes the hat from her face and turns on her side to face me. "I saw the photo of you with your parents in your dad's closet. She was gorgeous. You look so much like her."

"She was the most amazing woman. Even when she was sick, she comforted us. So smart and funny. She was happy if everyone around her was happy."

"I want to be that kind of mom someday. That's probably the best way to influence the world around you. My mom is not a good person."

I cringe. "Sorry to hear that. Do you think that's why you're so ... opposite? Did you make the conscious decision to be completely cool, or did it just happen?"

Maris smiles. "My dad was cool. It's genetic."

"Any siblings?" I ask.

"Only child. My dad said they got it right the first time, so there was no need to try again. Personally, I think my parents' marriage was doomed by the time I arrived, and they didn't like each other enough to have another kid. I'm sure my mother would have left my dad years earlier if I hadn't come along."

"So, it sounds like your family life wasn't the happiest," I say softly.

"I was always happy when I hung out with my dad. I regret not moving up north with him."

"That's heavy."

"It was, but I took full advantage of the wellness center at Florida State, and I did years of therapy. I've come to terms with it but regret sneaks in from time to time." Maris lifts her eyes to mine. "I'm not damaged goods, though. Not any more than anyone else. No one gets out of childhood trauma-free."

I chuckle. "So true. It took a long time to stop being angry at God for taking my mom. I was angry for years, but I have peace now. My dad helped a lot. He was there for me. I'm sorry you had to find your way back to good alone."

"What doesn't kill you makes you stronger," I say raising my water bottle.

"To growing up," she says, lifting her bottle.

"To blowing up," I say.

Maris emits a low-volume squeal and does a seated dance. "We're blowing up," she whisper-screams.

We each take a swig and Maris lays back down, but I remain seated with my forearms resting on bent knees as I watch the waves take over the sand and recede again.

"Thanks for caring about me enough to be curious about my past," Maris says softly.

Her comment makes my heart hurt. Is she used to encountering people who don't show her basic human caring? "I should have told you this before you took the job, I guess, but I don't think of us as just a band. My goal is to bring players together who complement each other musically, but also to cultivate a personal bond. I guess I don't know how to spend as much time together as we do without getting close personally."

Maris's hand finds my back. "You're such a good guy, Theo. Imma ask you again, how are you single?"

I nearly choke on the water I'm swallowing. "Evidently, it's because I'm an only child and everything was given to me, and I don't under-stand that everything isn't always rosy for everyone. Let me see, what else did she yell at me about while breaking it off?"

Maris laughs heartily. "Seriously?"

"Oh, yeah. And more. I was totally blindsided."

"I would have never guessed, as an *only* myself, that you're an *only*. It seems so natural to you to have your band brothers in your house. It was hard for me to adjust to dorm life because I never shared a room, but you share a whole house."

"Yeah, well, we'll see how generous I feel on tour if I have to share a bed with Max or Nico."

Maris sits up. "Maybe we can get two rooms with two doubles and one of you can bunk with me. We'll figure it out. Being well-rested is important if we're going to make a splash on this tour."

I look over at Maris to try to read any innuendo that might be behind her eyes. I shrug. "Okay, we'll figure it out."

"Wanna hit the water?" she asks.

"Absolutely. And it's close to low tide, so maybe we should bring those shell bags you packed."

Maris gears up in sunglasses and a hat, and I hide my eyes behind dark Ray-Bans just in case Maris gets ahead of me on the beach. We're just talking at this point, but I'm still a man. A Greek man, at that.

MARIS

WHEN THEO AND I GET home, Nico's in the studio playing guitar with headphones on. He's recording something, so I stand in the door-way and watch without him knowing. He wears a pair of loose joggers and a T-shirt that looks like it's been washed into soft submission. He has dark blonde stubble on his face and there's no product in his hair. He's gorgeous. I watch his fingers to get an idea of what he's playing, and I hear his music in the way a musician can hear with their eyes. I notice how precisely he strikes each note, and I imagine the sound that goes with each string he plucks. He's so talented. His skills weren't taught, but rather learned by doing, and I find his devotion admirable.

Theo passes me on the way to the stairs, and I put my finger in front of my lips as I point to Nico. Theo holds up a shaka and sticks his tongue out in a rock 'n roll way to show respect. Then, he winks at me as he heads for the shower. We talked all day long. Surprisingly, very little of our conversation was about music, the excitement over our band, or the upcoming tour. It was almost like a date in the sense that we interviewed each other and shared pieces of ourselves. It made me realize that, regardless of what Nico told *whoever* on the phone last night, he doesn't know me.

Nico finishes the take and turns to play back what he recorded. He sees me standing in the doorway and his mouth opens into a wide grin. I notice that when he has stubble on his face, the dimple in his right cheek is even more pronounced.

"There you are," he says. His voice sounds raspy. Like he hasn't spoken yet today, even though it's four in the afternoon.

"Working on something for the band or something of your own?"

"Funkengroovin'," he says, removing the headphones and holding them out to me. "Wanna hear?"

"Yeah, sure." I cross the studio and hold the headphones to my ears with the headband dipping below my chin, so it doesn't touch my salty hair. Nico presses play and I close my eyes to hear better, which makes Nico chuckle because he does the same thing.

I bop my head as I listen. It's just the music at this point, no vocals yet, but I start humming a melody line. I open my eyes and see Nico studying my face. The music stops and I relinquish the headphones.

"Nice," I say.

"Thank you. I got five or six fully flushed out songs in the can today. Amazing what you can do when you're left alone with your thoughts."

I look into his eyes. He's hard to read. Nico has that thing the best performers have, the ability to draw an audience in. He pulls me in the same way. He's alluring and everything about him attracts me to him, but when someone is always that way, I wonder if it's real. Theo is always sweet, but I don't question his sincerity. Am I unfair to Nico because he has a reputation?

"What kind of thoughts inspire such music?" I ask.

"Can we go up to your room?" he asks.

I bristle.

"Just to talk. Just to have some privacy to talk."

"Aren't you worried about the guys seeing us?"

Nico shakes his head. "I don't care."

I'm not sure what feelings are bubbling up in my chest, but I agree and lead the way upstairs. I'm glad to see that both Max's and Theo's doors are closed. What does it mean that I don't want them to see me in this moment? Then, Bartender Barbie's face pops into my head and I know. Nico made me feel like a fool. And yet, I have no claim to this dude.

Nico closes the door and locks it behind him. I gesture toward the bed but remain standing myself. I rinsed off with fresh water before we left the beach, but I'm still coated with sunscreen and salt.

"You got a lot of color. Did you and Theo have a nice day?"

I smile and nod. My stomach is suddenly upset, and I don't trust my voice.

"I'm glad." Nico rubs his lips together. "Maris, I wish I could go back to the night before last and make a different choice. I wish that I had told you the whole story about going back to the club before I jumped into your bed. I'm sorry that I intentionally tried to keep that information from you. That was wrong." He's looking right into my eyes as he speaks, and I feel like I can't breathe. I don't know what I want him to say next.

"In my defense, I didn't do anything to disrespect you. What I did made me realize that the only girl I want to see after the gig is you."

I scoff and roll my eyes. "Oh, thanks. It's an honor to be your first call hook-up."

"Woah, Maris. That's not what I'm saying. I'm trying to be respectful of what you told me yesterday in the kitchen. That you just got out of a long relationship and don't want anything complicated. I'm not trying to be presumptuous and imagine that you want another boyfriend right away, or that I'd be the guy you'd choose. All I'm trying to tell you is that what we have is enough for me right now."

I cover my face with my hands. "My God, Nico, you're just making this worse."

"How? I'm telling you that I don't want to be with anyone else, and I'll wait to see if you change your mind about wanting a relationship. If you do, I hope you'd give me the chance to be that guy."

"But in the meantime ... what? We sleep together every night?"

"The ball has always been in your court, Maris. I didn't set this up. To be honest, I didn't think ahead when this started. I knew we had chemistry. I wanted you so bad. In the past, when it was kind of about the conquest, it was easy to move on ... after. Shit, I am making it worse. I rehearsed this all day, too. There are at least five songs on the computer in the studio that say this better than I'm doing now." Nico stands up and walks over to me. He takes my hands. "I want to go backwards with you. I want to take you out to breakfast. I'd even go to the beach if it's your favorite way to spend the day. I was so jealous of Theo today. Everyone who saw the two of you together probably thought you were a couple and that ate me up inside."

"When I thought that you might have gone back to the club to see Barbie, my concern was that you two have a connection. That she knows you better than I do. That you have history." I start toward the bathroom and Nico follows behind. "When Dickhead cheated on me, I wondered if it was because I sucked in bed, and he needed someone more exciting. So, I naturally assumed you—"

"Oh, Maris, no. Don't do that to yourself. Guys like Dam—"

"Dickhead," I corrected him.

"That's important to you, isn't it?" Nico asks. "Noted. Anyway, guys like him will never be able to handle the amount of attention you get on stage. They might not even realize it themselves, but dudes like that feel emasculated by a woman who commands the attention of hundreds of people at a time. A guy like me, on the other hand, gets totally turned on by the fact that those suckers can drool all they want, but that fireball is coming home to me. Theoretically."

Nico's words land. He might be right. I think out loud. "But he encouraged me to drop out of law school to pursue music full time."

"How were you doing in law school? Pretty well? Were you competitive with Dickhead? I'm really not feeling that as a name, by the way."

"He wasn't a genius or anything, but I kept right up with him."

"See? Maris, if there's one thing I know, it's the male ego. I have one, so I'm familiar with it. I like to think I'm taming mine, but this is a classic case of a dude needing an ego boost. He might have a big-boy job, but brutha isn't grown yet in the psyche department."

I turn the shower on, aware that the minutes are ticking closer to rehearsal.

"I genuinely appreciate your perspective. That's a whole new ..." I raise my right hand to my head and make the *mind-blown* gesture. "So, thank you for that."

Nico leans against the vanity on the side of the bathroom that I don't use. Me turning on the shower didn't send the message that I want to be alone to think. But Nico is listening, so I talk.

"I wasn't thinking ahead the first time I texted you, either. I was hurt. Like you said, I felt undeniable chemistry with you. I'd been in a relationship for a long time and here was this incredibly sexy and talented guy right down the hall." My voice gives out like it does when I'm nervous. "I wanted to feel desired. And thinking that Nico Van Asten could want me was ... thrilling." The room is getting steamy now, but I feel myself arriving at the point, so I forge ahead. "The things you made me feel, physically ... holy shit, Nico. You know your way around a woman's body. And who wouldn't want to feel like that as often as possible? Being with you feels empowering and is a total confidence boost."

I stop talking because my throat is getting tight, and I feel my eyes starting to sting.

"We put the cart before the horse," Nico says. "This was never going to be just a fling. I should have known that. I should have held you and let you cry that first night. Hell, the first month. I should have been the friend you needed. The man you needed."

Like Theo was. That's what I'm thinking. Theo was that man my first full night in the house. He did what he thought was best for me, not what served his own purpose. My God, I'm so confused.

"I want to start over with you, Maris. I want to give you, give us, the beginning that we deserve. I don't want to hide my feelings for you anymore, but we can keep it on the DL for the sake of the band. In case it doesn't work out."

"What do you feel for me, Nico? You don't really know me."

Nico looks like I slapped him. "How can you say that, Maris? I know you intimately, and I'm not talking sexually. I know that you earned the space you claim on stage among dudes you had to outwork to get there. I know you respect hard work more than natural talent. I know you're confident in what you bring to the table when you collaborate. I know you care about people's feelings because you've taken Max under your wing. I know that Dickhead's betrayal devastated you, not only because you didn't believe he was capable, but mostly because you would never have done that to him. You're loyal. That's why you gave Backyard Breeder notice of your departure in an industry and a market where most musicians quit a gig via text hours before stage."

Nico stands tall and crosses the bathroom to where I'm standing. He tucks my sticky hair behind my right ear and lets his pointer linger. "I know that this music note tattoo behind your ear is a touchstone for you when you start to get upset. You touch it when you need to center yourself."

The tears fall now. I've misjudged Nico. I saw him through a superficial lens and deemed him a superficial person.

"I know that you feel safe with me because you let your guard down completely when we're alone together. I know that what I did the other night made you feel like you had to put that guard back up, and I'm so sorry about that. If you want to move forward with me, or backward," Nico chuckles, "I won't do anything to make you put that guard up ever again."

I tilt my chin upward to stare into his blue eyes. I see calm and strength. I see sincerity. He grabs the bottom of his T-shirt and uses it to dry my tears. It's as soft as it looks.

"That hot water isn't going to last forever, and I've said my piece, so I'll let you get ready for our session. Thank you for hearing me out, Maris."

Nico kisses my forehead and turns to leave. I watch him stuff his hands deep into his joggers as he saunters to the door.

"Nico," my voice is barely a whisper.

He turns around with a hopeful expression.

"Would you like to go out to breakfast tomorrow?"

He grins. "It's a date."

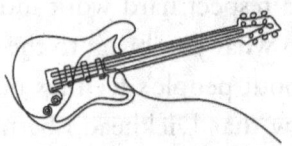

NICO

MARIS AND MAX BOLTED AFTER the gig under the guise of blazing the outdoor pizza oven to have multiple selections ready for Theo and me when we get home. Truth is, Max and Maris do very little to help with breakdown, outside of wrapping cords and encasing their instruments, anyway. Theo and I do the heavy lifting. I don't mind, and Maris went to the trouble of cleaning the pizza oven after we let it sit for a year. Divide and conquer. Also, I'm never going to discourage anyone from making me food.

"So, I got the contract from Phil while we were playing. I haven't opened it yet," Theo tells me as we stack the speakers onto a dolly.

"Want some moral support?" I ask.

"Dude, yeah. I'm half expecting to get dicked."

I laugh. "If we don't like the terms, the worst thing that happens is we don't do the tour, and we keep booking ourselves and making our music until the next opportunity presents itself."

Theo motions that he's ready to lift the left side speaker off the stand, and I follow him to grab one side.

"I guess I feel like we're at the mercy of whatever terms they offer to get on this tour. One, two ..." We lift and walk a few steps forward before setting the cabinet down.

"There's only one way to know what's in the contract, my man. We can read it once we're packed up. Unless you want Maris to read it first. She was halfway to being a lawyer. She got through contract law before she dropped out."

Theo gives me the side-eye when I mention Maris, so I say, "I think you and I should look it over first, though. As founding members of Funkengroovin'."

"This is a great problem to have, isn't it? Being nervous about an offer we've dreamed of for years?" Theo laughs and shakes his head.

"I knew we'd get here, brother. It was just a matter of time."

"And hiring Maris," Theo adds.

"She didn't hurt our chances," I agree.

"Revolution Records has a few artists on the tour, and Phil knows those guys. It would be great for us to get in front of that team."

"That's Phil's job," I say. "As far as I'm concerned, our job is keeping our noses to the grindstone to elevate the music we're putting out so we're undeniable."

Theo places the keyboard cases across the dolly, and I set the bass amp on top of them.

"I know. It's hard to relinquish control, though."

I slap Theo on the back. "Your management got us this far, but if we want to play at the next level, we have to expand the team. Are you having second thoughts about Phil's integrity?"

Theo shakes his head aggressively. "No. I'm just a worrier."

"Imagine how fun it will be for you to just play music. That's what you wanted to do in the beginning, but then you had to book the gigs, deal with the agents, hire band members, schedule rehearsals, incorporate so you could pay everybody. Man, you're not going to know what to do with your time when you have a team to chase down money for us. You do more business than music. This is gonna be a whole new world for you."

"I have been carrying you slackers, haven't I?" Theo says, smiling.

I throw the bag of mic stands on top of the second dolly as Theo stacks the lights on the dolly he pushes.

"Theo, sincerely, we wouldn't be in this position without your dedication and willingness to work your ass off for the band. I'm grateful, brother."

"I wouldn't have stuck with it during the hard times without you forbidding me to quit."

"You know I wanna hug you tight and long, but people are watching," I say, making Theo double over with laughter.

We yell our goodnights to the club staff and push our overloaded carts toward the back door where our trucks are parked.

The gear from my dolly fits into the bed of my truck, and Theo has a system for loading the remaining gear into his. We work wordlessly, going through rote motions we could do in our sleep. We close the tailgates in near synchronicity; not surprising for two guys used to being in step with one another for years running.

"My truck or yours?" Theo holds up his phone.

"I'm not that kind of girl," I say. "But mine."

Theo climbs into my passenger seat, and I start the truck, crank the AC, and turn my speakers down from their usual volume of 11.

"Do you want me to read it out loud, or—"

"Just hold it where we can both read it."

Theo and I dive in and my mind gets stuck on the dates. The tour starts earlier than I realized. That's okay, just a little bit of a surprise. It's a three-month run with a varying number of days off each week. The travel between venues is by coach bus with the other musicians on the tour. That will suck. Funkengroovin' gets two hotel rooms, and the list of hotels is included alongside the dates they correspond to. We'll share a greenroom with other bands and get paid on Fridays. Our per diem is measly, but it looks like the management company is taking care of three meals a day, transportation, and hotel expenses. All in all, it's not much more money than we make now with less luxurious living conditions, but almost anything would be. Our gain is awesome exposure on a bill with some other bands I respect quite a bit.

"Dude, I'm happy," I announce.

"Yeah?" Theo asks.

"Absolutely yeah."

Theo sinks back into his seat. "Are Maris and Max going to be okay? I want Maris to be comfortable. I have a feeling that Max is going to complain, but I can also see him gelling with the other musicians and having a great time being included, know what I mean?"

"I do. And it's only three months. I can stand on my head underwater for three months."

"Yeah, but you're you. You're used to punishing physical exertion in the hottest months of the season and riding a bus with other big, sweaty dudes. Showering with other men—"

"Okay," I say, holding up a hand. "I get it."

"Maris is comfortable enough with us, right? She won't feel like the odd one out?"

"We won't let her," I say.

"She'll have her own room, so that will give her a place to retreat to that's just hers."

I don't say anything. Maris and I have been carving out time together here and there, but it's hard to do when you live and work with the people you're trying to keep it a secret from. We discussed telling Theo and Max about us before the tour and now seems like the right time for me to tell my best friend and co-founder of our joint, successful venture.

"Theo, Maris might have company in her room from time to time if things continue going well."

Theo faces me. "What are you talking about?"

I put it out there. "Maris and I are together."

"Maris and … you? Are together?" Theo repeats. He laughs. "Nico, my guy, you almost had me."

"I'm serious, Theo. We're together. It's been going on for a couple months now. We didn't want to worry you and Max in case it didn't work out, but it's working."

Theo's face flashes from disbelief to anger. "What the fuck? What happened to not wanting a chick in the band because someone always has to get their dick wet and fuck everything up?"

I feel the tendon in my neck pop, and I put my finger in Theo's face. "Watch yourself, Theo."

"I should watch myself? That's fucking rich, Nico." Theo knocks my hand away. "I've *been* watching myself and I've been watching out for Maris. Sounds like I should've been watching you."

I try to compose myself, and Theo reaches for the door handle. "I expected you to be surprised, but I also thought you'd be happy for us," I say evenly.

Theo faces me again and his expression is pained. "You better not pull a Nico. You better not use her and toss her aside—"

"I don't do that—"

"I'VE WATCHED YOU!" Theo shouts. "You leave a wake of destruction behind you, Nico." Theo presses the palms of his hands into his eye sockets. "Listen. You're my brother, but if you fuck her over—"

"I love her, Theo."

His hands fall away from his face, and he falls back into his seat.

"I love her, too," Theo says, his voice cracking. "She doesn't know. I've never given her any indication ..." He trails off. Looks out the truck window.

My chest feels tight and I close my eyes, so I don't have to witness his pain.

"Theo, I had no idea."

"Don't." He opens the door to the truck and gets out. Before he slams it shut, he says, "Be the man she needs, Nico. Make her happy."

THEO

Nico beats me back to the house because I stopped on the way to buy a bottle of Dom. I was planning to celebrate Funkengroovin' executing our first festival contract, but I guess now we have two things to toast. Our first tour, and good guys finishing last, aka, Nico getting the girl. Because of course.

Max, Maris, and Nico are on the lanai by the pool when I come in the front door, so I grab four champagne flutes and an ice bucket and join them.

"Perfect timing, Theo. The last pizza just came out of the oven," Maris says, smiling.

Perfect timing, Theo. Excellent, impeccable timing. "I am a drummer," I say. "Did Nico tell you guys that we got the contract?"

Nico's eyes haven't left me since I broke the plane of the front door. His face is tense.

"No!" Max says. "You got it?"

"We got it and it's not terrible, so it looks like Funkengroovin' is on the bill. I bought some chilled Dom to celebrate. I have no idea if it pairs well with pizza."

"Aw, thanks, Theo. That makes the occasion more special," Maris says.

Nico opens the cabinet above the outdoor kitchen and retrieves a stack of plastic plates, but I stop him. "Nico, let's do real plates to go with the crystal flutes."

He puts the plates back. "Sure. I'll grab some from inside."

I remove the metal cage from the top of the champagne bottle. "Does anyone know what this thingy is called?" I ask, holding it up. Maris and Max look at each other with stumped expressions.

"A muselet," Nico answers, as he returns to the lanai. "It comes from the French word that means to muzzle."

"You're a man of the world, brother," I say.

"Family owns a tavern, remember? I started bartending at age eleven," he replies with a laugh. "Not that we sold champagne regularly in the Northwoods of Wisconsin, but we had a wine distributor who taught us things."

"Let me guess, a female? Must have been, or you wouldn't have paid attention." I shoot back. I know I'm being an asshole, but I don't care.

"Are you gonna pop that, or what?"

I smile and tell everyone to gather for the uncorking. "We're celebrating two milestones in our band tonight," I say.

Nico clears his throat and I snap my head in his direction. "What? Aren't we?" He stares at me and rubs his lips together. I know he does that when he's worried. "Yes, we are. We're celebrating signing the contract and …" I make the sound of a drumroll with my tongue, "the fact that Max and I are going to be roomies on the road due to two of us falling in love. Here's to Maris and Nico. May your love song echo through the ages." I've been twisting the cork as I talk and I feel the pressure build, so I push the cork with my thumb and hear a satisfying pop. Maris catches some overflowing bubbly in her flute and Max follows suit. I pour a glass and hand it to Nico, who accepts it with a stoic expression. I pour myself a glass and say again, "To Funkengroovin' and to Nico and Maris."

"Hear, hear!" Max says enthusiastically. Maris parrots the expression as she searches Nico's face for a clue as to what transpired between us. The four of us clink glasses, and I finish my Dom in one series of swallows. I raise the crystal flute above my head when it's empty and exclaim, "Opa!" smashing it on the pool deck. "Goodnight, kids. Enjoy the pizza." I head into the house and take the stairs two at a time before locking my bedroom door behind me. I jump in the shower and try not to think about what will probably be happening very soon under the roof I've shared with Nico for five years. In my dad's bed, no less. I've never even slept in the master, and Nico's been making his mark in there for months. That little bitch.

MARIS

I START CLEANING UP THE BROKEN glass, but Nico tells me to sit down and have some pizza before it gets cold. He kisses my forehead, and Max turns his face to the side as if he's witnessing something forbidden.

"I mean, we're still gonna eat, right?" he asks me. "I'm starving and I think we did an amazing job with these bad boys."

"Yeah, of course. Dig in," I tell him, taking my seat at the table.

"What do you think that was all about?" Max asks. "Did you notice Theo drinking a lot at the club tonight?"

"He's not drunk," Nico replies. "He's pissed. At me. Not you guys, just me. We'll handle it between the two of us, so don't worry about anything."

"I mean, I knew about you and Maris, but you don't see me getting all surly about it."

Nico looks up from where he's crouching over the pavers, and Max shoves some pizza in his mouth and chews.

Nico finishes the job and uses his phone flashlight to look for any shards of glass he may have missed. "Keep shoes on out here for now. I'll vacuum the deck tomorrow," he says. "So, which pie has the most meat?"

Max points to the one he topped with pork, salami, bacon, and Italian sausage. Nico lifts a slice from the pizza stone and inspects it.

"There's no pineapple, if that's what you're looking for," Max says.

That makes me chuckle, in spite of how terrible I feel after watching Theo melt down on a night that should be a celebration. Especially for him and Nico, and now the two of them are fighting. About me. Or at least about Nico dating me. I knew the band was afraid something like this would happen after they hired me, and I let it happen, anyway. I bear the responsibility. Theo held himself to a higher standard, but the band he nurtured and brought this far is faltering, anyway.

"Fuck," I whisper.

Nico places his hand on top of mine. "Theo and I have had rough patches before. We've fought about a lot of stuff over the years. At the end of the day, we both want the band to have an awesome showing on this tour. Once he sees that you and I aren't going to jeopardize that, or make the band dynamic awkward for everyone, he'll settle down. Please have some pizza. It's very good."

"Thanks," Max said. "I made the one you're eating."

I steal a look at Nico and almost bust out laughing because I can imagine what he's thinking. I help myself to a slice of pie with four cheeses, mushrooms, and shaved shallots. It's not hot anymore, but it is delicious.

The three of us eat with very little conversation, and then Nico and I clean up. I wrap the leftover pizza in foil and write *THEO* on top in Sharpie before placing it in the fridge.

We go upstairs and, when we're in front of Nico's room, he says he's going to shower and then come to mine. It feels wrong, knowing we don't have Theo's approval. I don't know yet why or how Nico told Theo about us. It seems it could have been done more gently, but Nico doesn't know that I went to Theo's room first that night. Nico and I had a secret, but Theo and I still have a secret.

I go to his door and tap softly. I don't hear movement on the other side, so I assume he's asleep and head down the hall. The door squeaks behind me and I turn to see Theo standing there. He looks at me like I'm a stranger.

"What's up?"

"Can I talk to you, please?" I ask, walking back to him.

Theo motions to the loft and I lead the way. I take a seat on a stuffed chair and Theo sits on the ottoman in front of it. He's facing me and our knees are only inches apart. He rests his forearms on his thighs and waits.

"I want you to know that I didn't go shopping door-to-door down that hallway for a boyfriend."

Theo's eyes stay on mine, but he doesn't say anything.

"I went to Nico. He didn't hit on me or take advantage of me. I thought he'd be the perfect revenge fuck, I guess."

Theo closes his eyes and I regret my words immediately. "What I mean is, I didn't intend for feelings to take root. I didn't think that was even possible with Nico. But I've seen another side of him."

"If I had taken you into my room that night," Theo says softly, "it would be us, Maris. There's no doubt in my mind. I hate Nico right now, but I love Nico like a brother ... that I hate. I think. What does an only child know about that, right?"

I chuckle.

"It wasn't my imagination, though, was it? It could have been us?"

"It wasn't your imagination."

Theo clasps his hands together and bites his lower lip. "I don't know what you want me to say, Maris."

"You don't have to say anything, but I want you to know that I didn't choose him over you. It just happened. Whatever *it* is. But we have to explore it and see if it's ... anything. I think I should get an apartment—"

Theo shakes his head. "You're leaving on tour for three months. Now is not the time to sign a new lease."

"It feels wrong to stay in your house."

"It's our house," Theo says. "It's a band house. You're an integral part of the band and, honestly, the reason we're taking off the way we are. We owe you a lot, Maris. You can't help that you have terrible taste in men."

I laugh and start crying at the same time.

"You don't have to be so perfect all the time, Theo. In fact, if you'll start fucking up more, it'll make me feel better."

"My *Opa* toast wasn't a fuck up? I think it was."

We laugh together.

"Are we okay?" I ask.

"We're okay," Theo promises. "Just give me some time to get used to this."

NICO

WAKING UP WITH MARIS'S HEAD on my chest makes me so happy that I want to suspend time indefinitely. I don't want to exhale her scent. I don't want the clock to advance another second. And yet, since my football injury happened, I've never been more excited about my future. The new music we're writing is going to hit with the festival crowd, and record companies are going to see that signing us to a deal is a no-brainer. As if that wasn't enough good fortune for one man, I have a beautiful, talented, tender-hearted woman at my side to share every step of the journey. I look down at Maris's sleeping face and my smile grows. She is the first girl I've loved who speaks my language and understands the essence of who I am because we're the same. I don't have to explain to her how much music means to me, or what a high it is to discover a progression that sounds like magic.

But I can't think about how happy I am without considering how unhappy I've made Theo. I try to recall whether he gave any hints that he was developing feelings for Maris. I can't remember him treating her any differently than he treats Max and me. Theo's kind to everyone. He treats everyone as if they're special to him. I think back to when he helped Maris move out of the condo. He was the one who volunteered to help her go get her stuff. I wonder if he was feeling something already, way back then. At the time, I just took it for granted that he was simply being the reliable, stand-up guy the moment called for.

I remember how upset he was to learn that Maris's ex had cheated on her. Should I have known then that he had feelings for her? If I had known, would I have developed feelings for Maris? I was attracted to her when I first saw her, but from the night I sat in with Backyard Breeder, Maris has had my full attention.

I push guilty thoughts from my mind. I haven't done anything wrong here. Maris chose me. She and I were free and single when we started hooking up, and a situationship turned into a relationship. Besides, I'm better for her than Theo would be. Maris needs someone who makes her feel safe, and that's my role. I will give her all the room she needs while having her back on stage and off. In Theo's last relationship, he kind of lost his individuality. Some girls like being half of a whole, but I see Maris as a woman who wants to join all of herself with someone else to be double who she would be alone.

"Stop staring at me so loudly," she whispers.

I chuckle and do a little sit-up to kiss the top of her head. "Good morning."

"I can hear you thinking," she says.

"Really?" I ask cynically.

"No, but your breathing changed. Are you worried about something?"

"I'm not worried about anything at all. Are you?"

"Mm." Maris pulls herself up my torso until her mouth reaches mine. She kisses me softly, with closed lips. I pucker my lips against hers and then let them deflate, then repeat the motion rapidly until she starts laughing. "What are you doing?"

"Ever wonder why I have such luscious lips? Lip presses," I say, demonstrating again.

"You are so much weirder than people realize," she says, but she's still laughing, and her eyes are sparkling.

"The world only knows super cool Nico, but you get to hang out with this guy." I do the lip thing again, and she presses the palm of her hand to my mouth.

"Stop that right now, or we're over."

Now I laugh. "Getting the ick?" I ask.

"Not even lip presses could make you icky," she says sincerely.

I cup the back of her head in my hand and pull her to me, kissing her fully. I lift my hips into Maris, and she feels that my whole body is awake, alert, and aching for her. She takes me into her hand and guides me where I want to be.

When we come together like this, like music and melody, I feel the same high that comes from the synergy of band and audience as they lift each other to frenzied euphoria. I will spend the rest of my life chasing this feeling.

THEO

I WAKE UP IN A HOUSE that doesn't feel like mine anymore. With Maris and Nico coupling up I feel like I'm intruding in their love nest.

I decide to go for a swim before rehearsal and when I step onto the lanai, I remember the broken glass from last night. I don't see any big pieces, and I don't want to wake anyone else up because I want to be alone for a while, but I drag the shop vac from the garage and turn the beast on to suck up any invisible foot stabbers, anyway. I leave the vac on the lanai, knowing that glass is great at hide and seek. Even though I think I did a good job, I'll do it again after everyone is awake.

I dive into the deep end of the pool and start swimming laps. It only takes me eight strokes to get from one end to the other. It's not a huge pool, but I switch up strokes with each lap and feel my muscles working. I fall into a rhythm that requires exertion and feel stress leaving my body.

I obviously didn't respond well to Nico's news last night. I had an emotional, but honest reaction, and I'm not embarrassed about it. Nico dropped a big bombshell on me. I thought we told each other everything and that's part of what sucks about this. Nico and I are the bedrock the band is built on. As long as we stick together, there's a Funkengroovin'.

As the cool water rushes down my body, I remind myself what Nico knew and what he didn't. He knew that Max and I would frown upon him getting with Maris. I can see how he rationalized that it wouldn't be a problem. Hell, on some level, I decided that when I was wondering if there could be anything between Maris and me. What he didn't know, because I didn't tell him, is that I was starting to have feelings for her. The truth is, it could easily be me in this situation with her, so I can't hold a grudge against Nico. I can envy him, but what good will that do?

I'm working harder with every lap and stay underwater for three in a row.

The last thing I want is for anyone to feel sorry for me. *Poor Theo is hurt because he didn't get the girl.* That's pathetic. And, who wants to be tied down on tour? We're going to be meeting so many people over the next few months. That's a lot of stress on a new relationship.

The exercise has the desired effect on my mind, and I imagine burning off the negative emotions. What's there to be negative about, anyway? My professional dreams are coming true. Being able to take this ride with Nico, Maris, and Max is the culmination of years of pounding the rock trying to break through the noise. The four of us have that indefinable thing that sets our music apart. We're on the precipice of playing music on a level few bands ever reach. Whether it lasts for a summer, or a decade, we owe it to ourselves, and each other, to enjoy every second and live the experience to the fullest.

I feel a disturbance in the water and see hairy legs dangling from the side of the pool. I stop swimming and tread.

"Sorry, man. If you're in the flow, keep goin'," Nico says.

I turn onto my back and float, taking in the cloudless sky and a single blue heron flying just above the pool cage overhead. "I think I'm good," I tell Nico. "Kicked my own ass a little bit."

He chuckles knowingly. "The hotels we're booked in for the tour better have a pool, or you're going to shrivel up and die."

I hadn't thought about that. I let my feet float to the bottom and stand, facing Nico. "Dude, seriously."

Nico extends his arms behind him and leans back. He's searching for the right words, I can tell, so I make it easy on him.

"Listen, I don't want to rehash last night. I've had time to process the news, so let's just move forward. Everyone knows now, so it isn't a secret. That has to be a relief. Let's just get ready for the tour and bang out some great rehearsals and shows so we can have fun and slay on the road."

Nico narrows his eyes at me. "Are you sure we don't have more to talk about?"

"I'm sure," I say with feigned confidence. "The thing I'm most worried about is replacing the crystal flute I broke. It was one of twelve and now there are only eleven."

Nico sits forward conspiratorially. "Or, we could break another one and you'd be back to an even number. Your dad isn't here often enough to know what the glassware situation is."

"If all else fails ..." I say, climbing the steps and retrieving my towel.

Max slides the lanai door open and pokes his head out. "Maris and I are going to the bakery. Do you guys want anything?"

Nico and I say, "No" in unison and we realize that, just like on stage, my voice is a parallel third below Nico's, forming a two-part harmony.

We make eye contact and Nico makes a disgusted face that I try to copy.

"Sorry, but Maris doesn't have a chance at being Nico's other half. Job's taken and it's you, Theo."

"Leave, before I get up, Max," Nico says.

"Hurry up, we're starting at eleven. Don't be late," I tell him.

"Yeah, yeah," Max says, closing the door.

"I'd rather have the band together, the four of us, than Maris," I say out of nowhere. I don't know where the thought came from, but it seems true in the moment.

Nico opens his mouth, and I think he's going to say something, but he doesn't.

I wrap the towel around my waist and drop my trunks to my ankles, stepping out of one side and using the opposite toes to kick the shorts up to my hand. I wring them out, waiting for Nico to tell me what he's thinking. He's letting his feet float to the surface of the water and pushing them down again. He stays quiet.

"I'm gonna hit the shower," I say on my way past him. Maybe Maris made the right choice, after all.

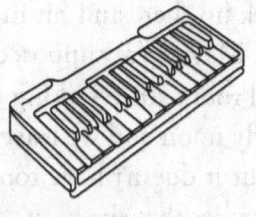

MAX

IT WAS UP TO US to get ourselves to Orlando, so we rented an SUV and drove up from Miami yesterday. We went to the venue for sound-check and got to see the set-up, which was awesome. Today seemed far away, but now that it's here, I'm feeling the weight of it. I've never been more nervous about anything in my life.

Funkengroovin' is well-rehearsed and our show is flawless. I could play it in my sleep. I'm proud of the music, too. We're doing some cool stuff. My concern is that other bands might outshine us, or that we'll go viral for all the wrong reasons. It's hard to believe that we haven't already peaked and that our spectacular rise can continue. All of this seems too good to be true. I wish I could think more like Nico and Theo who feel like everything that's happening to us was inevitable. That's the differ-ence between dudes who have been rewarded by meritocracy and ... me. I'm trying to get on board with the fact that I am like them now, but it's a struggle.

Maris seems to have the most well-adjusted attitude of all of us. She's living in the moment. She told me to do the next necessary thing and to boil it down to the basics. Sleep, eat, play, repeat. I wonder if it is that simple.

I keep reminding myself of how assured I felt yesterday at the soundcheck. The crew got us dialed in and the mix was sensational. It's so much better than having Nico trying to run sound and play at the same time. And ... the wall of sound ... it's incredible to hear our music through stadium speakers. It was so amazing yesterday that all we could do was grin while we were on stage. We took videos and posted them to get our audience psyched for the kick-off tonight. Maris, Theo, and

Nico can't wait to get back up there and hit in front of a crowd, but I've been throwing up all day. Maybe I'm supposed to be a studio musician.

I haven't left the hotel room since waking up. Theo got up early and hasn't been back. It's nearly noon and we leave for the venue in an hour. The hotel doesn't suck, but it doesn't have room service, so I text Maris to see if she's eaten. She replies that she hasn't and will walk down to the little lobby restaurant with me, so I splash some water on my face and meet her in the hallway.

"Sort of like at home, huh? Down the hall from each other?" she says when I open my door.

"Sort of, but not at all," I say.

"You feeling okay, Max? You look a little pale."

"Great," I say as we enter the vestibule where the elevators are. Maris hits the down button, and I check myself out in the mirror across from where she's standing watching the numbers light up. "Confirmed," I say. "I definitely do look like shit."

"Meh, have some tomato juice with lunch. It'll bring your color right back."

An elevator opens and we are by ourselves inside.

"Isn't that an old wives' tale?"

"I don't think so. If you eat a ton of carrots, your skin turns orange."

I lean against the railing in the elevator and try to keep my stomach steady as we descend. The continental breakfast bar is still open, so we give our passes to the hostess, then grab our plates and proceed through the buffet.

"Dry and bland are your friends," Maris whispers.

I go for plain French toast and scrambled eggs that look too yellow to be real. Maris seems happy to find cottage cheese and fruit. She adds a banana bread muffin, and we sit at a table for four, probably by habit.

"You're going to have a great time today, Maxer. If you need a reminder of how much fun you had at sound check yesterday, I have video evidence," Maris says.

I smile.

"You're the least likely to make a mistake playing and you'll be able to hear yourself better than ever, so your background vocals will be perfect."

"How can you be so confident?"

Maris thanks the server for the coffee she's pouring and searches the ceiling for an answer. "Honestly, I guess it's because I believe in you guys so much. You, Theo, and Nico are so talented that all I have to do is not fuck you guys up."

"Wow," I whisper. "You just unlocked some next level shit, Mare."

She giggles. "But it's true."

"Wow," I say again. "I have that level of faith in you three. Yeah, man, that's what it's all about."

Maris smiles and holds her coffee mug out, waiting for me to toast on it.

"I wish I had texted you earlier. I feel a thousand percent better," I tell her.

"Well, if it isn't the world-famous Funkengroovin'!" Theo walks ahead of Nico and sets his phone down on the table.

"What's good, Fearless Leader?" Maris asks. "Good workout?"

"No, the gym sucks, but our set will be a great workout, so I need to carb up."

Nico grins at Maris and palms the top of my head like a basketball as he walks past. "Be right back."

Theo follows him to the buffet.

"I feel so much better being with you guys. Time alone in the room wasn't good for me today."

"You can always call me, Max," Maris says sincerely.

"If I had known Nico was gone, I would have."

"Whether Nico's there or not doesn't matter. We're a band, my dude. If one of us needs the others, we're there. Especially on the road."

"I guess it's just first day jitters."

"That French toast looked so good, I had to get two plates of it," Theo says, sitting down next to me.

Maris pauses before taking a sip of coffee. "I'll never know how you stay in such good shape eating like you do, Theo."

He laughs and flexes his right bicep. "So, did I hear you're feeling a little anxious, Max?"

"I was. Maris said something that helped a lot. She told me that her faith in us sets her at ease. That perspective calmed me right down."

Theo looks at Maris and smiles. "That's really the heart of it, isn't it? If I ever get tired while I'm playing, I just suck it up and keep hittin' because you guys need me, and I want you to be able to do what you do at the highest level, so I keep pushing for you guys."

Maris reaches across the table with both hands and touches mine and Theo's. "Can I just say that I love you guys so much?"

"We love you, too." I answer for Theo because he shoveled a heap of French toast in his mouth as soon as he was finished talking.

"Break it up," Nico says as he sits down next to Mare.

"Don't forget we're wearing blue for the set today," she reminds us, retracting her hands after a final squeeze.

"Yeah, we said blue and white were okay, right?" Theo clarifies.

Maris nods.

"I'm wearing white joggers with a blue short-sleeve button down, kind of a geometric print with a few shades of blue, and my white prescription sunglasses."

"Sounds cool." Maris is always supportive.

"Damnit, Max, that's what I was going to wear. Now what am I gonna do?" Nico teases me, but his face tells me it's all in fun.

"I'm gonna wear something blue. Or white," Theo says, and Maris laughs, checking her phone.

"Oh, shit, you guys. The van picks us up in a half hour, so I need to get upstairs and get ready." She makes three *mwah* sounds and heads to the elevators.

Theo's nearly finished, and Nico is polishing off an apple, so I wait for them. When the food's devoured, Theo says, "Let's fucking go!" with a huge smile on his face. An hour ago, I wouldn't have been able to match his energy, but I'm surprised to find myself right there with him.

"Let's *Funkin'* go!" I say back.

Theo stops in his tracks. "How did we miss that? It's always been right there."

"Every now and then, I'm a genius."

"Every day, brother. I wanna see you showing off today, got it?"

I chuckle. "Got it, brother."

"Yeah, you do," Nico says. I look over my shoulder to make sure he's talking to me. He is. Fuck yeah.

MARIS

"THE GUYS ARE SO LUCKY, they don't have to do anything to get ready, apart from getting dressed," I tell the viewers joining my live. "Funkengroovin's first set of our first show on tour is just hours away, but we're playing during the daytime, so I'm going to let my hair wild out, because fighting humidity in Florida is a lost cause, as we already know, right, ladies? And, who needs eye make-up when you have a great pair of shades!" I pop the shades on my nose and model them for a moment. "So, I'm just going in with an old-school bronzer along my hairline at the top of my forehead, and across the bridge of my nose, like so," I trace a make-up brush across the areas as I narrate. "I'll hit my cheekbones, and then I like to hit my collarbones to make them pop."

I look into the camera lens. "I welcome any and all ideas you have for make-up looks. I need to watch all the tutorials, so link some that you like. I usually just try to make sure I have some sun on my face and add a lip gloss. I'm the first to admit my skills are hot garbage." I laugh. "I'm really looking forward to getting on stage later and slaying with the guys. We have an awesome show for you, so I hope you'll catch one of these dates."

I hear the hotel room door open and Nico calls, "I hope you're naked!"

I make an *oops* face into the camera. "And that's Nico. Come say hello to the livestream audience!"

Nico comes into the bathroom and sticks his face in front of the phone. "I need a shower and the van shows up in fifteen minutes, so unless you want this broadcast to be for mature audiences only, you might want to sign off."

The comments section starts rolling. I only started doing this a couple weeks ago, but it's clear my audience is mostly female. Any time one of the guys joins, the comments blow up.

"I'll post photos later. Be sure to get your tickets and come see us on the road! Love one another! Peace!"

I end the live and read Nico select comments as he showers.

"*Please, please, please turn the camera toward the shower ... Maris, you look beautiful, you don't need make-up*, aw that's so sweet ... *Maris, you're so fucking lucky, Nico is a snack ...*"

"Knowing that all of these comments are coming from ten-year-olds creeps me out," Nico says.

"Not all of them," I say defensively. "The one about watching you in the shower is a sixty-seven-year-old woman from Naples."

Nico turns the water off and steps out of the shower.

"Don't do it. I'm dressed and I don't want to get wet," I warn him.

He does the naked windmill anyway and I run out of the bathroom.

"Could you please grab me something blue and white?" he asks.

I'm wearing all white, a tank dress with high-top Converse, so I make sure Nico has some blue.

"How about a white muscle T with your Miami Dolphins pants?" I love making fun of his aqua, knee length joggers with orange stripes down the sides, but I also love how Nico's ass looks in them.

"Perfect, thank you," he calls. I smell his hair product, and it makes me feel at home.

I walk back to the bathroom and lean against the doorway. "Can you believe we're here?"

Nico is using his right hand to give his hair a controlled, yet casual look. "Yes. I can't believe I'm here with you, though. That's the part that makes me feel like the luckiest man alive."

He quickly brushes his teeth, then applies cologne. Watching Nico going through this routine has me enraptured. I can't get enough of watching him in private moments. The juxtaposition of watching him on stage, seeing him strut around, playing intricate solos, and making outrageous vocals seem effortless, is nothing compared to being able to watch him brush his teeth in his underwear.

"Is it okay?" he asks after he rinses and spits.

"Hmm?"

"Is my hair a mess, or what?"

I chuckle. "Not at all. I just love you."

Nico's face lights up. "That's the first time you've said those words to me."

I make a face. "That isn't true," I argue.

He takes me in his arms, and I melt. As usual.

"Maris, I've been waiting. That's the first time you've told me you love me."

I feel tears coming and I burrow into his chest. "I do, Nico. I love you so much."

He kisses the top of my head in the way I've come to adore, and he declares, "Best. Day. Ever."

"And we haven't touched a stage yet," I say, trying to lighten the mood so my throat doesn't tighten up and make it harder for me to sing later.

"Nothing that happens on stage is as important as what happens right here," Nico says. "But, unless I'm going on in my boxers, I need to get dressed."

"I have some internet friends who would love that. Just sayin' on their behalf."

"That would be a way to make news on the first day of the tour. Let's suggest it to Max."

"He has his 'fit all picked out. Leave that boy alone."

Nico pulls his shirt over his head without messing up his hair and steps into his half-pants as he speaks. "I'm being very brotherly to Max. I have brothers, so I know what I'm talking about."

I give Nico a sweet kiss. "I've noticed."

We grab our gig bags and meet Theo and Max at the elevators. Theo is wearing a silky navy-blue tank with matching joggers and white kicks.

"You guys look like a band," I observe.

"What gives it away?" Theo asks, tugging on the lanyard around his neck that holds the various passes we all have to wear.

"No one looks at us anyway, Maris. All eyes are on you, and you make us look great," Max says.

I throw my arm around him and give him a side hug.

The elevator arrives and we ride to the lobby in silence. A driver holding a sign emblazoned with *Funkengroovin'* waits for us by the door.

"Hey, man. I'm Theo. This is Max, Maris, and Nico."

We take turns shaking the driver's hand.

"I'll never remember your names, so I'm just gonna call you all Funkengroovin'."

Nico takes my bass case and puts it in the back of the van with his guitar and Theo's snare, then we load into the vehicle. Nico and I sit on the bench seat in the back with Theo and Max in front of us.

"I'm taking you guys to the green room, which is actually a tent behind the stage. Your set time pushed yesterday after sound-check, so you're going on an hour later, but that's a good thing. It means they like you."

We look at each other with pleased expressions.

The driver jumps on the interstate for less than five minutes and then exits again. As we approach the festival grounds, I see a field packed with cars and my spirit soars. I was worried that we would be playing to no one, but it looks like the music lovers aren't snubbing the opening acts. We pass another field filled with parked cars. Then another.

"Holy shit," Theo says. "Is all of this festival parking?" he asks the driver.

"Yeah. I have to take you in through the service gate in the back because the lines to park are so long. They started shuttling people at nine this morning."

I lean forward and put my hand on Max's shoulder. He covers it with his own but doesn't say anything.

Nico pretends he's going to vomit, and I glare at him, trying not to laugh.

As we get closer to the stage, we can hear the music and the crowd noise.

"Theo, who's playing right now?" Nico asks.

"The schedule says it's The Heathens."

The van driver rolls down his window, then confirms, "Yeah, that's still them. I left to pick you guys up right after they started."

Nico tilts his head to listen, and he nods.

"Their sound is a lot harder than ours," Max says softly.

"True," Theo says, "but the headliners sell the tickets, and our music is the same genre as theirs."

"Don't worry about what anyone else is doing, Max." Nico sounds like a dad. "We came to do our show, and everyone here came to celebrate music. Winning this crowd over is so much easier than any gig we do where the patrons want the band to turn down so they can eat in peace. This audience appreciates us, and they want us to melt their faces off."

"And the rest of them are too drunk or high to complain," the driver said over his shoulder.

"Thanks for the ride, buddy," Theo says as the van comes to a stop. "Are you taking us back to the hotel after our set?"

"Dude, I have no clue. Could be me, could be someone else."

Nico and I recover our axes from the back of the van and Theo grabs his snare. Nico pats the door twice after he closes it to let the driver know he can leave.

"Here we are." Theo's grin widens underneath his Ray Bans.

"Let's go rub shoulders." I lead the way to the entrance marked, *Backstage Passes Only Beyond This Point.*

Two security guards man the door and eye the bulky passes hanging from lanyards around our necks. "Have a good show," one says.

"Thanks!" I'm the only one who replies.

The tent is filled with rows of cafeteria style tables. Staffers wearing festival T-shirts serve food and run errands. Silver tubs of ice-covered beverages are randomly placed throughout the space and, at the far end of the tent, ping-pong tables, cornhole, and other time wasters sit unused. Musicians sit alone and in groups. A few sleep on tabletops here and there. Air conditioning units work hard to keep the temperature a few degrees lower than the temperature outside the tent. The sound of their mechanical straining combines with conversations and various instruments being played at the same time to produce an indistinguishable buzz.

"This isn't what I expected at all," Max says.

"Back of house is never as impressive as front of house, right?" Theo says, laughing.

"Wanna go out front and watch the concert?" Nico asks.

Before any of us can reply, a dude wearing a cougar print unitard and credentials bursts through the side opening of the tent, screaming, "It's hot as fuck on that stage!" He lowers himself into one of the ice-filled tubs, spilling water, cans, and bottles over the sides.

No one in the tent seems to notice. It's like nothing happened.

I look at Max, who is dying laughing.

"Still worried about going viral for all the wrong reasons?" I ask.

"What even is this place?" he asks.

"It's the land of no fucks," Nico answers.

Theo takes his phone out of his pocket and starts texting. "We have a handler, so let's have him take the gear while we go watch some of the other bands."

A female walks past us wearing a nun's outfit. She's doing a vocal warm-up.

"I suddenly feel terribly ordinary," I tell Nico.

"Oh, yeah, there are a thousand Marises in this tent. Look! Movie star gorgeous talents so secure in themselves that they don't have to present as *freeeeeaaaaks* to get attention."

I look into his eyes and see that he's enjoying teasing me.

"Same thing I told Max. Do you."

"Our guy will take our stuff backstage, so let's go to holding area D," Theo says, walking to the back of the tent.

"Funkengroovin'!" A tall, skinny kid with a huge straw hat waves us down. "I'm Kenny. I'm your man for whatever you guys need."

I like him instantly. Kenny is brimming with enthusiasm and excitement.

"I love what you did with Silver Springs," he gushes. "Can't wait to hear you guys play live."

Kenny promises to guard our gear with his life and then lets us through a gate beside the stage that leads to an area where festival employees get the best view in the house.

The stage crew is setting up the next band, and Theo and Nico comment on how meticulous they are. Theo got talked into leaving the majority of his kit and his cymbals with the drum tech last night, and he's watching the guy like a mother watches a nanny cam. The movements of the crew seem choreographed by experience and, on day one, they're already working with impressive efficiency.

"They know what the fuck they're doing," Max says.

It's been less than ten minutes since the musician from the last band took a cold plunge in the beverage well, and the next band is already starting their first song.

"Boys and girls, we're so glad you made it!" The female lead singer, a pretty Black girl with braids and black trench coat takes command of the stage. "We're called Hurricane Hellen, and we're here to blow some shit around!"

I count five people on stage; all dressed in black trench coats. If Unitard Man was hot up there, these guys are going to die. They start their first song, and it has a punk edge to it. The bass player is a stocky white guy, and his bass face is already on full display. I can't tell if he's a player or not because the song doesn't give him much to do, but Hellen, if that's her name, sings her heart out. She has a powerful voice, and she's fun to watch.

"What do you think?" I ask Max.

"I really don't know. I like the visual element, but I'm not blown away by the music. Chick can sing, don't get me wrong."

"She's really good," I agree.

"Drummer is solid," Theo adds.

I glance at Nico, who has his eyes closed. He's picking apart the pieces. When he opens his eyes, he sees me watching him and shrugs his shoulders nonchalantly, which I know means he doesn't hate them, but he's not terribly impressed, either.

We listen to four songs that sound alike and decide to go back to the shaded tent.

I notice that Max has a spring in his step that he didn't have on the way out. Nico's idea to give us a look at the crowd and another band was smart. Max knows he's talented and well-educated. His hang-up has to do with feeling like the cool kids are going to call him out, but everyone here is a cool kid in some way, so that means no one is cool. I feel better about what I came to do up there myself, so I'm sure Max is feeling it.

We grab beverages for ourselves and team up for ping-pong. Since there are several tables with no waiting, we devise a bracket and play singles. We call 21 a win and we're down to the final two in no time. I'm surprised that Nico and I are sitting out watching Max and Theo play for the championship. Theo is a pretty competitive guy, and he and Nico were going at it like life depended on the outcome of their game, but Max is a ping-pong ringer. He makes quick work of beating Theo, and then we still have two hours to kill.

We claim a table and sit down for Panera salads and sandwiches.

"Do you feel like everyone here knows one another?" Max asks.

I laugh. "I was just thinking that this reminds me of the first day of freshman year of high school." I scan the room with my gaze. "Some of these people recognize each other from middle school, and some of us have friends that we knew would be here, but most of us are just checking each other out. Wondering who's gonna be Top Dog."

Theo laughs. "That's so accurate!"

"Ah, great, a high school redux," Max says. Then, his expression changes. "But this time, I'm at the table with the captain of the football team, the hot chick, and the good-looking rich kid."

"And we're at a table with the Berklee Badass," Theo says.

"Talk about yourself like you're an outcast one more time and I'll haze you. That shit's over. You're a player now," Nico tells Max.

"Should I get a blinged out chain that says *Berklee Badass*?"

I roll my eyes as Max laughs with the guys.

"This is gonna be okay," Max says. "This is gonna be fun."

THEO

KENNY HAS US IN THE backstage holding area as the rock band ahead of us, Free Beer, from New Jersey, finishes their set. They have the crowd worked up, so all we have to do is keep that high going. We designed our set to start hot, stay hot, dip the energy down for Silver Springs to give us a breather, and then finish hot. I like that we're following a band that's handing us a hype crowd.

Music plays through the main speakers as the stage crew gets set up for us, so the four of us are in the wings, pretending we do this every day.

I look at Nico whose cocky smirk comforts me. I built this band around him, after all. He's never met a stage that intimidated him. Maris looks like a kid visiting Disney for the first time, and Max's face is determined.

"I want to thank you guys for sharing your talents and your hard work to get us to this moment," I say. "I'm so happy to be here, and I'm so psyched to be here with the three of you. I'd rather be here with you guys than anyone else."

Nico holds up his fist, and I bump it, and then Maris and Max add theirs.

I whisper, "Funkengroovin'," and it becomes a chant. We go until we bust out laughing.

The stage director whistles to get our attention. "You guys might wanna see this." He points to a backstage monitor.

Our band name appears on the screen, and the crowd reacts with cheers. The announcer's recorded voice booms through the speakers,

"*Ladies and gentlemen, when a band turns up the heat in Miami, everyone notices. This viral sensation has become a fan favorite—*" A clip of our Silver Springs video plays and the cheers crest again. "*The world has gotten to know Theo—*" the production team lifted a photo of me from our Instagram page, but they chose a good one, so I'm not complaining. "*Nico—*" the cheers crest again when Nico's photo replaces mine, and Nico laughs. "*Max—*" another crest of cheers drops Max's jaw to his chest. "*And Maris—*" Now the crowd goes nuts, and she looks at each of us with a petrified look on her face. "*But you're about to experience them first-hand. Please welcome to the stage ...*" Kenny starts clapping and tells us to have a great show as the production staffer points with both hands to the stage. We start walking and then Nico runs ahead, so we all pick up the pace. "*Funk-en-groov-in!*"

The stage seems bigger than it did yesterday, and Max, Maris, and Nico seem farther away from my drum stand than ever. We've played some small venues where we had to practically stand on top of one another, so this seems extra crazy.

"What's good, Orlando?" Maris yells into her mic and the crowd responds.

I count us into the first song on our set list, "Coming Around", which, fittingly, was the first song Maris played with us at her audition. That seems like years, not months ago.

The air is filled with our music. The thump of my kick drum is so loud it's tangible. The entire crowd feels it in their chests, and I'm providing the heartbeat for ten thousand strangers who are syncing to my rhythm.

Nico is *on*. His star quality is undeniable, and he has the audience enthralled. Every movement, every riff, and every note he offers up is received with ecstatic enthusiasm. He and Maris use the entire stage as they play to the audience. Nico solos and then calls an audible, introducing Maris and giving her a solo after he finishes. Just like I did on the first day we played this song together. This is standard gig stuff, and Max and I roll with it. The fact that we're already loose enough to be on our toes in this environment bodes well for the rest of the set.

It seems like the crowd grows larger with every song we play, but maybe I'm trippin'. All I know is, we're having as much fun as they are, and that's saying a lot.

Max is feeling himself and it's the first time I've seen him ignore the piano bench. He plays standing up with his head thrown backwards. Sometimes when I look over at him, his shades are hanging off the tip of his nose, other times they're on top of his head. He looks at the audience rather than keeping his eyes on his keys, which is his habit. I fucking love it.

If the festival grounds had a roof, Silver Springs would be blowing it off. The crowd is dead quiet during the beginning of the song, and they wave their cell phone flashlights back and forth in spite of the afternoon sun. As we play, I glance up at the viewing area for backstage passholders, where we watched Hurricane Hellen earlier. It's packed. For me, that's the best part. Other musicians checking us out and cheering us on.

Silver Springs ends and Maris turns around to face Max and me. She's beaming as the crowd cheers for her version of the song. She's glistening with sweat and the huge stage fans lift her hair into a wavy cape. Or maybe it's more of a veil. She's never looked more beautiful. She smiles at me and mouths, *thank you.* I wink at her and count us into the final song of the set. Nico sings lead and he slays it, leaving everything on the stage. I can't believe an hour has passed. Sixty minutes have never slipped through my fingers so quickly.

Maris thanks the crowd and we're backstage when the *encore* chants start.

The production team and the director huddle.

"Theo, what do you want to play if they send us back out?" Nico asks me.

"Ah ..." I'm blank.

Canned music starts playing through the mains.

Kenny comes over, shaking his head. "We can't do it. It'll throw off the timeline, and it will piss off the other bands. Sorry, guys."

Nico looks at me, and I shrug. What am I supposed to do?

"We get it," I tell Kenny.

"I'll bring your axes and the snare to the holding area." Kenny spins on his heel and runs back onstage.

Individual stage crew members go out of their way to tell us we didn't suck as we leave the wing.

"Dude, I'm so pissed they didn't let us go back out," Nico says loudly. He's pacing in a circle, blowing off steam.

"I know," I say. "But I get it, and that doesn't take away from what we just did out there. We fucking murdered."

"We're murdering motherfuckers!" Max yells.

Maris laughs, but she has tears rolling down her cheeks.

"You okay?" I ask. I search her face and I'm struck by the realization. "You're dad?"

She breaks down and I sweep her into a hug. "He saw that. He saw you."

Nico finally calms down enough to notice what's happening and he catches my eyes. He points at Maris and then makes an *okay* gesture with his thumb and forefinger. I nod, then see Max say something close to Nico's ear and his face softens.

"Okay, guys, I have your cases and Theo's snare." Kenny's balancing three awkward items, so Max and Nico help him.

Maris pulls away and wipes her eyes with the back of her hands before she replaces her sunglasses.

"You can't tell," I assure her.

Nico has his guitar and Maris's bass, so I take my snare and we tell Kenny we'll see him tomorrow in Jacksonville.

As we walk to the pick-up point for the hotel shuttle, I hear Nico ask Maris if she's okay, and she responds that it was just an emotional release after such a big moment. I wonder if she will tell him what was at the heart of it later, and I wonder why he doesn't *know*. He should connect the dots. I did.

"Ah, we're going viral again," Max says, holding up his phone to show us a video of the crowd chanting for an encore.

"Leave 'em wanting more. Isn't that the old showbiz adage?" I say, smirking.

"You want more?" Max says. "Buy a ticket for Jacksonville."

Nico looks at me and shakes his head, laughing. "Post show Max is different."

"True dat," Max confirms.

Show number one is in the books.

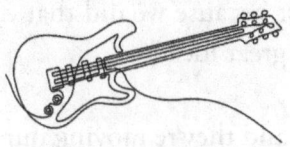

NICO

"I miss my truck," I tell Maris as I try to settle into the seat beside her on the bus. No matter how I sit, I'm uncomfortable. "I feel like the seat portion should be at least five inches deeper."

"I didn't know above average height came with so many inconveniences until I met you," Maris says sympathetically. She's sitting by the window for the ride from Jacksonville to Savannah, Georgia. The drive would take under two hours in my truck, but the trip from Orlando to Jacksonville taught me that "bus time" adds twenty extra minutes for every regular hour of travel. Plus, our driver seems incapable of driving over seventy or leaving the far right lane.

"Maybe you can stretch your legs into the aisle once we get moving," she suggests.

I shift sideways in my seat and recline backwards onto her with my legs extending across the aisle into Theo's lap. "Like this?"

"Dude. No," Theo says without looking up from his phone.

Maris giggles, so the gag was worth it.

"The show last night was even better than Orlando, don't you think?" Maris asks, showing me some photos that the audience members tagged us in.

"It feels really good up there," I say, squirming in my seat.

"I can't imagine playing these kinds of shows ever gets old, you know?"

I turn my face toward her and lower my voice. "Everything gets old if you take it for granted. We won't let each other do that."

Maris is scrunched down with her knees propped against the seat in front of her. She looks up at me, the whites of her eyes making her look doe eyed. "I don't take good things for granted, sir."

"Mmmm, I miss my truck," I growl.

Maris chuckles. "Just because we did that once and lived through it doesn't mean that was a great idea."

"Agree to disagree."

"Phil just texted me and they're moving our start time to five o'clock for Savannah and Myrtle Beach," Theo says, leaning across the aisle.

"I'll take it," I say.

"He also mentioned that some record reps RSVP'd for the Myrtle Beach show."

"Excellent. We'll be fresh after a day off and, by show four, the sound crew will know our set, so they'll be anticipating what we're doing rather than responding to it."

Theo nods. "The video guys, too. I was watching last night, and they cut to the action before it started. Made me think they took notes on who sings which songs and where you guys are soloing. It was only show two and they were all over it."

Maris finishes reading her book and closes the cover dramatically. "So great," she whispers. Leaning across me, she hands the book to Theo.

"Right?" he says, smiling. "The payoff was so worth every step of the journey."

"The willowy woman was Anna, don't you think?"

"Absolutely," Theo agrees. "That's how I took it. That Rostov and Anna were together in the end."

"Such a great book," Maris gushes.

"Thick book," I observe. "I'm glad you're finished with it, so I don't have to carry it in your backpack anymore," I tease.

"Max wanted to read it next, Nico, so you'll have to wait to join the book club discussions until after Max is finished," Theo tells me.

"Is it about music?" I ask.

"No, it's about this Russian Count who—"

"I'm out," I say.

Finally, the bus pulls away from the hotel entrance and begins to lumber down the road.

"Is Max asleep already?" I ask Theo.

He shrugs and leans forward so I can see past him. Max is wearing sunglasses and earbuds and uses a travel pillow to bolster his chin. The bus bounces from the driveway onto the road and his head sways along with the motion of the vehicle.

"That kid can sleep anywhere," I say. "I'm so jealous."

Theo smirks and tries to get comfortable in his seat. "Try to get some sleep now and we can hit the gym before the show. The later hit time is gonna feel more normal to us than having to get ready for work at noon."

I hold up my phone and text Theo so none of the musicians sitting around us overhears. *We'll just keep slayin' until we're the headliners.*

Theo reads it and holds up his fist, which I bump with my own.

"Goodnight, Johnboy," Theo says. He used to shout that down the hall at night when I first moved in with him. I had to Google it to learn he was referencing an old TV show.

"Then there were two," I say to Maris, who leans forward to check out our slumbering bandmates.

"They might have the right idea," she says. "We didn't get much sleep last night."

I tilt my face down to hers and kiss her slowly. "Sleep when we're around other people, don't sleep when we're alone."

"I like the plan," she says, kissing me back.

"Lay down," I offer, patting my lap.

Maris slips out of her shoes and pulls her knees up to her chest and then rests on her side, using my thigh as a pillow. I lean my seat back a whole three inches and rest my right arm across her torso in case the driver has to hit the brakes. I don't want her to get hurt.

I must have fallen asleep because I wake to the sound of someone getting violently ill in the bathroom a few rows behind where we're sitting. I do a head count, and it isn't one of us four, thankfully. I try to fall back to sleep, but it's so loud, I wonder if the sick person is actually in the bathroom or just yacking in the back of the bus.

"What the fuck?" Theo blinks a few times and turns to look at me. I shrug and he turns around to face the back of the bus. "Sounds like someone is losing some vital organs back there."

Theo looks down at Maris and then over at Max. I wonder if he's doing the same thing I did, or if he's wondering how they can sleep through the noise.

The door opens and then slams closed again and the heaving starts fresh.

Theo and I look at each other with big eyes.

A female with baggy camo pants, a neon pink tank top, and a camo ball cap uses her hands to steady herself against the seats as she walks down the aisle. I don't recognize her until I notice a hot pink braid dangling from under the back of the cap. She makes eye contact with me, and I smile and lift my chin a little to acknowledge the lead singer of the headlining band. *What the hell are they doing on our bus?* She notices Maris asleep in my lap, and she smiles sweetly at the sight. When she gets to the back of the bus, she knocks on the door.

"Nick? You okay?"

Theo and I look at each other. While we were sleeping, Nicky Knight walked past us on the way to lose his stomach. After the first two shows we played, we were too wiped out to go back to the venue to watch Dame Knight, named after their lead singer Dinah Dame and one of my contemporary guitar heroes Nicky Knight. I owe it to myself to watch him as much as I can to pick up whatever morsels he might drop.

Theo bounces his eyebrows and I try not to fangirl.

Dinah Dame gets some sort of muffled reply from the bus bathroom and heads back toward the front of the bus.

"Is Nicky okay?" Theo asks as she approaches our row.

"He says he is."

"I hope so. Playing sick sucks. We love you guys, by the way. I'm Theo from Funkengroovin and this is our guitar player—"

"Nico Van Asten," Dinah says. "We know you guys. We been watchin'." Dinah points to Maris. "She's ridiculous. I love that girl."

"I can't believe you know who we are," I say, chuckling.

"I was glad to see you added to the bill," Dinah says, winking.

"Well, you just made our day," Theo says. "Sorry about the circumstances that brought you to the back of the bus, though."

Dinah smirks. "Ah, Nick's been trying to kill his organs for years. He's tough. He'll bounce back."

"He's a pro," I say.

"See ya around," Dinah says.

"Dude," Theo says under his breath.

"She's so hot," Max says, startling both of us.

"I thought you were asleep, man." Theo laughs.

"Who could sleep through that yacking and then this yacking?" Max gestures to the back of the bus and then toward where Dinah stood a minute ago. Max leans forward and sees Maris cuddled up peacefully. "I guess Mare can …"

I look down at my girl, and I love that she feels so safe with me that she can fall into a deep sleep among other people in the middle of the day.

The bathroom door slams open, and I remain facing forward, not wanting to let on to Nicky that his misfortune is widely known.

He steps out of the bathroom and, in his thick British accent, puts a great spin on an old line. "Do not bloody go in there, mates. Sorry an' all that."

He doesn't walk past us, so Theo and I take turns looking toward the back of the bus under the guise of having a conversation. Nicky is passed out in the last row, sitting next to someone who is taking selfies with him.

I point and Theo follows my gaze. "Hey, my guy," Theo says to the dude posing next to Knight. "Cut that shit out and delete those right now."

The young punk laughs. "You gonna make me, Funkengroovin'?"

Theo stands up and I should, too, because I am supposed to have his back, but I don't want to wake Maris.

Then, the kid says, "Just kidding. Shit. Can't even take a joke?"

I turn to look at him, and I see that he's showing Theo he's deleting two photos.

"Little prick," Theo says as he sits down again.

"I wonder what band he's with," I say.

"Megaphone," Max says. "I can ID every musician on the tour. I studied."

Theo and I exchange disturbed expressions.

"Okay, well, keep an eye on that kid's social media," Theo tells Max.

"I will. I'm going back to sleep."

"Should we tell someone about Nicky?" I ask Theo.

He shrugs. "Dinah didn't seem that worried."

"MYOB," I say. "That's the key to getting through the tour."

Twenty minutes pass without further incident and then the bus exits the interstate. The change of speed wakes Maris, who smiles sweetly and asks if she missed anything, which cracks Theo and me up. I point to the back of the bus, and she sneaks a peek. I know she sees Nicky when she puts her hand over her mouth.

"Is he ... sleeping, or?"

"He hurled for a half hour and then passed out. Dinah came back to check on him." I squeeze Maris's thigh. "Dame thinks you're ridiculous, by the way."

"You lie," Maris says. "Seriously?"

"Yeah, ask Theo. He heard her, too. Anyway, she checked on him once, but didn't come back, so we figured this might not be unusual."

Maris looks concerned. "I hope he's okay. We haven't even seen them play live yet."

"Seriously. Nicky's known to divert from the recorded versions of their songs when he plays live, so I'm excited to watch him." I turn to Maris wearing a serious expression. "Maybe not tonight, though."

"Might not be their best show, or this might be his pre-game ritual," she says. "We don't know."

"When I was studying styles, I learned to copy every note he played on their first three albums. I'm a legit fan, so it feels weird to sit here doing nothing while he might be in dis—"

"Fuck all, it's comin' again, innit?"

Maris's mouth turns upside down, and I close my eyes while shaking my head.

Theo glances over and says, "Ruh-roh."

The bus pulls into the hotel portico and everyone offloads in a somewhat orderly fashion. We've learned that it takes a hot minute for the room keys to be dispersed to the band leaders, so we don't rush. I look for Dinah to give her an update on Nicky, but she's nowhere to be found. Probably in a Premium Uber headed to a better hotel. I don't see anyone from Dame Knight, so I tell the bus driver that Nicky is still in the bathroom and not to kidnap him by accident. He looks less than pleased.

Maris, Max, and I get our luggage, and Theo's, from under the bus and stand together in the lobby, planning to drop our stuff in our rooms and meet up again in the restaurant for lunch. Maris is fully charged after her nap, and she's coaxing Max to come to the gym with the rest of us after we eat.

Theo finally joins us and gives Maris our room key, so we head for the elevators, but before the doors open, we hear a deep baritone with a British accent shout, "Nicky Knight is dead!"

Maris and Max gasp, but Theo and I look at each other and dissolve into laughter. Without explaining, we leave our luggage with our bandmates and return with a very incapacitated Nick Knight between us hanging onto our shoulders.

Maris's expression is priceless. "What in the—"

"Hey, Love." Nicky attempts charm, but the odor that emanates from his mouth works against him.

"We're going to take him upstairs so he can lie down, and then we'll reach out to Phil to find out where he's supposed to be," I explain.

"I'm gonna stay in this shithole with you nobodies."

His reply makes all of us laugh. The elevator opens and we step inside with our luggage and our rockstar.

"It's like a big, wide mouth, innit? Who are you guys?" Nicky asks. He's eyeing our cases.

"Four-piece contemporary band called Funkengroovin'," I tell him.

"Ah, right. You're the Silver Springs girl. Good on ya with that one."

Maris's eyes get huge, and her cheeks start turning pink. "Thank you!"

The elevator opens on floor five, and we make our way to Theo and Max's door, while Maris and Max double back to grab all our gear.

"Ah, bed. How I've missed you," Nicky says before launching himself face down onto the closest one.

"That's yours, Theo," Max says definitively.

"Can you believe a week ago, we were at Theo's house in Miami getting ready for a gig at Club Fish and today we have a bona fide rock star passed out in our hotel room?" Maris whispers.

"I better tell someone he's here," Theo says, pulling up his recent calls. "Yeah, buddy, if anyone's looking for Nick Knight, he's in room 518 with us."

Phil's worried voice is an octave higher than normal.

"Okay. See ya." Theo ends the call. "Nick's two handlers, and Dame Knight's handler, will be up to *collect him* shortly."

"So, is he drunk?" Max asks. "All I smell is vomit."

"I don't think he's drunk ..." I say. "Anymore."

"Maybe one of us should stay with him while the rest go down for lunch," Maris says.

"I've got him," I say. "Guitar code."

"I'll bring you something," Maris says. She rises up on the balls of her feet, and I lean down to meet her sweet lips.

"Might as well just leave our stuff here and we can transfer it to our room when you guys get back," I tell her.

"Okay. Have fun babysitting your buddy," she teases.

"If he wakes up, you can read him *A Gentleman in Moscow*." Max gestures to the book on his bed.

"I'm going to pleasure myself on your bed," I say with a smile.

Max's face falls and he closes his eyes as Theo and I chuckle. Maris gives me the side eye as she walks to the door.

I hold my hands out at my sides. "Brother stuff," I explain. "Don't let him spit in my lunch."

The hotel door closes, and I'm alone with Nicky Knight's decidedly not dead, but not fully alive body.

MARIS

THE ELEVATOR DOOR OPENS ON floor five and we hear raucous male laughter. As we close in on Max and Theo's room, it gets louder.

"We're back!" Theo announces as he opens the door.

Nick is sitting on one bed, still wet from the shower and wearing a towel, playing Nico's guitar as Nico sits facing him on the other one. Nico's face is slightly flushed, and his smile is as wide as I've ever seen it.

"Welcome in, mates," Nicky says enthusiastically. "Turns out young Nico here is a damn good guitar player, and he's got me droppin' some tricks."

"You're seven years older than I am, Nick. It's not like you're an old man," Nico says.

"Musician years are like dog years, mate. Better bed as many ladies as you can while you still look like that, cuz this face ain't what it used to be."

Nico laughs and I roll my eyes playfully. Nick hands Nico's guitar to him. "Do it just like I taught ya."

Nico takes his guitar in his hands, and it becomes an extension of him. A feeling I know well. He rips through the riff that opens one of Dame Knight's hits and Theo instinctively snaps his fingers to keep time.

At a certain point, Nick yells, "Yes, mate. See? It ain't proper, but it's so right, innit?"

Nico's radiating happiness and it's contagious. I look at Max and Theo, and they're wearing the same smile I have.

"Okay, so then, the second bridge is ..." Nico plays guitar.

"Yeah," Nicky confirms when he hears it. "Everyone plays the seventh there, and I don't understand why they think they're hearing a bloody seventh, but you're on it, mate." Nicky turns to face us, which makes his towel open wider than I'd like it to. "He's good, your guitar man."

Theo nods and laughs. "I know. We played together at a jam night in Miami, and I fell in love with this dude. Kept him with me ever since."

"Nick, this is Theo Athanasiou. He's our bandleader and drummer extraordinaire. Really solid player, you'd love groovin' with him." Nico gestures toward Max. "On keys, we have the fabulous Max Anthony Castelano, a Berklee School of Music grad, and a mad musical scientist."

"Nice to meet you, Nicky," Max says, holding out his hand. Nicky shakes it respectfully and that makes me so happy.

"And this gorgeous badass bassist is Maris Humphries, who also sings her ass off."

Nicky raises his eyebrows and says, "We should get to know each other better, doll."

Nico saves me. "I wouldn't blame her if she dumped me for you."

"Oh, that's your girl, mate. You should lead with that."

I smile. "I'm a big fan. When we heard we had the chance to be on a bill with you guys, we couldn't believe it."

Nicky holds his hand out to Nico, who gives him the guitar.

"We're full circle here, mates. In seven years, unless you hit bigger than we did, you'll be sitting here with some young musicians who play better than you ever did and are on their way up the ladder, while you're trying to gracefully milk what's left of your best days as you descend the ladder. On our way up, we crossed paths with Zenith. Greatest fucking band of all time. Monsters, all of 'em. Great bunch of guys and prolific musicians. All of 'em had more music to give, but the industry moved on and then they died, one by one."

The room falls silent. I look at Theo, who searches my eyes for a clue what to do. Max looks like he's going to cry, and then Nico says, "That's rare air at the top, Nicky. I'm not sure we'll ever get there, but no one forgets the legends who do. The music lasts forever, and to be able to contribute to the songbook is what it's all about."

"True enough, mate. But get a good money manager so you don't have to play festivals when you're middle aged." Nicky's laugh is genuine, but I don't know if it's okay to join in or not. Nico seems to "get" him, and he shakes his head and smirks at him as he plays his guitar.

There's a knock on the hotel door and Theo goes to answer it. Three young guys wearing Dame Knight T-shirts are standing in the hall.

"Your bodyguards are here, Nicky," Theo calls.

"Time for a proper nap," Nicky says, standing up. "Thanks for the camaraderie, mates."

Nick hands Nico's guitar to him, picks up his clothes, and calls, "Thanks for the towel," on his way out the door.

"Fucking classic," Theo says after the door closes.

"I can't believe I just had a playdate with Nicky Knight," Nico says with a laugh. "What is my life right now?"

"He genuinely dug your playing," I say, handing him the box lunch we brought upstairs.

"He was out like a light and then stood up, saluted me, and went into the bathroom. I heard the shower turn on, and when he came back out, he was Nicky Knight." Nico shrugs. "He asked what kind of axe I had, and we were off. Just trading licks and riffs." Nico runs his hands down his face. "Insane."

"I wish he had showered before he slept in my bed," Theo says sadly.

"Call room service and have them bring fresh bedding," I suggest.

Theo points at me and nods like that's the best idea he's ever heard.

"Let me smash this and I'll get ready for the gym," Nico says, opening the box.

"I'm going to go to our room to change," I say. "Max, do you want to come with us?"

"Hell to the no," he replies. "I'm going to call everyone I know and tell them that Nicky Knight was just in my hotel room."

"Be careful how you present that," Theo warns. "Sounded kinda sussy just now, my guy."

Max laughs. "I'll work on the delivery."

"Come pick me up at my room, okay?" I grab my tote and my spinner suitcase. Theo gets my bass case, opens the door for me, and follows me next door to my room.

"Have you ever seen Nico that happy?" I ask him as I swipe my key card.

"I never have, but I bet you have," he blurts. Theo's face goes white, and he stammers, "I-I didn't mean anything disrespectful …"

I can't help laughing at him. "If Nicky Knight was a chick, I'd be single right now."

"Too bad he's a dude," Theo says. He turns back toward his room as I open my door, and his closes behind him before I can say more.

THEO

THE SAVANNAH CROWD IS VIBING with our performance, and they sing along with every song we play. That's a new development. Seems this crowd did their homework before coming to the show. The material we're playing is mostly new, written for this tour. It's heady to see the audience embrace the songs like they're old favorites. There are no nerves on stage anymore. Even Max is having a blast. The kid is officially out of his shell.

Maris is wearing jean shorts with a bikini top, and a sleeveless crochet duster that hangs to her bare feet. Her authentic hippie chick is on display, and I love it. Her vocals are so powerful tonight. It's as though the audience is physically energizing her and enabling her voice to do whatever she wills it to. Her playing is always solid, but players aren't at the mercy of the many unmanageable variables as singers are. A dry hotel room, too much pollen in the air, not enough sleep, or a post-nasal drip can derail a vocal performance, so I'm thrilled to see that Maris isn't affected by being on the road … so far.

Nico and I are always in sync and playing in a bigger pond has intensified our connection. I can read his mind and he can read mine. On stage, anyway. Like now, when he tilts his head back without looking at me and raises the neck of his guitar slightly higher than where he usually plays. He's going in for a big finish, and I stand by, waiting for the cues for the hits he wants and the crescendo that will take us home.

The festival producers asked us to announce our last song ten minutes before the end of our set so that we can do a built-in "encore" without throwing off the timeline. It works great and we're working toward that big finish right now. Nico and I are dripping with sweat, Max's smile can probably be seen from space, and Maris has all of us captivated as she delivers her final sustained note of the song. I see her raise the neck of her bass and I panic. The rule is: the band follows the singer, but I don't know if she's leading us right now. Nico usually cues the end of the night. The sound crew has me wearing a headset mic for my background vocals so I can't yell to Nico like I would on a gig. I try to get Max's attention, but he's looking at Nico, as per usual, so, along with the beat, I say, "Eyes on Maris" into my mic.

Both Max and Nico turn to face me, and I gesture to Maris who lets go of her final vocal note and holds the strings on her bass to make them silent on the next beat. We all follow suit and the song just … stops. It seems anticlimactic at first, but the spontaneous and dramatic ending causes the audience to lose their minds and scream their appreciation. Maris thanks the crowd, says goodnight on behalf of the band, and we make our way backstage.

"What the fuck was that?" Nico yells in my face as soon as we're out of sight of the audience.

"What are you talking about? I was following the singer."

"I end the night, not Maris," Nico says as if talking to a subordinate.

"Guys, guys." Maris makes her way to where we're standing. Her bass is still slung behind her back. "That was my fault. I was in the moment, and I had an idea—"

"I thought it was cool as fuck to end on the one," Max says. "Totally unexpected. I think we should do it like that again tomorrow and commit to it, so it seems intentional."

Nico runs his hands down his face. "Exactly. It looked like we fucked up out there and then just … walked off."

Maris has tears forming in her eyes. "I'm sorry, I should have communicated better."

"I picked up on it," I tell her. "We've gotten used to watching Nico for the end cues, but it's your song, so we should be watching you."

Nico shakes his head as he whips his guitar strap off his shoulder. "We'll just go back to me singing the last song."

Max scrunches his face up. "The order is perfect right now. We don't need to switch songs; we just need to smooth out what Maris hears for the ending."

"There's nothing wrong with the way we've been ending it," Nico counters.

"We labor it sometimes, man. We've been known to lay down a couple measures of rock opera," I say, laughing.

"You think this is funny?" Nico asks me. His eyes are cold and his mouth twists into a disgusted expression. "We look like amateur idiots right now. That ending negated everything we did on that stage tonight."

I roll my eyes. "That's a ridiculous exaggeration. We absolutely slayed tonight and no one knows that the ending we came up with just now was improvised." Kenny has my snare and is coming to get the axes. "What did you think of the new ending tonight, Kenny?"

"At first I was like—" he gasps. "And then I was like, dude ... rad."

"See?" I make eye contact with Nico. "Ask them to let you watch the video," I say gesturing toward the production table. I keep one eye on Maris who seems to be on the brink of sobbing. Her face couldn't be any redder, so I drape an arm across her shoulders. "Are we pros or not? Are we good on our toes, or not? We've never wanted to be the band that plays a live show like it's a canned track."

"There's a time and a place—" Nico starts. His expression changes, and I think it's because he's just registered that I'm standing up for Maris. He looks back and forth between us and rubs his lips together.

"Can I get your guitars?" Kenny breaks the tension. "Are both of you good for one more show with these strings, or do you want new ones for Myrtle Beach?"

"Mine are good, just the standard op, Kenny. Thanks," Maris says, her voice sounding shaky. After what she just did on stage, I'm so upset to hear her vocal cords sounding inflamed now. Fucking Nico.

"Yeah, new strings, for me, Kenny. Use the ones in my case, please."

"See you guys in Myrtle Beach." Kenny looks eager to leave us, but he stops short. "Oh, my God, I can't believe I almost forgot." There are little groups of people backstage, and he nods toward two of the handlers who came to my room earlier in the day to retrieve Nicky Knight. "Those guys have backstage passes for all of you to watch Dame Knight from the wings tonight. Make sure you get them before you leave. So, I'll see you tonight."

"Holy shit, that's so cool," Max says.

Maris is watching for Nico's reaction. I've known him longer than she has, so I know he's still steaming and that the conversation we were just having isn't over.

"I'll make sure we get 'em. Thanks, Kenny," I say. I pull Maris into a one-armed hug and ask if everyone wants to go back to the hotel for a couple hours before Dame Knight comes on, and she and Max answer affirmatively. "Nico, why don't you go grab those passes?"

He clears his throat and says, "Sure, boss."

"I haven't seen him this pissed since he didn't want to hire Maris," Max says.

"And the award for always saying the wrong thing at the wrong time goes to—" I say, which makes Maris giggle.

"Well, he was wrong about that and he's wrong about this," Maris says.

I hope she feels as confident about the statement as she sounds when delivering it.

"Exactly right," I say. "Great show tonight, by the way. Truly. You guys are on fire, and I'm honored to be here to witness it."

"I think the show is getting better and better every night," Max says.

Nico rejoins the group. "I have the passes, so we can catch a van."

The next band is starting and the noise level backstage jumps to deafening decibels. I nod at Nico, who leads the way. The ride back to the hotel is wordless. In the elevator, I ask everyone what time we want to go back to the venue. I tell the band that I'll set up transportation, and we split off into our rooms. I want to make sure Maris is okay, but she's walking far ahead of all of us. I hope she gives Nico a whole bunch of shit for what he just did.

MARIS

NICO FOLLOWS ME INTO OUR hotel room, and I walk to the bedroom, expecting him to be right behind me, but I hear the shower turn on, and I'm exponentially angrier than I was backstage. I am shocked that the man who says he loves me just pulled rank on stage and now, evidently, thinks he can avoid talking to me about it.

I want to go into the bathroom and confront him, but I pace the floor instead. Less than three minutes later, Nico appears wearing a towel around his waist, carrying the balled-up clothes he wore on stage. "When are you planning on doing laundry?" he asks casually. "I think I'm going to need clean clothes soon because my luggage seems to be mostly dirties."

I blink repeatedly while words jumble in my head. My words come out like knives, "If you're suggesting that I do your laundry—"

"What?" Nico's eyebrows pull together. "I figured we would do it together. I don't have enough clothes to make a full load ... why are you looking at me like that?"

"Why are you pretending that you didn't just embarrass me in front of Theo, Max, and the entire backstage crew when you exploded over me calling an audible on stage during *my* song, which bee-tee-dubs you do all the time, when our rule is the band follows the singer?"

"Fine, let's get into it." Nico takes a deep breath. "This was show four. We ended the first three shows the same way, with the hits and the sustain, right? Theo watches me for the timing. Max watches me for the timing. They've been watching me for five years. But you decided, during show number four, in front of a couple thousand people, you're going to walk us through your first show close." Nico sits down on the bed and puts his head in his hands. "We had no idea what you were guiding us through, nothing to reference, because you never did that before."

"I've called changes at gigs," I counter.

"At gigs, Maris. Lousy club gigs where the stages were so small we could communicate with each other. When Theo told us, through the stadium speaker mains, to watch you, I had no idea if you were going to count the way I've been doing it, or ... what the fuck. And then the one comes, and I see your hands close your strings, so I choke my guitar out ... I don't know how Theo stopped his foot from hitting the kick drum."

"He was watching me, that's how. He got it. Max got it. It seems the only person who was pissed off about it was you because you didn't get to walk us through the big build up you usually do."

Nico lays back onto the bed and stares at the ceiling while breathing in and out with sound. "So, yes, we do a big build up at the end of the night. Theo rides his crash, the rest of us slay ... you've been there. And then we finish the night in a way that makes sense musically."

"Oh, so my ending didn't make sense musically?" I roll my eyes. "So, any song that doesn't have a huge build up at the end doesn't make sense musically?" I start naming songs that don't have measures of music after the final vocal. When I get to "Fix You" by Coldplay, Nico clears his throat loudly.

"Like I said backstage, there is a time and a place to work things like that out. Live, in front of a festival audience, isn't either one."

"I wasn't trying to upstage you or take anything away from you. I was in the moment, and I thought it would be more impactful to end with a punch in the face, rather than our usual extended ending."

"If I had been given the opportunity to disagree, I would have, but you made the decision for all of us."

"You make decisions for all of us all the time. So, do you have the authority to do that because you're a dude, or because you've been in the band longer, or is it because you're a superior musician?"

"Maris, you're abundantly talented, obviously. This isn't a question of whether you have the skills to rewrite us on stage. It's a judgment call and a matter of protocol. If you want to rework the end of that song, we have all day to sit together and hash out a new ending. Springing it on us on stage—"

"You spring shit on us every night, Nico. You change arrangements on the fly, change solos on the fly, double choruses on the fly—"

"Those things are within the framework of the song," Nico says, raising his voice. "What you did tonight was something out of left field. If you can't see the difference …"

"Again, Theo and Max aren't pissed off over it."

"That's because they're both too infatuated with you to tell you the truth. I love you, Maris, so I'm going to tell you the truth."

I scoff and feel my throat getting tight. "Don't fucking gaslight me, Nico. You couldn't wait to show everyone backstage that you disapproved of what I did up there, so you could distance yourself. You made it very well known that you thought I had blown the whole show. But you did that because you love me, so it's fine? I should thank you; I guess." The sarcasm is so thick in my mouth I can taste it.

"We're conflating two different things, Maris. Did I handle myself well? No, I didn't. I'm sorry that I embarrassed you backstage. I wasn't trying to. I was genuinely pissed at a fellow band member who I felt made us look bad in front of an audience and other musicians. You're my girlfriend, yes, but you're also a fellow band member and sometimes we have to keep those things separate."

"What if I don't love everything you do on stage, Nico? As a fellow band member, should I tell you?"

"If it helps me musically or makes me a better performer, yes. Absolutely."

I shake my head and laugh. "I'll never criticize how you express yourself artistically because expression can't be right or wrong." I open my luggage and find a pair of jeans and a T-shirt to wear after my shower. "I won't take artistic license with the ending of the final song of the night again. I'm sorry I embarrassed you in front of your fans and fellow musicians." I walk past Nico and close, then lock, the bathroom door.

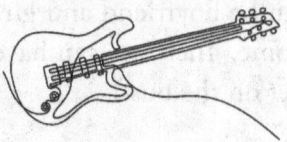

NICO

DOGHOUSE POPULATION: ME. FUCK. I regret losing my temper in the moment. I was pissed, though. What happened on stage earlier should never happen. The numb nuts we were playing for didn't know any better, but the other musicians know a train wreck when they hear one. Maris's interpretation of the song while she was performing wasn't catastrophic, but the way we usually do it is so much better. I should have been more sensitive. I should have waited until the four of us were alone to talk it through. Should have called for a Band Beating. Shit. I stand by my opinion, but I feel awful, and Maris isn't in the mood to let me try to reconcile.

When she comes out of the bathroom, she's fully dressed, so that shuts down any ideas I had about seducing her. I follow her lead and dress in jeans and a T-shirt. I like when we look like a pair. I know that's cheesy, but I don't care. Also, I'm from Wisconsin where cheesy things are revered.

Maris is laying on the bed by the window. We always sleep in the bed closest to the wall, so this is a signal that she doesn't want to be near me. She turns on the TV and begins flipping through the channels. She leaves it on a movie I've seen before. It's a comedy, and she giggles here and there, which makes me smile. I hope that means she's starting to feel better about things, but we've never had a fight like this before. There was the Bartender Barbie ordeal, but that doesn't really count.

We weren't a couple at the time and that was a misunderstanding. I'm worried that damage has been done.

"Hey, Maris?" I say softly. "Can I fix this? I'm scared that I broke something between us."

I hear her exhale. She mutes the TV. "I don't want to talk about it right now. Maybe we can be boyfriend and girlfriend tonight but leave the bandmate roles at home. Then, we can have a Band Beating tomorrow before it's time to get on the bus."

"Perfect. Thank you."

"Mm-hmm." She unmutes the TV.

"Hey, Maris?" I say softly.

She mutes the TV again. "Yes, Nico?"

"Is it lonely in your bed? Cuz this one is lonely."

"Nope," she says, unmuting the TV. I sit up to look at her and she's stifling a laugh, but when I swing my legs over the side of my bed she says, "I did not invite you over here."

"Okay," I say, stretching out to cover my whole bed.

We watch a half hour or so of the movie and then Theo texts the band chat: *If I have to eat vendor food again, I'm gonna puke. Wanna hit the lobby for dinner before the van picks us up?*

I text back: *YES!* Then I look over at Maris to gauge her reaction. My phone goes off and I see her reply: *Yes! X2*

She turns off the TV and grabs her purse as I grab my wallet. I feel relieved, yet worried at the same time. Being locked out of Maris's heart, even if it's only for a brief time, is painful as hell.

MAX

MARIS SAT ON MY SIDE of the booth at dinner, which made me believe that she and Nico were still pissed at each other. Initially, I told Theo not to invite them to dinner, but he scoffed at me. I don't like it when people aren't getting along. It makes me stressed. Nico sat across from Mare, and they engaged in conversation and everything, so it wasn't awkward, but usually they sit next to each other.

We had a decent dinner at the Italian restaurant at the hotel and then made our way back to the venue. It looks very different at night. The stage lights add a dramatic layer of coolness. The general admission area looks eerily dark, and I can't help but think how easy it would be for an audience member to throw something at the musicians on stage. That shit has to stop. You can't see into an audience when the stage lights are in your eyes, so you can't deflect. If the people are supposed to be fans, they shouldn't be abusive.

The energy is different at night, too. Our crowds have been happy and easy-breezy. They keep beach balls in the air and wear shorts, hats, sunglasses, and sunscreen. There are plenty of daytime attendees still bopping around the crowd, but the Dame Knight fans stand out in leather and boots. The mood is heavier. The crowd is drunker. I'm glad we aren't headlining.

Kenny is with us in the wings. We've never hung out with him outside of work, and he's cool. He has great stories about the other bands and keeps Maris and me laughing as we wait for Dame Knight to go on. Theo and Nico are huddled together watching the sound crew set the stage. Out of the corner of my eye, I see a splash of neon pink, and I tap Maris's arm to point out Dinah's arrival in the wings.

Maris doesn't try to hide her excitement. "She's right there!" Maris whisper-shouts.

"Do you see Nicky?" I ask.

Maris shakes her head as she scans the wings.

"Oh, my God. She's coming over here," I say. "Dinah's coming this way."

"Funkengroovin'!" she screams. "Thank you for sobering Nicky up this morning and for getting him back to us safely."

"Hey, I'm free to babysit Nicky anytime," I say sincerely and Dinah laughs. I made her laugh! "Would it be weird if I asked for a photo with you?"

"It would be weird if you didn't," she said, putting her head on my shoulder. After I click a few, she says, "Maris, get in here, baby."

"Really? Okay, yeah." Mare joins us and I snap a few more.

"That's gonna be my Christmas card every year until I die," I tell Dinah.

"We need to get together, Maris. I need some damn girl time. You up for a massage in Myrtle Beach?"

"Um, yes, please," Maris says.

"I have a guy who comes to my room. I bet the spa can send two over. Does noon give you enough time to get ready for your set?"

Maris looks at me and her eyes are sparkling. "Seriously? That would be awesome, Dinah."

"Can I come?" I beg. I make both Dinah and Maris laugh. I love it when Nico and Theo are too busy to cock block my game.

"Ladies only," Dinah says. "But I'll leave you with this, sweet boy." She kisses my cheek and I wink at her.

"Have a great show," Maris says. "I mean, of course you will, but have fun."

"Thank you, Maris. I love what you do, girl. You're a mutha bass player and you're sangin', too? Make me look lazy."

Maris laughed. "Yeah, well, if I was great at one thing, I wouldn't have to compensate."

"See you the day after tomorrow at noon. I'll have Phil get you my room number."

Maris and I trade incredulous expressions and watch Dinah greet Theo and Nico, who are even closer to the stage now. She hugs and kisses them both like old friends.

"Can you believe we're hanging with Dinah Dame?" I ask Maris. "I figured we wouldn't be allowed anywhere near the headlining bands."

"Honestly, I didn't even consider this side of the tour. I was so focused on our show, I didn't think about the opportunity to hang with other players. This is crazy cool. I'm going to Dinah's room for a massage, and we're only one week into a three-month tour."

I turn to Maris to acknowledge what she said and notice that her eyes are on Nico. Dinah is back-to-back with him measuring her height against his. She starts twerking and then busts out laughing. Maris laughs along and I'm relieved. Maris is a cool chick.

"The stories of my death ..." The British accent is easy to identify. Nicky's here. He makes his way to the stage, greeting roadies, stage crew, and musicians by name. He takes a second or two with each of them. I wonder if he'll remember us, since he wasn't exactly in tip top shape this morning.

"Oi! It's Max and Maris from Funkengroovin'! I'm so glad you were able to join us tonight."

"We wouldn't miss it, Nicky," I say. "I never thought I'd be back-stage at a Dame Knight show."

"Don't limit your expectations, Max. Every day is an adventure." Nicky turns to Maris. "What does Nico have that I don't have? Never mind. I don't want to know. All my solos are for you tonight, love."

"I can't wait to watch you play," Maris tells him.

Nicky moves on to say hello to Theo and Nico after he touches base with each person standing in between.

The crowd is getting restless. The last band finished their set quite a while ago. They start chanting *Dame Knight* over and over. I'm glad we're backstage and not out in the audience.

The monitors come alive and the video that introduces the band starts playing. Theo and Nico are standing behind the lighting truss, and Maris and I join them there. Nico opens his arm out to his side and Maris slips into place beside him. Theo looks at me and opens his arm the same way, and we die laughing.

Dame Knight's first song is one of their first number ones. It's an older tune, but everyone in the house seems to know it. I watch each band member for a few minutes. No one is phoning it in. All of them are engaged with each other and the audience, which I love to see. They're playing at full tilt. Dinah practically does a HIIT workout on stage. She's everywhere all at once, and her vocals never waver. Nicky plays to the audience as a whole and finds individuals up front to single out. The crowd is under their spell, but I have to say, we have the same relationship with our audience. They haven't loved us as long, but they love us as much, and I'm grateful that I've been able to experience that.

The band rips through the first four songs without any dead air. They play transitions like we do. I was surprised that some bands on the tour do hard stops and starts. Nicky puts his hand in the air, and the band drops to bass and drums.

"Mates, we have a special treat for you tonight!" Nicky yells into his mic. "We're going to bring up a special guest for this next song ..."

I sense someone behind us and turn to see Kenny holding a guitar that looks a lot like Nico's. I reach across Theo and tap Nico, then point to Kenny.

"Nico Van Asten from Funkengroovin' is with us tonight. He and I played this song together earlier today, and I thought you should hear the way he plays it because it's bloody beautiful ..."

Nico looks genuinely shocked, but he straps on his guitar and listens to what Kenny is yelling in his ear. He nods as Kenny speaks.

Maris looks over at me and Theo with her mouth and eyes wide. I make the same face back. Mare gets her phone out and starts a livestream.

"Please welcome to the stage ... . Nico Van Asten!"

The band starts the song, and the audience goes nuts. Nico walks out playing the signature riff, and Nicky joins in playing a harmony part in perfect sync with him. Nicky is center stage and Nico reaches him in a few long strides. They're both in a badass stance and are matching each other note for note.

"What the fuck is happening right now?" I'm shouting, but I can't even hear myself over the stage volume. I see Theo take his phone out of his pocket and I fumble for mine. My lock screen doesn't recognize my astonished face, so I have to type in the passcode to unlock it. I kneel down to get a good angle and frame Nico, but my hands are shaking. I can't believe he's out there trading licks with Nicky Knight. Nico alternately laughs and then his face changes to serious guitar player stank face. But then, he can't help himself and he's laughing again like a little kid. So are Theo, Maris, and me. We keep our eyes and our phones on him, but we sneak looks at each other. We're over the moon excited for our brother, and he is more than rising to the occasion. Nicky gives

Nico a solo and he walks to the front edge of the stage and rips, much to the delight of the crowd. Dinah walks over and dances against Nico and the audience eats it up. As the song comes to an end, Nicky and Nico tear it up, and the audience shows them how excited they are to share the moment with them. When the song ends, Nicky yells into the mic, "That's the most fun I've had since my fourth wedding night. Nico Van Asten, mates. Show him you love him."

I keep filming as Nico walks off stage, waving to the crowd. He hands his guitar to Kenny who gives him a big hug. Maris runs into Nico's arms and he's beaming. He says something into her hair, and they stare into each other's eyes for a second before they kiss. It's just a quick one; they don't do too much PDA.

Theo slams himself into Nico and they bro-hug. I hear Theo shout that Nico sounded awesome.

I'm still holding my phone up and Nico puts his face in it and then says, "Send that to me."

I keep rolling as Nico gives Theo and Maris a play by play. He's providing details of how he felt up there and what he experienced. His hands make motions as if he's playing guitar. This video is an important part of Nico's history, so I keep rolling.

NICO

MARIS WENT LIVE ON OUR band page while I was on stage with Dame Knight. I'm so grateful she did that because my brother Marcus gets alerts when she signs on. As luck would have it, my whole family and half our town was at the tavern, so they were able to watch me sit in with Dame Knight in real time. My phone started blowing up right after Maris ended the stream, but the only call I took was Marcus's.

I was so happy my family got to share that experience with me, and each of my brothers and both my parents insisted on talking to Maris, which sent my already high spirit into the stratosphere. Watching her on the phone with them, laughing and interrupting each other out of pure excitement felt like everything in my world had fallen perfectly in line. But I knew she was still mad at me.

When the band got back to the hotel, we were too hyped to go to our rooms, so we hit the lounge. After a few beers and a couple games of darts, we came upstairs. I'm kind of nervous to be alone with Maris. I want everything to be normal between us, and it seems like it is, but I donn't trust it.

We say our goodnights to Theo and Max and schedule a Band Beating for ten. Maris opens our hotel room door, and I follow her inside.

She says she'll be in the shower for a few minutes, and that's not exactly an invitation, so I watch the video from tonight while I wait for her. When I hear the water turn off, I shut down my phone and put it on the charger.

I'm sitting on the bed closest to the wall, feeling like an uncertain teenager, rather than the up-and-coming rocker the audience saw just a few hours ago. I inhale the fragrance of Maris's body wash and the distance between us is killing me. I can't wait any longer, so I knock on the half-open bathroom door. "Can I come in?"

"Sure," she says, sounding tired.

She's wearing the same T-shirt she had on our first night together. It's not overtly sexy, but the memory stirs me.

"I know we're going to talk about this tomorrow, but the part of me that's your man wants to apologize for the part of me that is your band mate. Maris, I'm sorry for the way I overreacted earlier. There's a wall between us now, and I want you to know that it physically hurts me to feel separated from you."

She closes her eyes, and when she opens them again, she looks into mine. "I love you, you big idiot. But that can't happen again."

I nod my understanding.

"Get in the shower because you have stage stank all over you and I'm not trying to get covered in that."

I'm out of my clothes and in the shower before Maris squeezes toothpaste onto her brush. By the time she's putting the toothbrush back in its case, I'm reaching for a towel. She playfully slaps my hand.

"No, sir. You shall not cover thyself."

I give her a look in the mirror. "What would the lady have me do?"

Maris smiles wickedly. "Everything. The lady will have you do everything."

I step out of the shower stall and pick her up, drenching the front of her T-shirt as it presses against me. I carry her to the bed by the window, knowing she isn't sleeping there tonight. Especially not after we mess it up. I pull Maris's T-shirt off with my teeth, and I'm pleased to see she isn't wearing anything underneath.

I hear a rasp in her voice when she says, "You were incredibly sexy on stage tonight."

"Were you screaming for me?" I brace myself on top of her and kiss her neck. Maris melts when I kiss her neck.

"Mm hm," she breathes, wrapping her legs around my torso and her arms around my neck.

I scoop her into my arms and lift her up, then I sit on the edge of the bed with Maris in my lap. I love being face to face with her so I can see every expression and feel every gasp. She pushes my chest and I fall backwards onto the bed.

"Are you going to take advantage of me?" I tease.

"Tonight is for me," she says. Maris starts moving on top of me, and I clench her hips in my hands. I watch as shockwaves pulse through her body and she lets her head fall backwards, her long hair cascading to the top of her perfect peach. The ecstasy on her face sends me over the edge. We sustain the feeling for longer than I ever experienced before Maris.

She leans forward and braces her arms on either side of my head, swishing her hair back and forth across my face. "You have five minutes to recharge," she says.

"Whatever the lady wants."

THEO

Judging by what I heard through the wall last night, Maris and Nico made up. I wore my earbuds to bed and listened to music to keep from losing my mind. I got up early and hit the gym alone, then had breakfast in the lobby. Time alone is hard to come by on the road and I enjoyed it. At five minutes before ten, I'm back in the room with Max, Nico, and Maris for the Band Beating. Maris sits in the desk chair, Max sits on his bed, which I told him to make prior to the meeting, and I sit on the TV stand across from where Nico sits on the other bed.

"The bus leaves in two hours and then we have the night off, so this is a good time to check in with one another," I start off. "Before we discuss yesterday's show, are there any matters that I need to take to Phil? Any problems with accommodations, food, per diem, anything like that?"

Nico raises his hand and we all chuckle. "Can we ever rent a car, at our own expense, and drive ourselves to the next gig?"

"I'll ask Phil, but I doubt it."

"Can't hurt to ask," Nico says. "Thanks."

Max raises his hand and I nod at him. "Our first payday is today, but I haven't seen the direct deposit hit. Any idea what time that will happen?"

I look at Max and wonder, once again, what this kid needs money for and why he never seems to have any.

"I'll ask Phil," I promise. No one has anything else, so it's time to get to the potentially ugly stuff. "Okay, let's talk about last night's show. Maris, I'd like you to start us off, please."

She recrosses her long legs and scans the room with her eyes. "First,

I'd like to thank you guys for following me yesterday and for trusting me in the moment. Sincerely."

Max nods and I wink at Maris, fully aware that Nico is watching me.

"But I recognize that the impromptu change was a bad call. I felt it would be more dramatic to end spontaneously and let the silence hang. I heard it in my head pretty much the same way it played out, thanks to you guys being Johnny-on-the-spot times three, but that doesn't make it the right call."

I watch Maris to make sure she's said everything she wants to say.

"Anyone else?" I ask.

"I want to apologize for losing my cool in public. That was very unprofessional of me," Nico says.

"Max, do you have any input before I give my take?"

Max shakes his head. "Not really. I thought how Maris ended the set was cool, but it could have gone badly, so I see Nico's point."

"Okay, so here's my take. I watched the video from yesterday. The whole set was technically great, and each member of the band gave the audience a great show. We were engaged with them and feeding off them the whole time. No question we were in that otherworldly, creative space. The question is, how disciplined should we remain inside that space, and does discipline kill creativity?" I watch to see how each person is reacting to my words and, so far, no one is responding verbally or nonverbally. "Every time we venture outside of convention, it's a risk. Like Max said, and like Nico pointed out, it could pay off or crash and burn. What we have to decide, as a band, is how much creative license we want to take on the fly, or are we going to stick to the script and wait for rehearsals to suggest changes?"

Nico raises his hand. "While we're on tour, I vote for weekly rehearsals where we can try out and nail down new ideas."

"Maris, what do you think about that?" I ask.

She looks at Nico, who glances in her direction, smiles shyly, and looks back at me.

"I understand the value of working things out before we're in front of an audience, of course. Personally, I feel stifled by the idea that I don't have the freedom to be creatively spontaneous, but if we make that rule for the duration of this tour, I'll abide by it. I just don't like the thought that we're going to reproduce the same show for three months without any deviation, regardless of the audience, or how we're feeling, or whatever indefinable thing happens in the moment."

"Like I told Maris yesterday, if the audible is within the construct of the song, extending a solo, or breaking down the music to have an acapella break where we ask the crowd to sing with us, that's fine. I just don't want to be in a position where I'm flying by the seat of my pants on stage."

"You flew by the seat of your pants last night when you sat in with Dame Knight. You didn't know if they do that song the same as the record," Maris points out.

"Yes, well, there's more latitude when you're sitting in. Everyone knows the person sitting in isn't a band member."

"Yeah, but the band trusted you to play the parts and go with the flow."

I don't want this to turn into a back and forth between Maris and Nico, even though I have to admit I like watching them argue. Just a little bit. I insert myself into the conversation, anyway. "I'm pulling the band leader card."

All eyes are on me now.

"Like Max, I agree with the points that both of you are making. Maris, your contributions to the band carried us to this level. I trust you, and I respect your musicianship. You have the same right to call an audible as any of us. That said, I think we should implement rehearsals while we're on the road so that we can find new ways of presenting our material, so we don't get bored or burned out."

Maris nods.

"Nico, I understand why Maris wanted to try something new to end the night because the build feels too drawn out at times to be an effective climax. People can't scream for three minutes straight. Let's land on something in between, see how it works, and adjust accordingly. From now on, the only audibles on stage have to be within the construct of the song *and* we have a hand signal for it. Is everyone amenable to that?"

"Does the band follow the singer, or does the band follow Nico when I'm singing?"

I wasn't ready for that very valid question. Now I understand what's at the heart of Maris's frustration.

"The band follows the singer. All the time. So, Maris, decide how we're going to end the last song."

Nico raises his hand again. "Maris brought up "Fix You" by Coldplay yesterday. What if we drop the music out and sing the chorus one last time acapella? Maybe even twice?" Nico is talking to Maris. "That gives us an intimate moment with the crowd before we go and maybe that's better than BAM, BAM, BAAAAAAM, BAM!" Nico imitates a big finish.

"I think it's worth trying," Max says. "Major chord harmony?"

"Or," Maris says, "a second melody." She closes her eyes and starts humming.

"Add harmonic color by adding a 9th there." Max demonstrates.

Theo and I watch as the two of them put their heads together and make sounds that don't sound compatible.

"Yeah, yeah." Maris laughs. "Instead of going up—"

Max hits a lower note and Maris squeals. "That's so cool."

"Nico and I can sing that while you and Theo stay on the melody and the third." Max sings a counter melody to Nico, who listens the first time and joins in the second. Then, they sing it again, splitting into their voices.

"Please tell me I don't have to sing that, because I'm never going to find the ninth," I say.

"No, you just follow Mare like always," Max instructs.

I snap the tempo. "Everyone together. One, two, snap, snap ..."

We sing the old lines, adding the second melody, and when I hear the blend, I say, "Holy shit!"

Max and Maris laugh, and Nico says, "Again ..."

I keep snapping and we run it a dozen more times so that it plants itself in our minds.

"That's really cool," Nico says. "I love it."

"I love it," I agree.

"That's the shit, Max. Nico, good idea. Theo, thank you for getting us here."

"Keep shining your light on things we can improve," I tell Maris.

Nico opens his mouth to add something and then coughs into his hand. He's not as dumb as I sometimes think he is.

"We have a four-hour bus ride, and then the rest of the day off," I say. "I need to shower and pack, so get the hell out of my room," I say.

"If it's a four-hour drive, that means five hours and twenty minutes by bus," Nico says.

"I might be able to finish *A Gentleman in Moscow*!" Max's face lights up at the thought.

I slap Nico on the back. "You need to find a hobby for killing time on the bus, my guy."

"I need to drive the bus."

"I'll find out if you can drive yourself to any of these dates."

"Thanks, brother. See you down there." Nico heads toward the door and Maris hangs back.

"Thank you, Theo. I appreciate how you handled that." Maris gives me a hug, and I hold her tightly to me. I just worked out, so I should have mercy on her and make it a quick one, but she doesn't seem to care. She makes a purring type of a sound and my heart beats faster. I kiss the top of her head like I've seen Nico do a hundred times before, and then I let her go. I watch her walk to the door, and she turns to smile at me again before she closes it behind her.

MARIS

DINAH HAS A KING OCEAN view room at the hotel in Myrtle Beach.

Our rooms have a parking lot view, so the minute I enter hers, I'm mesmerized.

"I'm such a beach baby, you don't even know," I tell her. "You have to sleep with the sliders open tonight to let the sound of the waves serenade you."

"Oh, girl, I'll sleep in one of those lounge chairs on the balcony. I'm a water sign. I need that shit." Dinah is wearing a hotel robe, and two massage tables are set up on the far end of the room. I see that she hangs her stage attire in the closet the way I do.

"That's a great outfit. Those sequined pants are going to look fantastic under the lights."

"Yeah, I borrowed them from Nicky." Dinah lets a loud cackle out and her laugh makes me laugh. "Maris, this is Don. He's mine, and that's Mark. He's yours."

"Nice to meet you," I say, shaking hands with Mark.

"Was Nico hoping you'd have a Mary rather than a Mark?" Dinah asks.

I chuckle. "He did ask if I knew whether the therapists were male or female, so I told him we requested nineteen-year-old male, college football players, since Nico played football in college."

Dinah laughs again. "So, he knows the breed. Keep him on his toes, girl. Are you ready for the most relaxing hour of your day?"

"I am so excited," I gush.

"Do you have any particular concerns or tenderness?" Mark asks.

I shake my head.

"There's a robe for you in the bathroom, if you want to undress to your level of comfort," Mark says.

"Thank you, I'll be right back."

When I reenter the room, Dinah is already on the table and Don is working his magic on her, so I drape my robe over a chair and lay prone on the table next to hers. The oil is warm and smells like gardenias. I'm in heaven before Mark even touches me, but when he starts kneading my neck, I drift into euphoria. I close my eyes and try to melt into the table, but Dinah wants to talk.

"So, how did you and Nico meet?"

175

Really? Ugh. "Through music, of course. We're all transplanted Miamians."

"How long have you and the big man been together?"

"Um, officially a few months. Unofficially, a few months longer." I chuckle.

"So, it's still new between you. That's such a great time in any relationship. When I saw you curled up in his lap on the bus, I thought you were just the cutest couple."

"Oh, thanks. We're happy." I'm speaking softly, hoping Dinah catches on that I want to relax. Then, I feel ungrateful. She invited me for girl time, and she made sure I knew she wouldn't accept me paying my way, since I'm her guest.

"How long have you been playing with Dame Knight?" I ask.

"Officially, ten years now, unofficially, about fifteen." She laughs.

"How did you become a band? I feel like I should know the answer to that question, but I don't think I do."

"We kinda snuck onto the scene, you know? Nicky was playing with Page One, right? I got hired to sing background vocals for them, and then Nicky and I started writing together, but Page didn't want any of our songs, so we started recording when we weren't on the road with them. We used the studio musicians to play gigs here and there, and then it just took off. I'm pretty sure Bobby Page still has a hit out on us in the UK."

I can't help laughing at the iconic story. "Were you and Nicky a couple at the time, or ...?"

"Oh, no. Nicky and I are like brother and sister. No offense, but I don't fuck with band mates." Dinah cackles. "Anymore."

"Ah, there's a story there," I prompt. If I keep her talking, I can just listen and chill.

"Girl, I was madly in love with the guitar player in my first band when I was in high school. I went to a school for the performing arts in New York. Best time of my life, no lie. Being surrounded by all those young creatives was exhilarating, you know? Well, there was this light-skinned Black boy who played the guitar with so many different personalities ... I thought he must have been a prodigy. He was good in bed, too. We formed a band and did gigs in the city." Dinah stops talking for a moment, and I wonder if she's lingering over a particular memory. "Then, he cheated on me. I was devastated."

I make an "aww" sound.

"But he was sorry, so I took him back. And then, he cheated on me again."

"Oh, that fucker," I say. "I bet he's sorry now."

"He took his life right after we graduated."

I turn my head to face Dinah. "I'm so sorry. I had no idea."

"Girl, it's okay. It was a long time ago, and I've been in love a lot of times since then, but I'll always be grateful to him, you know?"

"Mmmm."

"How long has Nico been with Theo and Max? You're the newest band member, right?"

She obviously already knows the answer to the second part of her question. "Yeah, I'm the newb. Theo and Nico started the band five years ago, and I think they picked Max up in the first or second year. I don't know exactly."

"So, is Nico committed to Theo, then?"

I'm unsure what Dinah's really asking, but I don't like the question on its face. "Yes. They're like brothers."

"Hmmmm." Dinah asks Don to concentrate on her lower back. Then, she says, "Is Nico indebted to Theo in any way?"

I feel myself tense up, which is counterproductive. "Indebted? No. They're partners in Funkengroovin' and close as brothers," I repeat.

"That's great," Dinah says, but her tone doesn't match her words.

"I feel so lucky to have landed in this band. Not only because the guys are great musicians and we collaborate so well together, but because we're like a family. We live together."

"I thought I read that somewhere," Dinah says. "You all live in Theo's house in Miami, right?"

"Our studio is there, so it's the perfect set up."

"I see," Dinah says.

Initially, I wanted to slow the hour down to extend my enjoyment, but now I wish it would end. Dinah didn't want girl time, she wanted dirt.

"Are you guys looking for a second guitar player or something?" I ask.

Dinah cackles. "Girl, I'm not trying to jack your man. I'm sorry if I'm asking too many questions. I just like to hear about the dynamics in other bands. Every one I've been in is so different. Sometimes the ties that bind are musical, sometimes personal, sometimes there's a hierarchy. It interests me, that's all."

"What ties Dame Knight together?"

"Age and history. We don't have time to start over with new bands, and we can keep ridin' what we've already done for another five years or so."

"Do you still enjoy it?"

Dinah exhales. "Some nights I love the shit out of it, and some nights I'm watching the clock."

"Which happens more often?"

Dinah cackles. "That's the question I need to ask myself. Good question, girl. I think I'd love it again, like really love it, if we started writing new material and made another album. Our label isn't going to give us the opportunity to do that though, unless we can guarantee that we'll be giving them something new, not just Dame Knight chapter 15, you know?"

"From my point of view, as a newb, I'm worried that I'll never have the success you've had and that I'm spending all of these years chasing a dream that's unattainable."

"If this doesn't work out, you can always go back to law school," Dinah says.

I'm glad she can't see my face because my expression is full-on *what the fuck*. "How do you know I was a law student?"

Dinah cackles again. "Girl, I told you we were happy when Funkengroovin' was added to the bill. We had a say in the lineup, so we did our due diligence. That's a legal term, right?"

"So, you helped choose us for the tour?"

"We gave our approval. I don't know if we helped choose you guys, but we looked at your channel and found out that all of you are pros with squeaky clean reputations. That's hard to find today."

"Like I said, I feel very fortunate to be with these guys."

"And with your guy," Dinah says.

"Girlfriend," I say without meaning it, "there's no luck involved there. Nico and I had plenty of options and we chose each other. The chemistry we have isn't luck." I think for a moment. "It's fate."

Dinah whispers, "Awwwww, girl. That's so sweet."

We go quiet until the timer goes off, ending the massage session. I gush about the experience and how grateful I am to have been invited and leave as quickly as I can.

I text the band chat from the hallway and the only response I get is from Theo. He's at the beach. Perfect. I want some sun and I have a lot to tell him.

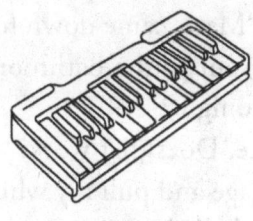

MAX

EVERYONE ELSE HAD STUFF TO do on the night off except me. I can guess what Nico and Maris did, and Theo caught an Uber to dinner and a movie. He straight up told me he needed some time alone, so I didn't ask to go along. I fell asleep on the bus ride to Myrtle Beach, so I didn't get to read much, but my book was my dinner date at the hotel restaurant and then I took a long, hot bath in the room. I was a little worried about the cleanliness of the tub, but I used a towel and a lot of body wash to clean it before I filled it. I knew Theo wouldn't be back for a while, so it was a treat. I'll do it again when I get the chance.

Theo got up early again today and hit the gym and breakfast alone. I'm starting to worry about him isolating himself. It isn't like him. Or maybe it is like him, and he never gets the chance to be alone with all of us living in his house. I wanted this experience of being on the road to make us tighter, not make us sick of one another.

I had breakfast and read in the lobby for a while, hoping I'd run into some other musicians from the tour. Everyone I recognized was paired up and even when I waved, no one came over to talk, so I went back to the room to take a nap before the show tonight. Theo said that some record execs are coming, so I want to be rested. When I wake up, I see that Maris texted the band chat an hour earlier, and that Theo was the only reply. I bet they're still at the beach, but we leave for the venue in an hour, so I hit the shower before Theo gets back.

I'm drying off when I hear the hotel door open. "Honey, I'm home!" Theo yells.

"It's about time. I was getting worried."

"Wait ... really?"

"No, not really," I say. "How was the beach?"

"So nice," Theo said. "Maris came down for the last hour."

"Cool," I say, clearing out of the bathroom. "What are we wearing for the record exec show tonight?"

"Maris picked all white. Does that work?"

I sift through my luggage and pull my white joggers out of the hotel laundry bag they've been balled up in for days. "I really should have used my night off to do laundry."

Theo glances over and laughs when he sees the condition of my wrinkled pants. "We have an hour or so. I bet you could hand wash those in the sink, wring them out in a towel, and hang them on the balcony to dry."

"The chicks online who call you a Zaddy don't even know how right they are."

"Hurry up and use the bathroom sink, so I can get in the shower."

I pump body wash into the sink and do laundry pioneer style.

Theo takes a phone call, and I hear him talking to Phil about driving ourselves to gigs. It sounds like Dame Knight had some issues with the bus situation, too, and Theo is clarifying that we aren't asking for a separate coach. From what I hear, Nico is going to be disappointed. Our pay showed up before Phil reached back out, so Theo doesn't have any further questions. Phil must be relaying some good news though, because Theo keeps saying things like, "Awesome," and "We didn't come this far to fuck up," and "Thanks, Phil. We'll make you look good."

"What was all that about?"

"Just some additional information on who's going to be there for our set tonight. Nothing to worry about or get nervous about. Same show as always," Theo says.

I finish twisting the towel my pants are rolled up in and head to the balcony to hang them. "I'm not nervous anymore, Theo. You can tell me who's coming tonight."

As he closes the bathroom door, he says, "Can't talk. Gotta make myself look pretty."

As if Theo doesn't always look good. Girls send him so many thirst traps on social media. He shows me some of them. If I was as good looking as Theo, I'd be hooking up on tour. I don't think he is. Unless he wasn't alone last night, like he claimed he wanted to be. Part of me thinks he's saving himself for Maris. I hope that's not the case because she's never going to leave Nico ... unless he pushes her away. Which isn't outside of the realm of possibility because Nico is always going to do what's best for Nico.

NICO

I spent the day sleeping, resting up for the show. I'm a little irritated at Maris for hanging out with Dinah, but I understand taking the opportunity. I'm more than a little upset that she went from Dinah's room to meet Theo on the beach. We have the biggest show of our careers tonight and both of them are integral parts of it. Didn't they want to be fresh? Also, I just don't like Maris seeking out alone time with

Theo after he made a big production out of taking her side yesterday in the Band Beating. To be fair, he didn't fully take her side, but he pandered to her a lot. I know, from the horse's mouth, that he loves her, for fuck's sake. Of course I'm not cool with them hanging out, but I can't tell Maris that, so I have to pretend I'm cool.

She seemed off when she came back from the beach, too. Something was bothering her, but she denied it. Her skin was already a little pink and the highlights in her hair seemed to have gotten brighter in the short time she was in the sun. She's so naturally beautiful. I missed her when she was gone, so I follow her into the bathroom when she starts getting ready.

"Tell me everything. How was the massage? I can't believe I was able to sleep while some other man had his hands all over you."

Maris gives me a look. "The dude was a professional. I'm sure he doesn't even see his clients' bodies anymore."

"You're adorable when you're being naïve," I say, crossing my arms and leaning against the bathroom vanity.

Maris steps under the warm water and it beads up due to all the oil on her skin. I have to take a deep breath because I'm having a physical reaction to imagining how it got there.

"Honestly, I couldn't relax with Dinah," she admits. "I feel like she's not a woman you can let your guard down around."

"Why's that?"

Maris is massaging her scalp aggressively as she washes her hair, making me more certain that something's bothering her. "Nothing I can put my finger on or say for sure without sounding paranoid. I just don't feel like she has a genuine interest in being friends. It was like she was on a fact-finding mission."

"Well, people have to get to know one another before a friendship develops."

Maris conditions her hair and piles it on top of her head, securing it with a clip. "Right, of course, but there's a difference between being interested in getting to know someone organically and bombarding them with pointed questions."

"Hmmm, about what?"

"Our band and how close we are. How devoted we are to one another. Stuff like that."

"Okay, well, that's an obvious place to start. It's what you have in common. When I was hanging out with Nicky, we talked music the whole time."

Maris points the razor she's using to shave her legs in my direction. "That's just it, though. You guys talked about music. She wanted to know about the *ties that bind* us together as a band. Her questions felt invasive, to be honest."

I shrug. "Maybe she doesn't get the chance to do girl talk very often and she either dives right in when she has the chance, or she forgot how to do it."

Maris turns straight on to look at me. "I'm telling you something was off, so stop making excuses for Dinah. Please."

I hold my hands up and nod slowly. "Yes, sorry. I didn't mean to do that. I guess I was hopeful that you would find a friend on the tour. That's all." I reach to the towel rack and grab a fresh one.

Maris finishes rinsing and turns off the water before stepping into the towel I'm holding open for her. I wrap her up and pull her to me.

"I missed you today."

She looks up at me and her face softens. "I missed you, too. Isn't that crazy? With all the time we're spending together—"

"It's not crazy at all. I'm secretly glad you didn't make a friend because I'm too selfish to share you."

Maris kisses me and I instantly feel calm. The touch of her soft lips evaporates any tension I was holding onto.

"You might want to change those boxers," she says.

"Oh, really?" I begin removing her towel and she laughs.

"No, sorry, I'm not flirting. We're wearing all white for our set, and those black boxers will probably show through."

"Ah," I say, tucking the end of her towel back into place.

"I'm going to wear my white mini skirt with the bralette top," Maris says.

"I call that your naughty tennis outfit."

She laughs and rolls her eyes at me.

I get out of Maris's way and pull out all the white items I have. "Do you know what Theo's wearing?"

"You know those European length pants he has that you always make fun of? Yeah, so those, and a sleeveless shirt."

"My God, he's going full Greek."

Maris giggles and comes to help me coordinate. She pulls out a pair of white jeans and a very lightweight tissue T-shirt. "This is a very self-serving choice because I get to look at your ass and your pecs all night."

"I feel so violated," I say dramatically.

"No, you don't," Maris replies.

"But I want to."

"After the show. When we have multiple labels making multiple offers for us."

I take Maris's face in my hands. "I am so happy that we're going through all of this together."

"Max and Theo, too," she reminds me.

"Yes, but I don't feel the same way about them." I show Maris what I mean, and she moans appreciatively.

THEO

Maris and I decided not to tell Nico that Dinah was sniffing around to determine his level of dedication to our band. Mostly because we genuinely don't know if that was her intention, and because Dinah flat out denied that they were looking for another guitar player. Secondarily, with record reps coming to our show tonight, we have to be laser focused. We're getting the chance to do what all of us came here to do; secure a record deal. Together. Dinah was talking about ties that bind ... contracts work pretty well. Not that we've ever needed anything to legally bind us together. We've been loyal to each other through the lean times; we're not going to bail on each other when we're finally getting recognized. Personally, I'd rather be part of an up-and-coming band than part of a project that already peaked. If Dame Knight was thinking about jacking Nico, I'm sure he would feel the same way.

From what Phil told me on the phone earlier, Dinah and Nicky aren't happy campers. Their management company failed to negotiate for private travel between venues, and they aren't thrilled to be staying at the same hotels as the bands further down the line up, aka, bands like us. I get it. They've paid their dues, and they deserve perks. Their name is driving ticket sales, after all. At first, I was thrilled that we were hanging out with Dame Knight, but now I think the farther we stay away, the better. There seem to be a lot of things imploding in their camp, and we don't need to get hit with any of the fallout.

I lied to Max when I said there wasn't anything to be nervous about tonight. I'm fidgety as hell, but I'm trying to cover it up by warming up on my drum pad in the van on the way to the venue. Maris is chatting with Max about the book we've all been reading, and I'm grateful that she's sensitive enough to know what he needs in the moment. Nico has the same energy I do. He's sitting next to me, bouncing his knees, and breathing in for four counts and out for four counts. I'm a drummer, I notice patterns.

"You ready for this, man?" I ask.

Nico turns his head to look at me, and I see his signature smirk. "Fuck, yeah, brother. I was just thinking about the first night we played with Jimmy." He laughs. "If you told me that night that we would be on the way to showcase for record execs who came to see us on tour ... dude, I would have relentlessly shaded you for being delusional."

I laugh so hard my drum pad slides off my lap. "That night was a perfect disaster in every way. I just kept looking at you like, *we can get through this, bro.*"

"I turned Jimmy all the way down in the mains," Nico says. "Like off."

I'm laughing so hard my voice comes out as a squeak. "He didn't even notice!"

"He's just up there smilin' and doin' his thing. And at the end of the night—" Nico is laughing too hard to finish his thought.

"He asks …" I'm hardly able to breathe. "How did I do?"

Nico and I explode with laughter. Maris and Max are turned around in their seats, staring at us with amused expressions on their faces. Maris takes several photos.

"Dude, I was so mad. I wanted you to fire him on the spot," Nico says in spurts.

"Nah, man. I knew he could play … a little. Enough?" I turn to Nico and the waves of laughter start all over again. "Like, I hoped so, because he had already moved in."

That last part kills Nico, and he stomps his feet on the van floor while putting his hands over his face. "That's right. You let him move in the day before the first gig."

"Not one of my better business decisions."

"Oh, my God, I wanted to murder you so badly. And then, I was just like, *Imma quit*." The look on Nico's face, like he was so sure that was the only move, makes me laugh harder, if that's possible at this point.

"What about … what about …" I try to catch my breath. "When you kicked my drumhead in on stage at Billy's Waterfront Bar and your foot got … stuck …"

Nico throws his head back and belly laughs. "And Billy was waving his finger at us … you guys are—"

I join in, "Fireeeeed-d-d-d-d!"

"Feel like we missed out on some pivotal moments in this band?" Maris asks Max.

"Oh, I was there for the drumhead incident. When Nico pulled his foot out of the head, his shoe came off inside and Theo wouldn't let him have it back."

Maris starts laughing. "This sounds like elementary school stuff, and you guys were how old?"

I shrug. "We were passionate young men."

Nico holds his right hand in front of me, and I clap it with mine.

"We've had some good times, brother," Nico says. His eyes are watering from laughing so hard.

"Nothing but love looking back and looking ahead," I tell him. "You better dry your eyes; people are going to think you cried all the way over here."

"I fuckin' did!"

Maris's expression is so cute. She's eating up every moment of our bromance. I mean what I said to Nico. I wouldn't be here, the band wouldn't be here, without him.

"Dude, I appreciate you," he tells me.

"Fuck off," I say, laughing.

The van stops and we head backstage. The band that plays before us is just starting, so we find Kenny and hang out in the holding area. Maris takes photos. We all mentally prepare. In a couple hours, this opportunity will be behind us, but right now, the outcome is in our hands.

MARIS

Dear Lord, please help me to perform to the best of my ability. Please let me be a blessing to my bandmates and let us find favor with the record execs who are here. If my dad's energy is around me, please let me feel him. Amen.

My bass feels heavier than usual, and I adjust the strap, but that increases my discomfort, so I slide it back to the original position, which is marked by a deep indent. I remind myself to focus on the audience, not the record people. Pleasing the audience and feeding off their energy is the magic.

Nico holds his guitar at his side and hugs me with his free arm. "Ready?"

I look up at him and bite my lip. "Ready as I'll ever be."

Nico kisses my forehead and then looks into my eyes with his steady gaze. "You are ready. Timing is everything and this is our time."

My heart feels like it's thumping out of my chest, and I don't know if it's because I love Nico so much or because my adrenaline is cranking.

Theo and Max walk over to us as our video introduction begins to play. Theo sticks his head between me and Nico. "Funkengroovin' ..." He starts the chant, and we all join in. We're in a circle, arms around each other, and the crowd is reacting to something. I look at the back-stage monitor and see that a camera is on us. Theo's handsome face exudes excitement, and he is the Greek god Nico predicted.

"Let's go get it, band family!" Theo yells over the crowd noise.

We all yell some version of *Let's goooooo* and we run out onto the stage where the crowd greets us with seismic rumbling. Or at least it feels that way. The set-up in Myrtle Beach allows the crowd to be closer to the stage, and it feels like the ground beneath us reverberates as they jump up and down.

"Myrtle Beach, what's good?" I shout into the microphone as Theo counts us into "Coming Around." The crowd recognizes the tune, and they react with screams of excitement. I pass Nico as I make my way to the opposite side of the stage from where my mic is set up. We make eye contact as we pass, and I know that everything will be okay because he will carry us all if we need him to.

As Nico sings lead, I make my way to Max's keyboard set up and lean into his mic as we sing our background parts. The camera is on us, and we ham it up. Max is wearing his white sunglasses and I grab them from his face and put them on, forgetting they're prescription. He and I have a moment of genuine laughter when I blind myself and give them back. It's silly, but the audience loves it. I move to the drum stand and jam with Theo for a few measures, and the girls go nuts when the stage screens become giant billboards of his face. As the first song finishes, I meet up with Nico at center stage as he solos. I hold down my bassline but add flourishes that compliment what he's doing. As we start the transition to the next song, he kisses me. On stage. In front of everyone. It's the first time we've acknowledged our relationship on stage. Anyone who follows our socials knows we're together, but we've never interacted this way during a show. I'm surprised, but when I hear the crowd explode into approving cheers, I play it up.

The next song is mine, so I go to my mic stand to sing lead, while Nico plays to the audience downstage. Max solos on this song, so I turn to him while he plays, and I see Theo in my peripheral vision. He's not wearing the same smile he was before the show. In fact, he looks pissed. Maybe he's just focused. But he looks pissed. I try to get his attention, but he keeps his eyes on Max, like we all do when one of us is soloing. It's the respectful thing to do.

We head into the next transition and Theo introduces the song and tells a quick story about how he and Nico wrote it on a boat, adrift in Biscayne Bay at three-thirty a.m. after running out of gas. The song is titled "Running Out of Gas," but they transferred the meaning to a relationship so the world wouldn't know what dipshits they are. But, when Theo gets to the part about them being dipshits, he leaves himself out and tells the crowd that Nico's a dipshit. Everyone laughs and cheers and Nico plays it off with a shrug, but that was a shot fired.

I'm on edge, but Nico seems entirely unaffected. He sings the song as perfectly as he always does, and we move the show along. Technically, we're like a well-oiled machine. I feel tension on stage, though, and I hope the audience can't feel it. Nico shouldn't have kissed me. That reduced the four of us to the two of us, and Theo obviously didn't think it served the show. I go back to the drum stand to jam with Theo the next time I'm free to do so, and he locks eyes with me and smiles. We play off each other and that makes me feel a little better. Maybe I'm imagining things. Stress does funny things to perception.

The crowd is digging us. Every song that we finish feels like we got another solid performance in the can. If we screw something up now, we've shown that our status quo is first rate. I feel like I can relax on the backstretch.

It's time for Silver Springs and the production crew plays our muted video on the screens as Nico and I sit next to each other on stools that Kenny and a stage tech bring out.

Max starts the song on piano and the crowd whistles, but quiets quickly before I start to sing. When Theo comes in on the drums, I look back at him because the hits are just so perfect. He smiles at me and it's a genuine smile. I keep singing and Nico's eyes don't leave me. I feel him watching me more than I see him.

When it comes time for the guys to add background vocals, I close my eyes and revel in the sound of all of us together. It's emotional. I feel like I can hear Theo singing the line about wanting to love someone but not being allowed to more prominently than usual. Nico's solo follows and I turn to watch him play. I look up at the screen and see that the producers have each of us framed inside four split-screen boxes. Theo's eyes are closed, and his face is red. He's either working really hard, or he isn't okay. We only have two songs after this, so if he needs water, he can get it soon. I hope he doesn't start cramping up.

The crowd goes bat-shit crazy for Nico's solo. They're right. His feel is haunting. I watch him play and he makes eye contact with me, raising his eyebrows and smirking. He knows what this does to me. I chuckle and sing the next lines to him as he and the guys harmonize with me.

At the end, the music breaks down and my vocal is more isolated. I'm so overcome with emotion that my voice cracks, but it's authentic, so I don't care. I'm thinking about the night that Nico and I first sang this song together, but I'm also thinking about Theo and the night he asked if it was his imagination that we could have been together. If he hadn't sent me away that first night. The night I went to him, but wound up with Nico by … an act of fate? Default?

The end of the song hangs, and the stage crew come to get the stools out of the way. Nico sings the next song, and then I'm singing the last song of the night with the new ending. The crowd is very gracious, and I thank them for taking the musical journey with us. I wish them peace, love, and happiness, and then our showcase is over.

Kenny is the first person to meet me as I leave the stage. I ask him for new strings before the next show, and he tells me that I was great. I feel a hand on my shoulder. It's Theo. I fall into his arms and we're both crying. Sobbing, really.

"What … the … fuck?" Nico asks, laughing when he comes up behind us. "Did someone tell you that we sucked because we were fucking awesome out there. No need to cry about it."

Max throws himself into our hug and starts crying with us. The release of emotion is mandatory after something as huge as what we just went through together.

"Thank you, guys, so much," I say. "All of you were so good and you lifted me up so I could do my best."

Max replies, "Thank you, guys."

Nico puts his huge arms around all of us and tries to move us off to the side. The other band is trying to get to the stage.

"Okay, okay, break it up," Nico says. "We did what we came to do. We did what we knew we could do and now the puppet masters know what we can do for them, so the hard part's over."

Theo lifts his shirt and dries his face. Max opens a bottle of water and empties the whole thing over his head, which splashes us, and we jump away. Theo's phone rings and he retrieves it from his pocket. It's Phil, so he answers on speaker.

"Yo, Theo. Great show, man. Can you guys come over to the VIP tent?"

We exchange smiles and Theo says, "Sure. We'll be there in a few minutes."

Phil ends the call, and Nico picks me up and swings me around as I laugh.

"Let's not get overly excited," I say. "We don't know anything yet."

"If the record reps hated us, they wouldn't want to tell us in person," Nico says, setting me down.

We have to ask directions to the VIP tent. It's fully air conditioned, and the food and beverage service is several steps above what's offered in the green room tent. I see Phil sitting at a satellite bar with three guys who look like they were just out hiking and a woman in holey jeans and a Blondie T-shirt. I like her already.

"The band needs no introduction. Band, this is the senior A&R team from Revolution Records Luis, David, Bill, and Stacey."

We shake hands, but I rub my palms against my skirt first, keenly aware that I'm a sweaty mess from stage.

"We liked what we saw," Luis says. "We like your social media presence; you guys created a big buzz for yourselves without any help from people like us. We're going to work with Phil to come up with an offer. I hope we can make some music together."

We exhale collectively and start shaking hands again.

"Are you guys hungry?" Stacey asks, pointing to the hot buffet table.

"Starving," Max replies on our behalf.

Luis laughs. "Help yourselves, and let's sit down and get to know each other over some food."

"I'm not sure I can eat," I whisper to Nico. "My stomach is so unsettled."

"Give it something to do and try to relax," he says, handing me a plate and getting me started in the buffet line.

Stacey is ahead of me, so I follow her to a long, empty table and sit beside her as we wait for everyone else.

"I really love what you do, Maris," Stacey tells me. "I'm a musician myself. Well, not anymore. But I played for years, and I love being on this side of the business to scope out talent that's deserving of recognition, you know?"

"What do you play?"

"Mm, guitar, bass, and keys. I worked in corporate bands mostly. Made enough money to record the stuff I actually wanted to play." Stacey chuckles. "We had a deal with an indie label and did some touring. It was fun. Hard, but fun."

"Which side of the business do you like better?" I asked.

Stacey pauses to consider her answer. "I think there was a time for doing what you're doing and then there was a time to settle in one place within the industry. Some musicians live on the road forever and absolutely love it, though. Speak of the devils." Stacey points to Dinah and Nicky, who are just arriving. I watch Dinah beeline straight to Nico, who was on his way to our table.

"I had the opportunity to spend some time with Dinah this morning," I say before taking a bite of risotto to stop myself from saying more.

"They really like you guys," Stacey tells me. "They advocated for you, which is almost unheard of these days."

"How kind of them. And how humbling for us," I say between bites.

Nico sits across from us and the rest of our contingent joins us, one by one, with full plates. Nicky and Dinah join us as well, which I didn't expect. They're sitting with the execs on the far end of the table, so I'm shielded from having to answer any more of Dinah's questions for the time being.

Luis addresses the table and immediately has everyone's attention. "Part of what we wanted to talk to you guys about is our vision for launching you. We think we have an exciting and unique crossover opportunity that will give Funkengroovin' a big advantage over other newly signed bands." Luis clears his throat by coughing into his fist. "Marketing is everything. There are so many ways that we can get you into households across the country, and honestly, you're already doing a good job of that. I think something that would set you apart from," Luis made air quotes with his fingers, "new artists is attaching you to a band that is already a household name and then doing a spin-off."

Theo sits across the table and a couple seats down from me, and he turns from Luis to make eye contact. I raise my eyebrows, and he mimics me before turning around again.

"Have you guys seen how many times the video of Nico sitting in with these guys has been played?" Luis laughs. "It's some crazy seven-digit number. If I say it, I'll be wrong because it probably just went up again." He laughs performatively. "That was a beautiful, unscripted, and organic moment, but maybe it shouldn't be just a moment. We're thinking that Nico should play with Dame Knight every night for the rest of the tour."

Theo clears his throat loudly and I scoff under my breath.

"Maybe not for the whole set. Maybe a few songs. It's not like Nicky needs another guitar player on stage, and maybe that takes away from what you're doing, Nick, but I think the crossover works for Dame Knight as well, just to infuse something new. What does everyone think? Nico? We should probably ask you first," Luis says, laughing too loudly.

I look across the table and see Nico's discomfort. It's obvious to me because it's so rare to see him uncomfortable.

"I think that's something we, Funkengroovin', should talk about," he says.

"Sure, sure, of course, you guys have to be on the same page," Luis says.

"I think it's a no-brainer for Funkengroovin'," Dinah says. "Publicity is the most expensive part of this business. A move like this would grab attention."

"How do you explain the mash-up to the fans?" Theo asks. "Nico appearing regularly with Dame implies he's a fixture, so how do you frame it?"

"Special guest star?" Luis suggests.

Nico scoffs. "I'm hardly a star, Luis. Especially to Dame Knight fans. I'm some kid who copies Nicky closely. Musically, that's just the truth. I'm proud of Funkengroovin' and my role in it. In Dame Knight, I'm just playing covers. Those covers are part of the rock lexicon. They're big, huge covers, but they're not mine, and Nicky shouldn't have to share them."

I feel my body relax. That is exactly how I hoped Nico would feel.

"What if we wrote some songs together?" Nicky asks, leaning into the table to look at Nico.

Fuck.

Nico looks at me, but I'm frozen. He says, "If Phil can make a deal with Revolution for Funkengroovin', that means we'll be writing every day. We'll need to have an album worth of material when we come off this tour."

"It's your first album. You haven't released the songs you're playing now. Your set is your first album," Luis says, solving the matter.

"We haven't gotten off the ground as recording artists. I don't want to lend my guy to another band," Theo says.

"And Dame doesn't need me," Nico says. "It doesn't even make sense for them to bring in a no-name."

I start feeling chilly, and I rub my arms to get some blood flowing. I was walking on air an hour ago and now I'm entirely deflated. I feel like these people are adversaries, not potential team members. I don't feel safe. I want to leave. Like, leave the tour. Go back to Miami with my guys and play Club Fish tomorrow night.

"Mate, the thing is, we can help you gain that name recognition. It would be fun to write together, wouldn't it? We got on like kittens in a sack. You have a more contemporary style than I do, so you can bring some fresh air. Give us some youth." Nicky is smiling and I believe his intentions are good. Unfortunately, he's not the person working the puppet strings.

"Listen, this is a lot for one day." Luis laughs again. "We're just throwing spaghetti against the wall, here. Eat up, everybody. We're celebrating … possibilities!"

"Hear, hear!" Dinah says, raising her glass. She looks down the table at me and winks.

NICO

MARIS WEARS THE SAME EXPRESSION she did that day in Theo's kitchen when she found out that I went back to the club without telling her. She makes eye contact with Theo, but not with me. Max won't even look at me while Luis is pitching his fucked-up idea. When Nicky called me on stage with Dame Knight, I was surprised, flattered, and thrilled, but I'm the exact opposite of all those things in this moment. I feel like the record execs, along with Dinah and Nicky, laid a trap. I try to read Phil's expression, but that fucker won't look at me, either, so he was probably hip to what they were going to present, and he didn't prepare us for this. He's supposed to be our manager and look out for our best interests.

Luis sees that the four of us aren't immediately receptive to his vision, so he pivots and says he's just spitballin'.

I reach across the table and tap my fingers beside Maris's plate. She looks up and smiles at me, but it's a vacant smile. I tap my fingers again, and she moves her hand from her lap and places it on mine. I blow her a kiss and she mimics the gesture.

Luis, Bill, and David are immersed in an animated conversation with Dinah and Nicky, and their laughter comes in bursts. No one at our end of the table has anything to say in front of Stacey, who seems to be the only person who can read the room. She finishes her meal and excuses herself to call home. Before she leaves, she tells Maris that Phil knows how to reach her if we want to reach out.

Stacey's departure gives us permission to follow suit, so we extend our thanks, fake our excitement about the potential offer Revolution might be making to sign us, and we walk back to the transportation hub where we get into a van to head back to the hotel.

As soon as the van door closes, I turn in my seat to face Maris, Max, and Theo. "I need you guys to know that I had nothing to do with what Luis just proposed, and I had no idea they were going to spring that on us."

Theo nods. "We know, man. We know that."

"I don't understand why they think it's good for us," Max says.

"I think it's good for Dame," Maris says. "I think they've gone stale creatively, and they see what Nico brings to the table, and they want some of it."

I take Maris's hands in mine. "You're biased, babe. That's sweet of you to say, but that's not even the genre of music that I write."

Maris shakes her head and looks at our hands. "You like to play harder stuff. When you sat in with Backyard Breeder you played rock."

I hunch lower to get Maris to look into my eyes. "I like changing it up sometimes, but our band is versatile as hell. If I want to play something with a rock edge, Funkengroovin' will write something with a rock edge." I look back at Theo and Max, who back me up.

"They haven't even signed us, and they're picking us off for parts," Theo says.

"Not if we don't agree," I say. "Don't forget that this team wasn't the only label at the show today. Phil said there were others lined up, right?"

Theo nods. "True, but Revolution is the biggest with the widest distribution."

"So what?" I ask. "Genuinely? So what? If we go with a smaller label, they might put more effort into us, whereas a major has bigger acts to focus on."

"No one else asked to meet with us after the show," Max points out.

"Just because Phil is already in bed with these guys doesn't mean we have to be," I say. "Theo, text Phil right now and make sure he follows up with the other execs he invited today. Tell him we want to hear their feedback. It's not his decision whether to put all our eggs in one basket."

Maris nods. "Definitely. And, if Phil tells Luis he's following up with other labels, that sends a message that the ball is in our court."

"Yeah, fuck Revolution," Max says.

"Fuck 'em," I echo.

"But what if we're holding you back from something that could launch you into another stratosphere?" Maris asks quietly.

"Why just me? If Dame really wants to help market us, they can move us up in the line-up. We could open for them, and they could join us on stage for a few songs. Maybe we write a couple songs with them as a super band. That way Nicky gets his new material, we have Maris and Dinah our front—"

"Two drummers?" Theo asked. "Two keyboard players? Two bass players?"

"Maybe Maris plays and Dinah sings. Maybe their drummer plays percussion on those songs. Maybe Max and their keyboard player divvy up parts …"

Theo laughs. "That's never gonna happen, my guy. Dame Knight is never going to join us on stage and then take a back seat."

I run my hands through my hair. "You're right, you're right, but there's some ground between Dame only using one member of Funkengroovin' to promote our band and them backing us up on a collaboration."

Theo's phone alerts and he reads a text from Phil. *Following up now. We should meet in the morning to talk.*

"All four of us, or just you and Phil?" Max asks.

"All four of us," Theo says adamantly. "I want you guys there."

"Have him come to the hotel for breakfast," I suggest, looking at Maris for her approval. She nods.

The van stops in front of the hotel and we walk, like zombies, to the elevator. When the doors close Max says, "We fucking rocked that show."

Theo grins. "Absofuckinglutely."

"I've never heard you guys play so well," Maris says with a giggle.

"That's what's important. We can't let them distract us from what we do together," I say, trying to cheer everyone.

"Fuck Revolution," Max says again. We all echo his sentiment and make plans to meet in a few hours for dinner. We seem to be pulling together instead of pulling apart, which is what I was afraid might happen. I feel better.

But, when Maris closes the door behind us in our hotel room, her eyes fill with tears.

"Whoa, Maris, what's this? More emotions to release?" I put my arms around her, and she holds on tight, so I lift her up and carry her to the bed. "Okay, love, tell me what you're thinking."

"They're going to force our hand, Nico. Dinah and Nicky want you to work with them, and you'd be foolish not to take the opportunity. I want what's best for you, but I don't see how this isn't the beginning of the end for us as a foursome."

I lay on my back next to Maris and pull her into me until her head is resting on my chest. "I want you to really hear me, okay?" I'm talking into her hair as she cries softly into my shirt. "I'm not leaving Funkengroovin'. Theo and I built this thing together. It's our baby."

Maris laughs a genuine laugh.

"I was happy in Miami. I was happy playing clubs at night and writing music during the day. I'm even happy with what Max contributes."

Maris makes a warning sound.

"I've been blissfully happy since I gave up my wrong minded notion that we shouldn't have a girl in the band. I can honestly say, these last few months have been the happiest of my life." I kiss the top of her head. "I'm a kid from the Northwoods of Wisconsin. I never thought I'd get this far in music. And I'm doing it with my friends and my woman. I don't need or aspire to anything *more*, whatever more might mean."

"I don't want to hold you back."

"Maris." I turn her head. "You got me here. I'll have Theo call Phil right now and tell him I thought it over and don't want to work in any capacity with Dame."

Maris starts crying harder.

"I will never understand your gender," I say, chuckling. I let her get out whatever it is that she needs to purge. Holding Maris to my chest has become my default setting. I hope it calms her the way it does me, even when she's upset. Having her in my arms and knowing I'd do anything to make her feel safe makes me feel like a man. For the first time, if I'm honest with myself. I feel a duty to her, but it's a responsibility I take on freely. It's so easy. Guarding her heart is my first concern. Her feelings are more important than my own at this point.

THEO

I TOLD THE BAND TO BE in the lobby, ready to go out to dinner, at nine. Myrtle Beach has a great live music scene, and I feel we owe it to ourselves to get a taste. The young woman who works as the hotel's concierge, a fan of our band, told me exactly where to go for good food and music. I know the atmosphere will feel like home, and stepping inside the place, I'm happy to be right.

We grab a table near the stage and order bar food that tastes like Michelin star cuisine after all the tent food we've been eating.

"Cheers to us and the best set we've ever played. I'm honored to share the stage with you fine musicians," I say, raising my beer.

"I love you guys!" Maris says.

Nico contributes, "Cheers, fuckers!"

"Cheers!" Max adds, slamming his beer mug into ours like a bowling ball striking pins.

"What is it with you spilling liquids all over the place today?" I ask.

Max giggles like a little kid, and I roll my eyes before taking a swig.

The band is already set up, and we try to guess, based on the gear, what kind of music they play. It's a game Nico and I used to play when we'd go out to see bands in Miami to scope out our competition.

"Three keyboards, so I'm gonna say top 40," Max guesses.

"Or," Maris holds a finger up," since there aren't any mics for horns, he could be covering horn parts, and they could be a funk band."

"I hope so," Nico says almost wistfully, which makes me laugh.

"Judging by the age of the person who told me about this place and the age of the crowd," I look around, "I'm going to say top 40 with a crossover to Morgan Wallen and Chris Stapleton as the room gets drunker and starts shouting requests."

"I do not miss requests, my friend," Maris says.

"How are you guys doing?" Our server stops by the table.

"Another pitcher," I say.

"Also, the band wants you to know, but doesn't want you to feel obligated, that their stage is your stage if any of you want to get up and play tonight."

I look at Nico, who turns around looking for the band. "Do we know these guys?" he asks.

"They know you," the server says with a laugh. "Pretty much everyone in here knows you."

"Are you shittin' me?" Max asks.

"Funkengroovin', right?" our server smiles. "Right. So, like I said, the invitation stands."

"That's really cool," I say sincerely. "Please tell them to feel free to come grab a beer with us if they have time."

"They're not allowed to drink on the job, and the boss doesn't like staff to harass patrons, especially famous ones."

"We're not famous," Max says.

"You kinda are," the server argues. "Another pitcher, then. Anything else?"

Nico locks eyes with me and says, "Four shots of Patrón, please."

I stare Nico down. "Thanks, but what are you having?"

He laughs and holds a fist across the table for me to bump.

"I've never had tequila," Max says.

"You're not driving. Don't worry about it," Nico says.

The band takes the stage as the server returns with our drinks. She takes away the empty plates, and we shift our chairs so we're all facing the stage. The drummer starts a groove, and the keys start the funky intro to Stevie Wonder's "Superstition". I howl and Nico yells, "Yaaaaas!" Maris is the first person on the dance floor, and, to my surprise, Max joins her.

I lean across the table and yell to Nico over the music, "That's the tequila dancing!"

He laughs and puts four fingers in the air when our server walks past.

I look at him and pretend to pass out. None of us are big drinkers, but we all need to let loose tonight.

Maris is lost in the music, and she moves as if it animates her. She sways her hips with each beat of the kick drum, just like she does when I'm playing. Her feet don't move, but she's the best dancer on the floor. Max is a little spastic, but he has his own thing going on, and he looks like he's having a blast.

The server shows up with four more shots, and Nico and I clink our shot glasses together and down the tequila. Maris looks over and Nico points at the remaining shots. Maris runs her finger across her neck and then gets Max's attention. He holds up both hands and shakes his head, so Nico and I tip another one back.

The band starts "Jungle Boogie" by KC and The Sunshine Band, and Nico and I clap and cheer them on. It looks like Maris and Max aren't coming back to the table any time soon, so I move to the chair next to Nico.

"That guitar player is killin' me, man," he says. "He's got that ..." Nico sings the sound he likes while he mimes playing the riff.

"Totally. I love the drummer's foot, too. Heavy as hell."

"You got that, my brotha," Nico says, lifting his chin for emphasis.

The band transitions into another song, and we applaud and yell our appreciation. I worry, momentarily, that Nico will strain his voice, but then I remind myself that Nico knows he has a show tomorrow. He's never been prone to vocal fry.

I watch Nico watching Maris and, suddenly, my chest feels tight. I love Nico and I love Maris, so I try to redirect my feelings away from the jealousy that's rearing up.

A girl approaches us and leans over to yell in Nico's ear. He smiles at her and shakes his head, pointing to me. The girl smiles at me and walks over. "Do you wanna dance?"

I smile and hold my hands together in a prayer position. "It's so cool of you to ask, but I'm not a dancer." I'm lying. I'm also sick to death of being everyone's second choice, but she doesn't need to hear that.

"Come on, please?" She smiles sweetly at me, and I consider how hard it was for her to come over to our table by herself. It feels like the whole room is watching … and she is hot. She's platinum blonde and has a rockin' body. She's wearing a lot more make-up than the girls in Miami wear. Must be a regional thing. I take the hand she has extended. She leads me to the dance floor and makes room for us beside Maris and Max, who scream with happiness when they see us.

"What's your name?" I ask.

"Ann," she says.

"I love your accent," I say. "I'm Th—"

"I know who you are, Theo," she says, smiling.

"I didn't know you could dance!" Maris shouts at me.

I shrug my shoulders and smooth it out even more. All Greek men can dance. At least the ones in my family, anyway. Maris notices and approves.

"How long are you guys in town?" Ann asks.

"Just tonight," I tell her. "We leave in the morning."

"Are you staying close by?"

I'm a little thrown by her forwardness. "I don't know, we came by Uber. Maybe?"

Ann laughs too hard and starts dancing against me. I notice her friend taking a video and I thank her for the dance and head back to the table, but Nico's gone. I instinctively look toward the stage and that's where I see him. The guitar player is showing him his pedal board and Nico is strapping on a guitar.

The band doesn't introduce him or anything, they just transition to another song and Nico starts playing the opening riff to "Purple Rain" by Prince. I take my seat and yell, "Get it, Big Man!" Nico nods at the band's singer, so he steps up to the mic. I've never heard Nico play this before, but I know the solo is out of this world, so I settle in and wait.

Maris and Max made their way to the foot of the stage and are swaying back and forth in front of where Nico stands. Part of me wants to join them. Part of me wants to throw my beer mug at him. I know he's digging this band, but can't he sit and appreciate them without getting on stage? Of course, he can't. Players want to play. And, holy shit, is he playing. Nico rips this guitar solo like he plays it every day. The place goes nuts, and I smile between swigs of beer.

As Nico plays, he throws his head back and closes his eyes. I know part of that is the performer in him, but part of it is the moment he's in. He feels music. He breathes music. I feel grooves, sounds, and rhythms. I wonder how different our experience of the same song is. It looks like he loves it more than I do, but when I said I'd rather have Funkengroovin' than Maris, he didn't agree. He didn't disagree, either.

The song ends and Nico yells into the mic over the crowd noise. "Give it up for this awesome band. Thanks for letting me play."

He quickly slips the guitar off and gives it back to its owner and jumps off the front of the stage by Maris and Max. The band starts playing a slow song, and Nico folds Maris into his arms.

Max comes back to the table, looking for beer. His cheeks are pink, and he's drenched in sweat. Or maybe he doused himself again.

"That girl was hot. Where'd she go?"

"You looking for a date?"

"Always, but she was into you, not me," Max says, sitting in Nico's chair.

"Nah, she was into Nico first. He passed her off to me," I say.

"Don't you dare feel sorry for yourself in front of me. Read the room, dude," Max tells me. "You could walk up to any girl in this place and ask them to go home with you and they would."

"Anyone can pick up a one-night stand, Max. That's not my goal."

Max's eyes went wide. "That's my goal. Teach me, sensei."

I can't help but laugh.

"Show me what your type is, my guy. Who do you like?"

Max scans the room. I try to follow his stare, and he seems to be focused on a girl with chin-length dark hair. She looks like the photo on his phone.

"You definitely have a type," I say. "Okay, so all you have to do is go over there and introduce yourself. Ask her if she's from here. Ask her if she likes the music. Just strike up a conversation."

"A whole conversation out of thin air isn't easy, Theo."

"It's like a muscle. The more you work it, the stronger it gets," I say with a shrug.

Nico leads Maris through the crowd on the way back to our table. "Are you guys ready?"

"Ah, no. Max was just going to shoot his shot with a honey."

Nico holds his hand in the air, and the server notices and nods at him.

"Dude, I said we're not ready to leave."

"Go talk to your girl, Max," Nico says. "We'll wait."

Max looks back and forth between us, and Maris gives him a quick hug. "You're a snack, Max. That girl is very lucky to have your attention. We'll stay as long as you want us to."

"Okay, I'm going." Max turns and beelines.

I smile at Maris, and she crosses her fingers.

"What happened to the chica you were dancing with?" Maris asks.

"I noticed her girlfriend taking video of us, and I don't know where that's going to be posted, so ..."

"Dude, that sucks. It's kind of nice that people are starting to know us, but that can feel invasive, too." Nico shakes his head.

"I guess you'll help us navigate that after you get all famous working with Dame Knight." I'm surprised to hear my thoughts spill from my mouth.

"I'm not working with Dame Knight, Theo. We've had this talk."

I press my lips together and tilt my head to the side looking at Nico. "Come on, man. You're putting on a good show that you're all about Funkengroovin', but when it comes down to it ..." I can't finish my thought.

Nico squares up in front of my chair. "When it comes down to it ..." He prompts.

I shake my head. The server shows up with the bill, and Nico and I both try to get her to take our credit cards.

"You trying to make yourself feel better about leaving us behind by buying us a meal?"

The server takes Nico's card and I laugh. "Even she picks you over me."

"Theo, my brother, you need to drink some water and move around a little bit," Nico says.

"I'm not drunk, Nico," I say, standing up, but wobbling a little.

"Well, then, you're better at handling your tequila than I am, because I feel quite drunk."

I roll my eyes. "You didn't play like you were drunk."

"Thank you, brother," Nico says. The server brings his credit card back and thanks us for coming in.

"I think we should get some fresh air," Nico says.

"I don't need fresh air, and we said we'd wait for Max."

Maris winks at me. "I'll wait for Max. You guys are probably making him nervous, anyway. Go with Nico and if Max strikes out, I'll bring him out front. If he hits a homer, I guess we have to hope he makes it back to the hotel for the meeting with Phil in the morning."

Maris's words are all jumbled together and I'm feeling a little spinny. "Fine."

Nico puts his arm around me, and I shrug it off. The band waves to us, and we both wave back on our way out.

The night air is crisp and salty. We must be somewhat close to the water. I'm suddenly homesick.

"I wish I could go for a swim in my pool," I say.

"I know."

"Oh, you know … everything. I forgot," I say with a laugh.

Nico walks to the back of the building and yells back to me, "We're across the street from the beach."

I follow Nico as I dictate a text to Maris and Max. *We're acrosh the shtreet from the beesh.*

Nico is already on the ocean side of the road, and he turns to wait for me. When I get to the sand, I take my shoes off. Nico chuckles.

"I don't mind the beach at night," he tells me. "It's better when it isn't blazing hot and there's no one here."

I start walking toward the water and Nico follows.

"I'm not going to dive in, if that's what you're worried about," I tell him.

"I'm not worried about anything," he says. "It sounds like you are, though, Theo, so I want to reassure you that I'm all in with what we started, man. I'm not working with Dame on the side. I'm not writing with them. I'm Funkengroovin' for life." Nico chuckles.

"You're gonna do what's best for you," I say.

Nico increases his stride and catches up to me. "Hold on."

I stop in my tracks and then I'm mad at myself for doing what he told me to do, so I start walking again.

"Theo, hold on," Nico says again.

"What the hell are you guys doing?" Maris's voice seems far away.

"We're having a Band Beating," I yell. "You're just in time."

Nico shakes his head. "What Luis said today doesn't change anything for me, Theo. This isn't a Band Beating. If anything, it's a reaffirmation of our dedication to Funkengroovin'."

Maris and Max run over to where we're standing. They look worried, so I tell Nico to tell them what he told me.

"I was reassuring Theo that I don't want to have anything to do with Dame Knight," Nico says.

"Oh, thank God," Max says, giving Nico a big hug.

"How'd it go inside?" Nico asked him.

"I got her IG," Max said. "If I ever come back to Myrtle Beach, I told her I'd let her know. But I'm glad to hear you say that about Dame because that could be a big opportunity, and I can see that it might be hard to turn down."

"It's not hard at all, Max. Theo and I didn't come this far together to leak any of our focus toward another project."

"To be clear," I say, "*Theo* doesn't have the opportunity to make that choice, but, if I did, my answer would have been a flat no. On the spot. I wouldn't have entertained it for a second. I wouldn't have tried to figure out a way to have my cake and eat it, too. Because I don't think of myself first."

"Are we waiting for an Uber, or ...?" Maris asks.

"No, we're having a Band Beating," I say.

"Let's have a Band Beating tomorrow morning before we meet with Phil," Maris suggests.

"I have some things that I want to say now." I look at Maris and she looks scared, so I put my arms around her and give her a hug. I let go and turn to Nico.

"Nico, my brother, I believe that you think you're going to stay focused on our band. But, when it comes down to it, you're gonna do what's best for you. And that's ..." I shrug my shoulders, "... what most people do. That's how people become winners. That's how a guy gets the girl, right?"

Nico is quiet. I want him to tell me what he's thinking, but he won't unless he's forced to. I want him to admit that I'm right.

"Listen, I'm not saying that taking care of number one is a bad thing, if you're the *one*, right? But let's say you're someone who counts on number one. Well, then, you're fucked."

"Theo, you're drunk. I'm drunk. This isn't a good time to talk. Let's go back to the hotel and pass out. We can talk tomorrow. This conversation isn't going anywhere good tonight."

I feel my face contort with anger. "You think you know everything, Nico, but you don't know shit. You don't know that Maris came to me after her conversation with Dinah because she was worried that Dame was trying to jack you. You didn't know that she came to the beach and confided her fears to me, not you. But, the really big thing you don't know," I pause for effect, "is that Maris is only with *you* because *I* sent her away."

"Theo!" Maris yells at me. "Stop it."

I see Nico's face change, and the pain that I see there is satisfying.

"You weren't Maris's first choice, my brother. She came to me first that night—"

"Theo, that's enough!" Maris yells.

"I sent her away because I didn't want to take advantage of her vulnerability. Her heart was broken. She was in pieces, but you did what was best for YOU, not her, didn't you? So maybe you're not the selfless hero you want us to believe you are, huh?"

Nico's words come out in a whisper, "Fuck you, Theo."

"When you get the chance to level up with Dame, you'll do it because that's what's best for you. And, Maris, if you think he won't be fucking Dinah within a week—"

My eyes had been on Nico, so the slap across my face was a complete surprise.

"How dare you?" Maris's voice is shaking, and she has tears streaming down her cheeks.

I can't understand her reaction. "I loved you enough, even way back then, to do what was right for you."

"That's bullshit, Theo," Max yells.

His voice surprises me because I forgot he was here.

"Mare, Theo saw Damon fuck that girl during your gig with Backyard Breeder. He told Nico about it, and they decided not to tell you. They were worried that you would resent them and not join the band, after all. So, no, Theo, you haven't always had Maris's best interests in mind. I did, though." Max turns to Maris. "I'm the one that sent you the anonymous DM about Damon."

Perfectly synced, Nico, Maris, and I all yell, "What?"

"Yeah, I overheard you guys talking about it in the pool. I couldn't keep Mare in the dark about something like that. And I knew when Nico and Maris started hooking up, but I also heard Nico tell his brother that he loved her, so I didn't say anything. So, both of you can fuck all the way off over who's motivations are self-serving because you're both pricks."

"You sent me that DM?" Maris is fully crying now.

Max blinks repeatedly. "I thought it was the easiest way for you to hear it. I didn't spend much time thinking about whether it was the best way. I sent the DM the same night I overheard them talking about it."

"You little shit," I say. "I give you free room and board, and you're fucking spying on everyone in the house?"

"I didn't do anything wrong, Theo," Max says forcefully.

Maris is sobbing and I look from her to Nico, who returns my gaze with rage in his eyes. Fine with me. I fucking hate him. He starts moving toward Maris, and I step between them.

"The Band Beating isn't over," I tell him.

Nico's right hook collides with my jaw, closer to my ear than my mouth. I hear something crack, and the next thing I know, I'm eating sand.

"It's over, *brother*."

Maris's crying is muffled now, or maybe my eardrum is broken. Max kneels beside me. I have a lot of pain, and some of it is physical, so I pass out.

MARIS

NICO STARTS WALKING BACK TO the bar and I'm frozen in place. The way Theo's legs went out from under him was terrifying, but I don't want Nico to leave alone. As if he's reading my mind, Max tells me he'll take care of Theo, and I should go after Nico.

I run to catch up with him. When I do, he has the Uber app open. He holds the phone with his left hand and taps the screen with his right, but he intermittently flexes and straightens the fingers on his right hand.

"Nico?"

He lifts his eyes from his phone screen to look at me, but his face is unreadable. I don't know what to say to him in this moment. I don't know if I should tell him why I went to Theo's room first, or why I told Theo my suspicions about Dame Knight's intentions before I told him. I don't understand what went into the decision he and Theo made not to tell me about Damon, but that all seems like ages ago. It feels like whatever I say next has the power to make or break us, so I say nothing.

"Uber is three minutes away, if you want to go back to the hotel."

"Okay," I say.

Nico shoves his phone into his right front jeans pocket and winces.

"Let me see your hand," I say.

"It's fine," he reassures me gently.

"Please, can I just look at it? The best parts of my life rely upon those hands."

Nico gingerly removes his hand from his pocket and holds it out. The knuckle of his pinky finger already looks like there's a marble under his skin, and the rest of his finger is starting to swell.

"Oh, my God. Are you going to be able to play tomorrow?" The tears waterfall from my eyes again and I instinctively reach for Nico's hand, but he pulls it away.

"Don't touch it. Please." He tries to laugh it off. "Remember how I told you that I bartended at my family's tavern when I was eleven? Well, by the time I was fourteen, I was big enough to be promoted to bouncer. And, I have brothers, so this isn't the first time I've had Boxer's Fracture."

"Nico! You think it's broken?" I have to touch him, so I place my fingertips on the side of his face.

He shrugs. "I should probably get it X-Rayed."

The Uber pulls up and I open the door and step back for Nico to get in first, but I'm talking to the driver from outside the car. "Is there a hospital with an Emergency Room nearby?"

"Uh, yeah, I think Grand Strand is the closest. So, you're not going to the hotel, then?"

"We are," Nico says. "Please go to the hotel first and then to the hospital."

"That's two different directions, are you sure?" the driver asks.

"Hotel first, hospital second, please," Nico says patiently.

"No, Nico, I'm going with you to the hospital." Then to the driver, "Hospital, please, not the hotel."

"Maris," Nico says calmly. "I want you to go back to the hotel and get some sleep. This isn't a major injury, so I could be waiting in the ER for hours before they see me."

"So ... the hotel?" the driver asks.

"Yes, please. It's settled," Nico says.

I'm at a loss for words again. I wonder if Nico would have gotten in the Uber alone if I hadn't come after him. I would give anything to know what he's thinking. But part of me is terrified that he thinks I'm only with him because Theo rejected me.

"Nico," I whisper. "Anything that happened before I loved you ... it feels like those things happened to two different people. I don't care about the Damon thing, and I ... I was intimidated by you when we first met. I didn't see you as a —"

"I'm not ready to have this conversation, Maris," he says softly. Nico inhales deeply. "I agree with you, though, the stuff that happened before we really knew each other doesn't matter today. But I don't understand why you went to Theo with your concerns about Dame rather than coming straight to me. If I suspected that another band had their sights on you, I wouldn't confide in Theo ..."

"We touched on it a little when I got back to the room after—"

"No," Nico says quietly. "No, you left Dinah's room and went straight to Theo. You didn't come back to our room."

"I should have. But Dinah didn't tell me outright what their intentions were. Like I told you, she was fishing for information. I didn't want to sound paranoid, or like a jealous girlfriend. And I don't want to be the reason you pass up an opportunity that could be really good for you."

"Now you sound like Theo. Questioning my loyalty. What's that based on, Maris?"

Nico turns to look at me, and this time I can read his expression. He's hurting. He presses his eyes closed and shakes his head.

"Fear," I say. "Fear of losing you. Losing the band." The Uber pulls up to the hotel, but I can't leave it like this. "Please let me go to the hospital with you."

"I'm a grown man, Maris. I can take myself to the ER. I've done it before. Go back to the room and get some sleep."

"I love you," I say. I sound desperate. I am desperate.

"Love you, too," he replies, but I wonder if he's just dismissing me.

"I'll be saying prayers that your hand is okay and that you can play tomorrow."

"I'm pretty tough," he assures me.

I lean in for a kiss and he obliges, but I don't feel much behind it. I know I have to let him go. Nico's suffering, he just had a huge fight with his best friend and business partner, he found out his girlfriend went to Theo behind his back … twice.

"Sleep tight," he says.

I get out of the car and slam the door behind me. As I walk through the lobby, I hang my head so that my hair provides partial coverage of my face. I opt for the stairs rather than risking having to ride the elevator with prying eyes. Once the hotel room door closes behind me, I go to Nico's suitcase and look for his University of Miami sweatshirt. It smells like him, so I put it on over my clothes and lay down in our bed. Alone.

PHIL

THE CONTRACT FROM REVOLUTION RECORDS was in my inbox when I woke up at eight a.m. It's a fifty-page boilerplate until the addendum regarding Nico's involvement with Dame Knight. They want him to commit to writing and recording ten songs with Nicky and Dinah and to tour with them to promote the resulting album. Every client I represent would think I was a godsend for presenting this opportunity, but I know these four. It's going to be a hard sell. To make matters worse, Luis added an expiry clause. If the band doesn't execute the agreement within forty-eight hours, the offer is automatically rescinded.

I tried to get Luis to make two separate offers, one for Funkengroovin' and one for Nico, but he wouldn't hear of it. He's counting on Nico feeling pressured to take the gig with Dame Knight as a means of securing a major label record deal for his own band. All Luis really cares about is keeping Dinah and Nicky happy and sellable for another few years. He's been going to that well for a decade, and he's going to keep going back until it's bone dry.

The lobby restaurant is busy, and I have micro-chats with people associated with the festival as they pass the table where I'm sitting alone drinking my second cup of coffee. It feels like I've been here for a long time, so I check my phone. It's 10:32. The band is over a half-hour late. For a meeting where they're expecting news from record labels. What the fuck is wrong with these guys?

I text Theo: *Hey, Rockstar, I'm in the lobby restaurant. You coming down, or should I come up?*

That should roll them out of bed. Three dots appear on the screen, and I tell myself I should have sent the text a half hour ago.

Theo: *Need a raincheck on the meeting, Phil. Maybe tomorrow in Charlotte.*

I'm so irritated by his response that I'm talking to myself, "Unfuckingbelievable."

No can do, Buddy. I have a major label deal for you with an expiration date attached, so get your lucky ass down here. You never had a better reason to get out of bed.

I know Theo's father is a wealthy man, but he never struck me as a spoiled asshole. Until now.

Theo: *Not happening today, Phil. I'll see you tomorrow.*

"Unfuckingbelievable!" I say quite loudly this time, drawing attention from other diners.

I march to the front desk and demand the room number for Theo Athanasiou, only to be told that the hotel can't give out that information. Honestly, I don't blame the desk clerk for not giving it to me. I'm sure I look as crazed as I feel.

It's ten forty-five now and the bus leaves at eleven, so I take a seat by the hotel entrance and wait.

THEO

I'M HUNGRY, BUT THE THOUGHT of moving my jaw and chewing food is so painful I don't want to try it in real life. I wait until Max leaves the room to get out of bed. I didn't shower when we got back to the room last night, so I should do it now, but I don't have time. Also, I don't care.

I throw my stuff into my luggage and go to the bathroom where I'm confronted by my reflection in the mirror. Holy balls, I look like shit. The entire left side of my face is swollen and bruised. My neck hurts like hell. It feels like the force of Nico's punch spun my head a full rotation. I was afraid to sleep last night, thinking I might have a concussion, so I sat up until sunrise. I wonder how terrible my head would feel this morning if three shots of tequila and a few beers had been the worst thing that happened. I remember the tequila and my mouth fills with saliva. I need water. And food. And sleep. But the bus leaves in ten minutes, so I check the room to make sure nothing is left behind and I ride the elevator to the lobby. The first face I see when the doors open is Phil's. Fuck. As I walk toward him, he's as unnerved at the sight of my face as I was at his.

"What the fuck, Theo? What happened?"

I don't stop to talk to him, but without moving my jaw, I say, "Don't know what you're talking about, Phil," and keep walking to the bus.

"Theo!" Phil yells at my back.

It hurts to talk, but I tell Phil I'll see him in Charlotte and board the bus, praying that he doesn't follow me. I see Max sitting in the back by the window, where we usually sit. I make eye contact with him, and he raises his eyebrows slightly as if asking if I'm coming back there. I don't know if my facial muscles are capable of expression and I'm too sore to try, so I take a seat near the front in an empty row. I don't want to talk to Max, or anyone else for that matter. I sure as fuck don't want to sit across the aisle from Nico. I didn't see him or Maris in their regular seats and that makes me sick to my stomach. But so does the idea of facing them today. Again, I wonder if it's the tequila, or just life.

I put my earbuds in to deter conversation, but judging by the looks I'm getting from the other musicians boarding the bus, my face is already doing that.

Then, Maris gets on the bus. I look down, but as she passes my row, I can't resist looking up at her. Her hand goes to her mouth when she sees my face and her eyes get watery. She blinks the tears away and pauses for half a beat but continues toward the back of the bus. I keep my head low expecting Nico to be right behind her, but he isn't. I expect each of the stragglers who board after Maris to be him, but none of them are, and then the bus driver takes his seat and closes the door. I panic. As much as I don't want to see Nico, I need to see Nico to know that we can move forward. Not just with our friendship, but with the tour. With the record deal, or not. The bus starts moving and I turn around to find Maris. She's looking at me and she shakes her head back and forth and then shrugs. Her face is red and she's crying as she looks out the window toward the hotel.

I glance over at Max and see that he's crying, too, but he's trying to hide behind sunglasses and a hat. He doesn't have anything covering his quivering chin, which gives him away. I face the front of the bus again and close my eyes. It should take three and a half hours to get to Charlotte, but adding bus time, it will be closer to four and a half ... or five. The longer the better. I need to rest up for the show. If we're playing the show. If the guitar player who sings half our songs is still in the band. If we still have a band. The bus goes over a bump and pain radiates from my head. It feels appropriate. I welcome it. Pain is honest. You can feel it. You can't feel love in the same way. You can't press your heart and feel love, but I can press my jaw and feel pain. Pain is real. I'd rather live in the real world than in some imaginary state built on a fallacy. I'll have to remember to write that down when I wake up. There's a song in there somewhere. First, sleep.

BANDMAGEDDON

Marci Viola

MARIS

My alarm goes off and I smell the Dolce and Gabbana fragrance that Nico wears. I smile in anticipation of seeing him next to me, but when I open my eyes, he isn't there.

"Nico?"

I scan the room and see his luggage where it was last night when I came back alone and went to bed. Then I realize that I'm wearing his University of Miami sweatshirt. It smells like him.

Memories flash across my mind like a terrible movie trailer for a film I never wanted to see. Theo telling Nico that he was my first choice. Nico punching Theo so hard that his legs crumpled beneath him as he fell to the sand. Nico leaving in an Uber, alone, to go to the Emergency Room to see if his hand was broken.

I pick up my phone and call Nico, but it goes straight to voicemail. The sound of his smooth, deep voice brings tears to my eyes. His message is lighthearted, and he sounds happy. The polar opposite of how he sounded when we last spoke and he insisted that I come back to the hotel to get some sleep.

"Hey … I'm worried. If you were waiting until I was awake to call, I'm up now, so please call me back. I love you. I love you so much." I hang up and watch my phone screen thinking he'll call back directly, like he always does. The minutes tick by and the stupid phone stays silent.

The band is supposed to meet with Phil at ten this morning, but there's no way I can face that conversation, and I'm not going without Nico. Could he be downstairs already? I call the front desk and ask to be transferred to the hotel restaurant.

"It's a beautiful morning in The Beach Café, this is Tina, how may I help you?"

"Good morning, Tina," my voice sounds like shit, and I realize that singing for ten thousand people a few hours from now is going to require a small miracle. "Do you by chance know the band Funkengroovin'?"

"The Silver Springs band? Yeah, I know them."

"Would you recognize the band members if you saw them in person?"

"I'm sorry, I'm not able to confirm or deny who may, or may not be, guests at the hotel."

"Tina, this is Maris from Funkengroovin'. I'm calling from upstairs in my room."

Tina giggles. "Oh, my God. So cool."

"I was wondering if you could tell me if you see Nico, Theo, or Max down there."

"I haven't seen them, but I'll put you on hold and check to make sure they didn't slip in, okay?"

"Thanks, Tina." I close my eyes and breathe deeply while the on-hold music plays. I will Nico to call me. Will him to feel me. We're never apart, so it's destabilizing to be separated, especially under the current conditions. We're experiencing bandmageddon and I don't know if we'll survive.

"Maris?" Tina whispers.

"I'm here."

"None of the guys are in the café or the lobby. I checked both places."

"Thank you, Tina, I really appreciate it."

"No problem. Feel free to call back if you want me to check again later."

I hang up, unable to remember a time when I've been less sure what to do next. I can't stomach the idea of seeing Theo or Max right now. I'm not necessarily pissed at Max, like I am at Theo, but I know he'll ask me a ton of questions along the lines of, *is everything going to be okay,* and I have no idea how to reassure him when I need reassurance myself. So, I'm quite sure I'm skipping the meeting with Phil. Theo can talk to him, he's the band leader. It's his job.

The bus for Charlotte leaves at eleven this morning. Should I get an Uber and go to the hospital? Do I have time? Fuck! Why didn't I insist on going along with Nico last night? Why did I agree to splitting up?

I can't even remember the name of the hospital that the Uber driver told us about. I do remember him saying it was the opposite direction from the hotel in relation to the bar we went to. I consult the map app in my phone and think the one with the word Grand in the name sounds familiar, and it's on the other side of the bar. I call the number for emergency care and hope to reach someone as helpful as Tina. The man who answers doesn't give his name and sounds annoyed before I've had the chance to speak.

"Good morning. My boyfriend, Nico Van Asten, sought treatment in the ER last night for a potentially broken hand. I'm wondering if you can tell me if he's still there."

"V-a-n ...?"

"Capitol A-s-t-e-n."

"Let me see ...," I hear some clicking. "... I'm not able to help."

"I'm not asking about private medical information, or anything, I just need to know if he's there. Or if he was there."

"I'm sorry, I'm not able to help."

I really want to try begging, but I know it won't work. "Thanks."

The map app tells me that the hospital I just spoke with is thirty minutes away. If it's the right hospital, and if Nico is still there, I wouldn't have time to get there and back before the bus leaves. And would I try to haul both sets of luggage with me? I dial Nico again, and it goes directly to voicemail, again. This time, the sound of his voice makes me cry.

I decide to take a shower and pray that he calls or comes back before I have to decide whether to get on the bus without him, and whether to take his things with me, or not. How can he leave me with all these questions? He wouldn't do that to me. Unless he's angry and he can't face me the way I can't face Theo. Or unless his injury was worse than he thought, and he needed emergency surgery to repair his hand if he's ever going to play guitar at a high level again. *Nico, call me!*

I step out of the shower and dress in the same outfit I wore on the bus from Savannah to Myrtle Beach. That bus ride was the beginning of the conflict that has overtaken the four of us. If Dinah Dame and Nicky Knight hadn't been on that bus, and if Nicky hadn't been drunk, then Nico wouldn't have helped him … I wish I could go back to that day and rent an SUV for the four of us the way Nico wanted to. Fuck Phil and his prearranged travel plans.

I start packing my bag. Once it's zipped, I gather Nico's toiletries from the bathroom and put them in his shaving case. His clothes are organized inside his luggage, but I don't zip the case closed.

I try his phone again with the same outcome as the previous two tries.

If he's okay, I'm going to kill him.

I try to decide what the likelihood is that Nico is incapacitated and can't reach me. Probably very low. He hurt his hand, not his head. Not like Theo. Oh, God, Theo. I can't understand why Nico hasn't been in touch. He knows what time the bus leaves and if he wanted me to take his luggage with me, he would reach out to ask me to do that. I tear a page out of my songwriting journal and write:

> *Nico,*
>
> *I've been trying your phone and called the ER, but I have no idea where you are or if you're okay. I considered taking your gear with me on the bus, but I don't know if you'd want that. Or if you're coming to Charlotte at all. I don't know what to do. I don't know if you want me to do anything. I'm so worried about you. I need to hear your voice. I need to know you're okay. Please call me. I love you, M~*

It's time to get on the bus, so I call the front desk and ask for a late checkout for our room. Hopefully, Nico makes it back here to collect his things. I can't believe I'm leaving Myrtle Beach without him. I look back into the room before I close the door, and it feels like goodbye.

Phil is in the lobby, and he tries to stop me to talk, but I blow him off. I've never seen him so pissed. He asks me what's going on and I'm not lying to him when I tell him I have no idea.

When I get on the bus, I look to the back hoping to, somehow, see Nico sitting there. He isn't. Max is, and he looks past me for Nico. His eyes meet mine and his face falls. Then I see Theo. The entire left side of his face is various colors of black and purple, and the proportion of the swelling is disturbing. I cover my quivering lips with my hand, and consider stopping to say ... what? What can I say? I continue to the back of the bus and sit by the window, leaving Nico's aisle seat open. Very few people board the bus after me, and I hope that every one of them is my tall, sandy-haired guitar player. The bus driver boards and closes the door. Theo turns to look back at me, and I shake my head and shrug a little. I look out the window, hoping to see Nico running out of the hotel, dragging his luggage behind him. He isn't there. I cover my face with my hands and sob.

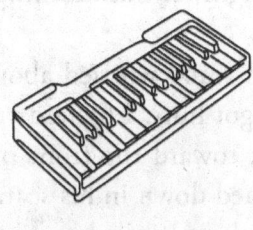

MAX

MARIS STARTS CRYING AS WE pull away from the hotel, so I move over to the seat beside hers ... Nico's seat.

"Mare?" My voice cracks because I'm on the brink of sobbing myself. I put my arm across her shoulders, and she turns to look at me. Her face is bright red, and her eyes are bloodshot. For once, our roles are reversed and she's looking to me for solace. I pull her into my chest and wrap my other arm around her. She sobs for ten minutes straight, then retrieves a roll of hotel bathroom tissue from her big hobo bag, and blows her nose.

"Good foresight," I say, pointing at the toilet paper.

"Yeah. I used all the tissues ..."

"So, is Nico ...?"

Maris leans back in her seat and closes her eyes. "After we left the bar, Nico had the Uber drop me off at the hotel and he went to the ER alone. That's all I know. He didn't come back."

I digest the information before I reply. "I was worried that he refused to get on the bus this morning, so, in a way, it's better than I thought."

Maris turns to look at me and her face says, *how?*

"I mean, if he made the choice not to come, that's more definitive than, I don't know, him getting delayed at the hospital or something."

"He hasn't called me, Max. His phone goes straight to voicemail. I tried calling the ER that I thought he went to, but they wouldn't tell me whether he was there or not."

"Maybe he told them not to release any information. A patient can do that. Maybe he was worried word would get out or something."

Maris seems to be considering the idea. "That still doesn't explain why he didn't call me all night, or this morning. He knew what time the bus was leaving."

"Nico must have been really worried about his hand if he went to the ER. I didn't know he got hurt. I figured you guys came back to the hotel like we did." I look toward the front of the bus, but I can't see Theo. He must be scrunched down in his seat. "I wanted Theo to go to the hospital, but he refused, so I called my mom and asked what to do for someone with a concussion."

Maris gasps. "Theo has a concussion?"

"I don't know for sure. He didn't throw up, which my mom said to watch out for. He stayed sitting up and awake until around seven this morning. I laid down, but I watched him all night. Once the sun came up, we both crashed."

"Nico thought he broke something in this part of his hand," Maris says, pointing to her first pinky knuckle. "It looked like a marble was underneath his skin here."

"Shit. What are we gonna do if neither of them can play tonight?"

"I'm not worried about tonight as much as I'm worried about every night after."

I puff air out of my cheeks and sit quietly for a few minutes. Then I feel my throat start to tighten up, and I know I have to get this over with. "Maris, I'm really sorry about how I handled the Damon thing. And if I stuck my nose into your business with Nico."

Her face is expressionless. I'm not sure she heard me, but then she says, "You did what you thought was right. I would rather have found out in person because I felt humiliated thinking everyone knew but me."

"I didn't consider that," I tell her. "I'm really sorry, Mare. I didn't want to pile more pain on you."

She pats my leg. "Dickhead caused the pain. And I don't wish away anything that brought the four of us closer together." Maris starts crying again and I try to think of anything that might bring her peace.

"I'm not too worried about Nico. I mean, it's Nico. He's okay, he's just okay somewhere other than on this bus."

Maris chuckles. "It feels so wrong without him. And it feels so wrong to have Theo sitting up there alone."

"I know," I tell her. "But he's probably sleeping because he didn't get any rest last night and he needs to power up before the show."

"If there is a show."

"Well, the worst thing we can do is stay awake worrying. If Theo and Nico are ready to go at show time and we're falling asleep, that's gonna look bad. I mean, the two band members who didn't sustain significant injuries last night are too tired to play? That's not gonna fly."

Maris nods in agreement. "Being unconscious sounds very appealing right now."

I stand up to go back to my row. "Stretch out and take advantage of not having two hundred pounds of beefcake taking up space next to you."

Maris tries to laugh, but she's too tired to emote. She curls up across both seats, and I position my neck pillow under my chin. I try to visualize all of us with our arms wrapped around each other backstage chanting *Funkengroovin'* the way we did last night. What a difference a day makes.

THEO

I WAKE WITH A START WHEN the bus pulls off the interstate. It feels like we're driving down a staircase, but that might be because my head feels like Jell-O. I check my phone and see fifteen missed calls from Phil and zero messages from Nico.

I don't know the musician sitting in the row across from me, but he has a six-pack of bottled water, so he's my best bud.

"Could I beg a bottle of water off you, bro?"

He looks terrified. Like if he says no, I'll start swinging. "Sure, man." He hands me two and I down the first in one go. I haven't eaten anything since last night, so I feel it hitting like I ran a hose straight into my stomach. I have Ibuprofen in my backpack, so I shake two into my hand and swallow those as well. My fingers feel thick, so I'm dehydrated, but my wrists, arms, and shoulders feel surprisingly good. Normal. My neck still hurts terribly, and my jaw, ear, cheekbone, and eye socket are killing me. I touch my face and decide not to do that again for at least a week. I feel like I got hit with a cinder block. How big is Nico's fucking fist?

I have to deal with this now, and I don't know where to start. I guess it all boils down to me and Nico. I don't feel like I should be the one to apologize. Sure, I said some hurtful shit aimed at what he holds most precious, but the fucker hauled off and assaulted me. I wonder if that's why he isn't on the bus. Is he too ashamed to face me? I've stopped myself from thinking about last night until now. What *did* I say? In a nutshell, I told him that he puts himself first and that he's only with Maris because I didn't take advantage of her when she was vulnerable, and then I insinuated that he did. So, basically, total character assassination.

What must Maris think of me? I'm an idiot to think this is only between me and Nico. I betrayed her confidence. Even if Nico shook my brain around, I'm going to heal before the damage I did to the relationships I care about the most, apart from my dad, will. The band is my family on this continent. That's why I have them living with me, if I'm honest. Sure, it's great to be able to record together and rehearse at the house, but I need people around me in Miami.

Am I the asshole? I was seething with jealousy last night; I remember that much. Fuck. How did I let this happen?

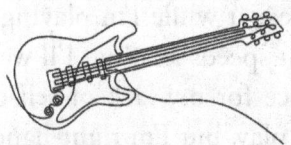

NICO

THE EMERGENCY ROOM AT GRAND Strand was packed when I arrived. The triage nurse assured me that my information and admittance would be kept private. In Theo's state, I didn't want him calling the hospital or, worse yet, telling Phil about our little incident and have him trying to track me down. The nurse gave me an ice pack and told me the wait would be close to two hours. She was off by three hours. I was glad that Maris hadn't come along for multiple reasons. First, there was no need for her to sit on a plastic chair in the refrigerated, loud atmosphere when the other option was getting some sleep at the hotel. Secondly, I wasn't ready to talk about what Theo divulged in his drunken rant. Hearing that Maris was interested in him first hurt, of course, but I didn't have enough details to know how hurt I should be. I knew how Theo felt about her, but I still don't know if she had any feelings for him beyond the bond we have as a band.

I was angry at Theo for expecting me to jump ship for the chance to work with Dame Knight. I devoted five years to Funkengroovin' because I believed that Theo was as talented and hardworking as I am.

Max gave us some credibility and Maris gave us … everything. Why would he think I'd leave now? Theo gave me no credit for trying to find a way for all of us to benefit from Dame's interest in me. If he really thought I was a totally self-centered asshole, what had we been doing for the last five years?

After four hours of rehashing everything that happened on the beach and trying to come up with the magic resolution for all of it, I finally got called back to have an X-Ray.

My suspicion was confirmed, it was a boxer's fracture, but clean, so it didn't require surgery. Thank God. The doctor repositioned the bone and it took the nurse forever to find a brace that fit me.

I won't be able to wear it while I'm playing because it stabilizes my wrist too much, but, if it speeds healing, I'll wear it during the day. I'm going to pay a high price for my lack of self-control. My left hand is more important while I play, but I'm right-handed. It's more important for everything else.

I looked at the clock while I was going through the discharge process and was shocked to see it was already nine am, but I was glad that Maris would be awake so I could catch her up. I hadn't wanted to wake her before her alarm. In keeping with my luck as of late, my phone was dead. Without access to my Uber app, I jumped in an available cab waiting outside the hospital. I was only thirty minutes from the hotel, so I was going to make it. Until traffic made it impossible.

So, now I'm trapped in the back of the cab and want my truck more than ever. The driver has opportunities to go make moves, but he's content to sit and wait.

"I need to catch a bus from the hotel at ten, my guy, is there another route, or can you use the shoulder?"

"Yeah, no, you're not gonna make it by ten."

"This is the only road that connects the hospital to the hotel?"

"Ya."

I feel my temper flaring up, but that hasn't served me well recently. "Okay, well, my phone is dead. Do you have a charger back here, or could I borrow yours to tell my boss to hold the bus?"

"Sorry, buddy. I don't let fares use my phone."

I'm ready to rebreak my hand. "Okay, then can you call for me?" Even as I ask, I realize that I don't know Phil's number by heart. In fact, I'm not certain of the last four digits of Maris's, and I'm not calling Theo.

"Just calm down, bud, or I'm going to have to ask you to get out of my cab."

"Dude, I'm just asking you to help me out. You picked me up from the hospital, so you know I'm not having a great day, and now I'm about to miss the bus to my next gig in Charlotte. You really don't have a phone charger in your cab?"

"I can't drive you all the way to Charlotte."

I inhale deeply and curse the partition between me and the steering wheel.

"Just, please, man. I'm begging. Whatever you can do."

"Yep."

I can see the sign for the hotel ahead, so I'm considering getting out of the car and running when the driver finally grabs his sack and uses the center turning lane to get us there. As we pull in, the bus pulls out.

"Is that your bus?"

I feel my blood pressure shooting skyward. "You're the worst driver in the history of driving," I tell him.

"You better leave me a tip; I used the turning lane. I could have gotten a ticket for that."

The fare is nineteen dollars and fifty-nine cents, so I dig a twenty out of my wallet, roll it tight and shove it through one of the round holes in the partition before bursting out of the car, which doesn't go smoothly using my left hand to work the door handle.

I hear the driver yell, "Asshole!" as I slam the door.

"Nico!"

I spin around and see Phil jogging towards me. Just when I thought things couldn't get worse.

"What the fuck is going on with you guys?" He clocks the brace on my hand. "Oh … oh."

"I need to go get my stuff and get on the road," I say stepping around him.

"Dame Knight's bus leaves in a half hour. You can ride with them."

"No, thanks." I keep walking, but I hear Phil following behind me.

"Who told you guys that you have enough collateral to make your own decisions? You don't show up for our meeting this morning—"

I hold my hand brace up, "I was otherwise occupied, Phil."

"Oh, it wasn't just you. No one showed."

I stop walking and turn around. "No one showed?"

Phil squares up with me but has to tilt his head upwards to meet my eyes. "No one. But I saw Theo's face as he boarded the bus this morning, and it seemed to have the imprint of your right hand on it. No one would tell me shit as they were walking to the bus and now you don't think you have to clue me in either, so let me remind you, I put you on this tour and I can take you off it."

"Everything is fine. It's an internal situation that will be resolved before we hit tonight. But I have to get up there, so I have to go get my stuff and get on the road."

"You're riding Dame Knight's coach." Phil says. "With me."

I stare him down and I'm suddenly exhausted. Getting a few hours of sleep sounds better than driving. "Fine. I'll be right back down."

"I'll come up and help you with your stuff." Phil gestures to my hand brace.

"Fine." I hoped to plug my phone in long enough to call Maris, but I don't want to have that conversation in front of Phil.

In the room, I find Maris's note and it pulls at my heart. I see that she gathered some of my things, and I feel how worried she must have been wondering what happened to me. I want to talk to her more than anything in the world right now. I plug my phone in, and I hear Phil talking on his in the hallway outside the door.

"Come on, juice up," I coax. I hit the head to freshen up a little, and then Phil's banging on the door.

"I gotta get downstairs, Nico."

This guy. I open the door with my left hand, and I realize how difficult it's going to be to adjust to my new normal. I try to remember to be grateful for this outcome. It could be worse. But I'm too tired.

"Can you grab my luggage, please?"

Phil seems to sense my surrender. "Are you going to be able to play?" He sounds concerned.

"I'm going to do my best," I say with a shrug.

"Glad it isn't your left hand," he says as he walks past me to get the gear. "Don't forget your phone."

I unplug it and follow Phil out of the room. Dinah is in the lobby and her face lights up when she sees me get out of the elevator with Phil.

"Nico! Did you miss your bus, baby?" She sees my brace. "Oh, shit. What happened?"

"Good morning, Dinah," I say.

"What happened?" she repeats.

"What happened? Who cares?" My British guardian angel rescues me. "It's just another rock-n-roll story. Let's get on the bus and get the hell out of Myrtle Beach."

"I couldn't agree more," I tell Nicky as he leads the way.

Their tour bus has bunks in the back and Nicky leads me to one that isn't being used. "No one will bother you in here, mate. You put this curtain down and it's an impenetrable sanctuary. Unwritten rule of the road."

"Thanks, Nicky."

"It's going to be okay, mate. Whatever it is."

I climb into the bunk and pull the curtain closed as instructed. I find an outlet and plug my phone in to charge, then turn the light out again. I intend to stay awake until I hear it turn on so that I can call Maris, but I pass out before the bus pulls away from the hotel.

THEO

I get off the bus first in Charlotte, so I don't have to wait forever for room keys. I trust Max and Maris to get my luggage as usual. I hope they do. As I wait to check-in, I listen to Phil's messages. The last one boils my blood. He tells me not to worry about Nico because he's on Dame Knight's tour bus, with Phil, and they left a half hour after we did. I laugh to myself imagining the conversation they all must have had on the way here. Dinah, Nicky, Phil, and Nico probably ironed out a great agreement.

I have the room keys, but I don't see Maris or Max in the lobby, so I go back outside to where the bus is still parked. I'm just in time to see Dame Knight's coach pull in behind ours.

Maris is waiting for the luggage to be unloaded from under our bus, so I walk towards her.

"I have your room key," I say softly, handing it to her.

"Thanks," she says, averting her eyes and suddenly becoming intensely interested in every bag that emerges from the hold.

I point to Dame's coach. "Nico's on board. He rode with Dame."

Maris looks at me now, and I can tell that she doesn't believe me. "Did you talk to him?"

"No. Phil left me a message."

I can see the questions percolating in Maris's mind and I shrug my shoulders.

"Yo!" Our driver pulls my case out and I step forward to take charge of it just as Max comes from the opposite direction.

"Oh, hey, Theo, I was gonna grab that for you," he says.

"He's your room key," I hand him a little folder with the room number on the front. "In case you want to wait for Nico." I gesture toward Dame's tour bus. "I'm going to the room. Please be quiet if you come in because I need all the sleep I can get before the show."

"Nico's here?" Max smiles, which triggers an eye roll from me.

"I'm going to the room."

"Nico's here?" I hear Max ask Maris.

"That's what Theo said. Max, maybe you should go to the room with him. I'll fill you in when I know more."

I hear Max agree and then the wheels of his spinner suitcase are gaining ground behind me. As I'm waiting for the elevator, he catches up.

"So, Nico rode here on Dame's tour bus?"

"Phil left a message saying so," I reply, watching the numbers light up above the elevator doors.

"Do you think that means he's, like, joining their band now?"

I look at Max. "I don't know anything more than you do."

He looks uncomfortable and shifts his weight from one foot to another.

"Do you *think* Nico's joining their band? I mean, he's your best friend, you know him better than any of us."

I want to bite Max's head off, but I can see how upset he is. Join the fucking club. "I honestly don't know. I need more sleep before I can play tonight. That's all I know for sure."

"Nico went to the Emergency Room last night. He thinks he broke something in his hand. Maris said his knuckle looked like there was a marble under the skin and his pinky finger was swollen."

I close my eyes and exhale loudly. "Fuck. I heard a crack," I say. "I thought it was my cheekbone. I'm still not ruling it out. So, can he play?"

The elevator arrives and Max and I board with a couple other musicians. He waits until we're alone to reply. "Maris doesn't know anything that happened after Nico went to the ER. She stayed at the hotel and had to leave this morning without having heard from him. She didn't know if she should take his stuff or leave it there ... he didn't let her know what was happening."

"How considerate."

The sun is blazing into our room, so I close the blackout curtain and call dibs on the shower. The water hurts my face. I should go see Nico before I lie down, but I don't have the proper mindset. I'd start another fight. That selfish asshole is proving me right, so I'll let him keep making my point for me. Poor Maris, having to spend all night wondering if he was okay and then having to decide this morning whether to stay behind or get on the bus. I'm relieved and gratified that she chose the bus. And me. And Max. That's very telling.

MARIS

I'M ANXIOUS AS I WATCH Dame Knight's band disembark from the bus. I'm not sure I trust the reporting that Nico is with them. Why would he be with them? Did he stay with one of them last night instead of coming back to our room?

Finally, Dinah gets off the bus. When she sees me, she beelines in my direction.

"Hey, girl!" she squeals before giving me a big hug that draws attention from the other musicians standing nearby. "Your man is just waking up. He'll be right out, but you can go get him if you want."

"I'll wait here," I say. I have sunglasses on, but I'm sure the evidence of last night's trauma combined with the uncertainty of this morning is visible on my face, regardless of my attempt to physically mask it.

"Girl, whatever is going on between you two, it's gonna be okay. Like you said, you guys are fate, right?"

Is Dinah gloating? Did Nico tell her that there was trouble between us?

"What do you mean?"

Dinah makes a sad face. "Girl, if you need an ear, Dinah's here, okay?"

"I thought you guys were going to be staying at better hotels from now on," I say.

She rolls her eyes and shakes her head. "One step at a time, I guess." She gestures towards their coach. "You saw the king rooms. I guess they're not so bad. More bed than one girl needs, you know?" Dinah cackles as if there's a joke in there somewhere.

I fake smile, but it turns real when I see Nico walking down the bus steps. He's wearing the same clothes he was last night with a brace that starts below his wrist and includes his hand and last two fingers. "See you later," I tell Dinah.

I move through the musicians who are still loitering outside the hotel entrance and approach Nico with trepidation. "Nico?"

My worries melt away when he sees my face and grabs me into a huge hug. "Maris, I can explain everything, I swear."

"Mate, take this to your room and fiddle with it," Nicky is handing Nico a soft guitar case. "Tape four and five together, mate. Lots of ice. Don't be a pussy."

Nico chuckles, "Thanks, Nicky."

"Hello Maris," Nicky says in a way that makes the greeting sound suggestive. He makes me laugh for the first time in the last twelve hours.

"I have our room key—" I wonder if I'm being presumptuous. "Unless you're staying with them."

"What? Staying with ... them?" Nico gestures to Dame's bus.

"I don't know ... anything," I whisper.

Nico kisses the top of my head. "Let's go to the room."

Instead of Nico taking most of the gear, we divide it evenly. I can see he's having trouble using his left hand as his primary. I'm simultaneously thrilled to see him here, and more worried than ever about whether he can play. I think about the performance he gave last night and can't imagine he's in any condition to do it again tonight.

Once we close the hotel door behind us, I find myself unsure. There is so much to say. Too much. First, the basics.

"Do you want to jump in the shower?"

"In a minute," Nico says with a soft smile. He takes the page from my music journal out of his left front jeans pocket and sits on the edge of the bed. "I can't imagine how upset you were this morning and how much of a shit you must think I am ..." Nico takes a deep breath and unloads, "I was in the ER until nine, my phone died, I don't know your number, the cab driver wouldn't make a call for me while he was driving, not that you can call what he was doing driving, the bus was pulling away as I got back to the hotel, and then Phil was there to greet me ... I couldn't talk freely in front of him, then he insisted I get on

Dame's coach rather than driving myself which, in retrospect was good because I slept the whole way and I'm still tired ..."

I walk between his legs and very gently intertwine my fingers in his hair, tilting his head upwards. My mouth on his calms us both. I'm so relieved that his actions weren't motivated by the desire to distance himself from me. Nico starts doing lip presses and I giggle without removing myself.

"I was so worried," I mumble into his mouth.

"I'm sorry. I anticipated a long night at the ER, but I did not anticipate being there all night. Oh, 239-872-2922."

I chuckle again. "534-423 ..."

"See? Our generation is fucked because we rely on technology."

I lightly touch his right arm. "How bad is it?"

"Not as bad as it could be," he says in his dad voice. "Nicky loaned me a guitar so I could get taped up before we leave for the show. That way I can test it and adjust if necessary."

"Have you tried playing yet?"

Nico rests his forehead against my lips. "No, not yet. I'm afraid to. What if I can't play at a high level?"

I take a deep breath. "Well, I'm sure Phil can get another band to take our place."

Nico shakes his head. "I can't do that to you guys. I can't be the reason we all have to go home."

I wrap my arms around his head. I have so many questions and I want to talk about last night, but I know this isn't the time.

"How about that shower?" I ask.

"Sounds good."

Nico's phone alerts and we see a text from Phil. "*Greenlight?*"

Nico growls. "This guy. I got off the bus five minutes ago. But I'm as curious as he is, so could you, please?" He gestures to the guitar case.

I unzip the case and take the guitar out. Nico lets it rest across his lap and removes the brace. He starts playing Purple Rain, but the guitar is slightly out of tune, so it sounds bad.

"That's not me," he says quickly as I laugh.

He plays *Coming Around* and then places his right hand across his stomach and covers it with his left. "It's an hour. I can do anything for an hour. Please text Phil that we're going on at five, as usual."

"Are you sure?" I ask. "Maybe we can get the bands before and after us to do an extra thirty minutes to give you a day, at least."

"Nah. There are people looking forward to seeing us. I'm going to give you a lot of my solos, though."

"No problem. Max and I will both step up."

"Thank you. I hope I don't embarrass myself or you guys, but I want to play."

I text Phil and he replies that he'll let Theo know.

"Have you spoken to Theo?" Nico asks.

"No. He sat in the front of the bus this morning. He looks terrible, Nico. He was the one who told me you were on Dame's coach, but that's all we said. I spoke with Max. He was worried, but he's going to be really happy to see you."

"Let's get through tonight and have a band beating tomorrow."

I flinch. "I don't think we should call it that anymore."

Nico makes a face. "Too on the nose, perhaps." He looks into my eyes. "How bad is he?"

"Max was worried that Theo might have had a concussion."

Nico closes his eyes and lets his chin fall towards his chest.

"But they stayed awake, and Theo didn't vomit at all."

"Not even the tequila? Because I fed him three shots, which was unwise, considering he drank most of the beer as well."

I shake my head. "He didn't vomit, but he looks like a truck ran over his face."

Nico hands the guitar to me and I lean it against the wall and follow him to the bathroom.

"First things first," I say. "We can sleep a little before it's time to get ready for the show. I'll order food delivery to the room. What do you want to do about transportation to the gig?"

Nico looks at me like I've asked a ridiculous question and says, "Same as usual."

"You and Theo riding in the same van, usual?"

Nico shrugs. "Yeah."

I don't think Theo is going to feel the same way, but I'm not going to say it.

Nico turns on the shower, and I help him pull his shirt over his head. "Thank you for coming back," I say.

"Maris, I never left."

THEO

MARIS TEXTED TO SEE IF I wanted her to come to my room with her make-up bag before the show, but I declined. She suggested team jerseys for stage attire. We discovered we all had them one day at the gym when we coordinated by accident. I think she wants us to remember how "in tune" we professed to be with one another at the time. I agreed to the attire. Not because I'm feeling in sync with my bandmates, but because mine is clean.

Max is full of energy and positivity as we get ready to go down to the van. He's driving me nuts. I'm wearing a Miami Heat jersey and he's repping the Marlins. He suggests taking a selfie for our Miami home slices. I stare at him, waiting for him to think that through. When he doesn't get it, I point to the left side of my face.

I don't want to see Nico, but I'm curious to witness his interaction with Maris. I couldn't believe she got into an Uber with him last night after watching him deck me. I didn't think Maris would condone violence. After what he pulled this morning, I bet she's seeing Nico a little differently tonight. Maybe that's why she wanted to come to our room. Maybe she was trying to get away from him.

The elevator doors open, and I see the back of a University of Miami football jersey, number 87, with Van Asten across the top. The last time I felt this much emotion was the day my mom died. The realization catches me by surprise, and it makes me angry to think that Nico can take me to the worst emotional headspace I've ever been in. Maris is next to him, wearing a Florida State Seminoles football jersey. It's a half shirt and she paired it with white denim shorts and Converse. As if she feels me behind her, she turns. I read her lips. *Here they come.*

Nico turns around and I see that his fingers are taped. He looks great compared to me.

He meets my eyes with a steady gaze and nods as Max and I get close to them.

"Hey, Nico," Max says.

"Ready to hit?" Nico asks him.

"Let's funkin' go," Max replies.

It's all too rosy for me. We're just going to let him walk back into the band like nothing happened?

Nico, Maris, and Max walk ahead towards the van as I follow closely behind. Maris is carrying a soft guitar case. Nico must have borrowed an axe to test his right hand. Maris and Nico take the back bench, and Max and I ride in front of them. Maris and Max are attempting small talk, but the tension is thick. At least I feel it, and I'm sure everyone else does, too.

When we get to the venue, we head to the backstage holding area where Nico and Maris pick up their guitars and I grab my snare. Max shows up with four bottles of water and hands them out. Everyone else is talking to one another, while I isolate myself. I don't know if I'm angrier at Nico, or Maris and Max for seemingly forgiving him so easily. But I guess he hurt me the most.

I try to reason with myself. If he wasn't here, I'd be far more pissed. I want to continue the tour, and Nico obviously feels the same. We still want the same thing. That thought makes me smirk. We really, really want the same thing. I decide that I'm more relieved that he's here after everything that happened than I am pissed off that he dared to show up after everything that happened.

I walk over to where he's standing, watching the stage monitor.

"Can you play?" I ask.

"I think so. Can you?"

"I think so."

We stand next to each other in silence. I'm waiting for an apology. Maybe he is too.

"Can we talk in the morning?" He asks, looking straight ahead.

"Yep," I say.

Nico walks away. *How fucking dare he walk away from me?* I hope Maris is watching and sees that I'm the bigger man. The one that approached him first.

I recognize the final song of the band ahead of us. As the stage crew resets, Maris comes over to where I'm standing. Her bass is slung behind her back. "Well, this is a test, huh?" she says.

I raise my eyebrows and tilt my head. "I'm going to do the same thing I do every night. Nothing different."

Maris takes a deep breath. "Everything's different. Offstage. But if we can be us for the next hour, on stage, that will give me hope."

"We're performers, Maris. This is what we do."

Our introduction video is playing, and the crowd is getting excited. Nico and Max stand behind Maris and me, and when we're announced, we go running onto the stage amid welcoming cheers.

"Charlotte! What's good?" Maris yells into her mic.

I count us into *Coming Around* and Nico starts the song. I look to the wings and see Phil standing there with Nicky Knight. I wonder if they came to see Funkengroovin, Nico, or whether we'll make it through the set. I'm curious myself, so I can't blame them.

Apart from a hellacious headache, I feel okay. I'm wearing ear plugs to try to blunt the pain of crashing cymbals and heavy thuds. It helps some. It's only an hour, and then I can go back to the hotel and get a solid night of sleep. But then I have to face Nico in the morning. I try to push that from my mind and stay in the moment.

I notice that Nico is divvying up his solos between Maris and Max. He takes a few and the audience thinks they're great, but it's not Nico at his best. Not Last Night Nico. No one else would notice, but I've played with him long enough. I watch Phil and Nicky as they listen in the wings. I see Nicky talking to Phil and making guitar playing gestures. He must be explaining the technical aspect of how Nico's compensating.

I keep the beat going and add some fills that I don't normally do. I'm not sure if I do it to bolster the band, take up the slack, or to drag Nico. All of us come to play, and the audience gets the best show when we each give one hundred percent.

I try to gauge how the show is going. The audience is totally into it and I'm not hearing any musical trainwrecks. We're lacking the spark that we usually have, but can anyone tell other than us?

It's time for Silver Springs and Kenny brings Nico's acoustic guitar on stage. Max starts the songs and I come in after Maris begins singing. The song is stripped down, and this is where Nico's playing really shines. Usually. He's covering the song, but he's sticking to the meat of the tune. No flourishes, no triples. I'm realizing that he doesn't have the dexterity he's used to in his right hand. He's still bending the notes beautifully, and even though his playing is simpler, it's still good. But it's not breathtaking. It's not Nico.

I watch him, smiling at Maris and singing his background vocals like nothing is wrong. I'm sore, but at least I can play at the level I'm used to. This is the first song that I've noticed a distinct change in his playing. Maybe because it's more stripped down, maybe the acoustic is harder to play, or maybe his hand is just killing him as the set goes on.

Only two more songs. Nico goes back to electric guitar and keeps his playing simple. He gives Maris two solos in the last song, and she puts on a master class in double time electric bass. The audience loves it, and we end the night to the same frenzied appreciation we've enjoyed every other night of the tour.

Maris says our goodnight and we run to the wings.

Nico goes straight to Nicky, and Phil cuts me off before I can juke him. "Is Nico going to be okay to continue?"

"You just heard the whole show, Phil," I say.

"He's playing differently, no?" Phil asks.

"Great musicians don't play the same shit every night, Phil. It's boring. And there are three other killer musicians in Funkengroovin', in case you haven't noticed."

"It was a good show, Theo, I'm just asking you, from the band leader's perspective, if Nico's going to ... be able to continue."

"Take care of the business, Phil. Leave the music to us."

I find Kenny and drop off my snare. Max and Maris are talking in the holding area, and I join them.

"Another excellent show, guys. Thank you for giving it your best once again," I say.

"He's gonna be upset," Max says to no one in particular.

"I won't let him be," Maris promises.

Nico walks down the stairs from the wings and sees us together. Nicky is with him and goes off in another direction after slapping Nico on the back. When he reaches us, he says, "Sorry, guys. Lotta pain."

"Dude, what are you talking about?" Max asks.

"Max. Don't," Nico says. "I'll sleep with my hand in an ice bucket and wear the brace every minute I'm not on stage, but if that's the best I can do …" Nico doesn't finish.

"I'll have the video production team send you the set," I say while texting. "It's impossible to evaluate your performance while you're performing. You know how it feels, but that's not always a true indication."

Nico clears his throat and Maris wraps her arm around his waist. "We all need sleep," she says. "Those people had a great fucking time watching us play tonight. We did our duty, men."

"Yeah, I feel like dog shit," Max says.

Nico and I look at each other, and for one second, we're us again. Unified in our mockery of our beloved, yet blissfully unaware keyboard player who has not been recently knocked out, nor is he nursing a broken bone.

We ride back to the hotel in silence. Exhaustion has claimed all of us.

When we get off the elevator to go to our rooms, Nico says, "Ten, Theo?"

"Ten," I confirm.

MARIS

I THINK OF ANY HOTEL ROOM I share with Nico as home. Closing the door behind us seals us off from Theo and Max, the tour, and every single facet of life that isn't Nico and me.

"Join me in the shower?" I ask as Nico removes his brace. I see pain on his face and sift through my toiletry bag to find Advil.

"I'll never turn that offer down," he says softly.

I start the shower and find a soft, romantic playlist. The stark bathroom lighting has two levels of brightness, on, or off, so I select off and turn the hall light on to provide a cozier atmosphere.

"Let me help you." I unbutton the top of his jeans and unzip them, slipping them over his hips. Nico lifts his jersey with his left hand, and I help him get it over his head.

"I'm stealing this from you, by the way," I say.

"You'd be the only female who has one," he says. "I never let anyone steal my jersey."

"Well, I'm honored." I fold it and set it on the countertop.

Nico uses his left hand to remove my jersey, inspects it, and tosses it into the hall while making a face. "'Noles," he says with disgust.

"Mad because we beat you guys all the time?" I make an upside down "U" with my hands.

"Yes," he admits. "I'll pick that up later, by the way."

"Get naked and get in the shower."

I grab my shampoo and conditioner and a bath towel to cover the bench seat. The hot water did its job and made the room steamy and warm, so I turn off the overhead shower and turn on the handheld spray. "Sit down so I can wash your hair."

Nico looks hesitant, but he perches on the edge of the built-in seat. I stand in front of him as I wet his hair, and his hands explore my body.

"Hold this, please." I hand him the shower wand and start massaging his scalp with my fingertips. As the shampoo lathers, I apply slight pressure, then I focus on his temples and the back of his neck. I can feel him relaxing, so I take my time.

I wash his face and talk him into letting me do an exfoliating scrub, which he hates and rinses off immediately, bringing some humor into our sweet moment. I sit behind him and massage his back and arms as he leans forward and melts.

I'm surprised when he says, "Can we talk about what Theo said last night?"

I put my arms around him. "Okay."

"Can you tell me what he meant when he said you went to him first?"

I feel like I'm going to cry, but I also know that both of us are incredibly vulnerable in this moment and that makes me feel safe. "It was my first full night in the house. I was reeling from finding out that Damon—"

"You didn't call him Dickhead!" Nico turns around to look at me. "That's progress. And I'm sorry we didn't tell you that he was cheating. We should have."

"We didn't know each other, yet. That's why all of this happened." I take a deep breath and continue. "Theo helped me move my stuff out that morning. I was struggling with feelings of rejection and humiliation. I didn't want to be alone. I wanted to feel desired. Theo was the one who first wanted me in the band. He fought for me. I felt like I already has his approval. So, I knocked on his door. I thanked him for the incredible session."

Nico doesn't say anything, so I keep talking.

"I didn't ask to go in, and he didn't invite me in, but my purpose for being there was understood. He told me that he had a terrible time with his recent break-up and said I should ask you how hard he took it. Then he said we should go to sleep."

I let the words hang there, waiting for Nico to respond.

"We had that moment on stage with Backyard Breeder and we bonded over Silver Springs earlier that night. What made you pursue him instead of me?"

I almost laugh. "You're Nico. You're the guy with all the girls. You're unattainable."

Nico exhales and sits up, pressing into me. "So, you were thinking that Theo was someone you could be with long term?"

"Oh, I wasn't thinking. I was reacting. I genuinely wanted to prove to myself that I wasn't repulsive. I saw Theo as a sweet, gentle guy. Maybe I thought he would be easy, or at least easier than you, to entice. But, to me, today is so much more important than that night. And I'm so grateful that fate stepped in and shut that door. Nico, I didn't know you back then. I know you now, and I choose you over everyone else." The tears come now. "The way that Theo said it last night made it sound like you and I are only together because he and I didn't work out. He and I didn't have ... anything. Nothing. Nico, I was with Damon for four years, and I never felt about him the way I feel for you."

"Why didn't you tell me that you and Theo had a moment?"

"I was embarrassed."

"But then you guys went to the beach together, and you hug and jam together ..."

"I cleared things up with Theo. My feelings for him are the same as my feelings for Max."

He nods. "Did you want to keep us secret at the beginning to spare his feelings?"

I give the question the consideration it deserves. "Maybe a little, but mostly I knew why you guys were reluctant to hire a chick. I'd never had a relationship with a band member before, but I didn't waste any time making your fears come true. And I didn't know if we were just having a fling. I didn't think you were the kind of guy who was looking for a commitment."

"I wasn't," Nico said assuredly.

"They say that's when you fall in love."

"Maris, I think I fell in love with you that night on stage with BB. I've never been so drawn to a woman like I was to you. I wish it had started the same way for you, but I don't mind that it didn't. Even if your reasons for choosing Theo over me that first night were ridiculous."

I press myself against Nico's back and wrap my arms around him. "I didn't think this was possible with you. Or anyone."

"But then you confided in Theo rather than me when Dinah was trying to find out if our band was solid."

There are no explanations that flatter me, so I tell the ugly truth. "I was stupid and impulsive. I texted the group chat and Theo was the only one who replied. I was very upset at the thought of Dame trying to steal you away, but, at the same time, I wondered if we had any right to try to influence your decision. Part of my worried that if I told you, you'd be excited about the possibility and pursue it. I wanted someone else to help me think it through and to help decode what Dinah said and didn't say because I wasn't sure if I was being paranoid."

"Maris," Nico says softly. I brace myself to hear a response that will end our relationship and break my heart. "Everything I have is pickled. Can we be finished with the shower now?"

"Are we okay?"

"I'll work on not punching people and you work on impulsivity. Unless it's with me. I want all your impulses."

I kiss Nico's shoulder. "Deal."

NICO

As I get ready to meet with Theo, Maris floats the same idea she mentioned earlier this morning.

"Are you sure it wouldn't be easier for the two of you if I was there to mediate?"

I take both of her hands in mine and grin at her. "My dear Maris," I start. "I truly appreciate your offer, but Theo and I have to resolve this alone. It's a man thing, okay, babe?"

Her mouth forms into a frown. "Okay, well, Max and I are going to grab some breakfast. Come find us in the restaurant when you guys are finished."

"If the gunshot wounds are pluggable." I laugh at Maris's angry expression. "Stop worrying, everything will be fine. We'll both come to the restaurant after we talk."

Maris opens the door to our room and walks down to knock on Max and Theo's. Max must have been waiting for her with his hand on the door handle, judging by how fast he opened it.

"Morning, guys," he says nervously. "Theo says you can go on in, Nico."

"Thanks, buddy."

Maris presses her palm to my chest as she departs.

When I walk into the room, Theo has the beds made, the room straightened up, and the curtain open. I like this side of him. He wants to make a hotel room meeting between friends and bandmates as professional as possible. He's sitting in the desk chair facing the door.

"Hey, man." I sit on the bed across from him, knowing that's what he expected. There's a little bit of a dominance thing going on, but I don't mind playing my role.

"What do you want to discuss first, the personal conflict or the band?" He asks.

I don't like his tone. He's trying to come off as though he has authority over me, and that's not going to be productive.

"Theo, we've been friends, roommates, partners in the band—"

"It's my band. Always has been. I bought the gear, booked the gigs, hired the musicians ..."

I'm mindful of keeping my expression friendly. "Okay. Let's deal with the personal stuff because if we can't fix that, there's no need to keep talking."

Theo's face changes. "Is that a threat?"

I shake my head. "What the fuck, Theo? Can we just talk? Just fucking talk to me."

"The last time I tried to talk to you, you smashed my face in, so ..."

"Do you remember what you were saying and how you were behaving? I'm not trying to justify hitting you. That was a Neanderthal move and I'm embarrassed and ashamed. I'm sorry, Theo."

"I told you the truth, Nico. That's how we got here."

I close my eyes tightly and shake my head. "Theo, your version of the truth dismisses everything that's happened between Maris and me over the last several months. She and I talked all of this through last night, so I know everything. I know about the night she knocked on your door. I know why she went down to the beach to talk to you after she was with Dinah."

Theo sets his mouth before saying, "So, did you punch her in the mouth or just me?"

"Are we going to put some effort into this conversation, or is it going to be a spat?" Theo's angry. He's still as angry as he was the other night. I thought a lot of his rage was fueled by alcohol, but I misjudged the situation. I shrug. "Well?"

"Phil got the offer from Revolution Records yesterday. It has a forty-eight-hour expiration clause, and we're already twenty-six hours into it. There's a whole section about you writing and recording with Dame Knight and then touring with them to promote the record."

"I thought we were starting with the personal stuff."

Theo rolls his eyes, "We can't separate the personal from the professional, Nico. It's five years too late for that. I've seen you toss people aside before, and I want to know if that's what you're going to do to us."

"Who did I toss aside?"

Theo searches the ceiling for names. "Bartender Barbie. For one."

I bust out laughing. "Do you think Bartender Barbie wanted an engagement ring because I assure you, she didn't."

"Maybe she didn't, but every other girl who thought they were hooking up with a wholesome boy from Wisconsin was probably pretty disappointed."

"What the fuck does my past sex life have to do with you and I?" I'm raising my voice now, so I take a deep breath to try to keep my promise to Maris not to punch people anymore. Besides, my left hook isn't as vicious as my right, and I need my left hand to play.

"We're in a situation now where I need to be able to count on you, and I don't know if I can. When a prettier girl comes along, you ditch the one you have. When a more successful band comes along, will you do the same thing?"

I feel my eyebrows rising towards my hairline. "Those two things aren't the same, Theo. I've never given you anything to worry about professionally. I've been offered other band jobs in Miami since we formed Funkengroovin'. I assume you've been approached by other guitar players who want to get in line in case you want to make a change. We trust each other. Or we always have. What's different now? We're finally getting what we've been working toward."

Theo bites his lower lip, and his cheeks redden. "Everything is different since Maris joined the band. We were on the same team before. But since Maris, you weren't even aware that there was a competition, or that I stepped aside. But I didn't step aside so that she could be with *you*."

I choose my words carefully. "If you want to go profess your love to Maris, I'm not going to stop you. I'm not keeping her captive. She's with me because we love each other. She's not some prize that I set out to win."

"You took advantage of her."

"No. Neither Maris nor I would agree with that. But, yes, our relationship happened backwards. We'd been sleeping together quite a while before we started dating. Then we fell in love. It's not traditional, but it's real. And if you can't accept that, or if you resent me over it, we can't continue working together."

"So, that's going to be your excuse for joining Dame Knight?" Theo scoffs.

"I'm not stuck on Dame, my man, you are."

"So, I'm the problem?"

"I'm not leaving Funkengroovin'. Unless I continue to play like I did last night." I hold my braced hand up.

Theo stands up and starts pacing. "Are you and Maris a package deal now? Professionally?"

I shrug my shoulders. "We haven't had that conversation because neither of us is thinking about going anywhere. To be clear, I am worried about my hand. That's the only unknown variable in the equation for me right now."

Theo slumps down onto the bed across from me and lies back. "I noticed that you weren't yourself yesterday, but you weren't horrible. I think we did the wrong thing by not telling the audience that you broke your hand and that you, I don't know, hope they don't mind that you stayed to play for them anyway. Then they can all scream and cheer and it's business as usual ... or as close as possible."

"But then they'll put my hand together with your face," I say.

Theo chuckles. That's how all of this started in the first place."

"Dude, I'm really sorry I hit you."

"I was trying to break up your relationship. I think. I don't know if there was a plan."

My hand aches, so I excuse myself to go fill the ice bucket. When I get back, Theo is playing the video from last night.

"Fast forward to Silver Springs," I tell him.

We watch and wince once or twice. Maybe three times.

"Fuck," I say.

"It really wasn't that bad," Theo says.

"Can you be around Maris and I, Theo? When we talked about this the first time, at home, you said you'd rather have the band than Maris. I choose her over the band. Now I have the perfect excuse to leave the tour. If you can't work with both of us until you ... feel better ... I'll go home for the summer. I'll heal up. Before I go, I'll even get the sub guitar player up to speed."

"But that wouldn't be a soft step into the world of Dame Knight?"

"I have no interest in signing the Revolution deal the way it's written. It's us, or nothing as far as I'm concerned."

"What if it's nothing? What about Max and Maris? Is it fair to make that decision for them?"

"We can always ask for their opinions," I say moving my hand around the ice bucket. "But Revolution isn't the only record label in the world."

"Once word gets around that they offered, I wonder if that helps us or hurts us?"

"That's a question for Phil. But I like your idea about being honest with the audience," I tell him. "Part of what I'm struggling with is people posting video of me playing shitty, and having the internet decide that I'm a studio creation. Maybe we should even have Phil do a press release."

Theo nods. "Should we say something about my face?" He turns to show me the purple and yellow splotches.

"Dude, I got ya good." I pull a handful of ice from my bucket and offer it to Theo who starts laughing.

"Do you think we'll have to do an interview about this when we're seventy and someone makes a documentary about Funkengroovin'?"

"I hope so, my guy. I just have to come up with a better reason for knocking your ass out."

"You had a pretty good reason. Not good enough, but when you factor in the tequila—"

"I was so worried they'd give me a sobriety test at the hospital. I didn't drive myself there, but I was paranoid that they'd find out I was drunk. And then I was sure a cop was going to come arrest me. I made sure the admission nurse kept my information private. I was sure there was a BOLO for me."

Theo's laughing. "I came to with a mouthful of sand and Max was stroking my hair," He laughs harder. "My first thought was I must be super drunk if I took a dive after getting hit by that skinny motherfuck-er. Man, my head did a full rotation. I'm pretty sure I have whiplash."

"I hit you really hard," I admit. "When you stepped between me and Maris, like you were going to rescue her from me … I didn't even know my fist was flying until I felt my hand break."

"I heard it!" Theo yells. "I heard it crack. I thought it was my cheekbone."

"Shit. Dude, this is a lifetime low, for me."

Theo sits up, but he does so too fast, so he grabs his head to steady it. "It's gonna make a great documentary though. We've only been on tour for a couple weeks and we already have our first rock-n-roll story."

I start laughing. "Let's go have some breakfast and get on the bus."

"What about Phil?" Theo asks.

"Fuck Phil," I say. "But he took pretty good care of me yesterday, so maybe not fuck Phil."

Theo's phone goes off. "Speak of the devil."

"I want to get through the gig before we have to deal with Phil. How do you feel about telling him we'll meet with him after the show tonight?"

"Good."

Theo sends the text.

We stand up and look at each other awkwardly. I open my arms wide, and Theo pretends to duck before he gives me a hug.

"I'm sorry that me being with Maris …"

"It's not your fault."

The door opens and Max and Maris find us hugging in the middle of the room.

"I told you before," Max says. "You aren't Nico's soulmate, Theo is."

"We got to-go breakfasts for you guys. The bus leaves in ten minutes, we gotta go," Maris calls through the door on the way to our room.

I look at the ice bucket and Theo reads my mind. "Take it. You need it."

"Max, leave a note and twenty, please," I say on my way out. "See you losers on the bus."

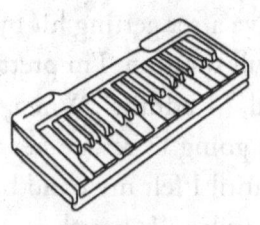

MAX

I'M GLAD THAT THEO AND NICO seem to be on good terms again, but their relationship is so weird to me. They fight, like physically fight, and then act like nothing happened. I mean, it's almost like fighting bonds them more tightly together through the alchemy of testosterone and … more testosterone.

We had a five-hour drive from Charlotte to Knoxville, Tennessee. There are a few dates on the tour with a later show time, and Knoxville was our first. Our hit time was nine 'o clock, but we didn't have enough time before the gig to see anything. I thought we'd have more time on tour to see the locations we're traveling to. We won't be here for twenty-four hours, so I'm not even counting it as a place I've visited.

The fairgrounds in Knoxville were the site of a World's Fair and it's the coolest venue we've played so far. It feels like a very big deal. I wish we could do a couple nights in this spot. The backstage areas are convention centers with air conditioning, real bathrooms, proper seating, and Wi-Fi. I could live here.

Going on after sunset means we might not sweat our asses off on stage. Maris thought we should nod at Tennessee with our stage attire, so she suggested we wear jeans with anything western we might have. She has a cool suede vest with fringe, but the rest of us couldn't make the theme work, so we bought matching Knoxville T-Shirts from a kiosk, and we got Mare a matching tank top. I wouldn't tell anyone, but this is my favorite look yet. I might suggest buying matching shirts in each city for the rest of the tour. Or maybe I should look into getting Funkengroovin' T-shirts for the band as a surprise. I like when we match.

Even waiting to go on is awesome here. The bandstand is permanent, and the wings are furnished. Theo is warming up on his drum pad and Nico is trying to decide if he has enough dexterity in his wrist with the brace on to wear it on stage. He said taping his fingers together last night didn't stabilize the injured part of his hand enough and, by the end of the set, it was throbbing and swollen. Maris is noodling on her bass and I'm taking some cool black and white photos to prove to my future grandchildren that this really happened.

"Five minutes!" Kenny gives us the cue, and we walk to the side of the stage.

"Everyone cool on the plan?" Theo asks.

I nod, not that I have a major part to play. Our intro reel rolls and Theo, Maris, and I run on stage when Funkengroovin' is announced. Maris runs to her mic and yells, "What's good, Knoxville!" Instead of counting us into the first song, Theo says, "Are you going to tell them Maris, or should I?"

"I can't disappoint them," she says dramatically. "Max, can you help me out?"

"I can't do it," I say. "Theo, you have to tell them."

"Knoxville, we're really sorry to have to tell you that Nico can't be with us tonight."

Genuine gasps and *awwws* echo through the crowd.

"He injured his right hand yesterday and—"

Nico comes running out from the wings and the audience starts shrieking with excitement. He goes to his mic. "What's good, Knoxville?" They scream like he's Harry Styles. "It's true that I'm not one hundred percent." Nico holds up his braced hand. "But I'm going to try my best to play for you anyway. Is that okay?"

The place goes nuts, and Theo starts counting us into the first song. The vibe on stage is far better than last night and we're interacting as band the way we usually do. It feels good. But it's undeniable that Nico is covering the basic guitar parts while adding nothing more. He solos a few times, but it's flashy stuff, not technically impressive. The audience doesn't know the difference, and they react with love and appreciation. I feel sorry for him. He's better than this. His vocals are fantastic though, and if that's all he contributes to the night, it's more than enough.

Silver Springs is better than last night because he tries to do less. We hype up the "encore" and leave the stage on a genuine high. It seems like we're over the hurdle. Like everything's gonna be okay. The audience doesn't mind Nico being a little limited. Maris and I get more featured playing time. Nico seems to be taking the humbling side effect of his outburst well enough. What a difference a day makes.

THEO

WE'RE WAITING FOR PHIL IN a conference room at the hotel after bribing our van driver to take us through DQ for old times' sake. Max is devouring his second burger, Maris is savoring her brownie sundae, and I downed two large fries with half of a large Blizzard. Nico said he didn't want one but then jacked half of mine … for old times' sake.

One of the contract attorneys in my dad's legal department is on my iPad, watching the whole spectacle. The four of us are sitting in a row on one side of the rectangular table like a junk food filled tribunal.

"I can't tell you how appreciative we are that you're up in the middle of the night to take this meeting with us, Mr. Demetriou," I tell him.

"Call me Alex, please. And I'm happy to be of help. Your father has done a lot for me and my family over the years."

"Do you have any advice for us, Alex?" Nico asks.

The tan, dark-haired man in a three-piece suit flashes a white smile. "Say very little. I'll do the talking. And if I touch my glasses, stop speaking immediately."

"Just to recap, we'll sign if they ditch the addendum regarding Nico working with Dame," I reiterate.

"Understood."

There's a knock on the door and Phil opens it and pokes his head in. "This is the place," he confirms. "I went to Red Oak Boardroom A, B, and finally found an unlocked door."

"Sorry you had trouble finding us," I say standing up and holding my hand out for formal handshake.

Phil seems taken back but shakes my hand. "Last time I saw you, I believe you told me to fuck off," he says with a laugh.

"Did I? I had a little bit of brain damage then, but I'm better now." I turn my iPad so that Phil can see the screen. "Phil, this is Alex Demetriou, he's our legal representation."

"Alex," Phil nods and takes a seat on the empty side of the table. "I didn't realize you guys had an entertainment attorney, but it's always good to have a lawyer on the team. So, is everyone up to speed on the offer?" Phil asks. "It's boiler plate because Revolution doesn't have to offer any special incentives. They have artists beating their door down, so we're in a unique position having them come to us. Frankly, if I didn't have the long-standing relationship I have with Luis, this wouldn't be possible."

"I take your point, Phil. The issue, as I'm sure you're aware, is that our clients flatly reject the addendum in its entirety. We're ready to execute the agreement, with minimal revisions, without the addendum." Alex says.

I inhale and hold my breath. Phil is supposed to be on our side, he's our manager, but I know he wants to remain in Luis's favor and delivering this deal to him would keep him there.

"Here's the thing Alex, Theo ... everyone," Phil sweeps his hand towards our side of the table. "Luis is invested in keeping Dame on the road. If they make another record and follow it up with a *good-bye* tour, their loyal fan base virtually guarantees they'll out earn every band on Revolution one last time." Phil puts his elbows on the table and leans forward. "This offer has very little do with you guys. Don't get me wrong, they like you. They admire the platform you've built and the attention you're getting. Stevie Nicks ... come on. But you guys won't earn Dame numbers for five years or more."

"Revolution can entice Dame to write and record new music without crossing purposes with our clients," Alex says.

"Dinah and Nicky have reached the precipice multiple times," Phil says. "They don't want to tread the same ground again and they claim to be tapped out creatively. Nicky loves Nico. He thinks he's a more deserving version of his younger self." Phil focuses on Nico. "Having you around takes him back to when all of this was new and thrilling. Dinah thinks you're an adorable puppy and she wants to play with you."

"Fuuuuuck that," Nico says.

"So, they're using you. You're … what? A muse?" Phil shrugs. "Who cares? Make the record, do the tour, and then launch your band straight into the stratosphere, instead of struggling to break through. You're young enough. You have time."

"Our clients understand the proposal, Phil," Alex says. "They reject that part of the offer."

"There are no parts to the offer. It's take it or leave it," Phil says without emotion.

"It's a half-step above extortion and you know it, Phil." Alex's delivery is calm, but stern. "There aren't even timelines attached to the commitment they want from Nico. It unilaterally favors Dame and Revolution. This isn't a serious offer, and I can't, in good faith, advise my clients to take it. You shouldn't either."

I didn't picture us walking out of this room as a Revolution Records artist, but now that I know it isn't happening, I'm a little disappointed. But grateful at the same time. I've heard that a bad deal is far worse than not having a deal at all. Honestly, being on this tour is an incredible opportunity and we if finish the festival dates and go home to Miami, we can capitalize on this experience and use it to keep climbing.

"I'm sorry to hear that you're so shortsighted, Alex. And you obviously don't understand how the music business works. One hand washes the other."

"I want to talk to the band members privately," Alex says.

Phil presses his lips together and stares at me without blinking.

"Can you give us a few minutes?" I ask. "I'll text when we're ready for you to come back in."

Phil pushes back from the table. "I'll be in the lobby."

"He's gone," I tell Alex when the door closes behind him.

"At this point, I think you guys have two options. One is full rejection of the offer, which ends negotiations between the parties, or we could counter. I reached out to colleagues who've been across the table from Revolution, and I'm told it is very rare for the label to negotiate terms, but we really don't have anything to lose." Alex sits back in his leather wingback chair. "What do you guys think?"

Nico speaks up first. "Phil just said that one hand washes the other in the music business. We're giving more than we're getting, but Luis believes that we can respark Dame's rise to the top of the charts. If he didn't, we wouldn't have this quid-pro-quo deal. I think we have more agency than Phil realizes."

"What do you guys want and what are you willing to give in return?" Alex asks.

"I don't want us to split up," I turn to Nico, "and I don't want to loan you to Dame."

"I still agree." He smirks at me. "Haven't changed my mind since this morning."

"Okay, so that's off the table." Alex moves onward. "How do you guys feel about collaborating with them on a writing project?"

I shrug and wait for someone else to offer an opinion.

"When Luis first floated the idea of having Nico work with Dame, it was pitched as a soft launch for Funkengroovin'," Maris begins, "The selling point was that our affiliation with Dame would raise our profile. Since then, we've learned that Nicky and Dinah are blocked creatively and worried that a new project might sound like recycled hits. So, they want to inject some new blood with a cross-over. But, what if the cross-over goes the other direction and we make them follow through on the original pitch?"

I tilt my head and narrow my eyes. "What do you mean?"

"What if, instead of Nico touring with Dame, Nicky starts playing with us now? He could fill in for Nico on guitar until his hand heals. Nico could sing and front the band to make room for Nicky. We could work up some new tunes with Nick, maybe write a couple for Dinah to sing. The sticking point may be that Nicky would have to work more. I don't know if he has two shows a day in the tank," Maris says.

"It wouldn't have to be two shows," Alex says. "We're restructuring, so we could restructure a max set. If Funkengroovin' and Dame are on the same label and the festival is getting two hours from each of you, overlap shouldn't be an issue for the festival organizers. In fact, it could be a draw. Theo sent me the festival contract before you guys signed it, so I can take another look to make sure nothing precludes the change."

I lean forward to look down the table at Nico. "This is close to the idea you had of combining the bands—"

"But Maris's take is actually workable," Nico jokes.

I think out loud. "So, our start time gets pushed, we open for Dame, they come out with time left in our set, we play the tunes we write together, and then we leave to let them finish their show."

"Would we write with them during the day then?" Max asks. "I guess we'd have more time since we're going on later."

"You should see their bus." Nico says. "They have the gear to write and make rough recordings on the road."

"Alex, what do you think?" I ask.

"What you think is more important." He says. "Are you comfortable with countering and would you be happy if they accept our offer?"

I bite the inside of my cheek while I read the faces in the room. "I'd be psyched to be on Revolution, and it would be cool to write with Nicky and Dinah and overlap our sets. That's definitely a win for us and I think it gives Luis what he wants immediately, rather than a promise for the future."

"And we test the new songs in the wild, which saves time and money in the studio," Max adds.

"Who agrees?" Alex asks.

"I like it," Nico says.

"I'm in favor," Maris says.

Max grins. "Yeah, man."

"Should I get Phil back in here?"

Alex nods on the screen as he scans something on another device.

When Phil comes back into the room, he seems surprised. "You guys are a lot giddier than you were when I left. I assume that means we're signing a record deal tonight."

I sit taller in my chair. "We're closer, but I'll let Alex explain."

After Alex outlines the contingencies included in our counter, Phil laughs. "No one counters an offer from Revolution. They won't even read it. It's insulting and it's a waste of time." Phill looks at his watch. "The offer dies in a little over eight hours anyway. That's hardly enough time to draft a counter proposal."

"That's not true," Alex says. "I've put deals together from scratch that have a lot more moving parts than this, with much larger numbers, in far less time."

"It's not going to work," Phil says.

"So, we have nothing to lose," I say.

PHIL

I KNEW REVOLUTION WOULDN'T ENTERTAIN A counteroffer. What I didn't expect was a vindictive response form Luis. I'm surprised and raging over his retaliation against talented, but green musicians for making a bad business decision. Luis is a powerful man, but he's proving to be unnecessarily malicious, which makes him look petty. He won't pick up the phone, so I leave another message.

"Luis, you've been doing this too long to take a business decision personally, and what you've done is, frankly, beneath you. The optics are not good. It looks like Revolution Records has a ruthless vendetta against these kids. Believe me, missing the opportunity to be on Revolution hurts them enough. Call me back or my next call is to Rolling Fucking Stone."

I end the call and imagine myself turning green and growing out of my suit. My therapist told me to count to ten, so I start the exercise. As I begin the fourth round, my phone rings and I see Luis's face on my screen. My rage comes back full force. "Does punching down make you proud of yourself?"

"I have no idea what you're talking about, Phil. Why are you calling my phone like a schoolgirl with a crush?"

"You know exactly why, Luis. This is a spectacularly shitty thing to do to these kids."

"What kids? Your four-piece bar band from Miami?"

"You've taught them a lesson by rejecting their counter. Leave it at that."

"They wasted my time."

"That's bullshit. You're pissed off that they tried to get a fairer deal for themselves. How dare they, right? Getting an offer from Revolution is like being touched by the hand of God, so how dare they?"

"They're unprofessional and ungrateful, and I had a professional obligation to inform the festival directors of my impression of them. I might have shared my opinion of them with some other label heads. Out of obligation."

"What sick satisfaction do you get from doing this to them?" I know I'm climbing into the band's coffin with them, but I don't care. "Do you kick your kids' puppy when they aren't looking, too? This is low, Luis."

"I can't hear you, Phil. You should call back, but when you do, you might not get through."

The call ends and I scream in frustration. I check the time and realize the band will be getting on the bus in a half hour, so I text Theo. I need catch them.

NICO

MARIS TRIES TO BURROW DEEPER into my chest, so I know she's starting to wake up. I comb her hair away from her face with my fingers and softly sing the opening lines to Bill Wither's *Lovely Day*. She purrs and I chuckle.

Maris half hums, half sings the background vocals, repeating the phrase *lovely day* over and over again.

"Good morning, lovely," I say softly.

"Mmmm ... it sure is," she says smiling. Maris kisses my chest. "What time is it?"

"The alarm goes off in a few minutes."

"Were you watching me sleep again?" She lifts her head and squints at me.

"You have me pinned down, so what else am I supposed to do?"

Maris wiggles up for a kiss. "Since we have a night off in Norfolk tonight, I found a sushi restaurant near the hotel, so I thought we could sneak away alone. Sound good?"

"Perfect," I say stealing another kiss. And then a series of sweet kisses.

The alarm goes off and Maris moans loudly. She does this every day when her alarm goes off, but I find it amusing. I love learning these little things about her and being able to predict how she will react.

My phone alerts and I reach to the bedstand to retrieve it.

It's a text from Theo that says: *Hallway. Now.*

"You get the first shower," I tell Maris. "Theo needs me for a minute."

I look around for something to put on and opt for the hotel robe hanging in the closet by the door. In the hall, Theo's wearing the same robe and my instinct is to laugh, but his face snuffs out my light mood.

"Our tour contract has been terminated, effective immediately."

I absorb the words, but I want them to mean something else. Or to be followed by more words. Better words.

All I can manage is, "Why?"

"Luis. Phil says he was pissed off that we countered his offer, so he contacted the directors of the festival and got us booted off the tour."

"We've been doing a great job every night." I hold up my hand. "Well, you guys have been."

"It has nothing to do with that," Theo says as he starts pacing. "Phil says that Luis wants to punish us and what's done is done, so … we're done. We're not going to Norfolk."

I lean against the wall and try to think. "Is there anyone Phil can reach out to?"

Theo shakes his head. "He told me that he's sorry, but Luis has the juice to influence these decisions. He said that he tried to explain what went wrong between us and Revolution, but the festival wants to keep Luis happy so that he doesn't pull Dame."

"Fuck. I feel like this is my fault. I let you guys down by not agreeing to the deal with Dame."

"Nico, I didn't want you to do it either. We came to this decision as a group. If anything, it's my fault for not getting us an entertainment attorney and taking advice from my dad's team."

I stop Theo as he paces by. "Dude, no. You got us this far. We owe you everything. We all agreed with Alex that the offer was garbage."

"I didn't tell Max. He's getting ready for the bus."

"Okay. Maris is in the shower. Should we both go tell Max now and then we can tell Maris?"

"No need," Max says pulling the door open to his room. "I heard."

"Fucking hell, Max, you're still eavesdropping?" I stop myself from breaking into a lecture when I see his chin quivering. "Aw, dude. This really sucks, but we're going to get through it together."

"We didn't even last a month!" Max squeaks.

I look at Theo and he's on the verge of laughing, like I am.

"We didn't, did we?" Theo says. "Fuck, that looks so bad."

I clear my throat, trying not to laugh at the situation we're in. "How are we supposed to get home?"

Theo makes a face that indicates he has no idea.

"You guys, this isn't funny," Max says sullenly.

"No, it isn't, but we have to keep our sense of humor. And we have to figure out what we're going to do next," Theo says.

"Does Mare know?" Max asks.

"Not yet," I say.

"She's gonna cry. I hate it when she cries," Max says.

"I'll tell her, Max. I'll make sure she's okay. How about we call downstairs for a late checkout and meet for breakfast after the bus leaves?"

"We can get a game plan together at breakfast," Theo agrees. "I guess I'll start checking flights back to Miami."

"Who's taking our place?" Max asks.

"Don't know, don't care," Theo says. "I hope all the Funkengroovin' fans boo them for the whole set every fucking night."

I open the door to my room, "See you guys downstairs."

Maris is pressing the water from her hair with a towel, and she has another one wrapped around her torso. "What's up with Theo? Is he okay?"

"Hotel towels suck, don't they? At least these hotel towels."

Maris knows my style too well. "Uh-oh. It's bad. What happened?"

I sit on the bed and pull Maris onto my lap. "Funkengroovin' has been removed from the tour, effective immediately. We aren't going to Norfolk."

"What? Why?"

"Luis pulled some strings to get us booted. He's pissed off that we didn't sign the deal."

Maris's face goes white. "Nico, that's my fault. I came up with the counter idea."

I shake my head and hold her chin between my left thumb and forefinger. "Theo and I already took responsibility and then talked each other out of it. It's no one's fault but Luis. He's a total cock. We don't have a plan yet, but we didn't do anything wrong, so we'll come out alright in the end."

Maris takes a deep breath, and it escapes as a sob. "This is so unfair."

"Yeah," I agree. "But look at it this way, at least we aren't contractually obligated to that asshole. We could be relying on him for the foreseeable future. I'm very glad that we dodged that bullet."

Maris looks into my eyes to see if I they agree with what I said. "That's a good point," she says. "But this still sucks balls."

"Yeah, but it's another great episode of our documentary."

"What?'"

"Theo and I are keeping track of the stories that have to be told in the documentary someone will make about us when we're rock icons."

Maris tries not to roll her eyes but fails.

"Get dressed, love. We're going to meet the boys downstairs for breakfast." I playfully push Maris off my lap, and she fights to stay there.

"In a minute." Maris wraps her arms around my neck and rests her forehead against my cheek. "This was really great," she says. "I'm not finished with this. I don't want to leave."

"Baby, we're not finished. Not even close. This was just a false start."

"Okay," she says. "You can go shower now."

I kiss her with all the emotion I feel for her in this moment. "This is just the beginning, Maris. I promise."

MARIS

MAX AND THEO ARE ALREADY seated and have plates of food in front of them when we arrive at the restaurant.

"Sucky morning, gents," I say as I lean down between their chairs and put my arms around both of them.

"Indeed," Max says. "I'm literally drowning my sorrows in carbs and syrup."

"Copying. Be right back."

Nico stays behind and sits at the table while I search the continental breakfast for food that looks less than a few days old. Truthfully, another two months of budget hotel food might have killed me. It's impossible to eat healthfully on the road. When I get back to the table, Nico is sipping a cup of coffee and my cup, at the seat next to his, is overturned and filled to the top with rich, black water. Budget hotel coffee also sucks.

Theo is reading his phone screen. "There's a direct flight at twelve-forty on American. Gets us home at four forty-eight, three-hundred ten bucks before taxes."

"The least they could do was fly us home," Max says.

Theo scoffs. "Yeah, right. There's a later flight that gets us in after midnight and then the next one is at five in the morning, but we'd have to pay to stay here another night."

I place my napkin over my lap and spoon my yogurt onto my pancakes, then add some fruit on top. "Whatever works for you guys, but I'd like to get the hell out of here as soon as possible."

"Ditto," Theo says.

I glance at Nico to see if he agrees. He has his elbows on the table with his available fingers intertwined in front of his lips. I can't read him.

"You guys are going to have to check bags too so that will cost more," Max says. "Carry on your instruments, though. You don't want the baggage dudes throwing your guitars around."

"Phil sent our cases over this morning, by the way," Theo tells me.

I hadn't even thought about my bass. I was leaving it with Kenny after each gig. I'm grateful the stage crew didn't leave town with it.

"So, should I buy the tickets? You guys can pay me back, or I can take the money out of your pay when we start playing gigs again."

"Hold up," Nico says. "I'm thinking." He turns to me. "This might be a blessing in disguise for my hand," he says softly. "I've been worried about playing while it's healing. Worried that it might not heal properly and effect the rest of my music career. I've already lost one potential future."

I see the concern in his eyes, so I place my hand on his shoulder. He reacts instinctively by kissing my fingers.

Then he faces Theo and Max. "You guys know, I've had to reinvent myself once already after an injury. I don't want to have to do that again. If football and music are off the table, I'm going to be Nico the bartender at the family tavern."

Max stares at his plate, as Theo nods understanding.

"I thank the football gods for blowing your knee out every morning. Just want to get that out there." Theo holds his fist across the table and Nico bumps it with his left. "But I understand completely. Not playing for four weeks—"

"Four to six," Nico corrects him.

Theo inhales sharply, but nods. "Four to six. If that ensures having you back one hundred percent, then that's what we do. Honestly, that gives me time to get some gigs lined up. We gave our calendar away on very short notice when we started the tour, so our old rooms are probably booked that far out anyway."

"Is that what we want to do?" I ask. "What did Phil say about the potential to get us on another tour? Could he set up a club tour for us? I'm just throwing other ideas out there before we go back to square one."

"I hear you," Theo says. "I get that, but how long can we each afford to stay unemployed while we wait for better offers?"

I feel my face fall. "Yeah, not very long. I've got my law school debt, and I was thinking about leasing an apartment."

Max's head snaps up. "No! Why would you get an apartment?"

I look at Nico. "I thought it might be better for everyone …"

"We have a lot of decisions to make based on something that happened an hour ago, so let's deal with the issue at hand, which is getting home," Theo says.

"Right, which is why I was starting to say that I might go home-home for a while." Nico looks at me again. "I haven't seen my family in over a year. I'm halfway to Wisconsin. It's summer, which is a great time to be there …"

I feel like the rug is being pulled from underneath me for the second time today, but I can tell this is something Nico really wants to do.

"You mentioned going home yesterday," Theo says. "I'd go see my mom if I could, man."

"Theo's right. Your mother would love that," I say.

Nico smirks. "I'm sure you've heard her on the phone. Every time I go to hang up, she says, '*Nicolas, when am I going to get to see that punim?*'"

"Your name is Nicolas?" Max asks, astounded. "Why didn't I know that?"

Nico shrugs. "I don't know Maximillian, Maximus …"

"It's just Max. I don't have a secret identity," he says sarcastically.

Theo lowers his voice. "You seem really upset about this."

"Did you know?"

"I give him a 1099, so yeah …"

"Anyway," Nico says. "I can't really afford to be in Miami for a month or more without an income. But I can crash at home. Also, I feel like if I was in Miami, especially with you guys, I'd be tempted to play every day. Almost definitely for more hours than I would have played if we were still on tour." He looks at me. "You're welcome to come with me. My family's dying to meet you."

I smile picturing it but yes dies on my lips. "I can't really afford to take a vacation right now, and I can't mooch off your family. I

267

want them to respect me. These circumstances would make for a terrible introduction."

Nico shakes his head. "They'd be so happy to see me, they wouldn't even ask why we're there or how long we're staying."

I laugh. "I bet they'd ask after week three. And then we'd have to tell them we're both unemployed and squatting at their house while they support us."

Nico chuckles. "I'm sure I'm going to have to work at the tavern to help out. Most of the drinks are tap beer, so I can fill beer steins, I guess." He mimics pulling a tap with his left hand.

"We could book ourselves as a trio until Nico gets back," Max says. "Not necessarily in clubs, but we could do, like, jazz brunch gigs, or hotel lobby gigs that require mostly instrumental music."

"Oh, look, he's fully recovered from perceived betrayal and he's back in business," Nico jokes. "Seriously, Max, you've been dying to do those types of gigs. Might be a good time to get them out of your system."

I lean my head against Nico's shoulder. When I woke up this morning, saying goodbye to him for an extended amount of time wasn't a remote possibility. I feel awful, but I know he needs to go home.

"Would you fly to Wisconsin?" I ask quietly.

Nico shakes his head. "I would probably have to connect through Minneapolis and again through Chippewa Valley, and the drive a couple hours … I might as well rent a car here. It'll be cheaper and feel like less of a hassle." Nico googles the drive time. "Only thirteen hours and twenty minutes from here to Minocqua, which means I can do it ten."

"Don't you dare," I say harshly.

"I won't. I'll just have a chill cruise and listen to tunes." Nico looks across the table at Theo and they both make faces and shake their heads.

"Yeah, good, Theo. Encourage him," I say.

"So, I'm buying three tickets?" Theo asks.

I look at Nico and it feels like my chest is cracking open and spilling my heart on the table. We both turn back to Theo and say, "Yes."

Nico winks at me, but I see sadness in his eyes.

"Tickets purchased and we're checked in."

"I'll come with you guys to the airport and rent a car from there."

"We better get moving," Max says standing up.

This is all happening too fast. I suddenly can't take a deep breath. Nico pushes back his chair and holds his left arm out for me to take. We walk across the lobby arm in arm, following Theo and Max. In our room, I look at our bed and wonder how long it will be before Nico is sleeping beside me again.

"I'm sorry for how quickly this is happening, Maris. I already feel adrift, to be honest."

"I'm glad to hear you say that because I can't imagine how hard it's going to be to say goodbye to you."

Nico presses me into his body and holds me there. "I'm always right here. In my mind, every minute, this is where I'm going to be. Right here."

I'm trying so hard not to cry. I don't want Nico to feel responsible for comforting me. He's embarking on a long travel day, and I want him clear headed.

"I love you so much. I'm going to miss you every minute."

He kisses the top of my head. "You understand why I feel like I need to do this, right?"

I pull back a little so Nico can see my eyes. "I agree with you. If you come back with us, you're going to play. You're going to set up and break down gear. You're going to write music, so that means more hours with the guitar. I respect your decision. It takes a lot of discipline."

He attacks me with kisses. "You have no idea how much discipline." Nico gasps. "Wait, I have an idea. I could come home, and you could pay me to be your sex slave."

I bust out laughing. "Why would I buy the cow?"

"Is that a Wisconsin joke? Because I feel targeted."

We kiss again and it's a whole-body kiss. It lasts until Theo bangs on our door and yells for us to get moving.

At the airport, I try to keep a smile on my face. I tell Nico to be careful, and to check in with us along the drive. But as I walk away, each step is more difficult. I turn around to look at him one more time, and he's still watching us. I blow him a kiss, and he performs a public lip press in return. So much of me lives in Nico now that I feel like I'm physically tearing apart.

THEO

I'm smiling under water. I missed this pool and my house. Granted, I wasn't away for three months as I planned to be when I left, but I was away long enough that everything looked weird and wonderful to me when I walked in last night. The house smelled so good, so new compared to musty hotels with old AC units. The kitchen seemed enormous. Having a whole room just for food? Crazy luxury. Sleeping alone in my bedroom, on my Tempur-Pedic mattress felt like heaven on earth after bunking with Max in smaller quarters. I hate what happened to us and I hate Luis, but, in this moment, I'm happy.

When I finish my swim, I lift myself out of the pool and lie on a chase to let the sun bake me dry. My phone rings, bursting my peace bubble. I lift my sunglasses to see the screen. It's Phil again. He wants to talk to Alex about suing Luis and Revolution for the income we lost when we were wrongly dismissed. I release an exasperated grunt and compose a text message through Siri: *Hey Phil, getting settled in at home. Still not sure what I want to do next. Thanks for looking out for us. I'll call soon.*

Maybe that will buy me a day. I'm surprised that Phil is so firmly on our side and willing to take action against Revolution. Luis must have really pissed him off because I thought Phil was Luis's boy. Maybe he's feeling guilty. Good. He can use that as motivation to get us some work.

"We're back!" I hear Maris through the sliding doors. She and Max went to Publix because the cupboards were bare.

I grab a towel and head inside. "What'd ya get?"

"Nothing served at the free Doubletree continental breakfast buffet," Maris jokes. "And we stopped at the Cuban Coffee Café and got the fresh blend we all love."

"I almost feel guilty about how happy I am to be home," I confess.

"I understand what you mean," Max says, filling his cabinet with his purchases. "I would have never left the tour, and I wish we were playing tonight, but if we can't be there, here is pretty great."

"I'm making a frittata," Maris announces. "Any ingredients you absolutely don't want in it?"

"Hold the peppers, please." I make an unsure face. "Unless you really love them."

"I can leave them out, but I'm making stuffed peppers for dinner, so you might want to make other plans."

I grab a grocery bag and start filling the fridge. "I just can't eat peppers first thing in the morning. Hits wrongs."

"Are we rehearsing today?" Max asks. "We could work up a jazz brunch set."

I look at Maris and she grimaces.

"Let's take a day to transition," I say.

Maris mouths, *thank you*.

"Besides we don't have any gigs." I laugh.

"Yeah, but we can't take a gig if we don't have the material," Max argues.

"I know. Personally, I need a day away from music."

Maris has my back. "I have laundry to do, and I want to take my Jeep for a drive. It's been sitting for a while …" she trails off.

"Okay," Max says. "I'll make a list of song suggestions and text them to you guys."

Maris stops what she's doing and faces me. "What would we call the trio? We can't be Funkengroovin' without Nico."

I finish stocking the fridge and freezer and start collecting empty bags. "That's a good point. Do you have any ideas?"

"Too Em-Tee," Max says, like he just struck gold.

Maris and I exchange looks.

"Maris and Max start with M, so two M and a T."

271

"Well, that's entirely awful, so there's nowhere to go from there but up," I say. I miss Nico right now. He would roast Max appropriately. I have to remember to tell him about *Too Empty* later.

"We don't have to live with the name or the material very long because when Nico comes back, it's full on Funkengroovin' again," Maris says. She gives Max a dozen eggs, a bowl and a whisk and starts chopping mushrooms.

"Have you heard from Nicolas? Also, you can give me something to do. I'm not entirely useless in the kitchen."

Maris uses her chef's knife to point to a bag of spinach. "Triple wash that in a colander and then chop it up," she instructs.

"The whole bag?"

"Yes, it cooks down. Nico made it home around midnight. He didn't tell his parents he was coming, and his father nearly shot him with a hunting rifle as he was entering the house."

I feel my eyes go wide. "Jesus!"

"He cut off an hour and twenty minutes on the drive time," Max said admiringly.

"Don't remind me," Maris says sharply.

"So, after they realized he wasn't an intruder, were they stoked to see him?" I ask.

Maris smiles. "Yeah. And Nico sounded happy to be there. His mom called his brothers, I guess they all live close by, and they all came over."

"At midnight?" Max asks.

I laugh. "They're close. When Nico got signed by University of Miami, he was the first relative to leave Minocqua in, like, two generations. When he left, his family took it hard."

I notice Maris smiling to herself and I wonder if she's thinking what it would be like to be part of that type of family.

"Maris and I have no reference for what that's like, being only children and only having one parent left."

"Well, at lest you have your dad, Theo. I haven't spoken to my mom in ..." Maris pauses her chopping to think. "Well, she met Damon once, so somewhere around four years."

"Sorry, Maris," Max says. "You can be my unofficial sister."

She winks at him. "Thanks, Maxer. For what it's worth, I already think of you as a brother."

"Aww …" Max smiles.

"How about me? Do you think of me as a brother?" I ask, raising my eyebrows.

Her face says, "*Really*?"

"Okay, fine, never mind. You don't have to answer. What do I do with all this green stuff now that it's clean and slashed?"

"Can you sauté the mushrooms while I chop the shallots?"

"In EVOO?" I ask.

She looks impressed. "Yes, please."

I grab my favorite from the cabinet. "First cold press. This is Greece's finest olive oil."

I get to work, and Maris adds the shallots as I continuously move the pan.

"Want to add sun-dried tomatoes? I have some in the cabinet next to the fridge."

"Great idea," she says. "Okay, the base is ready, you can add the sauté now."

"Or," I hold my finger up. "We can bake all the ingredients in the pan and just slide it into the oven. Cast iron," I explain.

"Sick!" Maris dumps as I blend. When she adds the feta, I do the hand gesture we use on stage for *keep going*. "I'm Greek."

Maris laughs.

"How long will that take?" Max asks.

"Twenty minutes," I say. "Maybe slightly longer."

"Okay, so I've never seen you cook in this kitchen," Maris says.

"I don't like cooking by myself."

She stares at me for a long moment and her eyes sparkle. I can't tell what she's thinking.

Max starts playing *The Girl From Ipanema* on his phone. "This would be a good song for us to play. Should I put in on our list?"

Maris looks away. "Every working musician knows that song, Max."

"Oh, good. That's a good start."

"I'm going to hit the shower. Maris, don't let our frittata burn."

Yeah, I'm happy.

NICO

ONE THING THAT I LOVE and hate about my hometown is that everyone knows everyone's business within minutes. The CIA could learn a lot about collecting and disseminating intelligence from the way the aunties in this town operate. By midmorning, my parents' mile long driveway was packed with cars, bicycles, and ATVs. Dad had the grills going and he served beer-soaked brats and burgers along with sides that showed up with each group of people who came by to welcome me home. Pro-tip, if you're inviting guests to a cook-out, put a couple Wisconsinites on the list, because they never show up empty-handed.

The Van Asten Place, as everyone calls it, is on the lake and two of my brothers are taking turns driving the boat for whoever wants to waterski. Marcus and I are sitting in Adirondack chairs on the dock watching the epic spills and laughing our asses off.

"I want to get out there so badly, but I know I'd mess my hand up even worse."

"Dude, it sounds like Theo had a reality check coming, but I still can't believe you clocked him." Marcus takes a swig from his green solo cup. We don't do red; Packers colors are green and gold.

"Oh, don't pretend you haven't beat on me, and washed my face out with snow. Remember when you tackled me from behind at the school picnic and kept my face in the dirt while Sarah Pavloski was watching?"

Marcus's face broke into a hug smile. "That was a beautiful day. Best school picnic ever."

"Asshole," I joke.

"Simmer down, she still went to Prom with you."

I turn away from the lake and scan the backyard. "This is cool. It feels like I never left."

"Except you're a big rock star now," Marcus teases.

"An unemployed rock star." I start to take swig of beer, then stop to add, "A broke, unemployed rock star."

Marcus laughs. "I wish I could have seen you play that festival, bro. Watching you on stage with Nicky Knight was the absolute best. All of us were losing our minds. You had us walking on air for days."

"It was fun while it lasted." I take a deep breath and enjoy the lack of humidity in the air and the smell of evergreens.

"What's next. What's the rest of the band doing right now?" Marcus asks softly.

"Well, big brother, time will tell. Theo, Maris, and Max are back in Miami. They're trying to find some trio work until I'm able to play again."

Marcus leans forward in his chair. "Don't take this the wrong way, but do you think it's smart to leave Maris with Theo for weeks on end? Considering he has feelings for her?"

I make a face like I've just heard the most ridiculous question possible, but, on the drive here, I had the same thought a few times. "If Maris and I can't be faithful during a couple weeks apart, then we aren't as in love as I think we are."

Marcus scrunches his face. "You're sure he won't pressure her? If she doesn't have another place to stay and she's relying on him for work and shelter—"

"Maris isn't a pushover. She isn't weak. She needs to work and that's the only reason she isn't here with me now."

Marcus puts his hands up. "I'm just looking out for you, Nico. It's a lifelong habit."

I laugh. "I know I can count on you."

"Shit, look out!" Marcus yells.

The boat is heading our way and then cuts back toward the lake as the skier behind the boat slaloms and drenches us with lake water.

I laugh, but I'm serious when I tell Marcus that our younger brothers are dead.

Marcus stands up and takes his shirt off, stuffing it into the waist of his cargo shorts. "I was about to get goin' anyway. It's almost time to open the tavern."

I spread my arms wide. "For who? The whole damn town is here."

Marcus laughs. "As soon as the sun sets, they'll be looking for pool tables, dart boards, and more beer."

"I'll swing by later," I promise. "I see a few new people I should say hi to."

Marcus shakes his head. "Take the night off. You gotta be exhausted after everything you've been through the last couple weeks." He comes in for a bear hug and says, "I'm here to talk if you need a sounding board, okay?"

"Thanks, Marcus. I love you, brother."

"If Sarah Pavloski shows up, give me call. I can be back here in five minutes, and I bet you'd be a lot easier to take down injured."

"Get the fuck outta here," I say with a smile.

Mom notices that our talk is over and doesn't waste a second before calling me back to the party. "Nicolas, the Kissners are here! Come say hi!"

I smile and chuckle to myself. It's nice to be surrounded by people who genuinely care about me and don't give a damn about what I do when I'm not home. It's helping my psyche already. I wish Maris was here receiving the same love and support. I really, really wish she was here.

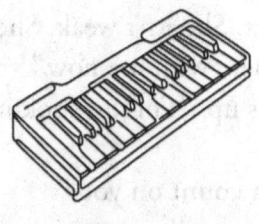

MAX

Maris made stuffed peppers for dinner, and they were awesome. I put a jazzy playlist together and the three of us listened while we ate, categorizing songs we all knew, songs we could easily throw together, and songs Theo would rather die than play in public. As usual, Maris was nice and gave every song I picked a fair shot.

I saw her texting a lot today and I assume that every time she's on the phone, she's talking to Nico. I miss him, so I imagine she's feeling his absence ten times more than I am. It seems weird around here without him. I'm so used to his roasts that I roast myself when I think of something he would say.

Dinner is over and the kitchen is cleaned up, but I don't want everyone to retreat to our rooms. "Do you guys want to watch a movie?"

"What did you have in mind, Maxer?" Maris asks.

"Ladies choice."

"Can't. I'm going out," Theo says.

"Where to? Checking out a band?" I ask.

"Ah, no …" It seems like Theo's going to say more, but then he doesn't.

Maris laughs. "You don't need permission, Theo, and you don't have to tell us where you're going."

"Thanks." Theo starts walking toward the stairs.

"Just kidding, tell us everything," Maris calls to his back.

"I'll tell you tomorrow. Maybe." Theo takes the stairs two at a time.

"Odd." Maris leads the way to the living room and turns on the TV. "Which streaming service should we try? We probably missed a lot of newly added content while we were on the road."

I lift the ottoman, pull out two blankets, and toss one to Mare. "Doesn't matter to me. Pick a genre first and then we'll narrow it down."

Maris laughs. "Process of elimination … no romances, no band movies or documentaries—"

"Nothing set in a hotel and nothing that features a bus," I add.

"Absolutely not," Maris agrees. "How about horror? Feel like a good horror flick?"

"Always." I hate horror, but it's Mare, and I want her to have a good evening.

She clicks the trailer for a movie about strangers trapped together at a house while the world is ending. When she says, "What do you think?" I know she wants to watch it.

"Let's do it."

Mare is in the leather recliner, and she extends the footrest. I lie on the couch next to her chair and prop myself up with pillows. The plot pulls me in, and I'm fixed on the screen when Theo walks past the living room towards the front door.

"Looking sexy!" Maris yells.

"I'm always sexy," Theo replies.

I tell him not to do anything I wouldn't do, and I hear Nico's voice in my head say, "*What, like go on a date with a girl?*" He has me brainwashed. I'm bullying myself now. As the movie gets tense, Maris's phone alerts and we both jump.

"It's just a Google alert," she says.

My phone alerts and we laugh at the coincidence. After five consecutive alerts, Maris pauses the movie.

"The hell's going on? Is the world actually ending?" She gestures to the TV screen before checking her phone. "Oh, my God, Max. Look!" Maris holds up a video of Nicky Knight on stage wearing a T-shirt that says, "*Fuck Revolution Records.*" He's banging on his guitar. The sound he's making is atrocious. He goes to the mic and yells, "Where's Funkengroovin', mates? Ask Revolution Records! Fuck off!"

Maris screams with laughter and my jaw drops.

"Holy shit! Way to go Nicky!" I yell.

Maris reads out loud, "Headliner Dame Knight's Nicky Knight throws a temper tantrum on stage in Norfolk tonight over the sudden departure of a band on the ticket."

"People are trying to figure out what happened to us," I say. "From what it says here, they didn't announce that we weren't playing and then Nicky came out and told everyone to fuck off."

Maris's phone rings and she answers a FaceTime call.

"Are you seeing this?" I hear Nico's voice and get off the couch to say hi.

"God bless Nicky!" Maris says laughing.

I stick my face into the frame next to Maris. "Hey, Nico. Miss you, man."

Nico squints and looks away. "You should warn people before you bomb, Max."

"Still an asshole," I say. "Good talking to you."

Nico laughs. "Miss you too, brother."

"Has Theo seen this?" Nico asks.

"He went out," Maris replies.

"That crazy Brit motherfucker ..."

"I'm going to make some popcorn," I tell Maris. "Want some?"

"Yes, please!"

"I would love to see Luis's face when he watches this for the first time," Maris says.

I hear Nico laugh at the thought of it. "That's what job security looks like," he tells Maris. "When you can go on stage and blow the show up without a concern."

"I hope they actually played their set though," Maris says. "People spent good money to hear them."

"They probably did. I bet Nicky wanted to get that off his chest and then he gave the crowd a great show. What are you guys doing?"

The microwave starts up and when the popping noises make it harder to hear the FaceTime call, I walk to the far end of the kitchen, closer to Maris's chair.

"Maxer and I are watching a movie."

"All right, well, I don't want to interrupt that, I just wanted to make sure you guys saw this."

"Can I FaceTime you back when I'm going to bed? I don't know how to sleep without you," Maris says softly, but I still hear her. "Your heartbeat lulls me to sleep."

"Oh, baby. You can always call me, but I might have another girl on my chest."

"Don't make me come up there," Maris threatens.

"Marcus's dog stayed here when he went to work. She's a golden and she likes to cuddle, so I plan to close my eyes and pretend she's you."

That makes Maris laugh. "What's her name?"

"Daisy Duke, so if you hear me talking to Daisy ..."

Maris laughs again. When she's talking to Nico, her laugh sounds like music.

"I love you. Call you later," she says.

"Love you," Nico replies. "Love you too, Max. I know you're listening."

Okay, fine, I'll let him have this one. "Love you, Nicolas!"

Maris busts out laughing and places her phone back on the table next to her chair. "I sent the video to Theo's phone," she tells me as I hand her a bowl of popcorn.

"Whatever he's doing must be important," I say.

Maris shrugs and points the remote at the TV. "Ready?"

I count us in, "One, two, three, four ..."

Maris presses *play.*

THEO

MY PHONE STARTED BLOWING UP last night and I loved seeing the video of Nicky calling out Revolution for getting us kicked off the tour. Phil left me a few messages, as did Alex, but I couldn't divert my attention to business. I was dealing with a sensitive matter.

Shana reached out to me when the photos of my pulverized face started circulating online. She was concerned. I didn't tell Nico because we weren't talking at the time, and I didn't tell Max because he doesn't forgive easily and I'm sure he still hates her for breaking up with me. If I had told Nico, he would have said that she just wanted me back because we're starting to become successful. I'm not stupid. I'm looking for signs of that, too, but the few conversations we've had felt like old times and Shana admitted that she made a mistake breaking things off with me. I think she realizes now that the things she let get to her were petty in the grand scheme.

Anyway, we met for drinks last night, took a long walk on the beach, and this morning she's waking up in my bed. I told her that I missed her, but I also told her there was no one special in my life right now, which was only half-true. But I'm working on making it fully true.

Shana didn't have the chance the chance to remove her make-up before we fell into bed, and that was my fault. She has racoon eyes this morning and my pillowcases need stain removal. I slip out of bed and start the shower. When I'm finished, Shana is still asleep, but I hear someone in the kitchen. I'm anxious to talk to Max and Maris about the video, so I close my bedroom door behind me and go downstairs.

"Good morning, sleepyhead," Maris says as I round the corner into the kitchen. "Have you seen the video of Nicky?"

"Ain't that some shit?" I reply as I pour myself a cup of coffee.

"Do you think Revolution will release a statement?" Max asks. He's sitting in front of the kitchen island with a plate-sized waffle in front of him.

"I found a waffle iron, and I made whole wheat batter from scratch," Maris explains. "Want one?"

"Ah," I look over my shoulder, wondering how much longer Shana will sleep. "Sure."

Maris pours batter into the iron. "What does Phil say about all of this?"

I stand beside where she's making my waffle and lean against the counter to face both her and Max. "He's feeling vindicated. But he still wants to pursue suing Revolution, regardless of Alex telling him we have no basis for a legal action."

Maris nods. "The contract was written to protect the festival organizers. They weren't violating the agreement by letting us go without cause. They could have fired us for any reason or no reason at all."

I point to Maris while speaking to Max. "Madame counselor is correct."

"That will be four hundred bucks," Maris jokes.

She opens the waffle iron and plates it for me.

"Have you eaten?" I ask her.

Max laughs. "Maris is still boycotting any food that was available on the hotel buffet."

I look at her with an expression of gratitude. "You did this for us?"

She chuckles. "I like having people to take care of. Does that sound very nineteen fifties?"

Max replies with a mouth full of waffle. "Not at all. It sounds awesome."

I top my waffle with sliced strawberries and whipped cream. "I'll make dinner, then. We can't have our bass player distracted by kitchen duty."

"Maris and I finalized a song list of traditional jazz tunes and classis instrumentals. Can we go over it today?"

My mouth is full, so I nod.

"Good. I also made a list of venues to pitch the trio to," Max says.

"Maris, excellent breakfast, thank you." I wink at her. "I let some of the local agents know we're back in town and what our situation is for the coming weeks. I heard back from a couple already. We'll have some dates on the calendar by the end of the day, I hope."

Maris brings her breakfast and sits next to me, so I'm in the middle. "In the past, I've played places that booked a jazz band, but then realized they really wanted Muzak."

I laugh, "Been there. Learned a whole bunch of jazz and then wound up playing instrumental versions of decades old pop tunes the entire time, and the manager was like, 'Yes! Jazz!'"

Maris and Max's laughs are cut short by the sound of Shana clearing her throat. I genuinely forgot she was here. The three of us look up to find her looking annoyed on the other side of the island.

"You're shitting me," Max says flatly.

"Nice to see you too, Max," she says.

I jump off my stool and go around to kiss Shana. "Maris, this is—"

"That's Shana," Max tells Maris. "Theo, you should have told us she was here. I would have stayed in my room."

"Max, stop it. Shana, what would you like for breakfast?"

"Nice to meet you, Maris," Shana says.

"A pleasure," Maris says smiling. I see surprise on her face, and I wonder if she sees the panic on mine. This isn't how I wanted this to happen.

"I'm not a breakfast person, Theo. It hasn't been that long, you should remember."

"It's been a while, hasn't it?" Max asks no one in particular. "Long before we hired Maris and started getting famous adjacent."

"Just say it, Max," Shana says. "Get it all out."

I notice Maris watching the confrontation and wonder how this looks through her eyes. Shana hasn't washed her face and is wearing one of my T-shirts. Her long brown hair is JBF styled. She's being as snarky to Max as he is to her. This feels very dysfunctional.

"I was here for Theo when you broke up with him for no reason and gaslit the shit out of him. He's too good for you. Theo, you're too good for her, man." Max sounds like he's pleading with me.

"Max, Theo and I had our issues, and I realize now that I wasn't mature enough to be in a serious relationship back then. But I've done the work and I'm in a better place now. If Theo is willing to give me a chance, you should be." Shana laughs.

"So, are you guys back together?" Max asks.

"No." I can tell by the look on Shana's face that I answered too quickly.

"I'm going to take a shower. Maris, nice to meet you."

I'm frozen in place. I know I should be following Shana upstairs, but I want to explain the situation to Maris and Max.

Max carries his dishes to the sink. "My guy …"

"Max, she reached out recently, and we talked."

"Be careful, Theo. I think you can do so much better. I'd like to believe you're just lonely, but I know you better than that," Max tells me.

My phone buzzes and I see that Amazon is at the gate, so I open it.

"I don't know where this is going or if it's going anywhere. But, Max, it's between Shana and me, okay?"

Max looks at me and rolls his eyes. "I'm not going through this again, Theo. She doesn't understand what you do for a living, she's demanding, she doesn't like any of us ... maybe she'll like Maris, but I doubt it."

Maris laughs. "What did I do?"

The Amazon delivery person is on the other side of the glass doors, so I take the package and thank him. "Maris, this is for you."

"I didn't order anything."

Maris opens the package and pulls out a stuffed bear with a tag that says, "Heartbeat Bear." She turns a white dial and a whooshing sound fills the room. Maris tears up and searches the box for a note.

"Nico?" Max guesses.

"To help me sleep until he gets home," Maris says smiling. "I have to go call him."

"Maris," I touch her arm as she passes me. "Please don't tell him who's in my shower right now. Not yet."

"If you have to keep a relationship a secret—"

"It's not a relationship, Max!" I calm myself. "Yet."

Maris walks out to the lanai, and I take the stairs two at a time. I feel conflicted. Like I owe Maris and Max more than I owe Shana. Part of me feels like I'm being disloyal to Maris, which is insane because she's on the phone thanking Nico for the replacement heart he sent to hold space for him. Fuck, this is complicated. Last night while I was with Shana, I really felt like we could get back what we once had together. What made me very happy. This morning, I feel like my happiness relies on Maris's degree of involvement in my life. Max makes a good point though; Shana resented the amount of time I spent with the band.

I hear her singing in the shower. Poorly. Like, painfully awful. When she sees me, her face lights up and she invites me in. I'm conflicted, but it's not like I have any better offers at the moment. I know what she likes, and she knows what I want. With her make-up mask removed, I'm reminded how pretty she is. It isn't hard to want her. She's tiny, yet perfectly proportioned and I lift her up with ease. She wraps her legs around me and whispers in my ear that I should put her up against the wall. She knows from experience that the towel rack is above her head, and she uses it to help hold herself up. The sex is urgent. Maybe we're making up for lost time. My heart is beating fast, and I hear it whooshing in my head, which reminds me of the stupid fucking heartbeat bear. Shana is too much in her own head to realize I'm rushing her. She comes and I don't try to last for another round.

"We're so good together, Theo," she breathes into my ear.

I cover her mouth with mine and kiss her slowly, meaningfully. I'm with the person I loved with my whole heart and grieved over losing. So, why do I feel like I'm losing my mind?

MARIS

NICO IS SITTING BY THE lake behind his parents' house. It looks like a movie set. I can see why he equates healing with home. Just seeing it over FaceTime makes me feel peaceful.

"Heartbeat bear is the sweetest thing anyone has ever given me, Nico. I make one comment and hours later," I hold the stuffed bear next to my face, "this guy shows up."

Nico looks amused. "I'm glad you like it. Damn near killed me to hear you say you were worried about sleeping without me."

"How many weeks has it been?" I ask.

Nico's face breaks into a huge smile. "Two days and that's two days too many." I hear his phone alert and his eyes to go a different location on his screen. "Max is texting me. He says it's a nine-one-one. Where is he?"

"He was here a minute ago."

"Now he's saying I need to call him ASAP."

I press my lips together and try to look oblivious.

"I'm going to add him to the call." Nico touches his screen and we're "waiting" for Max to join.

"Hey, Nico. Thanks for calling so fast. Oh, hey Mare." Max is pacing in his room. "Do you wanna be on this call, or do you want to leave it to the guys?"

"I was already on this call, Max," I explain.

"Oh. Sorry to interrupt, but this is important, and Nico will know what to do."

"Are you sure you're free to share this information?" I ask.

"He asked you specifically, not me, and you don't understand, Mare. This could affect all of us. Nico will agree with me."

Nico lifts the phone close to his face. "Will someone please tell Nico what's going on?"

"Theo brought Shana back to the house last night and she's still here," Max blurts.

Nico makes a face like he just got a whiff of something pungent. "Why?"

"She said that she was too immature to handle their relationship before, but she's grown or some shit. She reached out to him, and I guess they've been talking. She's trying to worm her way back in, that's for sure."

Nico chuckles. "Well, I don't like her, and Max, you don't like her, but Theo does like her, so that's what matters."

"Are you kidding me?" Max's voice gets squeaky. "She leads Theo around by the nose. Shana will have more to say about when and where we play than we do."

Nico shrugs. "I don't think Theo will let her get a leash around his neck this time. Maybe Shana really has grown up and maybe this is the right time and place for them to be together."

Max's walking pace quickens along with the cadence of his speech. "You're acting like she didn't absolutely destroy him when they broke up."

"I was there, my guy. And I'll be there for him if it goes south again, just like you and Maris will be."

"I can't believe you're saying this. In fact, if you were here, this wouldn't be happening."

Nico shakes his head. "It would be happening, just at her place. This is no different from you and your beloved jazz, Max. You and Theo both have things to get out of your system. You have to let it play out to know if you're missing out or not."

I can tell that Max doesn't love Nico's answer, but he can't formulate an argument for it either. He exhales loudly. "I'll let you guys get back to your FaceTime."

"Don't worry, Max. Theo won't get run over by Shana again. He's too smart for that," Nico says.

"We'll see. Bye, guys."

Max's face disappears and Nico's gets bigger again, which initiates my smile reflex.

"What do you think of Shana?" he asks.

"I met her for two super awkward seconds, so I don't have an opinion. I just want Theo to be happy," I say.

"He's probably pretty happy right this minute." Nico winks at me.

"Ew, I don't want to think about that." I laugh.

"This is good for Theo's ego. She dumped him, so he's getting some validation along with that bow-chicka-wow-wow."

"Anyway," I say making the word five syllables long, "what are your plans for today?"

"I'm going to do some left-handed gardening with my mom, then I'm left-handed driving her to the grocery store, and then I'm left-handed bartending with Marcus tonight at the tavern."

"That sounds so wholesome," I gush. "I love it."

"It isn't wholesome at all. We're growing weed, picking up illegal moonshine at the grocer, and the tavern will be the site of multiple deadly sins."

I chuckle. "Small town life is seedier than I expected."

Nico inhales deeply and turns the camera to the lake. "I need to get you up here. It's very easy to be stress-free and relaxed."

"So, exactly like Miami."

Nico laughs. "Truthfully, I'd rather be there because that's where my Maris is."

"This is already so much harder than I thought to was going to be, and I thought being away from you was going be like unplugging from my life source."

"Are you guys getting any gigs on the calendar?"

"We're rehearsing the jazz show today and Theo's put the word out."

"Once you start playing and getting back into a normal routine, the time will pass more quickly."

"Hurry up and heal, okay?"

Nico smirks into the camera. "I am fully motivated. Our family doctor was here yesterday for the cookout, and he said that bone broth, milk, and cheese will help mend bone, so I have the broth on the stove, and I'll have no problem finding milk and cheese in the dairy state. I'm one hundred percent sure his advice is based on an old wives' tale, but I'm doing it anyway."

"Oh, babe. I know you'll do everything in your power. It all comes down to time though. This, too shall pass." I try to look confident.

"I miss you, Maris Humphries."

"I miss you, Nicolas Van Asten." I kiss the phone screen and wave before pressing the red "x." I love seeing Nico's face and hearing his voice, but when the call ends, he disappears so fast that it upsets me.

"Maris?" I hear Theo calling from inside the house. When I turn around, he holds up his phone. I make the sign we use for "end" on stage to tell him I'm no longer on a call and he comes out onto the lanai.

"Nico?"

"Yeah. I wanted to thank him for the bear."

"Shana just left." Theo stretches out on the chaise next to where I'm sitting. "So, do you think I'm weak sauce like Max does?"

I let my mouth fall open in a shocked expression. "No!"

Theo puts both hands over his face. "What am I doing?" he moans. "We were having good conversations … when I got back, she wanted to see me … we fell into our old pattern so easily."

"Well, that's a good thing, isn't it?"

"I honestly don't know," Theo admits. "It didn't feel the same. It didn't feel as … perfect as before. Now there's all this bad stuff between us. The memories of things that were said and done as the relationship was dying."

I hate hearing so much pain in Theo's voice. I reach across to his chaise and place my hand on his shoulder. "If the love is strong enough, relationships can overcome a lot."

"I almost wish she had cheated on me. No offense. I'm not making light of the Damon thing. The reason she left me was that she didn't like how I look at life. She didn't like things about *me*. She didn't make an awful mistake; you know what I mean? I can forgive a mistake, maybe, but how do I forget that this is a girl who straight up documented my flaws in alphabetical order?"

"She said she's matured. Do you believe her?"

Theo turns to look at me, and he shifts his legs over the edge of the chair to face me. We're in the same position we were that night in the loft when he asked if he imagined we had an attraction to one another. "I don't know if I can trust her."

I scrunch up my face. "Trust is big. But if you're not worried about her cheating, what do you mean exactly?"

Theo looks up at me with his big brown eyes. He looks so vulnerable. "I don't trust that she's being genuine. She held a lot back before." He laughs awkwardly.

I take a second to think. "What brought you together in the first place? What made you fall in love?"

Theo chuckles and tilts his head back to look at the sky. "Initially? She was into the band. She and a couple girlfriends followed us around on the weekends. We started talking and it seemed like she was really into music, but once we started dating, her attitude changed. She tried to steer me away from *pipedreams* and brought up working for my dad every time the subject came up."

I scrunch my face up. "Our business can be hard on relationships. But what bonded the two of you? What did you love about her?"

Theo leans forward, resting his forearms on his thighs. "She's close to her family and I liked being around them. She's thoughtful, but some of that was baiting the hook. She can be sweet and fun … when things are going her way."

"Oh, Theo …"

"Yeah, I hear it. Starting over with someone new seems impossible though. And the process is awful, you know? You're attracted to someone, so you go on a few dates, if that goes well, you move to step two, but if it doesn't, you're back to square one. Being with Shana is like riding a bike without a seat. You know how to make it go and what to avoid."

I put my hand over Theo's. "You have so much to offer. You deserve to be with someone will reciprocate what you're willing to contribute to a relationship."

Theo scoffs. "You make it sound like there's an abundance of women who fit that description."

"There are … probably." I laugh. "Definitely."

"I want a Maris," Theo says plainly. "But you're one in a million. I couldn't believe that Damon, obviously a smart guy, considering his career, could be so fucking stupid to lose you."

"He wasn't built to be with a musician. Maybe Shana wasn't either."

Theo looks at me with a pained expression. "My dream girl is right in front of me, but I can't have her. So, what do I do?"

I don't have words right away, but I don't avert my gaze. "First, don't put me on a pedestal. I have a feeling that even I couldn't compete with the image you have of me."

Theo shakes his head. "We have so much in common. The make-up of our families, a burning desire to make music at the highest level, motivation—"

"And we will always have that foundation, Theo. I already know that I want you in my life forever. I feel so lucky to have found you. That's nothing to take lightly. I'll walk through fire for you. I mean that."

"But you aren't curious about whether we could be …"

I choose my words carefully because I have so much to say, and I don't want to get this wrong. "You know I was curious for a minute there. Theo, you're hot af, you're kind, thoughtful, generous, smart, sweet, talented, easy-going, steady …" I pause to squeeze his hand. "But when Nico and I opened up to each other—" Theo flinches. "Something clicked. Cosmically. When he let me in and I took him into my heart, it was like finding a missing limb."

Theo sits upright and looks to the sky again.

"I'm not saying this to hurt you, Theo, I'm trying to give you hope. When you find the right person, your person, you'll feel it."

Silence hangs between us. The moment stretches into minutes. Theo leans against his thighs again and clasps his hands. I rest my hand on top of his and wait.

"Nico told me to tell you how I feel ... that I love you." Theo looks into my eyes and bounces his eyebrows once. "He knows what you guys have is irreplaceable. That you're devoted to each other. That nothing anyone says or does can change that."

I feel tears forming in my eyes, but crying feels selfish.

"Theo, I love you. Fiercely. And Nico loves you in a way he barely understands because his bond with you is stronger than with his own brothers. He loves them, of course, but you guys need each other in a way that bonds you more than blood. It seems like you two share a brain on stage sometimes. You're soulmates in a way. Isn't that what Max is always saying?"

Theo smiles.

"To think that my presence has driven a wedge between the two of you feels so terrible. I think it would be easier for Nico to find another Maris than it would be for him to find another Theo."

"Then we'd both lose," Theo says. "So, what you're saying is that we're a throuple, but only two of the three of us are having the sex."

I snort. "I'm saying there is abundant love in this union. It's what holds us together. And if I was made for you, I wouldn't have clicked with Nico. God isn't a sadist. He wants you to love fully and be loved fully. Maybe you've already met the person He intended for you and maybe you haven't, but unless you release the idea that it might be me, you won't be open to her."

Theo chews on his bottom lip. "I spent a lot of the tour being jealous of Nico and that didn't serve any of us very well."

I consider whether I'm betraying Nico, but I decide he wouldn't mind. "He's struggles with the same thing in reverse from time to time."

Theo head snaps up in disbelief.

"Look at where you live. This is, what? House number two for your family?"

Theo looks embarrassed. "Three. Plus, the boat."

I nod. "Your dad is a multinational, sophisticated businessman and has resources at his disposal that he can offer you, while Nico had to forge his path alone. His family is everything to him, but they can't begin to relate to what he's trying to do with his life. That's another reason he feels closer to you than his brothers ... you understand him."

"What's mine is his, and yours, and Max's ..."

"We know. You show us every day. I guess what I'm trying to say is that what we all have together is lightning in a bottle. If you change one element, the magic is gone. And, for now, it might feel like Nico and I are our own fraction of the whole, but there's no Nico and I without the whole. And when you and Max fall in love, the circle will get bigger."

"When he kissed you on stage, that's exactly what happened." Theo's jaw sets as he looks at me. "Him displaying your relationship felt like a slap in the face to the band."

I nod my understanding.

"Wow. I just realized that was the rock that started this whole avalanche," Theo confesses.

"It surprised me too," I admit. "But I know it wasn't meant to throw anything in your face. I think he was in performance mode and gave that to the audience because he thought they would like it."

"And they did. Which made me madder than hell because the focus went from Funkengroovin' to Nico and Maris."

"You're right. Intentional or not, it was a miscalculation."

Theo inhales deeply. "I was looking forward playing house with you."

I don't know what to say, so I stay quiet.

"I didn't want you to see Shana this morning."

I wait for him to continue.

"I have to figure that out before it gets out of hand."

"Mmmm."

"Max is going to want to start rehearsal soon, so we better get back inside."

"Right," I say. As Theo shifts to get up, I touch his hand to get his attention. "Whoever lands your heart will be happy for life. And I'm sure I'll have my moments when I'm seething with jealousy over how beautifully you love her."

Theo pulls me to standing and we hold each other close.

"Be sure to tell Nico about this conversation, because I don't want to get knocked out again."

I giggle, then groan. "I love you, Theo."

"I love you, Maris."

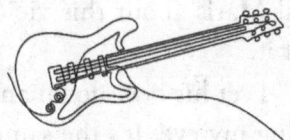

NICO

I LEAVE MY PHONE ON THE bar in case Maris calls, but every time the screen lights up it seems to be a solicitor. There are too many digits in a number I don't recognize, so I let the calls go to voicemail.

My high school teammate, Hank, is trying to make a point, so I give him my attention. "Jordan Love is the next Favre, and the Packers will never retire number 12 because of the way he left the organization."

"I don't agree, buddy. Love is going to be Love and he's gonna take us to the Superbowl more than once, maybe more than any other Packer QB, but we'll retire 12. He deserves that respect."

"Bahhhhh!" Hank stands up from his barstool and reaches behind the bar for the TV remote. I laugh at how normal that is here and can't imagine what would happen to Hank if he tried to reach behind any bar in Miami.

"I can't watch the Brewers lose again," he explains as he flips through channels.

"Nico!" A smiling face that I vaguely recognize approaches the bar and I try to imagine what this dude might have looked like ten years ago.

"Great to see you, buddy! How ya doin'?" I hold up my left fist for a bump.

"Good. Good. Marcia's pregnant again, so we're excited."

"Hey, congratulations ..." *The only Marcia I know is Marcia Holloway. Who did she date in high school? Got it!* "... Grant!"

"Yeah, thanks. The baby will be here around Christmas, so the kids say they're getting a brother or a sister for Christmas."

"That's fucking adorable. What can I get you, buddy?"

"Gimme a Schlitz. Hey, Hank, why aren't we watching the Brewers? They losin'?"

Hank dismisses the question by tossing a shelled peanut at Grant. I have to remember to tell Maris about this vicious bar fight. She'll love the wholesome nature of it.

"There ya go, Grant." I set his beer down and glance at my phone as it lights up again, catching my eye. It's the same long number again, so I grab it.

"Nico, mate, why the fuck do you have a phone if you're never going to answer it?"

I get Marcus's attention and point to the door to let him know I'm stepping outside.

"Nicky, holy shit! I didn't know you had my number, man. I thought I was dodging a scam."

"You got scammed, mate, but it wasn't by me. I want you to know Dinah and I had nothing to do with that nasty business and I'm mad as hell about it."

I laugh. "I saw the video. The whole band has. We couldn't believe it. Thanks, man."

"Ah, that's the least I can do, mate. And that's why I'm reaching out. To ask what more I can do."

I'm standing near the back door to the tavern and hold it open for a small group who's making their way in through the fire door, which is supposed to stay closed. "Well, Nicky, from what I understand, the festival directors have the right to boot anyone from the tour at any time for any reason, so there's no recourse there."

"Who cares about this twee tour, mate? We need to think bigger."

I laugh. "The rest of the band is in Miami, which is our home base.

They're going to play some gigs as a three piece until my hand heals. I'm visiting my family in Wisconsin until I can play again."

Nicky burps into the phone. "Every word you just said got sadder and sadder as you went on, mate."

I have a genuine laugh. "We thought our next few months were set, so, yeah, we're scrambling a little."

"What's Phil doing about this?"

"From what I understand, nothing productive."

"Fuck, mate. I'll see that weasel after the show tonight, so I'll light him on fire for you."

"Just don't swing at him, you could break your hand."

Nicky laughs hard. "I'll leave that to bucks younger and more passionate than I. You have my number now. Use it when you need me."

"Thanks so much for calling, Nicky. It means a lot."

"You got it, mate. Enjoy Wisconsin and get back to the states as soon as possible."

The call ends and I'm laughing my ass off all alone behind the tavern.

I text Theo: *Nicky just called! Don't know how he got my number, but he asked how he can help us out of this situation. Asked what Phil is doing and I told the truth. V cool to hear from him and wanted to share.*

I take a moment to stare at the stars and Theo texts back: *Dude, that's awesome. Call?*

It's not like I'm going to get fired from a job I'm not getting paid to do, so I call Theo.

"How ya doin', brother?"

The sound of Theo's voice brings a smile to my face. "It's nice being home, but I miss playing already."

"Remind yourself that we're playing music that puts me to sleep and you won't feel like you're missing anything."

"Sorry, man."

"It's not forever. We'll be back doing our thing very soon. So, what did Nicky have to say?"

"It was a quick convo. I thanked him on the band's behalf for backing us and he said he was going to light a fire under Phil tonight … he actually said he was going to light him on fire, but that's what I think he meant."

Theo laughs. "Never thought Nicky Knight would be Team Funkengroovin'. As much as things suck right now, life is still cooler than ever."

"That's true."

"I'll call Phil tomorrow and I was thinking about asking Maris to come along to meet with a Miami based entertainment attorney."

"She wanted that to be step one after we went viral, so, yeah, I think that's a great idea."

"Okay, good. Things happened so fast with Phil and the tour, but I think that's a step we can't afford to miss now that we have the time."

"Agreed. But Theo, Alex represented us well. Maris agrees that an experienced entertainment lawyer would have responded to that contract the same way Alex did. We're not here because Alex isn't versed in the industry."

Theo exhales with sound. "Thanks for saying that. Again. I think I agree with you, but I wants us to have someone with connections who knows how these deals work behind the scenes."

"Definitely. If there's a retainer, let us know. You shouldn't have to shoulder the financial burden."

"Yeah, we'll cross that bridge when we come to it. We have to find someone good first."

"Maris will know what to ask and what to look for."

"Exactly why I wanted to bring her along as my ringer."

"Let me know how it goes, man."

"You know it. Deuces."

I end the call and feel homesick, regardless of being at my actual home. I don't like to think about things that I'd rather be doing or places I'd rather be. I try to be mindful of staying immersed in the present, so I go back to the bar. The Brewers game is on again and they're leading as the game goes into the seventh inning stretch. I roast Hank about being a fair-weather fan. He throws peanuts at me.

It's the time of night that patrons want music, so Marcus mutes the TVs and turns up the sound system. The speakers in the tavern aren't new, but they have a round, warm sound which makes the music slap with an analogue vibe. I dig it. Until Marcus plays our version of Silver Springs. I can feel the heat rise to my face, and I don't know if I'm reacting to the overwhelming favor my hometown is showing me right now with cheers and applause, or if it's because I'm anticipating ... Maris's voice. It hits me like a punch to the heart. Fuck, I miss her.

MARIS

THEO'S BEEN ALL BUSINESS THE last couple days. I wonder if he's avoiding the Shana issue. Not that it's unusual for him to be professional, but I wonder if the distraction is an excuse. It's benefitting the trio because he has us booked four days a week for the next several weeks and he's charging the same as when Nico was with us. The three of us voted to set aside Nico's share, rather than dividing the extra money between us. It's not his fault he can't play, so we'll pay him his usual cut. He'll fight us, but it's three against one.

Today is our third consultation with entertainment attorneys. Neither Theo nor I felt comfortable with the first two firms. Both were megafirms with huge entertainment divisions, but we worried that we'd fall through the cracks. Repping big names shows the firms have juice, but we need someone who's hungry like we are. Someone who will put the time in and do the work necessary to shop for a record deal that will commit to growing our careers, rather than just releasing an album without adequate marketing and then drop us when sales are low.

I found the lawyer we're meeting today on LinkedIn of all places. She's brokered three deals in the last year, which isn't impressive in and of itself, but the deals were spectacular, and her clients are rising stars.

Nico asked me to drive his truck occasionally, so we're taking it today. It feels like he's with us. As I slide into the driver's seat, I realize I never driven it before, and it's considerably larger than my Jeep. Considering Miami traffic on I-95, I chicken out, and Theo trades places with me.

"I'm six-two and I still have to move the seat up to reach the pedals," he jokes as he powers the seat forward.

"Imagine me! I would have had to move it a foot closer!" I laugh.

It's funny how someone's vehicle is an extension of them. Nico's truck is neat. He had it fully detailed before he parked it in the garage and left on tour. His cup holders contain a few dozen guitar picks of various colors and weights. The passenger seat shows less wear than the driver's seat which makes me both happy and sad at the same time. The dash is spotless, and the only modification is a Green Bay Packers helmet that replaced the factory gear shift. When Theo sees that I'm looking at it he says, "Fucking Cheesehead" with as much love as he can muster.

Theo is wearing grey dress pants and a crip, white dress shirt open at the collar. I'm running out of business casual attire, this being our third meeting. I'm wearing a light blue short-sleeved wrap dress that hits mid-calf, with flats. I couldn't go to work as an attorney in it, but it's perfectly presentable for a business meeting. I'll have to repeat dresses after this one, though because the bulk of my wardrobe can be divided into three categories: Florida State, Beach, and Stage Attire.

Theo parks Nico's truck in a garage downtown, which I couldn't have done even with the back-up camera, and we walk a couple blocks to the offices of Lopez and Brice. The first-floor receptionist directs us to the third floor, via the elevator, and the law office is the first door we come to. Inside, the waiting room is decorated in expensive-looking art deco furniture and a young man wearing business attire and a pleasant smile greets us by name. His bright blue hair is styled in a corporate cut and that makes me, as an artist, feel welcome.

Theo and I barely sit down before Ava Lopez opens the door that leads to the offices. I'm an instant fan of her style. She has straight black hair, pulled into a long, sophisticated ponytail. She wears an elegant cream-colored tweed dress that looks like it came from Jackie Kennedy's closet. On Ava it looks both retro and cutting edge at the same time.

She's a bit shorter than I am, and her athletic looking calves inspire me to go for a run. "Good morning, Maris," she shakes my hand first, "and Theo. It's nice to meet you. I'm a fan, so I'll get that out of the way up front."

"She really is," the front office dude confirms. "We all are."

"That's super flattering," I say. "Thank you."

"You did the homework," Theo adds.

"No homework needed. I follow Stevie Nicks on Insta," Ava says.

Theo looks at me and we exchange a look that indicates we're both impressed.

Ava guides us into her office and offers Voss waters before we sit in thin, but comfortable deco chairs on the other side of a desk that is a plank of dark brown wood with a river of blue epoxy running down the middle.

"Wow, this is gorgeous," Theo says.

"You can touch it." Ava laughs. "I wanted to touch it when I first saw it."

Theo runs his fingertips over the smooth surface. "I love it."

Ava takes her seat, and we follow suit. "So, Funkengroovin' is looking for representation. Lucky me. What are your goals and what is your priority?"

Theo glances at me, so I begin. "We're presently under contract with a manager. The relationship is new, and we had a false start, so we can't say whether we're satisfied with that relationship, but it is ongoing."

Ava nods, "I know Phil. He's one of the good ones."

Theo and I exchange a look. None of the other lawyers we consulted gave feedback or offered their opinion of our management. I can see Theo likes Ava's transparency and I do, too.

"Phil is aware that we're looking for legal representation and we prefer a firm based in Miami rather than New York or LA."

"Why is that?" Ava asks.

Theo answers, "Honestly, because we understand how the industry does business in Miami. It's home, and we want to team up with people from home. We want someone on our side who knows us as people, rather than a lawyer who sees us as a product." Theo holds his hands up as he speaks, "I know we're a commodity, by the way, and we're asking to be bought and sold, but we want to be involved in the decisions and negotiations. Because we're just starting out, we don't want representation that will steamroll us into signing deals just to get a cut."

I jump in. "We're familiar with the development deals you negotiated for Scream, Wet Paint, and Hush Money. Those are the type of contracts we dream of signing."

Ava nods. "The industry is fickle, and I'd rather get my talent on a smaller label, with great distribution and marketing, than on a major right now. But the smaller labels have to be very particular because they don't deal in volume. Revolution can sign you and put a record out in six months, but if you don't produce big numbers on your first release, you're done. Getting dropped from a major is a tough thing to overcome."

I look at Theo and we're both nodding.

"Have you heard …?" Theo asks.

Ava makes a so-so motion with her hand. "Bits and pieces."

"I'd be happy to send you the contract Revolution offered us," Theo says.

"It was probably their boilerplate, but I heard there was a very unconventional addendum. If what I've heard was even close to the offer, I wouldn't have let you sign it."

Theo looks relieved. "Good to hear."

"Whether we move forward together or not, I would advise that you follow up on hitting Luis with a cease and desist. He's slandered you within the industry. I haven't seen that he's crossed the line to libel, but the sooner he knows that you aren't afraid of holding him accountable, the less likely he is to go there."

"I thought of that, but I wondered if we'd get blackballed," I admit.

Ava tilts her head as she considers what I said. "He's a powerful voice in the music business. He's been around a long time. But the old guard is turning over. The old ways of doing things are slowly becoming obsolete."

"Thanks to women like you who aren't intimidated to stand up to the good ol' boy network," I say.

"Maris, you're doing the same thing. Women in this industry need a tough center."

"I suddenly feel inferior," Theo says, making us both chuckle.

"We're standing on the shoulders of the women who came before us," Ava says. "There's no way my grandmother could have been in my position at age 28, you know?"

I nod my head in agreement.

"What about your intellectual property, copyrights, et cetera? I see when you post on YouTube that you have a watermark, and that's smart, but have you followed through with registering the work?"

Theo slides down in his chair a few inches.

"Tell her," I prompt him.

Theo bites his lower lip. "Are you familiar with the US mail?"

Ava laughs. "Vaguely, yes. Is that how you're proving ownership?"

Theo sits tall again. "My father's lawyer said if I mail myself the recordings and then don't break the seal, I have a time, date stamp proving I wrote the material." He laughs. "I still have a CD burner. I hoped an email time date stamp would do the same thing, but …"

Ava shrugs. "If you ever had to challenge misuse of your original music, that method would stand up in court. If we work together, we'll advance your copyright protections by four decades."

"But you knew exactly what I was going to say before I said it," Theo says.

Ava lets out a genuine laugh. "I did."

"Sometimes the old ways are the best ways," Theo says. "Not in this particular case, but I'm sure I can come up with an example, if I think about it long enough."

Ava's professional exterior cracks a little as she shares a laugh with Theo. I like her. She's prepared, she has a good track record, she's tough, but she's personable. I look over at Theo and I nod almost imperceptibly, but he reads me.

"Ava, if you're willing to take us on as clients, we'd be fortunate to have your representation," Theo says.

Ava shows her playful side as she makes a fist and says "Yes. Let's make Funkengroovin' the soundtrack for our times!"

I lean across the desk to shake Ava's hand and Theo does the same.

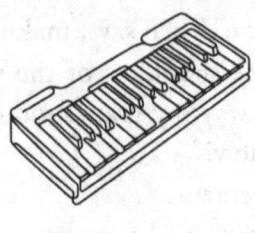

MAX

IT'S NOT MY FAULT THAT I overhear the conversations people have around the pool. I'm not trying to hear them, it's just acoustics. Regardless of how I know that Theo and Maris discussed the elephant in the room, I'm glad that I know. I'm relieved that I don't have to run interference or pick Team Nico or Team Theo.

I'm also happy about our upcoming gigs. Of course, I wish we were still on tour. I was just starting to feel comfortable playing in front of ten thousand people. Nico was right when he said that we didn't have to work that hard to win them over. It felt like the audience was there to support us and vibe on our music. But, since we're back in Miami, I'm looking forward to using a different music muscle to play a more sophisticated genre. That's how I see it, anyway. Theo is actually a great jazz drummer, and Maris has adapted to playing upright bass remarkably quickly. I think they might be enjoying the departure like I am. At least they aren't complaining about it.

Another positive development is the relationship Maris and Theo forged with Ava Lopez. I can't wait to get her input on my idea, but I have to sell it to Theo first. I'm sure Maris will agree to move forward with my plan, and she can probably talk Nico into it if he isn't sure. But I have to start with Theo, so I'm sitting at the kitchen island waiting for him to come inside after his swim. He's usually in a great mood after time in the sun and water.

"Hey Maxer," Maris strolls through the kitchen wearing a bikini and holding a beach towel.

"Are you going out to the pool?"

Mare stops walking and slides her sunglasses down to reveal her eyes. "You should be a detective," she jokes.

"It's just, if you go out there, Theo will probably stay longer, and I was hoping to talk to him about something before we get ready for the gig."

"Oh," Maris looks through the picture window at the lanai. "How long has he been in the pool?"

"Fifty-three minutes. He should be in soon."

Maris laughs. "You really should be a detective. You notice everything. I can wait another few minutes if you think that might help your cause." She leans across the kitchen island and points at my iPad. "Are you pitching music? Not trying to be nosy, just curious."

"Nope." I feel like it would be disrespectful to show anyone what I've been working on before I show Theo.

"Okay," Maris searches the fridge for a box of coconut water and grabs a banana from the fruit basket on the counter. She opens a package of almonds and stares at me while she snacks.

"If you're trying to get me to tell you what I want to talk to Theo about, I'm not going to."

Maris shakes her head and holds up her pointer finger while she swallows. "I'm just hanging out like you asked me too. I am curious about why you're so nervous and paranoid right now though."

"I have what I think is a great idea that could generate some revenue for the band, but Theo might not agree."

Maris tilts her head towards the lanai where Theo is toweling off. "Very cool, Maxer. Good luck."

Theo opens the slider for Maris and tells her that he's going to make a lasagna for dinner. I think it takes a while to put that together, so my timing is good.

"What's good, Max? You hyped for the gig tonight?"

"Yeah, man. I ironed a shirt."

Theo chuckles. "I've had to dress like an adult so much this week, it's kind of freaking me out."

"You're more a T-shirt and shorts guy on your time off."

"And on stage if it's appropriate, but these upscale jazz gigs ..."

Theo puts his nose in the air in a display of snobbery and then starts assembling the ingredients he needs for dinner.

"Speaking of T-shirts, I've been working on something for a few weeks that I'd like to show you. I was checking out some of the other bands' merch on tour ..." I bring my iPad to life, and the screen displays a Funkengroovin' T-shirt with our faces on it.

Theo moves closer to the screen. "Is that the photo we took in the studio the first day we rehearsed together?"

It's the one I look good in, the one with Maris's arm around my shoulder. "Yeah, but there are other designs too." I start the slideshow I made and Theo leans on the countertop to focus on the screen. He's smiling. I have the order memorized. First, the casual shot of the four of us, then there's a workup of just our logo, then one with four rectangles with individual stage photos of our first night of the tour, then separate T-shirts featuring each band member.

Theo laughs as each new image pops up. "These are cool, Max."

"I own the copyright for all of the photos, so we don't have issues there. And here is a sample," I unfold a cerulean blue T-shirt featuring the full band. "This is the weight and blend of the shirts that I think would be good quality, yet reasonably priced so we still make a decent profit on each unit."

Theo takes the shirt from me and inspects it. He's grinning.

"The company that would make the shirt or shirts for us is located right here in Miami and they can print on demand, or make the shirts in batches, depending on how we would decide to offer them for sale. It can be one hundred percent online through our website, or Amazon, whatever ecommerce platform we choose."

"What's our price per shirt?" Theo asks.

"Twelve bucks if we want colors, ten if we make the shirts all white."

"That includes the graphic?"

"Yeah, and the application process is screen printing, so the ink is absorbed into the fibers of the shirt, which washes well without fading."

Theo's eyebrows raise. "What price point do you think you could sell them for?"

"I think nineteen ninety-nine works. Remember when we bought the

Knoxville shirts on tour? They were twenty-five and Dame's tour shirts were thirty. In this retail space, I think we should stay under twenty."

Theo nods. "Did you show these to Maris?"

"No, I wanted to run it past you first, but if we're showing Maris, maybe we should show her this one." I hold up the teal Maris shirt. It's a beautiful photo of her face below her name with Funkengroovin' written in our signature script underneath.

Theo howls. "I love it! Maris, get in here."

"Or you could go with a Theo T." I hold up the sample featuring his face on cobalt blue. "Or the Nico." I paired a black and white photo of Nico playing guitar on a stone-colored shirt to show another option.

"What's up?" Maris comes through the slider and squeals when she sees the Nico T. "Oh my God, I want that!"

I hold it behind my back. "Do you have sunscreen on your hands? This is a sample."

"This is the idea, Max?"

"Show Maris the slide show," Theo prompts. "And the other shirt samples."

As Theo holds each one up, Maris reacts with little screams of approval.

"Max found a local company that will print these on demand. We could sell them from the ecommerce platform of our choosing."

"I want to talk to Ava about licensing the designs first and anything else I might not know about selling merch. But I thought it could be a good way to generate some revenue while we're in professional purgatory."

"I want the Nico one," Maris says. "How much?"

"Well, I guess there's a market." Theo says laughing. He refocuses on making dinner.

"So, can I talk to Ava about this and move forward with it?" I ask.

"Absolutely. Thanks for doing all the legwork, my man. I think it's a great idea. We can each post about them on IG once the op is a go. And, Max, you can take a cut for yourself. It's your idea after all."

"All for one and one for all, Theo. Just like us giving Nico a cut of the gig money."

I'm not sure what to do when Theo runs towards me, so I do nothing and find myself thrown over his shoulder and spinning at high velocity while Maris laughs and yells, "Whirlybird!"

My ideas, playing as a jazzy trio and selling the shirts, are coming in clutch and I'm proud of myself. If I resist barfing down Theo's back, I'll be even more proud.

THEO

I HAVE TO ADMIT THAT I'M digging playing with drum brushes. I've messed around with them here and there over the years, but the type of music we play in Funkengroovin' requires heavy hits with heavy sticks. Brushes are more dynamic and sensual. Dragging the brush across my snare is like painting a sound. It's kind of mesmerizing, but I wasn't joking when I told Nico it makes me sleepy. The jazzy music we're play-ing requires different techniques, so I'm challenged as a musician, but there's no adrenaline producing physicality. I don't necessarily want to be a sweaty mess in the lobby of the Ritz, though.

Maris had the biggest challenge to overcome when we transitioned to jazz. She kind of had to learn a whole new instrument. We borrowed an upright bass from one of Max's jazz friends, and Maris had to adjust to playing a fretless instrument that requires a lot more physicality than her electric bass. But she's showing out. The three of us toss solos back and forth. It's very low key. Maris has Nico on FaceTime so he can listen. Anyone else would think he's asleep in a hammock by the lake, but I know he shuts down the visual part of his brain when he wants the audio receptors on full alert. The moon is bright enough to light his features, so I play a cool fill, and his smile confirms what I already knew.

Three hours goes slowly without the band interactions we're used to on stage. We don't engage the guests who are having cocktails in the lobby lounge, either. In fact, the goal is to be as imperceptible as the fragrance the Ritz disperses into the space. I've decided this isn't a gig, it's a job.

We finish the six-minute-long song we've milked for all it was worth and, as I count us into the next one, Shana and her friend Emily clap loudly. I bite my lip due to secondhand embarrassment. No one else acknowledges our presence, which is standard in this setting. I try to remind myself that Shana is trying to be supportive and she's taking an interest in what I'm doing, but I don't look at her.

Nico is clapping too, but he has himself muted, so we can't hear him. Also, no one can see Maris's phone screen except us.

Shana is wearing a short, silver cocktail dress tonight. It fits like a second skin, and she looks gorgeous. I chuckle to myself when two lame looking dudes in suits invite themselves to sit at the girls' table. Emily must like one of them because she moves her purse from the chair next to her. One of the dudes is talking into Shana's ear and Maris looks over at me and laughs while rolling her eyes. I shrug. Of course, two attractive women sitting alone are going to get hit on. It's a law of nature.

We play for twenty more minutes, and then it's time for our only break of the night. Maris heads to the outdoor balcony to chat with Nico, and I press play on canned break music, then hit the head. Max follows. I know he will also follow me to the table to meet Emily, but I invite him anyway.

"Hello, ladies," I say as Max and I approach the table. The two dudes look offended that we're honing in. Shana obviously didn't tell them she's here to see me.

"The band sounds great," Shana says. "We're really enjoying the music. Are you from Miami?"

I smirk at her. I'll play. "We are. Are you visiting?"

Max rolls his eyes and sits on the arm of Emily's stuffed chair, placing himself between her and the dude she was talking to. "I'm Max," he holds his hand out.

"Emily. And this is David."

"Hey David, what do you do for a living?" Max asks.

"We're in investment banking," David says. "We're in town for a convention from Philly."

"Philly's a great music town," Max says. "Used to go down there for gigs when I was at the Berklee College of Music."

Shana and I look at each other and almost break character. She's familiar with Max's tendency to lead with Berklee.

"I wouldn't know really. I don't have a lot of time outside of work," David says.

I hold my hand out to the dude sitting next to Shana. "Theo Athanasiou." I can tell that he recognizes my last name. Maybe they really are investment bankers.

"Morgan," he says, shaking my hand.

"So, what do you think of the music, Emily?" Max asks.

"It's nice—"

"Do you guys normally bother guests by approaching couples?" David asks. "This is kind of like a bartender inviting himself to join our party, isn't it?"

I glance at Shana, but she doesn't say anything. "You're right, David. I don't want to lose the gig, so we'll say goodnight." Ball's in your court, Shana.

"Goodnight." David has an attitude.

I raise my eyebrows at Shana who smiles sweetly but doesn't tell David and Morgan that she and Emily are here to see us.

That's not how I thought this was going to go. I lift my chin in Max's direction. He looks at Shana and says, "You better not be in my kitchen in the morning, Shana."

"Her name is Monica," Morgan says with disdain.

I laugh and shake my head as we walk away.

"I fucking hate her, Theo," Max says. We go outside to where Maris is FaceTiming with Nico. "Shana just acted like she didn't know us, and she told those dudes her name is Monica."

Nico busts out laughing. "Is this part of a kinky sex game you guys play, Theo?"

"Man, I don't even know. At first, I played along, but she let those dudes diss us, so I'm pissed."

"That's fucked up," Maris says.

"I'm on a job, so it's not like I can cause a scene. I'm not going to jeopardize the gig," I say.

"She can't handle it when your attention is on anything besides her," Max says.

"Enough Shana talk," I say. "What do you think of the material, Nico?"

"I wish I could be there with an acoustic guitar, my guy. But the three of you sound awesome. I'm proud."

"You can join Weather Channel anytime you want to, Nico," Max says.

Nico laughs again. "That's what you're calling yourselves? Oh, wait, I get it ... Weather Report—"

"But not at all, no cap." Maris laughs.

"I like it. And I love what you're doing. Wish I could stick around for the next set, but I told Marcus I'd swing by the tavern to help him inebriate our friends and family."

"You're doing God's work, brother," Theo says.

"Go play your ass off and don't look at Shana once," Nico says.

"That won't be hard." I throw a shaka at the screen.

"Bye, Nico!" Max calls.

"Love you, babe," Nico tells Maris.

I can't help myself. "Love you too, babe."

Maris rolls her eyes and blows a kiss before ending the call.

"It feels like he's here," Max says. "I'm glad we get to talk to him and see him so much."

Maris agrees as I hold the door open for all of us to go back to the lobby stage.

"The dudes are still sitting with the girls," Max reports.

"Whatever." I take my place and call a song.

Halfway into it, Shana and her party of four stand up and start for the exit, but not before Morgan comes over to the band stand holding a twenty. He looks for a tip jar, and when he doesn't see one, he lets the bill fall to the floor in front of my drum set. I laugh and shake my head but keep playing.

"Goodnight," Maris says into her mic.

Morgan then flips me off and walks to where the other three are waiting for him. Shana is looking at me with excitement in her eyes. Like she's anticipating something. I go against Nico's advice, and I smile at her and then nod, then sweep one of my brushes twice in her direction as if removing her from the scene. Her face turns to stone. I've seen this look before. She's not getting what she wants. I can't hold back my laughter and her face turns redder. Whatever.

They leave, and the kicker comes at the end of the night when the lobby server brings me Shana's bar tab. She treated her new friends to quite a few libations at Ritz prices. What a witch.

On the way home, she calls four times, but I don't pick up. When I pull into my driveway, her Nissan Altima is blocking the gate. Max and Maris rode together in the Jeep and they're right behind me, so I toot the horn to signal Shana to back up. Instead, she comes to the driver's side of my truck. She struts through my headlight beams with a seductive look on her face.

"I left Emily with Morgan and David and came straight over," she says.

"So, you're a shitty friend. Congrats. Move your car, Maris is right behind me, and we'd like to relax after an unnecessarily trying job."

"The code isn't working," Shana explains.

"You don't know the code anymore," I say. "And you don't need to, since you won't be coming here anymore."

Shana looks stunned. She looks away from me and then looks back, eyes blazing. "I was just trying to spice things up, Theo. God! Overreact much?"

"You haven't matured at all, Shana. That's not spicing things up, that's a childish attempt to humiliate me in public, and then you left your girlfriend with two strange men. Terrible judgement. We're not getting back together." I stare into her eyes, so she can see that I'm serious. "Leave, or I'll call the cops. You're trespassing."

"Oh, my God, this is just another one of our stupid fights, Theo. The longer we stay out here, the longer we have to wait to make up."

Maris pulls up, but her Jeep doesn't fully fit behind the two cars between her and the gate. She parks on the road and gets out of the Jeep. "What's up? Is the gate broken?"

"Nope," I say. "It's blocked and the person blocking it won't get out of the way."

"Shana, can you please move your car? I want to take a bath and go to bed."

Shana looks back and forth between Maris and I. "Ohhhhhhhh. Okay. I get it. You're together now."

I feel my face scrunching up in confusion. "No. I'm single. And looking. Just not looking in your direction anymore."

Maris makes a hand signal that swoops around where Shana's car is parked next to the call box. I nod as Maris walks over to the keypad and types in the numbers I shared with her the morning after we recorded Silver Springs. The gate retracts and I drive around the Altima, followed by Maris in the Jeep. When I park in the garage, I look into my rearview and see headlights sweeping across the front of the house, indicating that Shana turned around.

What did I ever see in her? Did I really think our relationship was normal?

"Good riddance," Max says as he steps out of the Jeep. "Good job telling her to skedaddle."

When Max comes into the garage, I drape my arm around his shoulders. "I wish you had told me she was a terrible person sooner, my guy. Could have saved me a lot of time, heartache, and money."

"That's not funny, Theo."

I laugh anyway. "This time is easy. I'm already over it. She talks a good game on the phone, but in person, she immediately started her shit again. Ain't nobody got time for that."

Max repeats even louder, "Ain't nobody got time for that!" He takes a deep breath. "She will rue the day, Theo. Our stock is on the rise and she's gonna have to watch from the cheap seats."

"At least I know, now." I turn around. "Maris, where the hell are you?"

"Theo! Max! I need you!"

MARIS

I THOUGHT IT WAS JUST CRAMPS. Even though I take birth control continuously and only have a period every three months, sometimes I still get monthly cramps and spotting. We don't talk about it enough, but being female hurts a lot, and often. It's normal. I took Ibuprofen to get through the gig, but it didn't help. In fact, the pain in my abdomen got worse as the night went on. All I could think about on the drive home was a getting relief in a warm bath, but when I tried to get out of the Jeep it felt like something inside me … burst.

"What's wrong, Mare?" Max is leaning in the passenger door, and Theo is by my side.

I'm shaking uncontrollably. "I'm bleeding." I slide my hand between my dress and the driver's seat and show them the thick, dark mess.

"Oh, my God." There's panic in Max's voice.

"Max, pull my truck out and park the passenger door right next to Maris," Theo says softly. "Maris, you're going to be okay. We've got you."

My breathing starts to feel restricted, and my vision goes down to a pinhole. My fingers feel tingly.

"I need you take a deep breath, okay? Look at me," Theo says sweetly. "I need you to breathe with me. Breathe in for four … good."

Max backs Theo's truck next to us.

"I'm going to lift you up slowly. If it hurts, tell me, okay? I'm going to move very slowly."

"But your truck …" my words come out staggard and shaky. "There are towels in the back of my Jeep."

"I don't give a shit, Maris," Theo says as he effortlessly lifts me out of the Jeep. "You okay?"

I nod and bury my face in Theo's shoulder.

"You're okay," he whispers. Theo gently places me on the passenger seat of his truck and tells Max to get in beside me.

"I got you, Mare." Max wraps one arm around my shoulders and the other around my midsection. "Theo, go to Florida Mercy."

"I'm so scared," I tell them. "I don't know what's happening."

Max tells Siri to "*Call Mom,*" and he puts the phone on speaker.

The call is answered on the first ring. "How was the jazz gig, honey?"

"We're headed your way with a twenty-six-year-old female who is experiencing sudden vaginal bleeding."

"Maris?"

"Yes."

"How far away are you?"

"Just left Theo's house. Ten minutes, the way he's driving."

"I'll be waiting for you at intake."

The calls ends and Max sees the question in my eyes. "All of my parents are doctors."

My questions will have to wait. "Ow, oh my God."

"It's okay, Mare. Mom will know what to do."

Theo takes his right hand off the wheel and intertwines his fingers with mine.

"Almost there, Maris, almost there," he says as his thumb draws slow lazy circles in the palm of my hand. "Blowing this red light," he warns. "And now we're following the signs to the ER."

"There's my mom," Max says. Before the truck comes to a complete stop, Max opens the door, and his mother rolls a wheelchair closer.

Before I realize that Theo left the truck, he's gently transferring me from the truck to the wheelchair.

"I grabbed your purse, Mare," Max says.

"Hang onto it for now," his mom says. "I'll come get you guys from the waiting room."

The chair is moving through the sliding doors, and I feel a blast of arctic air as we enter the building.

"Maris, I'm Sylvia Castelano, aka Max's mom. I'm going to take you straight back to an examination room."

"Thank you," I manage.

"When did this start, honey?"

I try to estimate time, but I'm coming up clueless. "I felt cramping during the day, and it got worse as the evening wore on. I've been spotting, but that's not abnormal. I didn't start bleeding profusely until I tried to get out of my Jeep ... about fifteen or twenty minutes ago, I guess."

"Are you pregnant?"

Hearing the words out loud make me cry. Of course, that's what this is ... what else could it be?

"I—don't know. I didn't think so. I take birth control pills continuously for three months ... what if I ..." I can't get the words out.

Dr. Castellano closes the curtain covering the door to the exam room and squats down in front of the wheelchair. "Are you wondering if continuing to take your birth control pills after becoming pregnant causes a miscarriage?"

I choke on my sobs and cover my face with my hands.

"If that's what's happening, taking birth control would not be the cause. Repeat that back to me."

"Taking birth control if I was pregnant would not cause a miscarriage."

"That's right. Let's get you out of that beautiful dress and into this elegant paper wrap around."

I hear myself say thank you, but I don't feel like I'm in my body right now. The word *pregnant* is looping through my mind in 4/4 time. *Preg-nant, preg-nant.* There's heavy clotting in my underwear, but I have heavy periods. That's why my doctor recommended reducing the frequency of them.

"It could be just spotting, right?" I ask hopefully. "I'm not necessarily losing ..."

"We'll find out, honey. We'll get an ultrasound. Is there anyone you want to be in the room with you? Or anyone I could call? Your mom, maybe?"

"No." I say sharply, reacting to the suggestion of calling my mother. "Do you think Theo and Max would freak out if I asked them to come in? Considering the nature of the exam?"

"We have a privacy screen that I can use."

I nod and Dr. Castellano promises that she will be right back.

I'm alone with my thoughts. Or maybe I'm not alone. I lay my palm across my abdomen. I wish Nico was here. I need him so badly. I try to picture him beside me, holding my hand. I try to imagine what he would say if I discovered I was pregnant in a conventional way. Would he be happy? Upset? We've never discussed the possibility because I was on the pill. I could be carrying Nico's baby. *Nico's baby* replaces *pregnant, pregnant* and begins repeating in my mind. A little Nico. I picture a chubby blonde toddler. My heart swells, but I can't let my mind stay fixed on that image. I try to figure out how far along I might be, but skipping cycles like I do makes it impossible.

Max appears in the doorway followed closely by Theo. "Mare."

"I don't know anything yet," I tell them.

Theo leans over the railing of the hospital bed and kisses my forehead. His white shirtsleeve has blood on it.

"I'm sorry, Theo," I whisper.

"Oh, Maris. Just be okay. Don't worry about anything, just be okay."

Dr. Castellano is pulling the curtain back and two nurses come into the room behind her with the privacy screen and an ultrasound machine.

"Gentlemen, if you'll help the patient relax, we'll see what we're dealing with," she says. A few minutes later she softly touches the inside of my thigh and tells me that I'm going to feel some pressure.

Theo strokes my arm and Max's hand doesn't leave my shoulder. I press my eyes closed and brace myself to hear whatever comes next. In this moment, I realize that I very much want to be spotting and I want to hear the pregnancy is viable and stable. I start praying. Minutes drag past. The room is quiet. Too quiet, I decide. If Dr. Castelano was seeing anything reassuring, she would have announced it by now. The tears stream down my face and someone brushes them away. I hold my hands out and Theo and Max immediately grab them. I feel that the exam is finished, but there is no communication from the other side of the privacy screen. I don't need to hear what I already know. I open my eyes and see that Theo and Max both have tears running down their faces. The three of us hold onto each other, bracing to be hit by the words.

Dr. Castelano comes to our side of the privacy screen, and I can see it on her face. She takes in the sight of the three of us, two brothers and a sister, and she almost smiles. "I'm sorry, Maris. You experienced a random, yet common medical event that we refer to as miscarriage."

Theo and Max tighten their grips on my hands and Dr. Castellano's face softens.

"You must be a tough woman because it probably started a week or so ago. Tonight, you passed what we call 'the products of conception,' which means that the process is over. You'll have some cramping and spotting for a few days, possibly longer. I'll give you plenty to read, but I don't want to flood you with information right now. Do you have any questions for me?"

I don't know where to start. "How far?"

"Very early. I'd estimate four to six weeks."

"Why?"

Dr. Castellano shakes her head. "It's usually chromosomal and a miscarriage doesn't mean that your next pregnancy won't be perfectly healthy. It only means that this particular combination of egg and sperm didn't have the chromosomal material it needed, for whatever reason, to develop. It's very unlikely to recur."

I can't speak, so I nod my head. When I look into Dr. Castellano's eyes, I see so much compassion there. She nods back to me. "You can call me anytime in the coming days or weeks if you have any questions or concerns. If you develop a fever, or have pain, let me know, okay?"

I nod again.

"Unfortunately, there is some paperwork that we have to complete before we discharge you."

"You're sending her home?" Max sounds pissed.

"Home is the best place to rest and recover," his mother tells us. "And, I get it now, Max. When you talk about the band being family. I understand it now. But don't forget you have blood family and family by marriage, too. We would like to see you every now and then."

Max squeezes my hand before releasing it and gives his mom a quick, dutiful hug.

"How's the jaw, Theo? I had Max on watch for signs of concussion not too long ago."

"Totally fine, doc, thanks."

"Is all of that … animus resolved now? You're going home to a safe and peaceful environment?"

"Completely resolved, ma'am," Theo says.

"Is Nico still in Wisconsin?"

"He's on his way to Miami as we speak." Theo turns to me. "I hope you're not mad at me, but I called him from the waiting room. Marcus is driving Nico to Green Bay tonight, but the first flight out isn't until five am, so he's going to get a room. He'll be here before noon."

"I'm so relieved, Theo. Thank you." I feel like a coward, but I'm glad that I don't have to tell Nico what happened. And I'm glad that he's with the brother he's closest to. I can't predict what his feelings will be about the pregnancy, but I'm so happy that he's coming to be with me. With us. I need my family around me right now, and in a relatively short time, these men became the people I can rely on most for love and support.

"Maris, I can get you some scrubs from the vending machine. There's a shower down the hall if you feel ready, and I am sending you home with a week's supply of disposable underpants and pads, okay?"

"Mare, if you get your insurance card and other info from your purse, Theo and I can fill out the paperwork while you freshen up … if you want."

I clear my throat and find my voice. "Yeah, that would be great, Maxer. Thanks."

"I'll bring a plastic bag for your dress," Dr. Castelano says.

"Mmmmm. No, thank you. I don't want to take it with me."

Max's mom switches into mother mode again. "I'll take care of it for you, honey. Do you think you can walk down the hall, or would you like a ride?" She grabs the handles of the wheelchair.

"Can I walk? Will it be okay?"

Dr. Castellano nods. "But if you're feeling dizzy or weak, you shouldn't try."

"I want to try," I say.

"Max and Theo, go to the front desk and ask for Maris's paperwork, then fill it out to the best of your ability. Maris can fill in the blanks when she's finished. Maris, I'll walk you down to the bathroom and get you those scrubs."

"Thank you so much."

I wait for the boys to leave the room before I uncover my lower half and sit up. I'm a mess. Part of me doesn't want to wash the clots down the drain. It doesn't feel right, knowing what could have been. The other part of me wants to expunge all evidence of this from my awareness. Not that I'll ever fully be able to do that.

Max's mom points out how to call the nurse's station if I need help, and she leaves me with a set of dark green scrubs, mesh underwear, and a pad that is bigger than anything I've seen. The shower gel is antibacterial, of course, and it smells like a hospital, but it's a colossal improvement to my present condition. I use the harsh medicinal soap to wash my hair and face, and then I scrub my body twice. I can't cry anymore and I'm so tired. I want to be unconscious and stay that way until Nico comes.

I towel dry my hair and slip into the medical attire Dr. Castelano brought, complete with socks that have grip on the bottom. I don't care what happened to my shoes. I'd never wear them again, even if they were wearable.

When I emerge from the private shower room, Max and Theo are standing in the hallway.

Theo wraps me in his arms and whispers, "Remember what you told me, Maris. God isn't cruel. He isn't into torturing us. We have to trust Him." He releases me and offers his elbow.

Max falls in alongside as we walk towards the exit. "We're all set, Mare," Max says. "I'm going to borrow my mom's car because it's lower to the ground. Easier to get into. Theo will follow us home in the truck."

I don't question the plan.

Max is carrying a stack of papers and pamphlets, and what looks like several plastic blankets. The car is waiting at the entrance to the emergency room, and Theo opens the passenger door for me to get in. He tells us that he's right behind us, and we drive home.

NICO

WHEN THE UBER PULLS UP to Theo's house, the gate is open. I texted him when I landed to tell him I was on the way. There's a truck wrapped with advertising for car detailing parked next to Theo's truck. A man is working on Maris's Jeep and the tangible reality of what happened hits me in the chest. He's cleaning Maris's blood. My heart is in my throat as I open the front door and take the stairs two at a time to get to her room.

The door is open, and Max and Theo are on either side of her on the California King. Maris is asleep, so I hold my finger to my lips. Theo gently, slowly gets off the bed and Max stays put. I nod to Max and follow Theo out into the loft. After the fear, worry, and stress of getting here, I'm overwhelmed by the sadness that permeates the house. Theo hugs me and I bear hug him back.

"Thank you for being there for her, brother. I was losing my mind, but I knew she was in good hands."

Theo doesn't let go. "I'm so sorry, Nico. For everything. I'm so sorry."

We stay like that for a minute before slapping each other on the back.

"How is she?"

"She fell asleep an hour or so after we got home. Max made her some oatmeal this morning. One or both of us have been with her every minute."

"Does she hate me for not being here? I hate myself."

Theo shakes his head. "She's worried about you. She's not sure how you're going to take all of this."

I run my hands down my face. "Worried about *me*?"

"You know Maris," Theo says with a chuckle.

"I saw the detailer downstairs …"

"It was … pretty terrifying. She was scared. We were all scared, but Max called his mother who is an ER doctor, did you know that?"

I shake my head.

"All of his parents are doctors, evidently. We need to unpack that at some point, but his mother took charge once we got to Florida Mercy, and she was great. I told you everything she told Maris, and she gave us a bunch to read." Theo focuses on me. "Are you okay?"

"All I could think about was getting here and now that I am … it's real now. You know? My first concern is Maris."

"Yeah. All of us, man. We're going to get you guys through this."

My eyes start to sting. I clear my throat and lock that shit down but knowing that Theo and Max are feeling this as deeply as Maris and I adds another layer of emotion.

Theo's phone goes off. He takes it from his pocket and looks at the screen. "Delivery at the front door."

"I think it's from the Van Asten clan. They all wanted to come, like all of them, but I said they'd have to settle for sending flowers for now."

Theo places his hand on my shoulder as he passes to head downstairs.

I go back into Maris's room and Max creeps out of bed without waking her. He meets me in the doorway and gives me a hug.

"Thanks for being there for her brother, and thanks for hooking her up with your mom."

"Of course, man. Glad you're home. She's been having some discomfort. The heating pad seems to help, and she can take pain reliever as needed. Mostly, it's emotional pain, though." Max presses his lips together. "My mom told her that what happened isn't her fault, but I think we have to reinforce that."

I nod in agreement. "Thanks, buddy. Anything else I should know?"

"She thinks she's playing the Ritz gig tonight."

A smile spontaneously takes over my face. "So, she's still Maris."

Max laughs. "Still Maris. She told me to wake her up when you got here, but I'll let you do that." He closes the door behind him.

I'm wearing the joggers that Maris refers to as my cuddle pants because they're soft. I take off the long-sleeved T-shirt I layered over a tank for the flight and get under the covers next to my girl. Instinctively, she places her head on my chest. Pure love radiates through my entire body. I sing her favorite Bill Withers tune softly into her hair.

She lifts her eyes to mine and gasps. "Nico."

I kiss her forehead. "I'm here."

We hold each other tightly for several minutes, just breathing each other in and luxuriating in physical togetherness.

"I'm glad you're here."

"I'm so sorry I wasn't here last night. I'm never going to be that far away from you again, Maris. Not ever." I kiss her forehead once more and play with her hair. She smells like the hospital, forcing me to rethink about everything she went through last night without me. "I'm never leaving your side."

"I'm so sorry you had to find out over the phone from Theo," Maris's voice breaks.

"I'm glad he called when he did. Gave me the time I needed to be here now. How do you feel? Are you in pain?"

Maris rests her head on my chest. "It comes and goes. Just feels like menstrual cramps at this point. It's tapered off a lot."

"But you had pain last night?"

Maris exhales. "Yeah. It was so scary, Nico. I didn't know what was happening and once I understood, I was hoping that somehow everything would be okay."

I've had hours to come up with the magic words to end Maris's anguish, but I have nothing. "Love, it wasn't meant to be this time."

"Would you have been … happy?"

I move her hair aside and massage the back of her neck. "Yes. But also terrified. I'd love to have a baby with you when the time is right. I spent the night thinking about what a little person who came from us might be like. How could that kid not be totally awesome? But I don't have anything to give a child right now. I barely have anything to give you. And what would happen to our music?" I brace myself for Maris's reply. Maybe it's too soon to be talking like this. Maybe I should let her steer the conversation.

"We're not married. It might be old-fashioned, but I'd want to be married first, if I had the choice. But if the pregnancy had been viable—"

"We would have welcomed that baby and loved that baby with the same devotion we have for each other."

Maris starts to cry, and I can't hold back any longer. I haven't cried yet, and now I know it's because the only person I could share my tears with is her. We lay in the bed together, intertwined and let it all out in the safety of each other's arms. It wasn't the right time. I firmly believe that, but it still hurts. And knowing that Maris has emotional and physical pain adds to mine. As awful as this is, there's nowhere I'd rather be than here, with her, in this moment.

I can barely form words, but I choke out, "I love you completely, Maris."

"I love you all the way too," she says.

I guide Maris's face to mine and kiss her tenderly. Our tears mingle and our noses run, and we stay this way for hours.

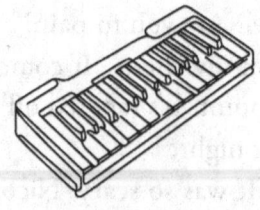

MAX

I'M GLAD NICO'S BACK BECAUSE I know he takes good care of Mare. Not that she needs anyone to take care of her, and not that Theo and I weren't doing a good job, of course. There's just no one who can play Nico's role but Nico. He appreciates how we handled things in his absence too, which feels good. I hate seeing the big man suffer though, and I heard them crying when I went up to my room earlier. Mom called to check on Mare and said it was okay for her to be up and around, so Theo and I are firing up the pizza oven to make dinner for everyone before we have to do the Ritz job.

I know Nico wants all the meats on his pizza and Mare likes cheese and mushroom with scallions. Theo's making a *Greek Masterpiece* for himself, and I told him that I'll be happy with whatever he wants to put on mine. While Theo cooks the pies, I set the table on the lanai. I put the flower arrangement that Nico's family sent in the center and find candles to light. I want everything to be perfect.

I hear Theo using talk-to-text: *Hey fucker, time to come down and eat.*

"That is no way to talk to Mare," I say, which makes Theo laugh. It's a nice sound. No one's been laughing today. "What do you want to drink?"

"I'll have a Corona. Thanks, Max."

"Mare will have water, but what do you think Nico wants?"

"A bottomless bank account and the ability to burn off calories like when I was a teenager." Nico's voice carries across the pool.

"To drink, was the question," I say.

Maris notices the flowers and the candles. "Aw, this is so nice. Thanks, you guys."

"The flowers are from Nico's family." I give her a hug. "You have color in your cheeks again. That's really good to see."

She squeezes me. "Thanks for everything, little brother."

"Okay, Max, that's enough huggy-huggy with my girl."

"I'm grabbing a Corona for me and Theo, want one?" I ask him.

"Yes, please and thank you, bro."

I want to be irritated with him, but I can't be. It's so good to have his snarky ass home.

When I come back from the kitchen, everyone is seated at the table, so I pass the drinks around and take my seat.

"I don't want to get too heavy, but ... I'm happy to be here with you guys, even though the circumstances suck. I missed you assholes and I love you. Thanks for having my back." Nico lifts his Corona bottle, and we toast.

"Welcome home, brother," Theo says.

"It feels right now that you're back, Nico."

"Speaking of backs and having each other's, Nico seems to think I shouldn't gig tonight, so will you guys please tell him that my doctor said I could do whatever I feel up to doing?"

Theo and I exchange looks and reply with individual versions of *absolutely not.*

"Are you guys serious? Not you too!" Maris protests. "The Ritz is expecting a three-piece."

"We already decided that I'm playing left hand bass on keys and we're doing the gig as a duo tonight, Mare. You're outvoted on this one."

"It's settled," Nico says. "Is a night off home alone with your man all that bad?"

Maris smiles. "Of course not. We don't miss gigs though."

"Maris, honestly, you've done this gig. We're wallpaper. It doesn't matter. Max and I will give them two great sets and we'll be outta there. Stay home and rest."

Mare looks at Nico and he winks at her before he leans over for a kiss.

"No sex, you guys. Not for a couple weeks," I remind them.

"What the actual fuck, Max?" Nico says.

"I'm just saying. I don't know if Maris read the pamphlets."

Nico busts out laughing. "That's the Maxest thing you've ever said."

Theo's eyebrows raise. "Oh. Yeah. That reminds me of another Max thing. What's up with having doctors for parents and never mentioning it before?"

I roll my eyes and use my napkin to wipe my mouth. "There's some family drama there and some trauma. Mostly momma drama trauma. I wrote a few cathartic songs about it."

Theo makes the hand signal for *keep going*.

"I don't tell people this stuff, but we're family, so ... when I was about eight, I noticed that when my dad went away for medical conventions, my mom's friend always came to stay with us. Like, every time. And once I asked if it could be just mom and I home alone. She said she needed time with her friend and that her *friend*," I made air quotes with my fingers, "loved spending time with us. I didn't want the friend to come, so I asked my dad to talk to my mom about it and he said he would. Well, they had a big fight in their bedroom, so I listened by the door and realized that my dad hadn't known the friend was coming over when he was away."

"Eavesdropping started early," Theo notes.

"Let me finish. This is why I have trust issues. So, my dad went on the trip and my mom's friend came over again. After they went to bed together, in my parent's room, I sat outside the door and figured out what was going on."

"Oh." Mare bites her bottom lip.

"Yeah. So, when Dad came home, he asked me, not mom, if her friend came over and I said yes because honesty is the best policy. He packed his stuff and left. Mom didn't say a word to me about it. A few days later, Sylvia moved in, and I started seeing my dad at his apartment on weekends. None of them told me what was going on. I knew because I found out for myself, but I didn't know mom and Sylvia were married until I saw Dr. Castellano on Sylvia's nametag."

"Dude!" Theo's eyes are bulging. "So, the woman who took care of Maris last night was your stepmom? I thought she was your bio mom because she has the same last name."

"All three of them use the last name Castellano and all three of them still work in the same ER."

"Wow." Nico draws the word out for eight beats. "That's either entirely dysfunctional or the most elevated example of uncoupling and recoupling known to man."

"It's the first thing," I confirm. "Dad never remarried. My moms want me to pretend that they handled everything perfectly. They thought I was too young to understand. I didn't care if my mom was bi or lesbian or cheating … who cares? I was a kid who had no idea what the adults in my life were doing, and I learned early that no one tells the truth, and you can't trust anybody."

"Where is Dr. Phil when you need him?" Nico says. Maris elbows him in the ribs. "What? You don't think unfucking that mess requires some therapy?"

"I got out of there as soon as I could, which was college. All my parents wanted me to play orchestral music or be a Broadway musician … you know, something respectable that they could brag about. My attitude was, they were the three worst decision makers on the planet, so they didn't get input into my life choices."

Mare reaches across the table for my hand. "You turned out great,

Maxer. You're honest, loyal, loving … all the things you didn't see modeled for you growing up. I'm prouder of you than ever."

I clear my throat. "It's not like any of them abandoned me, they just kept things from me, and that made me feel unstable."

Theo looks over at Nico who hides his eyes with his hand. "You're thinking it too?"

Nico chuckles. "Yep."

Theo takes a swig of Corona. "Max. Do you remember when Nico and I were in our *your mom* jokes phase?"

"Oh, yes," I say. "I recall."

Nico starts laughing. "Dude, you can hardly hold us accountable for being insensitive, because you didn't tell us."

I can't help but laugh. "Imagine if I had told you—"

"Oh, it would have been ten times worse," Theo says. "Nico had some of those zingers with me that almost made me cry." He laughs hard. "I was like dude, my mom's gone, that's not funny."

"Okay, well I'd only do that when you made jokes about dairy farmers milking my mom, or, no, the worst one was the cottage cheese joke. Dude, I still want to hurt you over that one."

Nico and Theo are laughing like little boys. Mare and I make eye contact and roll our eyes, but we're both smiling widely. When we need them, they're dependable and serious, but there will always be this side of them that emerges when they're together. At least I hope it lasts forever.

"We need to get ready for the Ritz," I tell Theo.

He checks the time on his phone. "Okay, yeah. By the way, Ava is coming tonight."

"I can ask if she's had time to look at the T-shirt stuff I sent her."

"We'll clean up," Nico says. "Go make yourselves look sexy for your gig."

"I wish we were coming with you. So much," Maris says.

"This is weird, but it's not forever," Theo says as he gets up from the table.

"This too, shall pass," I say. "It's great to see you smiling, Mare."

She blows me a kiss, and I follow Theo up the stairs.

THEO

THE WORD IS OUT THAT the jazz group playing at the Ritz, Weather Channel, is ... us. Funkengroovin' enthusiasts are crammed into the lobby, and the lounge manager isn't happy about it. The few followers who order drinks take up space, while inappropriately dressed, and nurse them, making table turnovers rare. They're requesting our originals by yelling them across the lobby like we're in a nightclub. It's great. But I think this will be our last night playing jazz in the Ritz lobby.

Ava, appropriately attired in a long satin slip dress, saves Max and I seats at the table she's been watching from. I notice a few brave men approach her and she seems to graciously dismiss them. No one leaves angry, in other words. The first hour and a half of the gig takes three days, but it's finally break time and I'm geeking over being able to talk to Ava. If Max lets me get a word in, that is.

"You guys sound so great," Ava stands up to hug each of us and give us air kisses. "I can't believe the two of you make so much music. It sounds like a full band."

"Thanks, Ava," Max takes the seat next to her, so I'm left with the chair across.

"Truly. I love your originals, but it's interesting to witness the musical depth you have. I imagine if Nico and Maris were here, it would be even more mind-blowing."

I smile at her as I lean back in the tall chair and cross my legs. There's room for both of us to do so in the seating arrangement only because Ava is tiny. I know women like my height, so why not use it to take up the distance between us?

"I emailed all the information I have on the T-shirts I plan to sell," Max starts. "Did you have a chance to look it over?"

"I took a very cursory look, but merchandising is straight-forward. It's a great idea for generating income," Ava makes a circle in the air with her pointer finger, "probably better than this."

I chuckle. "Working musicians need to work."

"Understood," Ava concedes. "But the sooner you get me a mastered demo, the sooner I can start shopping a deal for you. That's my top priority for you guys."

"I thought it would be the T-shirts," Max says.

"I'll put Russo on that Monday morning." Ava turns to me, "You met him at the office."

"Seems like a very professional cat and he's into fashion, Max."

"Okay, good to know." Max looks pleased.

"How soon do you think you can get into the studio?"

I press my lips together and tilt my head. "It's going to be another couple weeks. We don't want to compromise Nico's recovery, but as soon as his X-Rays show the fracture is resolved, we're at it."

"It shouldn't take us very long to record the songs," Max says. "We played the material on tour, so we know exactly how we want to do it."

"Video of you guys live on tour might be even better than a demo." Ava is thinking out loud. "I'll ask Phil to get me some cuts from the production crew. Cross your fingers that the quality is good."

A server named Kelly drops off a round of drinks for our table and tells us they're courtesy of two women at the bar who are smiling and waving in our direction.

"That's a boss babe move," Ava says. "Takes stones. Max, you should go over and chat to them. It would make their night."

"Really?"

"Of course," Ava encourages him.

"All right. Theo, see you up there." Max grabs his drink and makes his way to the bar.

"Well played," I tell Ava, raising my rocks glass before taking a sip.

"He thinks I'm here for business. So, you kept your promise not to tell anyone."

"I only told him that you were coming tonight," I say coyly. "He doesn't know in what context."

Ava smiles at me mischievously. "It's for the best at this point. Thank you for protecting my reputation."

I lean forward and run my hand down the front of Ava's leg and then up her calf. She shivers.

"This is moving fast. Let me know if it's too fast," I say.

"I was the one who called you, remember?"

"To make an appointment for me to sign the representation contract, not to have me take you on that gorgeous desk of yours. I'm very happy that we didn't damage that beautiful piece of furniture, by the way." I squeeze her calf and lean back into my chair again.

"I've never done this with a client," Ava says. Her chin is down and she's looking up at me through full, flirty eyelashes. "I hope you don't think I'm ..." she shrugs.

"I think you're a woman who goes after what she wants and I'm pretty fucking lucky you saw something in me that you wanted." I take another sip. "I just hope that getting to know me better doesn't change your mind."

Ava's face gets serious. "Theo, everything you told me about what you all went through last night with Maris is all I need to know. You're a genuinely good person." Ava lets her words land. "How is she today?"

I spread my fingertips around the rim of my rocks glass and rotate my writs in small circles, keeping the ice away from the center. "Nico got home around noon, so Max and I left them alone until dinner. We ate together at the house and the dynamic seemed normal. There's still a cloud over all of us and I'm walking on eggshells around Maris, but I think that's to be expected. Hell, last night at this time, the three of us were here playing and everything was fine."

"I've been around a lot of bands and there's always this push-pull dynamic among the members. It fascinates me. The pull with Funkengroovin' seems to be that you guys truly care about one another."

I smile. "We do. We hate each other every third Thursday, though. The music is the other component of the pull. For example, I'm not doing this Ritz gig as a duo if Max isn't the guy on keys, playing left-handed bass."

Ava looks over her shoulder at the bar and I follow her gaze. One of the girls is standing next to Max and she's draped all over him.

"Get it, Max," I joke.

"Now, if he wants to bring her back to your house tonight—"

"No." My tone is sharp. "Not while Maris and Nico are healing. It's a sanctuary not a brothel." I see compassion in Ava's eyes. "Sorry, I went full Zaddy there."

Ava busts out laughing. "You embrace the Zaddy?"

"All of it but the age part. Girls my own age are calling me a Zaddy."

"I'm going to call you Zaddy from now on," Ava threatens.

I look into Ava's eyes and laugh. She's gorgeous, intelligent, independent, and totally out of my league, but she's been on my mind since the first day we met. I don't know how long I can keep her interested in me, but I'm all in to try. As if she can read my mind, she leans forward. I glance at Max and his back is turned, so I rest my forearms on my thighs and make myself available for kissing. Ava makes it sweet and appropriate.

I lower my voice. "By the way, in case you were wondering, I'm not worried about my professional reputation, so whenever you're comfortable going public ..."

"Theo, having sex with your entertainment attorney would only bolster your reputation."

"When my lawyer looks like you, I agree."

Ava laughs and I get up to go back to the stage.

"I'll be here listening," she says. "And then I'll be at the condo."

I run my fingertips down her arm as I walk away and I feel that shiver again, but this time, I'm the one shivering.

MARIS

NICO INSISTS ON CLEANING UP after dinner, so I'm in the living room choosing a movie for us to watch. He's singing to himself, so I mute the TV to listen. I close my eyes and notice how my body reacts to the sound of him vocalizing. Every cell in my body seems to be vibrating with love. He has such an amazing voice. So effortless. And it's not a video that I'm watching alone in my room to keep me company. It's Nico, and he's here.

"I love you!" I yell.

He stops singing and laughs. "I love you, too. Did you find something to watch?"

"No." I turn the TV off and walk into the kitchen where Nico is stacking the dishwasher.

"At the tavern, we have a three-step method for cleaning the drinkware. First you wash, then you rinse, then dunk in quat sanitizer for a minute and set it on the rack to dry. At least that's how you're supposed to do it. Marcus has been in the business so long that he was washing, sanitizing, which throws off the chemical balance because you've just added dish soap to the sanitizer, and then he'd rinse, doubly negating the sanitizer. I don't know how they stay open without me." Nico laughs.

"I'm sorry you had to cut your time at home short," I say.

"No, no, no, don't say that. After three days there, it's like the movie Groundhog Day."

I laugh. "I'm sure that isn't true."

Nico closes the dishwasher and comes to my side of the island. "It's pretty true." He hugs me, but he doesn't hold me as tightly as he normally does. "I can't stop thinking about how awful it would have been if this happened while we were on the road." He takes my face in his hands. "Everything happens for a reason. Think about everything that happened that led to Max's mom being able to take care of you in Miami."

"God is large and in charge. That's the only explanation."

"They call Wisconsin God's Country because there's so much natural wonder, but my favorite part is star gazing at night. Next time I see that sky, you'll be with me."

"We have stars in Florida," I remind him.

Nico sweeps his arm under my knees and carries me to the lanai doors.

"Be careful with your hand!" I say through squeals and laughter.

Nico lays me down on a chaise by the pool and I make room for him beside me. We lie on our backs, my head resting in the crook of his shoulder. He gently rests his left palm on my abdomen.

"How do you feel?"

"Every day is going to get better and when the physical part of it is over, maybe the mental part will start to heal too."

"That's why I brought you to the stars." Nico turns his face to mine. "Maybe the energy that started heading our way will find us and tell us when it's coming back." He kisses me softly and whispers, "Maybe that energy will sprinkle a little star dust on us to set the stage for a return."

His words take my breath away. "Your way of looking at life is my favorite thing about you." I stare into Nico's blue eyes and wonder, for the millionth time, how I'm so lucky to have his heart.

"There are no coincidences, babe. It's all part of the plan." He winks at me.

You know if anyone one else heard you talking like this, they'd think you'd lost your Niconess."

"Marcus already took my bachelor card."

I giggle. "Every time I don't know what to expect from you, you give more than I dared to hope for."

"Because having you by my side is the most important thing in the world, so I'll do whatever it takes to make you want to stay there."

I roll so my body is flush with his and I put my hand under his shirt. When I go to kiss Nico, he pulls away. "Um, what the nuts?"

"Max says we can't have sex."

I laugh so hard I have pain. "Oh, not good."

"Shit, I'm sorry. I'm just trying to keep your spirits up."

"Well, then kiss me. And then kiss me again. And then—"

Kissing Nico is the most wonderful thing in the world.

THEO

Ava's condo tracks with her sophisticated taste. It overlooks Biscayne Bay, and the décor is modern Miami with tasteful throwbacks to the city's art deco roots. My truck is the only such vehicle parked in the resident's garage among Bentleys and Rolls Royces. I'm not intimidated by money, obviously, but I am keenly aware that Ava makes more of it than I do.

"Can I get you a nightcap?" she offers, after showing me around.

"Whatever you have is fine, thanks." I follow Ava to the self-standing bar in the living room.

"I'm sure this is much smaller than your house," she says as she pours.

"But I didn't buy the house."

Ava hands me a glass of brandy and we get comfortable on one of her white, leather couches.

"How old were you when you started playing music?"

"I got my first drum set for Christmas when I was ten, but I can't call what I did with it playing music."

Ava's sitting next to me with her feet underneath her, bent knees pointing towards me. I rest my arm across her thighs, and she inches closer.

"I think you either have a musical gift, or you don't," she says. "Otherwise, how do people make sense of instruments? There are so many wrong things you could do with them; you know what I mean?"

I have a genuine laugh. "That's a hilarious take, but accurate. To some degree, the curiosity has to be there. That's the gift, the curiosity. But then it's just hours spent practicing and learning from people who are better than you are."

"I really admire your dedication," Ava says.

"It's no different from deciding that you want to become a lawyer and committing yourself to studying law."

Ava touches my biceps. "It is though because I was almost guaranteed a career if I followed the curated path. You guys give your all to something that boils down to luck."

"That's where you come in. You make luck happen for the musicians you represent. Was entertainment always the area you always wanted to practice?"

Ava shakes her head wildly. "No. I wanted to be a criminal defense attorney. To make the big bucks."

I nod, "That's where the money is."

"Yes, that's also where the murderers and drug lords are though. I didn't think that part through. I took an exploratory course my first year of law school at UM—"

"You're a Hurricane too?"

Ava cocks her head to the side.

"It's just that Nico went there, and he still backs their football team. He played for them. You guys have me surrounded."

"I know. I'm his lawyer, too. Can I finish my story?"

I feel the smile breaking my face. "I apologize. Proceed, counselor."

"Thank you. So, I happened upon this class, and they brought in an entertainment attorney to give a lecture, and everything clicked into place. I love music. Since I was a girl, I took dance classes, all styles, and there was music in our house growing up. No TV, only music."

"It's great that you have a genuine appreciation for what your clients do."

"I love representing a group that deserves exposure and watching their careers take off."

"Does your family live here in Miami?"

Ava's face is expressive, and it lights up when she talks about her family. "I am one of three sisters, we all live here, I'm the youngest and the last single daughter. I'm tía to four nieces and two nephews, and my parents live in Naples, but we see them a lot."

"That's awesome. I really miss having family close by."

"Ah, but the band is the family you choose, right?"

"Very true."

Ava moves her hand from my arm to my face. She guides my eyes to hers. "How do you feel about our age difference?"

"It's not that wide a gap."

"Almost five years. It might not seem like much now, but when you're thirty-five and I'm already forty, you might want someone younger."

I smirk. "You're going to get bored with me and toss me aside long before I'm thirty-five. But …" I place my hand over hers and turn my head to kiss her palm, "I'll take whatever time you give me."

Ava sets my drink on the table behind the couch before she straddles me. "I can't imagine getting bored with you."

I grab her hips as she kisses me and unbuttons my shirt. As Ava nuzzles my neck, I stand up and carry her to bed. She lifts her dress over her head as I step out of my pants.

Ava smiles as she lies back and devours my body with her eyes. I place my flat hand between her breasts and trace downward and across her abdomen until it's between her legs. I stroke slowly as I run my tongue around her nipples. Ava cinches my waist between her thighs and pulls me on top of her, guiding me inside. I try to take my time, but she rolls me on my back and whispers in my ear, "Next time can be slow."

I watch as she moves on top of me, and I use my thumb to make sure the most sensitive part of her has continuous stimulation. Her cheeks flush and she exhales with sound as she moves faster. I cup her breast, pinching her nipple lightly between my fingers. She's not going to last much longer, but neither am I. Ava was right about letting the first round be a little frantic.

"Next time, I want to taste you," I say. That does it for both of us.

Between rounds, we explore each other's bodies, kiss, and make each other laugh. When Ava is ready to go again, she uses her mouth to bring her *Greek god* to life. I don't care if that sounds like a line from a low-budget porn flick, I'll let her have my *Greek god* anytime she wants it.

* * *

I wake up to the sound of typing on a computer and, when I open my eyes, I see Ava sitting up in bed next to me with a computer on her lap. She's wearing a T-shirt, and her hair is in a ponytail. She looks adorable. I sit up to massage her neck and shoulders. "Are you working already? What time is it?"

Ava faces me with a perky smile on her face. "I'm repping this new band and I just got the footage I requested of them. You should see the drummer, he's a world-class musician, smokin' hot, sweet, has business savvy," Ava pauses for effect, "and he's phenomenal in bed."

I lean forward, placing my chin on Ava's shoulder, and watch video of Funkengroovin' in Myrtle Beach.

"God, that seems like a year ago," I laugh. "Can you turn it up?"

"My pleasure."

"That's what I thought. We need to listen through studio speakers. Let's go to my house."

Ava moves the cursor to the top of her screen and points at the time. It's 4:44 am. "Can we wait until after breakfast?"

I look towards the window, but the blackout screen is doing its job. "You wake up in the middle of the night to work?"

"Only for one very special person."

I lift Ava's computer from her lap and close it, then set it on her bedside table. We lie side by side staring into each other's eyes until we can't keep them open any more.

NICO

MARIS AND I SLEPT IN my room last night and I think it's silly for two of us to take up two rooms in Theo's house, so we moved her things down the hall this morning. My bathroom doesn't have a soaking tub, so I'm sure my girl will be having spa days in her former space once she's able. My room overlooks the driveway, so she won't have a balcony, or a pool view anymore. Hopefully having me as a roommate compensates for the downgrade. We were trying to be quiet as we tracked past Theo and Max's rooms in the hall until we realized that neither of them came home last night.

I text Theo: *Need bail money? If you're with Shana, I'm chopping your dick off. Max is MIA.*

Maris texts Max. The tone of that message is different from mine. She seems better this morning. There's still spotting, but she slept well last night. I stayed awake reading the pamphlets Max's mom gave us, and I feel better now that I've educated myself. That was the first non-music related material I've read since college, and I could ace the shit out of an exam on the subject.

Theo replies. *Proof of life. Don't know about Max. Last saw him with a honey from the Ritz.*

"Maris, love?" She's sitting next to me at the kitchen island while we have breakfast together. I take her hand in dramatic fashion. "I have news about the boys."

She looks concerned, so I don't draw the joke out any longer. "They both got some sexual healing last night."

Maris folds her hands in prayer and looks at the ceiling. "Thank you, patron saint Marvin Gaye."

"Let's get it on," I stand to sing, snapping the fingers on my left

337

hand. *"Ohhhhhhh, baby, let's get it on."* I hold my left hand out to Maris as an invitation.

She presses herself to me and we sway as she harmonizes, *"Let's get it oooooonnn, sugar ... "*

"What did I tell you guys about having sex?" Out of nowhere, Max is in the foyer lecturing us.

"This is called dancing, Max." I tell him, grabbing Maris. "It's a romance ritual, but it doesn't always lead to sex." I dip Maris with my left arm. "Speaking of sex, my guy, do tell ..."

Max turns redder than a Delicious apple. "I mean, yeah ..." he smiles.

Maris gives me a cease-and-desist look. "Is there potential for anything ... relationship-wise?"

Max struts across the great room and goes into the kitchen, so Maris and I sit down and resume breakfast.

"I mean, I don't know. She likes me, which is cool. We stayed up most of the night talking—"

I cover my mouth with my hand to make a sound effect, "Whomp, whomp."

*"After ... we stayed up talking *after*, Nico."

Maris gives me another look ,and I press my lips together in compliance.

"But it was a nice night?" Maris asks.

Max's phone goes off and he looks at the screen. A huge smile erupts across his face.

"Looks like it," I tell Maris.

"She's a cool person. She's twenty-two, so a few years younger than I am. Had a high school boyfriend and a college boyfriend, but she's been single for a while now. She's working outside her field of study, she was a psych major, but she's working in sales for a salon haircare line. She goes around to salons taking orders and teaching stylists about new products."

Maris is beaming. I love her heart. "Sounds like you two made a genuine connection," she says.

"I don't want to get my hopes up, but she's pretty cool."

"I'm going to give you some advice, okay?" Maris gets Max's attention. "Make your next date with her right now. And have a plan. Ask her out on our next night off and tell her where you're taking her. Like, *my next night off is Sunday, and I'd love to take you to dinner at Piccoli's.*"

I shake my head at Max, but Maris sees me.

"Don't listen to Nico," she says, laughing.

I slow blink. "There was a time, a long, long time ago, Before Maris, when I was really, but really, good at this."

"Were you?" Maris teases. "We're not talking catch and release here. We're talking landing a fish."

I let my jaw drop and I clutch invisible pearls. "How dare you?"

Maris and Max both laugh.

"Whatever. Do it Maris's way."

"Tonight's our next night off, though, is that too soon?"

Maris's eyebrows scrunch together. "What about the Ritz?"

"Oh, yeah, we got fired. The place was full of Funkengroovin' fans last night who didn't order anything from the bar and shouted out requests for our originals, so yeah ..."

I shrug. "That gig isn't what we do anyway."

"But it was income," Maris points out.

Max is composing a text on his phone, but he mumbles, "I think Ava and Theo are working on putting our promo together. Didn't he tell you about it this morning? They went for a drink after the gig last night to talk about it."

Maris's eyes light up. "Ava, huh? She's ... amazing. I'm a big fan of Ava."

"The boys are on a roll."

"Say less, Nico," Max mumbles. "How's this: *Hey Rachel, if you're free tonight, I'd love to take you to dinner at Piccoli's. Does 7:00 work?*"

"I like the confidence," I tell him.

"I'm asking Maris."

"All of a sudden I have no game because I'm coupled up?"

Maris playfully grabs the inside of my thigh. "I like it too."

Max sends the text and raids the fridge.

"Good morning, kids!" Theo bursts through the front door with Ava behind him.

I love Maris's reaction to seeing her, and that the feeling is mutual. The two women hurry to hug, and they rock back and forth while holding on tightly.

"How are you doing?"

"I'm going to be great." When they pull apart, Maris says, "You have to meet Nico."

Ava strikes me as a Latin version of Maris. They're both exuberant, beautiful, confident, and smart. Ava's wearing an expensive looking shorts outfit, which matches Theo's persona well. I trust Maris's judgement, so I like her already.

"Great to meet you, Ava," I hold my right hand out, but then remember about the brace, so I hold both arms open wide, and she gives me a hug.

"Nice to meet you, as well. I know these guys are very happy to have you back in Miami. Also, go 'Canes."

"Go 'Canes," I echo. I like Ava even more now.

She waves towards the kitchen. "Hey, Max."

"I'm having dinner with that girl from last night," he announces.

"Okay, then we better get to work," Theo claps his hands together. "Ava got us every minute of footage from our tour performances. We're going to edit our favorite takes together to make a demo reel."

"Thank you, Ava," Nico says. "A studio day sounds so good."

"I want everyone's input, so do what you have to do to be in the studio in fifteen minutes. I'm going to change." The look he gives Ava makes me chuckle and the look she gives him back tells me what I need to know about the two of them. Theo kisses her and it's not a performative, obligatory kiss the way he kissed Shana.

I catch Maris's eye and she smiles at me. I know we're thinking the same thing; we hope they can have what we have. Max too, if that's possible. Maybe Rachel is the perfect brand of goofy for our bro. My grandmother always said there was a lid for every pot, no matter how crooked the pot.

"I'll go power up the studio," I tell Theo as he heads for the stairs. Today feels normal. Hopeful. What a difference a day makes.

MARIS

AFTER THEO WENT TO HIS room, Nico and Max went into the studio, which gave Ava and I some girl time.

"Are you a coffee drinker? We have a house favorite."

Ava smiles. "I would love a coffee, thank you."

I refresh my mug and grab one for Ava. "This little coffeehouse was the first place we went when we got back to Miami after being fired from the tour. They roast their own ethically sourced beans, but the coffee is so good, I'll admit I'd buy it if there were no ethics involved."

Ava laughs. "Now I have to try it."

I sit down at the kitchen island and Ava follows suit.

"Thank you for being so welcoming, Maris. I'm not sure what I would think of me if I were you. Sleeping with my client is the least professional thing I've ever done."

I shake my head. "Ava, Theo isn't just any client. He's Theo. He's unique. I'm happy for both of you. He deserves a serious woman, and I think any woman would be lucky to be with him."

Ava's face relaxes. "I was worried about what you'd think the most. Women can be brutally judgmental of other women."

"Tell me about it. Have you read the comments on our social media posts? The ones criticizing me are overwhelmingly female. It makes me so sad because I root for women. I had so many girlfriends in college, but it's been hard to make friends in Miami."

"I grew up here, but my best friends are still my sisters. I have two."

I place my hand on my heart. "You're so fortunate. I spent my whole life wishing for a sister."

"You can have our middle one!"

I crack up at how excited Ava is at the proposition.

"But, really, thank you for separating the personal from the professional."

"Everyone's entitled to a personal life. Nico is the first musician I've dated, but I've never been so in love, so I'm the last person to frown upon meeting someone through work."

"Theo is such an old soul, you know?" Ava's almost whispering. "He's younger than I am, but he has a confidence and a calmness about him that makes him seem older."

I nod. "Spot-on. Most twenty-three-year-old dudes are running around like chickens with their heads chopped off, but he's very goal orientated, very into family. He's not superficial. Theo's reliable and loyal. I love him to pieces."

Ava giggles and her cheeks turn pink. "I'm really smitten. Do people still say that?"

I shrug. "We do, so who cares about anyone else? We're just a couple of smitten kittens."

"We'll see where it goes," Ava says.

"I'm team Thava. Or maybe your name should go first … Avath? Avatheo?"

Ava laughs and makes a face. "Avatheo sounds like a pharmaceutical drug or something."

I try it out, "Ask your doctor is Avatheo is right for you."

We bust out laughing.

"Having you two in cahoots can't be good. World domination would be within your reach," Theo says as he comes into the kitchen. He's wearing a light blue short-sleeved knit shirt with tan linen shorts. He and Ava look like a well-matched set. I'm surprised I didn't see it the first time we met her.

Theo pours himself a cup of coffee. "Ava, would you like a cup of—"

"You're waaaay behind," I say.

"Of course." He smiles at me. "Let's go see if we have anything usable in that footage."

Theo steps aside and I lead the way to the studio with him and Ava in my wake.

Nico has the 65" monitor synced with Theo's computer and he's playing music through the Tannoy studio speakers.

"It's in Dropbox, Nico," Theo says.

"Do you want to watch them in chronological order?" Nico asks.

I sit on the stool I use in rehearsal and Ava takes the one next to me after I pat it. "Theo and Nico won't sit while they're listening. They're going to stand in the middle of the speakers, which is unity. They will both be into the sound, so they'll probably have their eyes closed most of the time. It'll be up to us to watch the video."

Ava nods. "But you're going to hear elements that will go right over my head."

"Occupational hazard, but it can be entertaining. Watch the four of us when we listen, it's almost like we're hearing a foreign language, and we'll all react the same way to the same things. It's quite comical."

Ava chuckles. "Thank you in advance for translating."

While we were chatting, Max suggested we start with the Myrtle Beach show and Theo and Nico agreed. Nico presses play, and the four of us are running across the screen to our places on stage. I watch myself yell, "What's good, Myrtle Beach?" The crowd reaction gives me goosebumps.

"Oh, my God, I can't wait to get back out there!" I say as on-screen Theo counts us into *Coming Around*.

Nico smiles at me. "Ditto."

The video starts on a wide shot of the stage including the screens on either side. It's an impressive set up. The sound quality is excellent; it must be directly from the main mix. As I watch us play, I'm transported back to that performance. We knew record execs were there. We were bursting with showmanship and musicality.

"Damn, we're good," Max says.

I wink at him.

The camera zooms in on Nico as he sings, and I fall in love with him for the thousandth time. He deserves to be on a national stage.

"Fuck, man. Wanna be in my band?" Theo holds his fist up to Nico.

Video Nico gives Max a solo and he tears it up. Two bars in, he starts sizzling and all of us laugh appreciatively.

"So, that's what you were talking about?" Ava asks with a chuckle.

"Woah, back it up, Nico." Theo says.

"Yeah, I heard that too. Maris and Max, listen to the background vocal." Nico replays the segment.

"It's echo, but it sounds out. Like a tritone," I say.

"Play it again," Theo says.

Nico grabs a pair of headphones before he does so. "It bothers me," he declares.

"Okay, so mark that," Theo says.

I lean over to Ava. "We're keeping track of imperfections and the version with the least wins."

"That's backwards," Ava says. She retrieves her phone and opens a note app. "I'm going to keep track of the big, beautiful standouts. We want the performance with the most of those."

I like the approach. Between the two analyses, we'll home in on the best representation of Funkengroovin'.

Video Theo throws in an off-time fill and we all yell.

Max tells Theo that was a tasty bit, and Ava makes a note.

Watching us on the screen is surreal. I'm immensely proud of my performance and our collective collaboration. We're giving the crowd a great musical show and each of us is fun to watch. The audience is an important ingredient in the magic we try to create on stage and they're vibing with every song we play. It's so rewarding to watch from this point of view. I have tears running down my cheeks, but the realization makes me laugh. Nico is watching me closely, so I blow him a kiss to let him know these are happy tears.

Video Maris is singing her heart out and then she joins Nico center stage for a guitar and bass jam.

"That's the sexiest thing I've ever seen," Ava says.

"That's my girl!" Nico's eyes flash with desire. I've seen that look before.

"I can't believe that in a few hours, that guy is going to knock out that guy on the beach," Max says dully.

Nico groans loudly and Theo says, "Really, Max?"

"It was after this show?" Ava asks. "I guess I imagined it was after a bad show."

"There were no bad shows," Max says.

"He's right," Theo tells Ava. "Even when Nico didn't have full use of his hand, every show we did was balls to the wall."

"Whatever caused that to happen, let's not go there again because a band that does this consistently, is a band I can get signed to a nice development deal."

"It won't happen again, Ava," Nico assures her. "Not for that reason anyway."

Theo slow-motion punches in Nico's general direction and they laugh.

"You'll have to get used to that," I say.

"Sibling rivalry and sibling love are two sides of the same coin," Ava says with a shrug.

"Exactly," I confirm.

As the hours pass and the footage rolls, we realize the hard part of making a reel will be deciding what to leave out rather than what to put in. It's a great problem to have. Watching the shows brings up a full spectrum of emotions. The highs are otherworldly, and the lows physically hurt, like watching Video Theo's face when Nico kisses me on stage. I glance over at him while it's playing, and Theo's eyes meet mine for the briefest second. He looks down at the board and I say, "Mark it."

"Agree. Flag on the play. Unnecessary PDA," Nico says.

By the time Max has to go upstairs to get ready for his date, we have the reel whittled down to an hour. We picked our favorite performance of each song. Nico and Theo will use these clips to edit further for a ten-minute highlight reel, which Ava says the A&R execs will listen to first. If they're interested, they can dive into the longer reel.

Max steps into the studio before he leaves to get our opinion of his 'fit. He has a lot of product in his hair, and it looks perfectly tousled. He's wearing white jeans and a black dress shirt with his white-framed glasses.

Nico is the first to compliment him. "I love the style, my man."

I thank Nico with my eyes. "You look great Max. Be yourself and have fun," I add.

"Myself still drives a 7 series BMW because I haven't returned my mom's car yet. I don't want to be frontin', but it can't hurt. Last night, Rachel had to drive me to her place and drop me off here this morning."

"Under the circumstances, I'm sure your mom would rather you keep the car for tonight," Theo says chuckling. "It's too early for Rachel to know you don't have wheels."

"Get out of here!' Nico yells at him. "Text if you aren't coming home. We don't want to stay up all night worrying about you."

I let my face fall into my hands and laugh.

"What?" Nico asks. "That's just basic courtesy."

"I don't let you know if I'm not coming home," Theo says.

"You're not Max."

Max rolls his eyes and heads out.

"He's leaving for dinner and none of us had lunch. Want to order in?" I ask.

"I hate to say this, but I really should get going. I have two meetings tomorrow that I need to prep for," Ava says. "I know you guys will choose the best moments for the short reel."

Theo moves from his place behind the computer. "I'll walk you out."

"Thanks for letting me be part of the process, guys. I had the best time."

Nico gets up to give Ava a hug, and they part by making two handed Us as a type of salute.

"That's not going to get old," I tell Theo. I start doing the Florida State war chant to even out the energy in the room.

Theo laughs and slips his arm around Ava's waist.

"What do you think?" Nico asks after they leave.

"It makes sense," I say. "Theo needs an older woman. I didn't realize it until now, but it makes sense."

Nico sits down and pats his lap, so I cross the room to snuggle up. "You don't think it has anything to do with losing his mom as a kid?"

I shake my head. "I think navigating that is a big reason that Theo is as mature as he is, but, no, I don't think there's an Oedipus complex happening, if that's what you mean."

Nico chuckles wickedly. "He is Greek."

Watching his lips on video all day without being able to put my mouth on them was torture, so I take his bottom lip between my teeth.

"You must be hungry," he mumbles into my mouth. After we make up for lost time, Nico says, "We can make dinner faster than having it delivered. How do you feel about a stir-fry?"

The front door closes, and we leave the studio to meet Theo in the kitchen.

"I'm thinking a stir-fry is quicker than delivery. You in?" Nico asks him.

"Sure. And then we can get back to work."

Theo and I have a rhythm in the kitchen and Nico falls in place perfectly, because of course. Bring in sync with one another is what we do.

"How long have you and Ava been a thing?" I ask.

Theo makes a face and bites his lip. "Um, well, since the day I went to sign the contract of representation."

"But you didn't go out that night. We three had dinner together." I pause my chopping to look at Theo. "Unless ..."

"It was ... spontaneous," he says carefully.

"My man." Nico holds out his fist.

"At her office?" My voice is three octaves higher than normal.

"You can never, and I mean never tell her I told you guys. I shouldn't be—"

"Theo, you sexy beast," Nico says playfully.

Theo laughs. "We took care of business—"

"And then you took care of business," Nico says.

I hold my chef's knife in a threatening manner. "Stop interrupting."

Nico smirks at me and I'm sure my face gives away that his smile melts me.

"Actually, yeah, that's what happened." Theo starts cooking the shrimp in a skillet. "Ava's attractive, obviously. I was looking forward to seeing her again, but part of that was being excited to start the partnership. When she met me in the waiting room, I took one look at her and suddenly my mind went blank, my mouth dried up … it was crazy."

Nico delivers the chopped veggies to the counter beside the stove and leans back against it with folded arms while he listens.

"I felt like she was flirting with me while we were signing and then we shook hands and the second we touched it was like lightning." Theo shrugs. "And then it was just on."

"So, was there a cosmic click, or …?"

Theo turns to look at me with a wide smile on his face. "It certainly felt like there was a click."

"Well, I think she's incredible," I say. "I feel like I'm watching the beginning of a love story that ends happily ever after."

"We'll see where it goes." Theo uses the same phrase Ava used when she and I were talking earlier.

"I'm happy for you man. Genuinely. Ava is an accomplished, grown woman and she fully supports your career. She's beautiful, she's a former 'Cane—"

"No one's perfect," I say.

Theo finishes the stir-fry and Nico hands him plates to fill. The guys eat standing up in the kitchen like there's a prize for finishing first.

I take my seat at the island and I'm struggling to stay awake. "Would you mind if I dip out after dinner?" I ask. "I'm suddenly exhausted."

"We don't have do this tonight," Theo offers. "If you and Nico want to spend some time together."

"Don't take this the wrong way," I say, looking into Nico's eyes, "but I'm so worn out all I want to do is sleep."

"Maris, your body is recovering. You need to listen to what it's telling you." Nico says. "If you don't take time to recover, the recovery will take more time."

"Spoken like a man who's been through the rebuilding process more than once," Theo jokes.

"As much as I want to be part of selecting the clips, I know you guys will isolate the best ones."

Theo washes his plate and places it in the dishwasher, then he soaks the skillet. "See you in there, man. Maris, sleep well, okay? Text us if you need anything."

"Thanks, Theo."

Nico sits beside me as I finish my meal. I haven't been able to eat too much the last couple days.

"Did the day take a toll on you? We spent most of yesterday lying down, but you've been sitting on a stool with no support all day today." Nico uses his left hand to massage my lower back.

"I felt great today, really." I assure him. "Watching the videos was a fantastic distraction and motivation to get back to fighting shape, right?" I chuckle. "But sitting down and getting some food in my stomach KO'd me."

"Leave your plate, I'll take care of it after I get you settled upstairs in your new love nest."

I giggle. "You don't have to—"

"Nonsense." Nico lifts me off the chair and carries me upstairs.

"I can walk, you know."

"I haven't been to the gym, so this is my real-world glute workout."

Nico carries me until we're in our room with the door closed. "Have I told you what a Maris fan I am?" He stands in front of me and holds my face in his hands. "I would love you if you had no musical ability at all but watching you on stage lights a fire in me, babe."

I chuckle and lift myself on my toes to reach his lips. "Are you kidding me? I stole the Nico shirt from Max."

Nico kisses me slowly, gently, and passionately for a few minutes.

"The thing is, I know I'm not the only woman in the world who's in love with you and that number is going to grow with our careers. I feel like I have a target on my back."

"What *other women*? There are no other women." Nico stares intro my eyes. "And if you don't think there's already a line of dudes waiting for me to fuck up, you're oblivious."

"I guess we're going to have to disappoint some of our fans," I joke.

"As long as I never disappoint you. I love you so much. You're genuinely my other half."

I exhale and linger in Nico's arms for another few minutes. "You better go help Theo. Wake me up when you come to bed, okay?"

Nico kisses me like he's departing on an extended journey.

"I love you, Nicolas."

MAX

MAX ANTHONY CASTELLANO IS ON a roll. The past month has been the best of my life. Dating Rachel over the last four weeks was worth every year I spent waiting for her. She's the sweetest, most thoughtful person I've ever met. My moms love her, and my dad says that she's out of my league. I take that as a compliment to my desirability, because Rachel was the one who wanted to define what we are to each other. She wanted to be able to tell people that I'm her boyfriend, so, I'm in a mutually fulfilling relationship. She fits in well with the band, too, which is probably even more important than my family liking her. I spend more time with the band. Maris made her feel welcome at the house and the guys don't diss me in front of her.

We aren't playing jazz gigs anymore. That was a short-lived pleasure, but I like having my evenings free to spend with Rachel. Once Ava set up a corporation for us, we went live with T-shirt sales and made over ten thousand dollars the first four weeks. None of us could believe it.

Maris physically recovered from the miscarriage, and she seems to be doing well emotionally. She seems happy when she's with us. Maybe she's struggling when she's alone with Nico, but if anyone can bring her through this, it's him.

Having Nico back in playing shape resurrected Funkengroovin' to its full potential. It's great to hear his guitar again. I think the time off actually enriched his playing.

I have the feeling that the good fortune is continuing tonight because Ava and Phil are taking us to dinner. We're going to MesaMar, which is a pretty fancy seafood restaurant. Since the rest of the band will have their significant others there for business purposes, Ava said I could bring Rachel. Something's definitely brewing.

The four of us are driving over together in the Bimmer that I still haven't returned, and my moms haven't asked to have back. We're ready early, so Theo pours four Spiced Jump Shots and we're toasting to coming through some really tough shit.

Maris bought a new dress for tonight and she looks absolutely stunning. Her tan is back, and the bright yellow color makes her skin look extra bronzed. The off the shoulder dress hugs her curves and hits below the knee. She's wearing heels that make her about six feet tall, so she's towering over me, but that's okay. Her hair is in a low bun, and she has more make-up on than usual. Maris looks glamorous.

Nico is perfect arm candy for her in his black suit with a black dress shirt underneath. Of course, he leaves a few more buttons of the shirt undone than anyone else would, but he's pulling off the Chris Hemsworth look.

Theo is dressed in a gray suit with a white dress shirt underneath. He recently cut his hair and Funkengroovin' fans are torn. I think he looks older with short hair, and maybe that was the plan. The truth is, Theo's the type of good-looking that doesn't depend on styling.

I splurged on some new threads myself. The cut of my suit is a little slimmer than Theo and Nico's; a little more modern, I think. It's a deep burgundy color and I'm wearing a white dress shirt with it. I don't like dress shoes, so I bought a new pair of white slip-on sneakers that look pretty smooth.

"Here's to us, gang. To overcoming the bullshit and sticking together," Theo says with his glass raised.

"To us!" we echo before downing the tasty rum shot.

"We look too good not to make a post," Maris says. She gives her phone to Nico whose wingspan is the broadest. We strike our poses and Maris drops the photo to all of us.

When I look at the pic, tears form. I'm thinking about the night on the beach and the night in the ER. I'm so grateful that we're still together and better than ever. "I really love you guys," I say, fully expecting to be ridiculed.

Instead, Nico grabs me and slaps me on the back. "I love you too, little brother. We wouldn't be where we are today without your contributions."

"Thanks, Nicolas," I say.

"No."

"Understood."

Theo and Maris crack up, but they both hug me and tell me they feel the same way.

"Should we get going?" I ask, leading the way to the front door.

"Can't believe we're letting Max drive," Theo says.

"The car fits the façade we're projecting tonight," Maris says, as Nico opens the rear passenger side door for her. "And it's a good thing Ava chose a restaurant in our neighborhood because we'll be there before the shot hits."

"I'll be DD," Nico says as he seats himself next to Maris. "I'm back in the gym after taking a break for my hand and I have gains to get."

Theo laughs from the passenger seat. "Man, you took a month off and you're still my gym goal."

"Do you guys want to be alone?" Maris asks sweetly.

"So, what's this dinner about Theo?" I ask. "You have to know something."

He holds his hands up and shakes his head. "Ava hasn't told me anything. I swear."

"It has to be good news." As I finish speaking, the car begins to read a text from my phone. "*Just got here, but I don't see your sexy ass. ETA?*"

"Ohhhhh, Max has a sexy ass," Theo teases.

"You're just trying to avoid telling us what you know," I say. Then I reply through Siri, "*Two minutes, baby. Can't wait to see you.*"

I look in the rearview expecting Nico to say something snarky, but he's kissing Maris's hand. I like that all of us are loved up in serious relationships. I also love that Theo is finally with someone we all like.

I pull into the valet stand and I see Rachel outside waiting for us.

The sight of her makes my heart jump. She's tiny, only five feet tall. I've never dated a platinum blonde before, but her bobbed hair matches her sunny disposition, and now I love blondes the most. I mean, she's in the salon industry, so the cut and color will probably change a lot; I reserve the right to shift my stance. She's wearing a light blue strapless dress the same length as Mare's, with heels. She meets me before I get to the door. "Hey, handsome."

"Hello beautiful." I give her a kiss and step aside so Maris can hug her new friend.

"You look stunning, Rachel. Blue is your color."

"Thanks! You look gorgeous. Thank you all for inviting me. It's exciting to be on the inside of this band stuff." Rachel lets out a nervous laugh.

"You're band family," I assure her.

When we walk into the restaurant, it's clear that the hostess is waiting for us and that many of the staff and patrons recognize us. Since getting back to Miami we haven't gone out much, apart from grocery shopping. It feels weird to have people turning around to watch us walk to the table where Ava and Phil are waiting. Weird, but cool. We all look great tonight, so soak it up, people.

Ava stands up and greets Theo first, but then hugs each of us, and Phil is going around pressing palms and kissing cheeks.

"Sit down, everyone, sit down," Ava says.

"Thank you for getting us out of the house," Maris says. "We get pretty single-minded when we're in writing mode. It's nice to be out of the studio and I'm really tired of stir-fry."

Our server appears tableside and takes a drink order. Nico's the only one abstaining. We make small talk until the drinks arrive, and that's when Ava tells us why she brought us together.

She gently taps her knife to her wine glass to get our attention, and Nico uses the cue to kiss Maris.

"Phil and I have some good news. We took a very targeted approach to subbing you guys to labels. Very targeted."

Phil holds up his pointer finger. "We pitched you to one label and gave them a twenty-eight-day exclusive."

"We asked for a 50/50 split from the first record and 70/30 from each one after that. You guys bear the cost of recording, but in exchange for that, you keep your publishing and copyrights. The label will handle marketing and sales, and they have major-label distribution partnerships because they're a subsidiary of a tiny little company you may have heard of called …" Ava pauses and looks at Phil. "What was it called again? It was just on the tip of my tongue."

Phil taps his fingertips to his lips. "It's a start-up, but I think they're going to make it …"

"Yeah, time will tell …"

"I'm dying," I say. "Please tell us."

Ava and Phil look at each other and then say, "Sony!" in unison.

"What?" Maris covers her mouth with her hand.

Nico stands up and meets Theo who was already on the way to him. They smash together like gladiators. Gladiators who hug.

Rachel squeals next to me and kisses my cheek before whispering in my ear, "My boyfriend is a recording artist on a Sony label."

I laugh. "Yeah, he is!"

On the other side of me, Maris grabs my hand. "We did it, Max."

I look into her gleaming eyes and words escape me. All I can do is smile.

"There are details upon details, obviously," Ava says once Theo finishes squeezing her. "But the contract has been back and forth a few times and we're ready to sign. I'll come over tomorrow and go through it line by line with all of you, but I'm very happy with it. It's the best deal I've ever made for a client. Phil's inside knowledge made it possible and when you guys have the chance, call Nicky Knight to thank him, too."

Nico and Theo sit back down, and Nico rests his arm on the back of Maris's chair. He swats my shoulder every fifteen seconds. I don't mind.

Phil leans his forearms on the table. "You guys know that Luis pissed me off. That was a miscalculation on his part because I have friends in the industry, too. Dame Knight hasn't been happy with Revolution for a while. Luis made a lot of promises that never came to fruition." He gestures across the table at Nico and Maris. "I think you guys know how irritated they were at the start of the tour about their hotel and travel accommodations."

Maris nods.

"Nicky's level of rage towards Luis increased ten-fold when he got you guys fired from the tour. He came to me and told me he wanted out of the Revolution deal, so we got the lawyers doing lawyer stuff and they found several instances of breach from Luis's side, and then we were free to shop for a new label."

Ava chimed in, "There's more to it, but ... yes."

Phil chuckled. "For us non-lawyers, that's essentially the story. We were able to present Dame Knight and Funkengroovin' to the Sony parent company. There's no cross-over, by the way. It wasn't a package deal. But being able to represent two very attractive products didn't hurt our credibility."

"I have to call Nicky," Nico says.

"He knows you're hearing this for the first time tonight, but I'm sure he'll take the call when you get the chance." Phil laughs.

"There are probably questions I should be asking, but I trust our team, so I'm moving on to the celebration portion of the evening." Theo catches the server's attention. "Champagne for the table, please."

"No one announce anything on social media until you get the go-ahead from me," Ava says. "I don't want you to tell anyone, not even family, at this point. Your label will release the news to the press, so you won't be able to talk about this until they do so. That could take several weeks."

"Back into the studio for us," Maris jokes.

"Back in the hole," I add, which makes her laugh.

"Oh, you might like this detail. There's a nice advance. You'll have to earn it out, but I'm sure you will," Ava says as the server pours.

Theo takes his glass and whispers, "Funkengroovin'. . ."

Maris, Nico, and I join with harmonious whispers while Ava, Phil, and Rachel watch with amusement.

I know that we've worked hard for this, but I also know we've been very lucky. As I sip champagne, I look around the table and feel over-whelmed with gratitude.

Rachel leans over and kisses my cheek again. "Congratulations, Max. I'm very happy for you."

"I'm happy for us," I reply. "What's good for me is good for you, too."

Rachel looks at me with the same dreamy expression that I've seen Mare give to Nico. Hot damn. Max Anthony Castellano is on top of the world.

NICO

TALKING TO NICKY WAS ENTERTAINING, as usual. The conversation lasted about six seconds. He said that Revolution hadn't done fuck all for him in years and he thanked me for giving him a reason to part ways with Luis. He said he'd see me soon and hung up.

I really want to tell my family the good news, but they would tell everyone in Minocqua and before too long TMZ would be in the Northwoods interviewing the Auntie Network. It's kind of nice that we have time to get used to the idea before sharing it with everyone, though. It feels like we're in this magical in-between time.

I drove Maris home in Max's mom's BMW after dinner. Theo went to Ava's and Max left with Rachel. We have the house to ourselves, which is great because, as Maris said earlier, we've been in the studio with the band for long hours lately. That's a lot of togetherness. I need time alone with my girl, and time to miss my brothers.

Maris went inside while I called Nicky and when I open the front door, I see her shoes on the entry rug, and her dress draped over the couch. Her underwear is farther down the trail leading to the sliders. When I look out to the pool, Maris is floating on her back in the moonlight. Her breasts rise out of the water as her long legs propel her across the length of the pool. Her hair floats around her. I leave my jacket, socks, and shoes inside and walk out to the lanai.

"Maris the Marvelous Mermaid," I say.

She giggles. "Will you join me?"

"In a minute," I promise. I sit on the end of a chaise lounge and watch her move through the water. The pool light is on, and I take in every inch of this woman who has been the center of my thoughts, actions, and plans since the first time were on stage together. Her physical beauty takes my breath away, but her heart is more gorgeous. I would give my life for hers so easily. I'd do anything to protect her. And tonight, I learned that I'll be able to provide tangible things as well. Like, food, clothing, and shelter. A year ago, I would have given anything for a record deal. It meant fame, money, admiration ... now all it means is that I'll be able to take care of her. As long as we do well, anyway. But I'm confident that we will.

"What are you thinking about?"

"How great everything is and how thankful I am."

Maris swims to the side of the pool and rests her folded arms on the edge in front of where I sit. "Me too. I feel like I'm in a dream. It's all very surreal, isn't it?"

I nod. "I've been living a dream since we fell in love, Maris. The record deal is the icing on the cake."

"It's true. I'm grateful for every wrong turn that brought me to this moment." Maris smiles and uses her arms to lift her torso out of the water. I lean forward to kiss her as droplets cascade down her naked body. We finish the kiss and stare into each other's eyes for a moment before she disappears under the water again. She uses her legs to push off the side, and I watch her perky peach swim away from me. She pops up at the far end of the pool.

"You're going to regret teasing me," I say sternly.

Her response is laughter. "I doubt that."

Maris sinks beneath the surface again and I jump out of my clothes like they're on fire. I dive in behind her and hear her squeal under the water. She slows her pace and turns to face me. I wrap her in my arms as we float to the surface, and she locks her legs around my midsection.

I lean back and kick us to a depth where I can stand. Maris traces my lips with her fingertips, and I kiss them. Her hands linger on my shoulders, down my chest and across my back. Her touch makes my mind go blank. There's nothing but Maris now. I kiss her neck, and she tilts her head to give me full access. I use my fingers to show her where I'll kiss next and when I get to her breast, she moans in anticipation. There's a floating lounge chair in the shallow end and I walk us over to it and lay Maris on top of it. Her legs dangle in the water and I gently separate them, tasting her, mixed with pool water. I gently rock the pool float back and forth, adding to the stimulation and within minutes, Maris's legs stiffen and her body shudders. Her hands are in my hair, and she releases a sound of total ecstasy. The waves rock through her and around her for a few minutes and then she exhales. I use my fingers to make sure she feels every bit of electricity.

"Let's go upstairs," she says.

MARIS

I LOVE HOW NICO WATCHES ME in the pool. Like I'm the only thing in the whole world that interests him. I wonder how much self-control he has left. He's still wearing the black dress pants and shirt that he wore to dinner tonight. He looks so handsome. His top buttons are open and his white gold chain with a guitar pendant hangs in the middle of his chest. His blue eyes never leave me.

I feel so free and so safe. I've never had this before. I swim over to him and lift myself out of the water for a kiss. The moonlight finds his face like a spot on stage. The blonder pieces of his hair stand out more in this light. I swim away from him, and his patience threshold is reached. I am so in love with this man. His humor, talent, fierce loyalty, confidence, and generosity overwhelm me. But the essence of Nico is protectiveness. He's a gentle and loving man, but he would never let anyone hurt me. I have supreme confidence in that fact.

He makes my body feel so much pleasure that I think I'm going to explode. The feeling lingers, crests, and wanes before I emerge on the other side.

"Let's go upstairs," I whisper.

Nico floats me over to the steps and takes my hand as I walk up the stairs. He grabs two towels from the basket and wraps one around my shoulders before tucking his around his waist. My legs feel like Jell-O and I'm the tiniest bit buzzed. I don't know if it's from the champagne or Nico.

"What am I going to do with you?" he says laughing.

"I know what I hope you're going to do with me," I say.

Nico bends down and tosses me over his shoulder before heading for the house. I'm laughing my ass off, and then I'm revealing asses. Or at least, I reveal his by yanking his towel off and dropping it behind us on the stairs.

"Didn't need it anyway," he says.

Nico leans forward and flops me onto the bed. Our bed. This isn't his room anymore, it's ours.

"You're in so much trouble," he says with a smirk.

"Do your worst." My anticipation erupts as laughter.

Nico kisses the inside of my thigh and works his way up my body, concentrating on my breasts for a few breathless minutes before he finds my mouth. Our kisses are passionate, but slow. We have time. I reach between his legs and feel he's ready. Nico's been cautious with me lately, but I want him to know it's okay for us to be the way were before. I tighten my grip on him. "Please. Don't hold back."

"Promise to tell me—"

"I will."

We make love like it's our first time together. It's somewhat cautious and sweet, but there's an urgency that comes from missing being together without restraints.

In the shower afterwards, we lather and rinse wordlessly, but our bodies and minds are still in sync. Nico holds a towel open for me and hugs me dry. I go back to bed and get under the covers. A few minutes later, Nico still hasn't joined me.

"Van Asten?"

I hear him chuckle. "Yes, Humphries?"

"Where are you?"

Nico comes into the room wearing a Maris T-shirt and boxers.

"Oh, my sweet man," I say laughing. "I look good on you. And you look good wearing me."

Nico smiles, but it's not his typical cocky smirk. He seems … unsure.

"Maris, this evening was the most memorable of my life. And it could be perfect if you'll do one thing for me."

I sit up in bed with the sheet tucked under my arms. "Anything." The look on his face is making me nervous.

Then he drops down to one knee and opens a ring box. "Will you marry me?"

I open my mouth wide, but nothing comes out. I'm stunned. Now I'm crying, because of course. "Yes, Nico. Yes, yes, yes."

Nico's face shifts and he starts crying too. He's smiling through it, but we're both overcome with emotion. "We never talked about what kind of rings you like. Max and Theo helped me pick it out."

I intermittently laugh between sobs. "All three of you?"

Nico shrugged. "I've never bought jewelry for a anyone besides my mom, so yeah."

I throw my head back and laugh.

Nico slides the ring on my finger as I look into his eyes. The tears are coming hot and heavy now. I glance at my left hand and see a platinum eternity ring with two crossover rows of diamonds.

"Let me explain," he says. "Since our relationship has always been a little backwards, I hope you don't mind getting your wedding band before the engagement ring."

I must look confused because Nico rushes to explain.

"I know most women want a big-honkin' rock and I can't wait to buy you one of those when we get the advance, but I kept coming back to this one because the two rows intertwine, like us, and because it flows like Silver Springs and I—"

I smash my mouth into his. Our tears are mingling together again, but for a beautiful reason this time.

"I could never love another ring as much as I love this one. It's perfect. It's us. And I don't know if you'll understand this, but I play bass for a living, so wearing a large ring won't work for me."

Nico laughs. "You deserve a planet sized diamond—"

"I'm starting to get angry. I love this ring and the reasons you chose it makes me love it even more. Stop insulting my engagement ring."

"I didn't want to propose without any hardware at all—"

"Nico Van Asten, stop it."

"As you wish, future Mrs. Van Asten. If you decide to take my name. You don't have to."

I take Nico's face in my hands. "I want to be attached to you in every way possible. I may even change my first name to Nico's Wife."

He smirks and my cocky, confident man returns. "Maris Van Asten sounds better."

"I'm going to be Maris Van Asten!"

THEO

It's midmorning by the time Ava and I arrive at the house. I'm going to need to keep some extra clothes and toiletries at her place because I'm starting to feel like a dirty stay-out each time I come home wearing the same clothes I wore the night before.

"Anybody home?" I yell.

"Dude!" Nico calls from the studio. "Way to ruin a take."

I make an *oops* face and Ava laughs as she follows me through the kitchen to the studio. Maris removes her headphones and sets her bass in the stand before coming to greet us, and Nico stretches in the office chair in front of the mixing board.

"Good morning!" Maris hugs Ava first, then me.

"Does the news feel real yet? Because I have the contract with me as evidence," Ava says.

"We have news too," Maris says.

One look at Nico's smirk tells the story.

"Aw, she said no at first, but you finally convinced her?" I guess.

Maris laughs and holds out her left hand as Ava jumps up and down clapping.

"Really? Oh my gosh. Congratulations, you guys." Ava inspects the ring. "This is beautiful. I love the eternity setting and the infinity nature of the bands intersecting."

"Thank you, Ava," Maris says smiling widely. "I love it. And Theo, thank you for helping Nico pick it out."

"I was just there for moral support." I shrug. "And to make sure he didn't buy a Ring Pop. He was all, *it should be bigger!*"

"No, no, no," Ava says seriously. "Timeless sophistication beats big every time."

"Exactly!" Maris agrees.

"Congratulations, You guys." I give Maris a hug and it feels different from previous hugs. It feels like I'm hugging my sister. A sister I love with my whole heart.

Ava is hugging Nico and when she lets him go, he gets to me in a few strides.

"Did you do the candles and the flower petals like you planned?"

Nico laughs and holds his hand up for me to crash my palm into it. I'm still mindful of his recent injury, so I hold back.

"I couldn't wait, brother. I didn't do anything she can tell our children about." Nico shakes his head and looks genuinely disappointed.

"That's not true at all." Maris slips her arm around his waist. "He was wearing a Maris T-shirt when he proposed. I think that's far more memorable than a few candles or whatever."

Nico's cheeks are turning red, and I can't help laughing at him. "You're such a dork, my guy. You used to be so cool!"

"It's going to happen to you too." He kisses the top of Maris's head.

"What were you guy working on?" I gesture to the board.

"Play it for them," Maris says.

When Nico hits play, the song opens with Maris's voice and at the point I feel the music should come in, I clap an intro fill. Nico nods with his eyes closed. The song is a ballad. A love song. Not what we typically write, but this could be our own Silver Springs. It's guitar and bass right now with some sustained string chords on it, but Max will color it in.

"I love it," Ava says. "It's a real showcase for your voice, Maris. Who wrote the lyrics?"

Maris and Nico exchange a knowing smile.

"We put our wedding vows to music," Maris says.

I look at Nico. "You romantic bastard."

He laughs. "It's for the band though, if you guys want to record it."

"You have to!" Ava says. "That's a hit. It will be the first dance song for every wedding from this point forward."

Maris laughs. "We're not really a ballad band, so it would be crazy to be known for this song, but I'll take it."

"It's not sappy and we'll make it cool," I say.

"Hello?" Max calls from the entryway.

"In the studio!" I yell.

He hurries through the door with Rachel following behind. "Am I missing anything? You're not writing without me, are you?"

"Nico and I were just laying down a skeleton. Good morning, Rachel."

"I brought applesauce crumble muffins." Rachel holds up a brown paper bag.

"She bakes!" Max announced excitedly. "They're really delicious."

"The way to Max's heart is through his stomach," Maris tells Rachel.

"Ava has the contract, so what do you say we go into the dining room and have some coffee and muffins as she walks us through it?" I suggest. "Oh, and not to bury the lede, but Maris and Nico have news."

"You popped the question?" Max guesses.

"She said yes," Nico confirms.

"Of course she did," Rachel squeals. "This is so exciting. Congratulations, you guys."

Maris's face is flushed. Her eyes are sparkling and she's glowing. It makes me happy to see her this way after everything that's happened recently. I've known Nico a lot longer than I've known Maris, and it's still hard for me to believe that the guy who wasn't looking for a girlfriend is taking a wife. Of course, she's a stand-out, and any man would be an idiot not to change his ways to keep Maris by his side. Then I turn my focus to Nico. His eyes are on Maris. His demeanor is calm, and he seems content to let her tell their engagement story. She shows Rachel the ring and explains how the design relates to their relationship. Nico's eyes are filled with amusement and admiration. He's not the one in the spotlight for a change and he seems to enjoy watching Maris. This is a different Nico. A dude content to play a supporting role rather than the guy who seeks attention. And yet, lending support has always been his strength, whether in the band or as my best friend. He's the guy that I've leaned on and he's the guy that Maris can rely on in the same way.

"Why the fuck are you crying?" Nico asks me.

I wipe the tear from my cheek. "I'm just so happy for you guys."

Nico bear hugs me and lifts me off the ground. "You're such a wuss!"

I laugh and break loose. "I'm not the one with a ball and chain, brother."

"What did you say, Theo?" Ava asks teasingly.

"I would love a ball and chain," Max tells Rachel. "Just want to be clear."

"Dining room in fifteen," I say in my stage voice as I head upstairs to change.

Maris and Nico are getting married. And I'm genuinely excited for them.

NICO

I DIDN'T PROPOSE THE WAY I wanted to. I wanted to live up to all the Insta proposals and give Maris a great story that matches how much we love one another. I feel like I kind of blew the engagement, so I'm not going to do that for the wedding. I'm impatient, but I will get this right.

Maris is adamant about not involving her mother. I have to trust what she's told me about that relationship and let Maris handle it the way she needs to handle it. My mother, on the other hand, wants to be the wedding planner and she's had some ideas that aren't terrible. For example, hosting the event at the Van Asten place. Maris loves the idea and I love that we don't have to reserve a venue a year in advance. I want to marry Maris as soon as possible. I don't want to wait until after our record comes out because then we'll have to tour to promote it, and we won't have time to be newlyweds.

Maris was born and raised in Florida. She's never seen snow and she has a very romantic idea of what it's like. I agree with her, mostly. I don't think she understands how cold it is in Wisconsin in the winter, but she loves the idea of getting married around Christmas. So, all we have to do is record an album full of number one hits for our label while planning a wedding that takes place in two months. But I'm not going to complain that all my dreams are coming true at the same time.

MARIS

"Hello Funkengroovin' friends!" I hold my phone up to show Theo, Max, and Nico behind their instruments in the studio. "We're busy writing and recording new music for you. I love the new songs, and we can't wait to share them with you."

I focus on Theo. "Big announcements are coming in the next few weeks, so watch this space," he adds.

When it's Nico's turn, he says, "Thanks for all the good wishes for Maris and me. For those of you who wanted to marry my girl and you're commenting with back-up proposals, sucks to be you." Nico smirks at the lens.

"Or you could buy a Maris t-shirt to keep her close," Max says. "Check out all the Funkengroovin' Ts on our pinned post. Beach balls and sunglasses are coming soon."

I frame my face in the shot again. "We wanted to pop on to say hello and let you know that we're working hard. Thank you for your support and encouragement. It means a lot to all of us. Much love!"

I scan the room behind me. Nico gives a peace sign, Max waves, and Theo holds up his drumsticks.

"Bye for now!" I end the live. "Thank guys. I want to stay current with our followers."

"Of course," Max says. "We track the merch sales and there's always a bump after you do a live."

"That's so exciting," I say. "I swear if I ever see anyone wearing a Funkengroovin' shirt at Publix, I'm going to hyperventilate."

Theo stands up behind the drum kit and stretches. "That would be crazy. I hope I'm on that errand with you when it happens."

"Speaking of food," Max says.

"Yeah, man." Nico sets the studio guitar in its stand and waits for me to walk in front of him. As I pass by, he grabs my waist and stops my forward progress. Pausing for a kiss from Nico is my favorite thing. I marinated some chicken last night and Max and Theo are carrying the dish to the grill on the lanai. Nico pulls salad ingredients from the fridge, and we make quick work of filling the huge salad bowl with enough for everyone. Nico grabs plates and follows me to the lanai as Theo finishes the grilling.

"We're a well-oiled machine, aren't we?" Max asks, placing drinks at each table setting.

"Indeed," Theo says as each of us takes our seat at the lanai table.

"I'm looking forward to releasing the record, of course," Max says, "but I'm not looking forward to the time when we don't live together anymore."

I make a sad face at Max. "I know. It will be nice to be successful enough to get our own places, but I love our lives now. Wake up, record, lunch, swim, record ... this is heaven."

"We can add another wing if we need to," Theo jokes.

"You're kidding, but I would love that," Max says sincerely. "When the big bucks start rolling in, maybe we should all go together and buy a mansion on Star Island."

Nico laughs. "Those monstrosities could house the six of us and the whole Van Asten Clan."

Max holds up a finger while he swallows. "Speaking of your family, have you made any more progress with the wedding plans?"

Nico nods at me, so I fill Max in. "Nico's mom knows everyone within a fifty-mile radius and she's calling in favors left and right. The Van Astens know a family who owns an event business, so they lined up a weatherproof tent with heat and electricity for the reception. It even has chandeliers in it."

"It's transparent, so we'll be able to see the stars," Nico adds. "They're going to set it up beside the lake, so the views will be spectacular. Depending on the freeze, we might be able to set it up on the lake, but that will be up to Mother Nature."

Theo laughs. "Are you serious? I don't want to spend the whole evening listening for the sound of cracking ice and waiting to die of hypothermia when we all fall into the lake."

Nico covers his mouth with a napkin as he laughs. "We drive trucks out there all winter … build shacks for ice fishing. It's thick, dude."

Theo shakes his head. "I know my vote doesn't count, but I vote for the event tent to stay on shore."

"I'm excited to see Wisconsin," Max says. "I've never been, but I liked what Nico showed us on FaceTime."

"We're all Wisconsin virgins," I say. "I'm learning a lot about Wisconsinites though. We had to set the wedding date around the Packers' schedule because Nico said no one would come on a game weekend."

"No one would be in town. Including my parents," Nico clarifies. "We do want to talk to you guys about something important though."

"Yes," I say, putting my fork down. "Set aside the traditional constructs of a wedding because we're going to do some things differently. For example, I'm inviting girlfriends from college to share the day with us, but none of them know Nico. We want people standing up for us who have witnessed our journey. Instead of having a Maid of Honor, I'd like to have a Best Man. So, Max, would you consider being my Best Man?"

Max's eyes double in size. "Really? Are you serious? I'd be so honored, Mare." He pushes his chair back and comes to my side of the table to hug me. "I've never been in a wedding before."

"And, obviously, Theo, I'd like you to be my Best Man, if you're so inclined."

Theo looks confused. "Nico, it has to be one of your brothers."

"I'm asking one of my brothers. The one who watched all of this unfold. The one who knows Maris and I the best."

Theo's eyes well with tears and he brushes them away as quickly as they form. "Damn, man. Are you sure you don't want to think about this some more?"

Nico laughs. "I've thought about it. I'm asking you. Will you stand up for me at my wedding?"

Theo leans back in his chair and puts his hands over his face. "I don't deserve it, man."

"Shut yo'. Don't turn me down. I want you beside me that day."

Theo emerges from behind the napkin after wiping his eyes. "Of course, Nico. Are you sure your brothers aren't going to carve a hole into the ice and get rid of me out of jealousy though?"

"Marcus agrees that it should be you and all of them will be grooms-men. The two youngest knuckleheads are still in their beer, babes, and brawling phases, so Marcus will be busy making sure they're on their best behavior." Nico grips Theo's shoulder. "It's a full-time job, so that's another reason I'd like you to be my Best Man."

"Okay, then. It's a done deal. I'll start Googling what I have to do," Theo says. He finishes his lunch and tosses his napkin over his plate. "I assume we're bringing the gear, right? You can't find a better band than us to play for the reception."

I shake my head. "We don't want to work the wedding, and we don't want you to work it either."

"I have it handled," Nico says, pushing his chair back from the table. He grabs Theo's plate and his own and takes them inside.

"Do you know who he's getting to play?" Theo asks.

I shrug. "He wants to take that off my list, so I'm clueless, but I trust him."

Max laughs. "Can you imagine being a bandleader in the Midwest and getting a call from Nico?"

Theo points at Max. "Anyone with the audacity to take the job has the chops to do it well, right?"

"Exactly what I'm saying." Max nods. "So, Mare, how many of your college girlfriends are coming to the wedding? I can't believe you didn't bring them around while I was single ..."

"You didn't need anyone's help to find a fantastic girl. I love Rachel," I say, smiling.

"Yeah, I do too," Max says.

"Have you guys said the "L" word, Max?" Theo asks.

"Oh, yeah." Max nods enthusiastically.

"How about you and Ava?" I ask.

Theo's face twists as he tries to hide a smile. "We've admitted that we're falling in love ..."

"Awwwwwwwww!" I sing. "I love Ava too. She's going to keep you on your toes, Theo. She's a force. I think the two of you are a good match."

Theo's cheeks flush. "We've been talking about how she can come visit on tour and write it off as a business expense."

"So, you're talking about the future," I say. "That's promising."

"I like everything that I'm learning about her. We're going to Naples next week so I can meet her parents."

Nico closes the sliding door behind him as he returns to the lanai. "Meeting the parents? That's a big step. Especially since it sounds like Ava's family is tight."

"I've met her sisters, their husbands, and all the kids so far. It's wild watching all of them together. Very loud, but awesome."

"I'll tell you the same thing I told Maris," Nico says as he pulls his white T-shirt over his head and drops it in my lap. "It's overwhelming until you realize that the only way to fit in is to embrace the chaos. You don't have to match the energy but understand that to get anyone's attention in a house full of family, we had to learn to be loud and we had to fight for food."

Theo throws his head back and laughs. "That explains a lot about you, my man."

"Yeah, maybe that was just my house with four boys. Maybe that wasn't Ava's experience. But I stand by the loud thing." Nico leans over me and I tilt my face upwards towards his for a quick kiss before he hits the water.

"Oh, no," Max says, scrambling to his feet. He stacks my plate on top of his and is two steps away from the sliding door when Nico's cannonball splash rains down on the lanai. "Can't ever walk into the pool like a normal person," Max mumbles.

Theo sheds his shirt and dives into the deep end and I'm right behind him. When Max comes back outside, I float a lounge chair to the shallow end for him to use. He's into tanning since he became Rachel's person.

"I'm really going to miss this," Max says again.

"Dude, we have a lot of great times ahead of us," Nico says. "Years and years of experiences we'll share together that we can't even conceive of now."

Max sits up on his float. "You guys are going to be like uncles to my kids."

Nico laughs mischievously. "I'll teach those little shits everything they need to know."

I dive beneath the surface to capsize Nico's float. "Auntie Maris will make sure he only teaches the proper lessons. Like guitar lessons. And that's it." I laugh as Nico surfaces, running one hand through his hair to push it from his forehead.

Theo is swimming laps along the edge of the pool, so we stay on the other side. I steal Nico's float and he recreates the Rose and Jack scene from Titanic as I repeatedly refuse to share with him. I know exactly what Max means. These days that we're spending together writing music, sharing meals, and coexisting the way we do are precious. Music bonded us in a way that is hard to understand unless you experience it. We respect each other for the talent we've cultivated individually and share freely. We understand how lucky we are to have the chemistry we do both onstage and off because you can't fake that. The four of us came from different backgrounds and experiences, but the rough edges we have filled each other's gaps.

The day I auditioned for the band, the guys worried that adding a female would break them up, and it almost did. But we made it through that, and I can easily visualize the scenario Max is talking about. We'll watch each other get married, become parents, raise children, lose our parents, become grandparents … if we're very, very lucky. But I can see having these men in my life as a touchstone all the way until the end. And we will always reminisce about the beginning and the ride we've been on together. It's so much more than making music, but music is how we express our love for one another. We strive to be the best we can be for each other. We push each other and carry one another when necessary.

I'm feeling emotional, so I let Jack, aka Nico onto the float because I know he will lay back with his legs hanging off the sides, making room for me, and he does. I lean back into his chest, and he wraps his arms around me. I feel so fortunate, and I'm hyper aware that I'm on the precipice of monumental life changes, but these guys are on the journey with me, so it's going to be great.

THEO

AVA'S PARENTS REMINDED ME OF my own so much that it hurt a little. They're still in love. They're easy-going and welcoming, but her father grilled me a little bit about the timing of getting involved in a serious relationship as my career is taking off. I think I set his mind at ease. I was honest and sincere when I told him that his daughter is one-in-a-million and that having her as a professional and personal partner is a far too valuable to lose. I think he was satisfied that I understood his concern and that I'm not a fame obsessed asshat.

Ava has Face Timed with my dad, and they got on like old friends. Ava says he's a more experienced version of me. Dad is letting Nico and Maris stay at the house in Athens for a couple weeks after the wedding, and he's coming here to meet Ava and her family. I'm really looking forward to that.

We delivered the mastered album to our label last week and they loved it. I feel like I just passed the biggest exam of my life. The record is quite good and we're all very proud of our first release. With that out of the way, the next milestone is Maris and Nico's wedding, and we're ready. The six of us are traveling together and our luggage requires its own Uber. My foyer looks like an airport baggage claim. There's excitement in the air and we're ready early, so the celebration starts now.

"You didn't replace the twelfth champagne flute," Nico observes as he pours. He's referring to the one I smashed the night I found out that he and Maris were together.

My mouth forms an O. "You're right, but I think your idea of making the set an even number is better." I raise a crystal champagne flute above my head and get everyone's attention as I yell, "Opa!" I don't want to have to clean up broken glass because the cars are on the way to take us to the airport, so I throw the flute into the empty trash can. It breaks, and everyone yells, "Opa!"

"That was somewhat anticlimactic, but it still counts," Nico says, handing out five glasses of champagne. "Thank you all for traveling with us to the frozen tundra to celebrate our upcoming nuptials. To friends who have become family."

Ava, Maris, Rachel, Max, Nico, and I clink our glasses together and sip champagne at eight am.

"Are you all sure you don't want mimosas?" Maris asks after the first sip.

"We're leaving Florida, and its oranges, behind," Ava says. "Also, I'm not a great flyer, so I don't want to dilute my buzz."

I wrap my arm around Ava, and she rises to her tiptoes to give me a kiss. "I'll keep your mind off the fact that we're rocketing through the stratosphere in an aluminum tube. I promise." I wink at her, and she rolls her eyes playfully.

"I hope I packed enough clothes," Rachel says. "I've never been up north in the wintertime. I hear your boogers freeze inside your nose when you breathe in."

"Seriously?" Max looks alarmed. "Nico?"

He shrugs. "Blow your nose before you go outside."

My phone goes off and I buzz the cars through the gate. "It's time to load up." A limousine and a Suburban park in front of the double doors.

Ava smiles knowingly. "The limo is courtesy of the label, and they arranged for a limo bus to take us from the airport to Minocqua."

Maris's jaw drops and she giggles with excitement. "That's totally unexpected," she tells Ava. Maris starts typing into her phone and I know she's sending a thank you text to our liaison.

"Boys, let's help the driver load the luggage." Nico takes charge of two suitcases and Max and I follow suit. It's a little chilly by Miami standards, even for an early morning in December, and I'm already shivering. I can't imagine what it's going to feel like in Wisconsin.

The limo driver holds the door open for the ladies, and we join them once the bags are stowed. As the car pulls away from the house, I play *Going to the Chapel* on my phone. I'm taking my job as Best Man seriously.

Everyone sings along, but the four-part harmony that's happening scares the amateurs and it's just the band singing by the end of the first chorus.

Maris places her head on Nico's shoulder, and he lowers himself to be more accessible. It's instinct now. I'm probably never going to stop noticing things like that. Watching him to make sure he's taking care of Maris in every way. But I don't think that's a bad thing. It doesn't hurt anymore.

"I can't wait for you guys to see the cottages we're staying in," Nico says. "Each one has a fireplace, and they're lined up on the edge of the lake, so we're close together."

"That sounds so cozy," Ava says hugging my arm.

"I hope there are enough blankets," Rachel says.

Max pushes his glasses farther up the bridge of his nose. "I packed a comforter."

Rachel's expression is a combination of shock and appreciation. "This is why I love you, Max. You think of everything."

Max shrugs. I know he brought the comforter because he's terrified of the subzero temps, but I'll let him have his hero moment.

"I can't wait for you men to see Maris's dress," Ava says, changing the subject. "Dressing for a formal occasion in the cold is a tough enough assignment but then add shopping for the occasion in Miami. It's Mission Impossible, but not only did our bride nail it, she set a new standard." Ava leans across me to look at Nico. "You're gonna die. Like, your heart's going to burst and you're just gonna ..." Ava sticks her tongue out and cocks her head to the side.

Nico laughs. "That would be my luck, right? I'm minutes away from marrying the girl of my dreams after delivering the best debut album in music history, and I keel over before I can wrap my arms around any of it."

"You're gonna be on that alter, or ice sculpture, or whatever, wearing your signature shit-eating grin and everyone is going to see what a sweetheart you really are in spite your tough exterior," I say. "In fact, twenty bucks says you cry during the wedding before Maris does."

Maris doubles over laughing.

"Real men cry at their weddings, Theo," Nico says forcefully, making everyone laugh.

"I'll have a hanky in my pocket if you need it, brother." I grab the back of his neck and squeeze.

"Thank you. I might."

"Your family must be so excited, Nico. It's really cool of you guys to get married up there," Ava says.

Nico looks at Maris. "It made the most sense."

We pull up to the curb at Miami International and I tip both drivers before we check our bags and head to the gate. As we go through Security, I notice heads turning in our direction. Nico makes eye contact with me, and we exchange knowing looks. By the time we're on the other side, it's clear that several people know who we are, and the knowledge is contagious.

The first person to approach us is a sweet mother. "Could my daughter get a selfie with the band?"

We oblige and quickly realize that was a mistake. A line forms and Nico and I herd our group down the concourse.

"So sorry everyone, we're running late," I keep saying as Nico repeats something similar to the people on his side.

When we get to the gate, the agent is waiting for us and opens a door to a private waiting area.

"That was crazy," Maris says. "Do you think they all know who we are, or was that just mob mentality?"

Ava bites her bottom lip. "The label has been splashing a lot of Funkengroovin' online ahead of the release. I think that's a sample of what your lives are going to be like from now on, but we'll broaden the team as needed."

"I don't think we'll have anything to worry about on the other end. Residents of Green Bay don't care about celebrity status. In fact, it will be humbling how much they don't care, but they'll be so kind you'll assume they're all stalkers."

Maris smiles. "Nico was telling me that when it snows, if you only plow your driveway and don't do the neighbors, people automatically think you're from Chicago."

Nico chuckles. "Or another big city filled with self-centered assholes."

"I genuinely can't wait to get there," Max says. "I'm not excited about the weather, but I'm ready to experience Inverse Miami."

The gate agent popped her head in the door. "Would your party prefer to board first, or last?"

As the Best Man, I answer for everyone. "Last, please."

"Absolutely."

"Wait until they see we're all flying economy," Maris says with a chuckle.

I raise my hand, like we're in a band beating.

"Theo?" Nico says. "Do you have a confession to make?"

"I upgraded our reservation to First Class."

"That's insane, Theo," Maris tells me. "You and your dad already provided us a whole house for our Honeymoon."

"Just doin' my job as Best Man." The excitement in Maris's eyes makes me smile.

Ava tugs on my arm and her face is radiating. "Well done, baby."

"I'm practicing to be your Best Man forever, baby" I say. "How cringy was that? Super pathetic, or merely baseline ick?"

Everyone laughs and Ava presses herself into me. "Taking care of people is sexy," she whispers. "And now you have someone to spoil you back."

I bend down so that our lips are almost touching. "I could go for some of that spoiling tonight," I say quietly before kissing her.

"Oh, you're going to get spoiled," she promises.

"Imagine what I'm going to have to do to top all of this when they get married," Nico tells everyone.

Ava and I stare into each other's eyes and agree without words that

Nico's prediction is likely. I shake my head in wonder ... how did life get this good?

The gate agent opens the door again and tells us that we can board the flight.

Nico asks us to get together for a selfie, and he tags all of us in his post. He created the hashtag Marrying Maris, and it's trending. Once we board the plane, I make eye contact with Nico, and he has water in his eyes. I see gratitude written all over his face. I reach my fist across the aisle and remember doing the same thing on the tour bus. He bumps my fist, and we laugh together. It's been a whirlwind, and it's only begun.

NICO

WATCHING MY PARENTS GREET MARIS was more emotional than I expected. They ignored me entirely and descended on her with so much love. I overheard my mother say that she's waited her whole life for a daughter, and that idea never occurred to me before. Of course, my mom is happy to have another woman in the family. I know Maris is hoping to have a close relationship with her too, and I think their intention will make it a reality.

Dad hooked the trailer to the tractor and Mom made gallons of hot mulled wine, so they're taking us, along with my brothers, on a hayride. When in Wisconsin ...

"This is a first for me," Theo says as he climbs into the hay. He reaches behind him to help Ava aboard.

"Make a nest and grab one of those blankets," I tell him.

"It's seriously freezing," Max complains. "It got so much colder after the sun set."

"Snuggle your girl, you're gonna live right through this." I toss a wool blanket to him and Rachel.

The wine mom pours gives off steam, and Max places his cup so close to his face that it clouds his glasses.

"You Miami boys are so tender," my brother Oliver teases.

"Guilty," Max replies. "Come down in August and we'll have the reverse conversation."

"I almost didn't wear a jacket," Peter tells Ollie. "We're gonna be sweatin' after a few sips of wine."

"Help Mom," I instruct, as I go through the motions of knocking their heads together without doing so.

"This is so fun," Maris says as I sit on the side of the trailer behind her. She snuggles between my legs and leans back into me. I tuck her into a wool blanket and Ollie brings her a cup of mulled wine. "It smells so good," she gushes.

"Where's mine?" I ask Oliver.

"You aren't injured anymore, get it yourself."

"See what I deal with?' I ask Maris.

"So, who's the youngest?" she asks. "Marcus is the oldest, then Nico ..."

"Then me, then Peter," Oliver replies. "It goes, M, N, O, P."

Theo's jaw drops. "I never put that together before."

"Obviously the quality gets better with each son," Peter says, then Oliver attempts to stuff hay in his mouth.

My dad yells from the tractor seat, "Is everybody ready to get underway?" We all answer affirmatively. "Honey, will you do the honors?"

My mom goes to the front of the trailer and counts, "Three, two, one!" She flips a switch, and several sets of wedding bells illuminate the trailer.

Maris covers her mouth with her hand and looks back at me. "Oh my gosh, this is so beautiful."

"Wait until we get out into the woods, and you see the snow clinging to the trees and the way the moon makes the ground cover glow," I tell her.

"Mr. and Mrs. Van Asten, thank you so much for this. I'm never going to forget tonight," Maris says.

I lean forward and wrap my arms around my fiancée.

"You can't call us Mister and Missus," my dad calls over his shoulder. "We're happy with anything you choose, but that's too formal. You'll be our daughter-in-law in a few days."

Maris giggles and looks back at me with a huge smile.

"How do you feel about having four brothers?" Marcus asks her.

"Like I won the lottery," Maris replies seriously.

"Well, with two of us you did," Peter says. "The older ones are boring, but Ollie and I will make sure you have fun."

Dad puts the tractor into gear and we're moving across the frozen lake towards the tree line. The tent is set and ready to host the wedding. Maris said it was more elegant than she imagined it would be.

"Are we, like, on ice right now?" Theo asks.

I nod to him, and he crosses himself.

"There's a good twenty-three inches of freeze already," Marcus tells him.

"Only twenty-three inches?"

"The boys spent so many hours in this lake or on it," my mom tells Maris. "Swimming and boating during the summer, and ice fishing and hockey during the winter. It was like having an adventure park in our back yard."

"That's really special." I can hear the smile in Maris's voice.

Once we enter the woods, the conversation stops. No one wants to break the spell of the hush. The tractor chugs, but it's not a "city" sound so it blends. I notice Theo's foot is moving with the engine cycle.

"Hey, Dad?" I cup my hands to yell at his back.

"Ya?"

"Can we make the stop on the way out, rather than on the way back?"

My dad's shoulder bounce like he's laughing, and he nods.

"It's not cold anymore," Max says.

Marcus laughs. "Congratulations! You're drunk!"

Dad takes us through a tree tunnel of snow-covered branches. Maris looks up and around, taking it all in. I squeeze my legs more tightly around her and she looks over her shoulder. The moonglow illuminates her pink cheeks and I lean over to kiss her to see how cold she is. I rearrange the blanket so that it covers her ears, cheeks, and nose.

Through the blanket, I brag, "Van Asten ATVs and dirt bikes made these paths. This is the result of years and years of hard play."

Maris nods and her eyes twinkle. Her words are muffled. "It's beautiful. I can't wait to see it in the summertime."

I love that my beach girl is connecting with the place I have roots.

"It's up here, Nicolas, but you're going to have to walk in," my dad says over the puttering tractor engine. "I'll get you as close as I can."

A few minutes later, the tractor engine stops, and the world is silent.

"I have something to show you," I tell Maris.

She gets to her feet, and I jump off the trailer into the snow. She isn't wearing snow boots, and we have a short hike through drifts to get where we're going, so I turn my back to her and tell her to get aboard. She jumps on my back, giggling, and we set out into the night. My boots make crunching sounds as I trek through the sparkling snow.

"Tell me about the couples' tree," Maris says softly.

"It's serious business," I say solemnly. "You can't add to the tree unless you're married. But everyone who gets married in Minocqua has a plate made with their initials and their wedding date on it; some are stainless steel, some are wood, whatever works. It has to be small enough to hang from a small, single stainless nail so the tree doesn't get injured."

"That's a sweet tradition," Maris says.

I'm getting closer, so I start looking for the car battery and the power inverter. Marcus said it's on the right side of the trail just a few feet from the tree and that I can't miss it. My big brother's footprints are partially covered with fresh snow, but I see where he walked around the tree and where he kneeled to set up the power source. It's on a wooden crate a few feet ahead.

"We're here," I tell Maris. "I'm going to set you down."

She slides off my back and slowly turns three-hundred and sixty degrees to take in the beauty of the setting. When I flip the switch and the tree lights up, she whisper-screams with delight. Marcus must have brought a ladder out here because the lights go up at least fifteen feet.

"What in the world?" She laughs as she studies the tall tree whose trunk and lower branches are adorned with small plaques.

I open my phone and press play on the song that I wrote for this moment. Maris listens to the first line, and her chin starts to quiver.

Today we're just beginning, a lifetime of love …

"Maris Humphries," I take her hands and get down on one knee as the song continues, "before we stand in front of family, band family, and friends, I want to promise you that I will always put you first. I will always make your happiness my priority, and I will always do my best to show you how loved you are. I want you to know that you have my heart forever. And I want to ask you again, more properly this time, to be my wife." I take the ring box from my jacket pocket and open the top. "This was my grandmother Van Asten's ring. My whole family wants you to have it."

Maris's eyes are brimming with tears, but her expression is pure joy. "I can't wait to be your wife, Nico." She looks around again at the lights and the tree where so many before us expressed their love for one another. "This is like a fairytale. It's almost too much." She laughs.

I take the ring from the box, "May I?"

Maris kneels too and takes my face in her hands. "Yes. Yes, to everything, always."

I kiss her like it's the first time and I've been anticipating the moment forever. Nothing has ever felt so right.

I slip the ring onto her finger, and it fits. I hold her left hand on top of mine, and we look at the ring. It stacks nicely on top of the first ring, and it adds some bling without taking anything away.

"Oh, my," Maris says. "It's so unique! I've never seen anything like it."

The two-carat oval cut diamond is set sideways in a polished platinum band.

"It's a hand-me-down," I say.

"It's breathtaking and I'm honored to wear it." Maris chuckles.

"Thank you for being the first brother to get engaged. My future sisters-in-law are going to hate me."

"You're the OG Van Asten wife," I tell her.

"How long does it take to ask a question you already have the answer to?" Oliver yells from a few yards away.

Maris laughs and I close my eyes tightly to try to maintain my composure. "Marcus's wife will understand, and the knuckleheads won't find anyone worthy of the family ring, so … come on out!" I shout behind me.

My mother brought bells along and our friends and family emerge from the trees ringing them enthusiastically. Dad holds the plaque he engraved and a small hammer.

"Once we hang this up, you kids have to tie the knot because we can't lie to the tree," Dad says, holding up the plaque.

It says: *Nico and Maris Forever.* I asked dad not to date it because I want our love to be a thing of the present.

Maris turns to the tree. "We're a little early but we're legit."

Everyone laughs.

"I vouch," Theo tells the tree.

"The tree is legally on my land, so I can change the rules if I want to." Dad thinks his statement is hilarious and we all laugh along with him, as if it is.

The bells ring as Dad pounds the nail, and I pull Maris close to me to keep her warm. I worry that her feet are getting wet and cold, so I bend my knees to make it easier for her to jump on my back.

"Hold on, Nico," Theo yells. He crouches down for Ava and Max quickly follows suit.

"I'll show you kids a thing or two," My dad says, but when my mom tries to get on his back, they both fall sideways into the snow. Their laughter fills the forest. Sadly, Ollie and Peter win the race back to the trailer.

When my parents finally make it back, Maris greets them both with huge hugs and thanks them for trusting her with grandma's ring. My dad isn't typically sentimental, but his words come out shaky. "She would love you, Maris."

I tuck my future wife between my legs again and wrap the wool blanket around her. Peter refreshes everyone's wine and we move slowly through the night.

Maris leans back and mouths, *thank you.*

I kiss the top of her head. "No, thank you."

THEO

NICO IS THE MOST CHILL I've ever seen him, and I'm a nervous wreck. The wedding is in two hours and I'm with the Van Asten men, and Max, at the tavern. It's closed, but this is where we're gathering to shoot pool, play darts, get dressed, and generally stay out of the way. I have both of Maris's rings in the pocket of my jeans and I tap the front of my pants every six minutes to make sure they're still there.

I suppose this is true of most people, but seeing Nico with his family reveals a different side of him. He's surprisingly obedient around his parents. Not in a subordinate way, but in a supportive way. If one of them asks for help, Nico drops what he's doing to take over. It's true of the whole family. They function like a unit. Miami Nico is always available to help with anything I need, but he's also wildly independent, whereas here, he stays close to the hive. Knowing he has this natural, yet invisible tether with his family helps me to see him as a family man, which I really couldn't visualize before.

Nico removes the triangular shaped rack from the pool balls on the far end of the table. "Your break, brother."

I lean over the table and take aim at the cue ball. I spank it with my stick and listen to the satisfying smack as it crashes into the arranged balls on the far end of the table.

"How are you so calm?" I ask Nico.

He smirks as I relocate for my second shot. "What do I have to be worried about? In a couple hours, I'll be married. Mission accomplished."

"The ceremony though, or the timing of everything running smoothly …" I miss my next shot. "Damnit."

Nico eyes the table and then walks to the other side for a better angle on the shot he wants. "As long as the priest doesn't die before he declares us man and wife." He aims and blasts the intended ball into a pocket, "I'm not worried about the rest. And Maris isn't particularly precious about everything being perfect."

"Her friends from school seem cool. It's funny that so many of them are lawyers. Ava's feeling right at home."

Nico tries to pull off a double shot, and it almost works. He laughs at the attempt. "Ava's a chameleon, and I mean that in the best way. She's one-hundred percent Miami, but she's embracing the North Woods and the Wisconsinites. Big city people don't always get it when they come to the sticks, but she's all in. I like that about her."

I smile. "She's very cool. Honestly, I think it all boils down to family for her. She relates, man, in a way that Maris and I are going to have to learn."

Nico boos the shot I sink. "I'm trying to be aware of when the Van Astens are too much."

"The Van Astens are too much and never enough at the same time," Marcus says as he drops off a round of beers.

"Do we have to wear the cucumber bunds?" Ollie emerges from the men's room holding a piece of his tuxedo.

Marcus and Nico both reply without looking his way, "Yes!"

"I can help with that," Max says. "And it's called a cummerbund."

Ollie brings the waist sash over to where Max is perched on a bar stool watching our game.

"I was worried that my parental situation would be a deal-breaker for Rachel, but she wasn't fazed by it," Max says as he shows Ollie how to adjust the formal wear.

"Maybe you'll let us meet your other mom and your dad sometime," I say as I send the ball across the table.

"He's ashamed of us," Nico says.

"That's the only logical explanation," I agree.

"Brothers, I'm just now getting to a point where I'm comfortable around them again." Max slaps Ollie on the back. "You're good to go."

"Let's get this party started," Ollie says grabbing a beer. "I've scoped a few of those hot lady lawyers I'm gonna introduce myself to. I'm the brother of the groom, after all. It's like I'm hosting this thing." Ollie turns to Max. "And you know how women get at weddings. They all want to catch the bouquet and be next."

Max laughs along politely with Nico's younger brother and, for the first time ever, I see Max as mature.

"So, you gonna tell us who you got to play tonight?" I ask Nico.

"Nope." He shoots again and starts a run to clear the table.

"Unbelievable suspense," Max declares. "Are we gonna sit in at any time?"

Nico laughs and shrugs. "If we feel like it, I guess, but this is my wedding, not a Funkengroovin' concert."

"If only your bride understood the pull musicians feel to play …" I say shaking my head.

"Mare will probably be the first person on stage." Max says, taking a swig of beer. "By the way, this is righteous beer."

"God-damn right! Wisconsin does beer and football better than anyone!" Peter shouts from the dart wall.

"Language," Mr. Van Asten yells.

"Sorry, dad."

I make a face at Nico, who laughs. I point to myself to ask if I've been swearing, and he shakes his head. I genuinely don't notice anymore.

"I better get over to my side of the wedding," Max announces.

"Can I come, please?" Ollie asks. "The ladies are going to need things … I can get things."

"Sorry, Oliver, I'm the only man allowed."

"Give Maris a kiss for me, man," Nico says.

Max puts on a Northern Face coat that he borrowed from Peter. "I will."

"On second thought, if your lips touch my wife, I'll kill you, but you can give her a hug." Nico smirks.

"Blah, blah, blah …" Max says on his way to the door.

Nico finishes running the table and we place the sticks in the holders on the wall.

"Are you taking a guitar to Greece?"

"Absolutely. Maris is taking her axe too. It was so hard not playing while my hand was healing, I don't want to deprive myself now. And if we write a song, we can drop it to you guys, and vice versa."

"Max is going to stay with Rachel while my dad is in town. It's going to be so weird not having you guys at the house."

Nico smiles. "We'll all be back before you know it."

We're quiet for a moment. Marcus, Ollie, and Peter react to a development in their dart game and Mr. Van Asten is using the office to dress.

"It's a big day," I say.

"Big day, brother. It wouldn't be happening with you."

I chuckle. "For a while there, I hoped it wouldn't be happening because of me, but now I realize that the two of you were made for each other."

Nico presses his lips together. "Thank you."

I search his face for a clue as to what he means, specifically. "None of the good things in my life would be happening without you," I tell him. "So, thank you."

"Fuuuuuuck," Nico says as his eyes get moist.

"Language!" the voice comes from behind a door.

We chuckle together and Nico holds up his fist for a bump.

"I'm happy for you guys," I say. "Truly happy for you."

MARIS

I WILL BE WALKING DOWN THE aisle towards Nico in an hour. As

Rachel does my hair (it turns out she's picked up a lot of styling tips while working as a sales rep) I reminisce on how fast our situationship turned into a relationship. I looked to Nico for physical comfort, but I never anticipated he would provide emotional support, professional encouragement, and protection of my heart, mind, and body the way he has. I'm embarrassed to admit to myself that I thought of him as an emotionless stud. I was so wrong. He seems that way on the surface, but he is so tenderhearted that I want to love him as completely as possible. I never want him to question whether I love every part of him, because I do. I can't believe I'm so lucky.

"What do you think?" Rachel holds a compact for me to look at the back of the intricate updo she created.

"Wow, Rachel. I look like I've been in the chair of a high-end Miami salon for hours, rather than a dining room chair in a living room."

"Ah, so gorgeous!" My friend Mimi from Florida State squeals along with the rest of the 'Noles crew.

"Very elegant," Ava says. "Perfect for the dress, Rachel."

Rachel pulls her shoulders to her ears as she beams with pride at her creation. She pulled my hair straight back off my face, which is not something I ordinarily do. I like my hair wild, but the style makes me feel like a bride. In the back, Rachel twisted and tucked sections of hair into and around one another with pearl tipped spiral hair pins. It took fifty to get the job done and I'm grateful that she brought options for me because I intended to wear my hair down the way I do every day, but this isn't an ordinary day, and elevated style is required.

"I think she's all yours, Ava," Rachel announces.

"Thank you, ladies, for helping me get ready. I'm hopeless when it comes to this stuff."

"No, you aren't," Ava says. "You're a natural beauty and a minimalist. That's why I think we should keep your look understated to make sure you shine through. We just want to enhance what God gave you."

I laugh. "Yes, please. Nothing too heavy."

"I got you, girl." Ava winks at me.

"If you need any nudes, I have this pallet," Mimi shows Ava.

"Oh, you have to use the Nars orgasm blush." Another girlfriend brings a compact to the dining room chair I'm seated upon in the middle of the Van Asten's living room salon.

"Who needs champagne?" Nico's mom is carrying a tray with multiple glasses.

"You're spoiling us, Momma V," I tell her. "Homemade Danish for breakfast and now champagne?"

"I have olives and figs with brie and bread coming up. It will be a while until we sit down for dinner, and I don't want anyone getting woozy."

"You have three other sons, right?" Mimi asks. "I want to marry into this family."

Nico's mom chuckles. "At the present, only Marcus is marriage material. He's a good man. Hardworking and very easy-going. I was sure he'd get married before Nicolas. No offense, Maris."

I try to hold my face still as Ava applies foundation, but I can't keep myself from laughing. "No offense taken, Momma V. I didn't see him as marriage material when I first met him either."

"I followed your band before we met," Ava says as she presses a pigmented sponge into my skin. "Both professionally and because I liked your music. Also, we had that local connection. But I genuinely saw Nico as a playboy."

"I did too," Mimi admits.

My eyes are closed, but I think it's my friend Tara who admits, "I hoped."

Wicked laughter fills the living room.

"I love the honesty that comes out when women gather together to do hair and make-up," I say. "I wish you guys were on the road with us. I need some female energy from time to time."

"Nah, you're living in rarified air. It's so cool that you're the only chick." Mimi says.

"I'm glad that Theo and Max brought Ava and Rachel into our world though. And the rest of you keep saying you're coming to Miami, but we need to plan a weekend."

"Your schedule is about to get nuts, Maris," Ava reminds me. "You'll probably have an easier time meeting up with friends while you're on tour."

"Could we come backstage?" That's definitely Tara.

"Obviously," I reply.

There's a knock on the door and Momma V yells, "Who is it?"

The voice on the other side is muffled, but recognizable. "Max."

"Come in!"

"Hello ladies!" Max stomps snow from his shoes before he enters the house. "How's it going on the bride side?"

"Rachel did my hair, Maxer. Come take a look."

I hear Max plant a kiss on Rachel as he makes his way to where I'm sitting. "Wowza, Mare. You look gorgeous. Amazing job on her hair, babe. I've never seen Mare look so elegant."

"That's the idea," Ava says. "We're bringing out Maris's elegance."

"Nico sends a kiss, Mare, but he says if my lips touch you, he'll kill me."

Rachel laughs. "He's all talk, but don't kiss her because you'll smudge her make-up."

"How's it going at the tavern?" I ask. Ava is applying eyeshadow with a soft brush, so I keep my eyes closed while talking to Max.

"They're chill over there. The boys were starting to get dressed when I left, so I figured I should get over here to get ready myself."

"Is Nico nervous?" I ask.

"Hell no," Max says emphatically. "He's exactly the way he is before a show. Pumped and ready."

I smile knowingly.

"Max, you can use the master bedroom to get dressed if you'd like," Mrs. Van Asten tells him. "Also, help yourself to refreshments."

"Nice. Thanks. The only refreshment the guys have is beer. It's great beer, but you ladies have the nosh."

"I'd better text my husband to monitor Ollie and Peter's intake," Momma V says.

"Marcus is on the case, Mrs. Van Asten. They're taking it light."

"Okay, good because today is an important day for our family."

"Well, prepare yourselves ladies because next time you see me, I'll be Max Anthony Castellano, 007."

"Be still my heart," Rachel says.

I hear Max give her another smooch.

"Take a look, Maris, before I do the other eye." Ava hands me a compact mirror. "Just make sure you like what I've done, and if you don't, we have plenty of time to start over."

"Okay, J-Lo." I inspect the blended neutrals set off with an under-brow highlight that has a hint of sparkle. "How do you get that dimension? Seriously, this is an art I don't understand."

"You keep writing and playing music and we'll make sure you have a make-up artist for videos and appearances," Ava says.

"Videos!" Mimi exclaims. "Our girl is going to be in videos, y'all."

"I have videos of Nicolas playing guitar when he came home from college. He was so nervous to play at the tavern," Momma V. recalls.

"He never told me about that," I say. "You have to show me the videos, Momma V."

She chuckles. "I'm going to wait until after you say *I do* because he looks like a scared puppy. He didn't start out as self-assured as he is today. When I see him on stage now, I can't believe that's the same boy."

"He is sooooooo good now," Mimi says. "A great guitar player, a great singer, and his confidence is so sexy—"

"Calm down, Mimi," I tease. "He's taken."

We all laugh.

"I don't want to do lip color until you're right about to walk, so I think we're finished." Ava takes my hand and walks me to a mirror that hangs over the couch.

"Oh, my gosh!" My reflection surprises me.

The girls gather and gush. "So beautiful."

"You're glowing," Rachel says.

"Absolutely stunning," Ava agrees.

"I'm not one to stare at myself in the mirror, but the longer I look, the more I notice. Thank you so much, ladies."

Rachel and Ava bookend me and give me careful hugs.

"Time to get into your dress," Mimi says. "I cannot wait to see you in your gown."

"Good thing I brought waterproof mascara because I'm not going to be able to handle it," Tara says.

"Waterproof mascara?" Momma V. thinks out loud. "May I borrow that?"

"Of course, Mother of the Groom," Tara says. "In fact, I'm happy to help with your make-up, if you'd like."

"Oh, that sounds like fun!" Mrs. Van Asten takes the chair I just vacated, and Tara starts choosing colors.

"Do you need help getting into your gown, Maris?" Ava asks.

"I don't think so, but I'll shout if I get stuck."

The bedroom I'm using to change in used to belong to Marcus and Nico and it looks like the Van Astens didn't change much when the boys moved out. Nico's football awards take up several shelves and his photo form Freshman year at UM, wearing jersey 87, is framed among them. I inspect the shot and chuckle over how young he looks. The middle and high school football photos evoke belly laughs, and I wonder if our sons will look like their dad. I'm fortunate to be surrounded by Nico's memories and his family. It feels special to be using the room he grew up in to dress for our wedding. Far more meaningful than getting ready in a nondescript hotel room or cloak room at a church.

I unzip the ivory garment bag, and the sight of my dress takes my breath away as if I'm seeing it for the first time. If we were getting married in Miami, I probably would have gone for something slinky that showed some skin, but this dress was chosen with the climate in mind. I felt like a bona fide princess when I tried it on, though. I'm glad the circumstances encouraged the style that will live forever through our wedding photos. My dad loved the movie Dr. Zhivago, and I get Julie Christie vibes from my sophisticated, winter wedding ensemble.

The dress is white lace and body conscious with a mermaid train. It has long sleeves and a bateau neckline. It looked simple on the hanger, but when I tried it on at the bridal shop, Ava, Rachel, and I unanimously voted to stop shopping. Just in case the heat in the tent isn't enough for my Florida blood, I ordered an uber-cool full-length wedding shawl.

It's made from synthetic white fur, and it has a hood, a la Dr. Zhivago. I didn't want a veil, so this is perfect. I can wear it up as I walk down the aisle and gather it around my neck after the ceremony.

I splurged on French lingerie for under the gown, and it makes me feel incredibly sexy. I step into the gown and zip the side. The boys don't have a full-length mirror in this room, so I take a selfie. The photo gives me chills. I have never felt so beautiful, and I think a huge part of that comes from how happy I feel in this moment. I don't want to wait another minute to run down the aisle to Nico.

I slip into white boots that hit mid-calf and I realize they will look sexy as hell with the lingerie when I shed the dress later. That's a bonus I didn't plan. I take the shawl from the hanger and place it over my arm before I walk back to the living room.

Max is the first person I see. He places his hand over his mouth and his eyes brim with tears. "Mare …" he circles me as I chuckle. "Mare …"

"What do you think, Maxer?"

"I think Nico is going pass out when he sees you. He can't handle this. I can barely handle this …"

The girls heard us chatting and are gathering at the end of the hallway. "Girl!" The squeals make me laugh as I walk between walls lined with photos of the Van Asten boys chronicling their time from infancy to when Nico was home a few months ago.

"You're the most stunning bride I've ever seen, and I have two married sisters," Ava says. "Don't tell them I said that."

"Thank you, Ava." I give her an air kiss.

"Maris, I'm speechless," Rachel says.

"Yep," Max agrees, slipping his arm around her waist.

"And you look hot, af, my man," Rachel says cuddling close to Max.

"Everyone looks stunning," I say. "We have to do a photo, but no one can post tonight, okay? We're going to do a Press Release after the wedding and then we can post tomorrow with Nico's hash tag."

"I'll take a photo of you ladies, and then, Rachel, can you take one of the wedding party?" Max asks.

We gather in different configurations and smile for the cameras, but I'm becoming impatient. I want it to be time.

"Maris, honey," Momma V. says after we take a photo together. "Do you have your something old, new, borrowed, and blue?"

I freeze. "Um, my clothes are new …"

"It's bad luck if you don't have those four things," Ava says with a serious expression.

"Don't worry, I've been ready for this since 1994," Momma V. says. "I'll be right back. She ducks into the master bedroom and emerges with a small, blue satin pouch. "My mother gave me this on our wedding day. It's a lucky penny and it covers your old, borrowed, and blue."

"I can't cry right now, Momma V.!" I say trying to manage my emotions.

She tuts and suggests slipping the pouch into my boot.

"That's perfect, thank you," I say. "For everything. Especially for raising Nico."

"Well, I guess we're going to test that waterproof mascara, huh?" Mrs. Van Asten says, dabbing her eyes. "Thank you for loving my son so well, Maris. You're the daughter-in-law I prayed for."

"Awww!" The girls and Max share the sweetness of the moment.

"Okay, now I really want to marry into this family. If I'm not seated next to Marcus at dinner, I'm switching the place cards," Mimi says.

"Do I hear my name?" Marcus appears in the living room. When our eyes meet, his face softens. "My brother is one lucky man."

"I'm the lucky one," I assure him.

"The guests are seated, and the harp player is keeping them entertained, so … anytime you're ready, we can get this wedding underway," Marcus tells us.

"We better go take our seats," Ava says. "You're stunning, Maris. I can't wait to capture Nico's first look on video."

"See you afterwards, Maris," Rachel waves as she follows Ava.

"Ladies, wait, I have the golf cart right outside," Marcus tells me. "I can take five at a time."

"I'm ready to go over to the tent," Mimi says breezily. When we laugh, she innocently asks, "What? We don't want to keep everyone waiting."

Marcus makes two trips. Then comes back for Max, Momma V., and me. We ride across the back yard in silence. The tent is glowing from within, chandeliers and candles ablaze. I see people seated on one end and long tables set up in the middle, dividing the stage and dance floor from the site of the ceremony. I haven't given much thought to what the venue will look like, but it's gorgeous. My singular care is that my Nico is there waiting for me. When Marcus stops the cart, Max holds his arms out for me. Marcus helps his mother, and then we're in the back of the tent behind drapes.

"Just like backstage, huh?" Max chuckles.

"Eerily similar," I agree.

The wedding march begins, and the first bridesmaid begins walking down the aisle. I take a deep breath, say a quick prayer, and then it's time for Max to walk me down the aisle.

NICO

WHILE PLANNING THE WEDDING, MARIS and my mother kept using the words *Winter Wonderland,* and they succeeded in bringing the theme to life. Dad, my brothers, Theo, and I arrived at the wedding site before the guests to walk through and make sure everything was perfect. Theo and I also wanted to make sure the sound company I hired set the gear up properly and we sound checked everything to our satisfaction.

The tent is divided into three purposes: the ceremony, dinner, and the reception, but the entire tent smells like gardenias. I can't imagine where my mom got fresh gardenias or how much it cost to ship them to Wisconsin in December. But the flowers might be another piece of the puzzle that was gifted by friends. I have a lot of free concert tickets and backstage passes to distribute to show my appreciation for the whole town contributing to our wedding. I know that my parents have personal and professional relationships with a lot of the people who offered things from the tent itself to rental tables and chairs, but the generosity on display chokes me up. These people who are lifelong family friends wouldn't think of charging for their services even though it's their livelihood.

The tent has clear picture windows, and the view of the snow-covered lake and trees surrounds us. Mother Nature provided most of the stunning decorations and all of the atmosphere. There is a white silk runner between rows of silver chairs and the raised alter has four tall posts on each corner with lit evergreen boughs draped between them. It's a beautiful place to take my beautiful Maris as my wife and I'm so excited to share the moment with my family and the friends who have become family to both of us.

Theo is hiding cords that snaked across the stage, so I walk to the far end of the tent to help him. "Wanna make some noise? Just to check the gear, of course," Theo asks with a guilty smile.

"Just to check the gear, of course," I say strapping on the guitar.

Theo sits on the drum throne, and I laugh at the site of him doing so in a full tuxedo. His foot presses the drum pedal, and a thick, booming sound fills the tent. Theo adds the snare and then reaches into his tux jacket pocket for a drum key.

"My Best Man has everything covered," I say smiling. I turn on the guitar amp and start to play while he tunes the snare, and my brothers come to the foot of the stage and cheer me on like the supportive psychos they are. When Theo gets the sound he wants from the drum kit, he joins in, and the devoted audience reacts with louder cheers.

"That's enough, that's enough." My Dad waves his hands over his head. "Guests are starting to show up."

Theo raises his eyebrows and bites his lip while I laugh at him. "Sounds good, brother."

"Your dad is right; we don't want to give any sneak peeks, and you don't want the guitar strap to wrinkle your tux jacket." Theo places the sticks on top of the snare drum and comes to the front of the kit to smooth the shoulder of my jacket. "You have a whole Gatsby thing going on," he tells me.

"I used product in my hair and everything," I joke. "It's not surprising that you look like you were born in a tuxedo, my man."

Theo rolls his eyes and gives me a half smile. "Whatever, dude. You've got leading man energy and the gorgeous face to go with it." Theo laughs wickedly.

"Hey, Marcus, can you get a pic of me with Theo?"

Marcus focuses his camera as Theo and I mug for the shot.

"That might be the only photo today without Max bombing," I say.

"He's so excited to be Maris's Best Man," Theo says, checking his pants pocket for the hundredth time.

"She was adamant that he has an important role. As he should," I say, "but don't ever tell him I agree."

"Obviously."

Dad approaches and puts his arms around both of us. "Well, are we ready for this?"

"I've never been more ready for anything," I say with a smile.

"I'm proud of you. You chose well son. Make each other's happiness more important than your own. When the going gets tough, love more, and when you're wrong, admit it." My father slaps me on the back.

"Thanks, Dad."

"He makes it sound easy." Theo chuckles.

"Write it down because it looks like you're next. I see the way you and Ava look at one another. No point in wasting time because life is short." Dad walks towards the entrance to the tent to join Marcus, Ollie, and Pete who are greeting guests and ushering them to seats. The harpist begins playing and the music adds a heavenly feel to the setting.

"Are we supposed to be backstage?" Theo asks.

"It feels like yes, but I don't know where that would be, so maybe we should just go help greet and seat."

"Okay," Theo says.

The guest list is sixty total, but we have to pull out more chairs. I think word got out and some extras showed up, but Dad says we planned for that, and we have enough food. We were strict about not allowing phones or cameras inside the tent, so the only photos will be from the professional Maris hired, and our closest friends.

"It looks like everyone's arrived, and then some. And it's time, so ..." Marcus places his hands on my shoulders ... "this is it."

"You're going to bring the girls and Max over in the golf cart?" I ask, smoothing my hair and straightening my bow tie.

"Yep. I'll go get your bride."

"Holy shit," I say.

"Holy shit, indeed," Marcus echoes.

"When you get back, we'll line up at the alter and then we can cue the harpist to start the wedding march, and the girls will come down the aisle."

"Got it," Marcus says.

Theo, my brothers, Dad, and I try to make small talk in the back of the tent, but the moment is too big for frivolous chatter. Ava and Rachel make their way in with mom, and they all look gorgeous.

When my dad sees my mother he says, "I'd marry you again, Hot Stuff." I would have cringed at that a year ago, but now I see it as a goal.

"You ladies look fabulous," I say, giving hugs.

"Nico, you're the quite the dashing groom," Ava says.

"Are you nervous?" Rachel asks.

I hold my hand out to show that I'm steady, and everyone laughs.

The bridal party arrives, and they line up in the order they're walking.

"Shall we?" My dad holds out his arm for my mother, and he escorts her to their seats.

"Let's gooooooo!" I whisper shout. We form a single file line and Peter leads the way followed by Ollie, Marcus, and Theo with me bringing up the rear. As I walk to the alter, I see friends from high school, cousins, and a few people I'm sure I've never met. The parish priest who baptized all the Van Asten boys greets me at the alter and shakes my hand. Then the harpist concludes Cannon in D and begins playing the wedding march. The music lands in my heart and I forget how to breath. All the faces that I just registered blur, and my eyes are focused on the drape in the back of the room. Max's hand appears and he pulls the drape aside. My breath catches when I see her. I'm overwhelmed by the sight of Maris. I try to take a deep breath, but swallowing air is difficult while my heart beats so wildly. I feel my lips quivering and I blink rapidly to clear my vision. Maris smiles at me, and I feel my face explode with joy. Max offers his arm and guides her down the aisle, but I can't wait, so I start walking towards them, which makes everyone laugh. I don't care that I'm doing it wrong; I just need her by my side. Max steps away and I take Maris's hand. She is stunningly regal in the white lace gown that outlines her silhouette, and the cape she wears is the glamorous touch that makes her look like the star she is. I forget that everyone is watching us and that we're supposed to be on the alter, rather than standing in the aisle.

"You're the most beautiful bride I've ever seen," I tell her.

"You're pretty gorgeous yourself," she says smiling up at me.

"Wanna get married?" I ask.

"Right now," she says, and people who are seated near us chuckle.

I take Maris's hand and weave it through my elbow. We climb three steps to the alter and I see that both Theo and Marcus have tears in their eyes. Theo pats his pocket again and then stands with his shoulders back and his chin high at my side.

The priest smiles at Maris and begins. "We are gathered here to unite Nicolas Van Asten and Maris Humphries in holy matrimony. I had the opportunity to meet with the bride and groom yesterday and I'm pleased to say that I don't have to ask the question whether they have each come freely and willingly to join their lives together." The guests laugh politely. "In fact, Nicolas asked if I would wed them yesterday in my office, which would make today a vow renewal of sorts."

There's more laughter as I turn to look at my mother. "He said no," I tell her.

"Smart move, Henry," My mother says.

"I've known Nicolas his whole life, and I just met Maris, but I am confident that they are ready to join themselves, heart, mind, body, and soul to one another until death parts them. They understand that marriage is a marathon and not a sprint. They've already proven that they will stay together through good times and bad, and they promised to stay together whether their first album goes to number one or doesn't break the top one hundred."

The guests chuckle again, and Maris and I turn to Theo and Max who make number one gestures with their pointer fingers.

"Nico and Maris have written their own vows, and I invite Maris to recite hers first."

Maris's eyes don't leave mine and she smiles at me as she speaks. "Nicolas Van Asten, it's impossible to put into words how much I love you, so I promise to spend the rest of our lives showing you. You will always be my first consideration. You gave me your heart, and I will protect it forever. I will double your joys and carry half of your burdens. I will tell you the truth." Maris's voice shakes. "I will be your home, your devoted wife, and the mother to your children if we are so blessed. I will do those things with my whole heart. I will be your partner, and your collaborator ... you're biggest fan on stage and off." The guests chuckle again. "I will be your sounding board and your playmate, and although I'll never be a Miami Hurricanes fan, I will dedicate my NFL loyalty to the Green Bay Packers and proudly wear green and gold and cheer *Go Pack Go* with you during the season."

The tent erupts in cheers, whistles, and choruses of *Go Pack Go* as I throw my head back and laugh.

I look at Fr. Henry, "There's no way I can top that."

He places his hand on my shoulder and shakes his head. "I'm sorry I didn't let you go first," he says, which makes the guests laugh again. "Good luck, son."

I take a deep breath and lightly squeeze Maris's hands between my own. "My dear Maris, today you make me the luckiest man in the world. You have surprised me repeatedly since the day we met, and I wake up every day excited to witness how you'll amaze me next. You turned a very self-focused man into a partner just by being yourself. Caring about you, loving you, working with you, and getting to know your heart made me want to support you in every possible way. Before I met you, my focus was working towards the ultimate professional goal. When you came into my life," I turn to Theo and gesture towards Max, "Our lives."

Max nods, "Our lives."

"You were the ingredient that made my wildest dream come true, and that's still very important to me, but my greatest source of pride is that a woman as incredible as you," I clear the emotion from my throat, "loves me. I will never take your love for granted and I will work to earn it, and keep it, every day for the rest of our lives. I always have your back, I will always care about the things that are important to you, I will learn from my mistakes, and I promise to put your needs first. I will be your husband, your bandmate, the father to your children, your lover, and your best friend until my last breath. I love you so much."

Maris is smiling through her tears, so I remove my pocket square and dab at her eyes as she chuckles.

"With that, it's time to exchange the rings that symbolize a love that has no beginning or ending," Fr. Henry says. "Maris, you'll go first."

Maris turns to Max who hands her a ring I've never seen before. I genuinely hadn't considered that I'd acquire a wedding ring today. I look at Maris's hands and feel a confused expression on my face.

"I have two versions of wedding rings for you," she says. "One will be comfortable when you play guitar, and the other is jewelry for when you're an off-duty rock star."

I hear Theo chuckle behind me.

"I'd like to have them both blessed, so ..."

Fr. Henry nods. "Nico, why don't you place the work ring on your right hand, and then Maris can place the other one on your ring finger."

Maris hands me a ring that looks like brushed nickel, but feels like silicone, and I slip it on my right hand. "Maybe we need to get you one of these," I whisper, which makes Maris laugh.

"We can talk about it later," she whispers, which makes the wedding party chuckle.

"Maris, repeat after me ... with this ring, I thee wed."

My bride looks into my eyes, and I feel my chin quivering again. "With this ring, I thee wed." Maris is crying and I feel my tears brimming over as well.

Henry nods at me and I turn to Theo who looks relieved to hand over the rings he's guarded with his life for the past several hours. We make eye contact and he's crying too, which evokes a chuckle from both of us.

I hold my left palm up and Maris places her left hand on top of it. "With this ring, I thee wed." I slide the rings onto her finger and feel my life settle into place.

We're staring into each other eyes as Henry says, "I now pronounce you man and wife." We're kissing before he gives permission and Henry says something to the guests about congratulating the newlyweds. I hear everyone cheering and the harpist begins playing a beautiful version of *Coming Around*, the first song Maris played with Funkengroovin' the day she auditioned for the band.

"Yeah!" Theo yells when he recognizes the song.

I hear Max laugh and the guests start singing in unison.

"You're my wife!" I tell Maris between kisses.

"You're my husband!"

We hold hands and walk down the aisle as our guests cheer and sing. While we were all facing the alter, the band took the stage on the far end of the tent. Maris's jaw drops when she recognizes them.

"You've gotta be kidding me!" She shouts as Dame Knight strikes the first chord of their biggest hit. Our guests scream and scramble to the dance floor.

"Congratulations, Nico, you lucky wanker!" Nicky says into the mic.

"Congratulations, Maris, or should I say, *Mrs. Van Asten*?" Dinah Dame says, waving at us.

"It's so good to be back in Canada!" Nicky yells as if he's in a stadium.

I laugh my ass off because, even while *in* Wisconsin, Nicky doesn't know where it is. "Nicky said he'd be happy to do a favor for us," I tell Maris as I sweep her into my arms to dance. "I don't think this is at all what he had in mind when he offered, but when I asked, he said yes immediately."

Maris throws her head back and laughs. "I can't believe Dame Knight is our wedding band!"

"Baby, this is just the beginning of a long life of making unbelievable memories," I tell her. She kisses me and I try to freeze time. I never want to forget this moment. How I feel right now. Grateful, ecstatically happy, hopeful, blessed, and loved. There's so much love in the room. Through our kiss, I mumble, "I love you, Mrs. Van Asten."

MARIS

WHEN I SAW NICO WAITING for me at the altar, I felt like I was in a movie. The handsome leading man, decked out in a tuxedo, showing a spectrum of emotion on his face … it was like a dream. But when I smiled at him and he smiled back, he became my Nico again. The guitar playing, ball busting, easy-going philosopher with a wicked sense of humor who loves me. As I walked towards him, on Max's arm, I thought of all the things he has become to me. Nico is my strength, my calm, the edge that sharpens my skill, the wave that carries me, and the safety I didn't know my life was lacking. I laughed as he came towards us, like a magnet that couldn't resist the pull. We didn't have a wedding rehearsal, but practice wouldn't have confined Nico's impulses.

I tried to be present in every moment, but as I stared into his eyes, all I could see was our future. I saw Nico as a husband and pictured us looking for a house to make our home. I saw him as a father, holding our child after shredding on stage. I saw him old, when our shared experience would be a stronger bond than we feel today.

Before I knew it, we were married. And then Dame Knight was playing, and I had to remind myself again that this wasn't a lucid dream.

When Theo and Max took the stage and called for everyone's attention, we took our seats for the Best Men's toasts. Nico and I didn't want to be isolated from our guests during dinner, so the "head table" included Max, Theo, Rachel, and Ava. The Van Astens sat at the table behind us where we could easily chat between courses.

Theo gently taps his champagne flute with a knife and silences the room. Nico and I indulge in a kiss because it's rude not to kiss when someone clinks a glass at a wedding.

"Good evening, everyone," Theo begins. "For those of you who don't know me, I'm Theo Athanasiou—"

"Funkengroovin'!" Someone shouts from the back of the room.

Theo laughs and shrugs. "Also, Nico's best man." Theo walks across the stage as he speaks. "When Nico asked me to be his best man, I was worried that the Van Asten brothers would disappear me upon my arrival in Wisconsin, so I'm thrilled to have made it this far alive." The guests laugh politely. "The reason that Nico bestowed this honor on me is because I've been a witness to this love affair. And, if I'm being honest, I'm not merely a witness, but the entire reason we're all here today." The guests hoot and cheer and Theo smiles slyly towards Nico and me. He stands still at center stage and has command of the room. "When I discovered Maris, Nico and Max didn't want a female in the band." Loud boos fill the air and Theo nods in agreement. "Yeah. But then Nico dropped in on one of Maris's gigs with Backyard Breeder and the band asked him to sit in." Theo is hitting his stride. "To hear him tell it, the minute they played music together, Nico became enamored with Maris's … talent." Theo raises his eyebrows to the guests, and they laugh.

"I was though," Nico yells. "My wife is ridiculously talented." The guests react with applause, and I mouth *thank you* to Nico.

"With Nico on board, we hired Maris and, like women do, she came into our lives and started making changes. If you weren't aware, we all live together in Miami. When Maris moved in, we three dudes became more civilized. We had meals together and we started using real dishes instead of paper plates. We learned how to use the dishwasher. We wore swimming trunks in the pool." Someone whistles. "But Maris had the most influence on us on stage and in the studio. As she was reinforcing our bond as band brothers, she was elevating us musically and creating possibilities that weren't available to us before she joined. I think we all wanted to be better … for her. At her audition, Maris stated that she was also auditioning us because she wasn't going to leave her band unless the move was a step up, and I think we all wanted her to be proud to be one of us."

"I'm so proud!" I call to the stage.

Theo laughs and raises his flute in my direction.

"I think we all loved Maris from the start, but when Nico told me that they were together, I had to take a step back and observe how

Nico's love for Maris had changed him. Nico was a fun-loving musician. He was serious about one thing and one thing only … music. He took life as it came at him, he wasn't really a planner. I thought of him as a happy-go-lucky guy, and he's still that guy, but Nico is centered in a way that I've not witnessed before. His priorities have changed. He once told me that if he had to make a choice between giving up Funkengroovin' and Maris, he would walk away from Funkengroovin' without a thought."

I look at Nico. "You did?"

He leans back in his chair and touches my face with the back of his hand.

"That may not mean a whole lot to many of you, but when you put five years into a band and you're starting to take off, you don't know if you'll ever find that magic again, but Nico didn't care. What he cares about is Maris. And she cares deeply about all of us, but her attachment to Nico is cosmic and undeniable. Until recently, I didn't know that two people could fall so deeply in love so quickly." Theo looks at Ava. "I thought it took years, but a very wise man, Mr. Van Asten, recently told me that life is too short to waste time. And I'm proud of and happy for Nico and Maris that they didn't waste time on their way to the alter. Because when it's right, it's right." Theo raises his glass. "Thank you, Nico, for asking me to be at your side today. Thank you, Maris, for being my favorite band brother, and thank you both for showing all of us what love makes possible. I love you guys." Theo takes a sip of champagne and then raises the mic again. "I'm Greek, but I was told in advance that the pieces of our table settings are borrowed, so I can't break anything, but Opa!"

Nico and I yell "Opa!" and take a sip of champagne.

Theo hands the mic to Max. "Good evening, everyone, I'm Max Anthony Castellano," Max's voice fills the room and Rachel cheers loudly for her man while everyone claps. "Thank you, thank you. I'm honored to be here as Nico and Maris's band brother, but I'm most honored to be here as Mare's Best Man. Um, what Theo said about Nico and me not wanting a chick in the band is true, but, back then, we didn't know Maris isn't just any chick. She's Maris, you know?" My girlfriends make some noise, and I smile at their expression of love. "I mean, here's this gorgeous girl who's a monster bass player, a fantastic vocalist, and she's also the coolest chick on the planet. Who knew such a person existed?" Max shrugs his shoulders. "We didn't. We'd never heard of such a creature, let alone encountered one in the wild." I chuckle along with the guests. "What Mare brought to the band was priceless, and what she brought to the house was priceless. Her presence changed us in the ways Theo mentioned, but she added a nurturing quality to our dynamic as well. For me, personally, Mare provided the validation I was thirsty for, and my confidence grew, so thank you for that, Mare." I blow Max a kiss and smile at him. "I knew, before they told us, that Nico and Maris we're an item." Nico scoffs beside me. I know if I look at him, I'll bust out laughing, so I keep my eyes on Max. "I was worried that their situationship would run its course and ruin the band. I mean, I was really worried, but I caught Nico creeping out of Mare's room one morning ..." Nico clears his throat loudly and Max holds up his flute to reassure him as the guests chuckle. "The way that Nico reacted to getting busted told me a lot." The guests laugh now. "This big, intimidating, snarky guy who doesn't miss an opportunity to joke or make fun of anything and anyone, didn't say a word to me. The look he gave me was enough to let me know the subject of him and Mare was off limits. To a guy for whom nothing is sacred, that was sacred. And this happened very early on, so what I've always known about Nico and Maris's relationship is that it was serious from the start. Whether they said that out loud to each other, or admitted it to themselves, it was serious from the start. I've watched them tackle a lot of things together, tough things, and I know these two will cross the finish line of life married, grateful, and with no regrets. I can't wait to witness all the years between then and now. I love you guys." Max holds up his glass, and everyone applauds including Nico.

Mimi asks Max for the microphone. "I'd like to make a toast if that's okay." She looks at me and I press my palms together to thank her for the gesture. "I'm Mimi Juliano, and I went to FSU undergrad and almost two years of FSU law school with Maris." This evokes applause from the guests. "I will always be able to say I knew Maris when ..." Everyone laughs. "Our first year at Florida State was tough for all of us, of course, but it was tougher for Maris because she didn't have support from her mother. By then, her father, who was her best friend and mentor, had passed, and I know he's with us in spirit today. I know he's so happy that Maris didn't give up her music and that she married a musician. Cheers to you, Daddy Humphries." Mimi raises her glass towards the sky. "For those of you who haven't known Maris as long as I have, I want you to understand how much she deserves this. She fully deserves to be adored and loved, and she deserves to have a supportive family behind her." The room is dead quiet. "I respect the boundaries that Maris set with her mother and the rest of her family. She had to do that to have the life she has today, but it wasn't easy. Sometimes you choose the devil you know because it's comfortable and familiar, but Maris recognized how toxic the people closest to her were, and she chose to go it alone. She took out student loans and worked her way through college playing in bands and traveling the whole state of Florida on the weekends while the rest of us were partying. She went without a lot of things and made do with what she could afford, but she never, ever complained. In fact, she was the person we all went to when we needed to be cheered up."

Several of my girlfriends confirm with shouts of *True! Yep! That's right!*

"I think, even back then, when all of this probably seemed impossible, Maris knew that she would forge a path to happiness and success. She was never a quitter, well, she quit law school, but that was because a musical talent like hers shouldn't be there in the first place." Guests cheer. "So, that's not really quitting, that's redirection. Maris, Mrs. Van Asten, I just wanted to say that I admire you, respect you, love you, and I'm so damn happy for you."

I blow a kiss to Mimi as Nico leans over and kisses the top of my head. The love around me squeezes out more tears and I'm destroying Nico's pocket square. We will have to replace it.

"Can you handle the first dance right now? Nico asks.

I start to laugh. "The song we wrote together with our vows as the lyrics? No!" I dab underneath my eyes again. "I think that would dissolve me into a puddle. What a terrible idea that was."

Nico circles his finger above his head, the signal we use for *keep it going* on stage and Dame Knight starts playing.

Nico lifts my chin with his pointer finger and gazes into my teary eyes. "Thank you for finding me. Thank you for being so strong and not giving up. Thank you for letting me love you the way you deserve to be loved." Nico slips his hand behind my neck and gently pulls me to him. Kissing Nico is my favorite thing in the world.

* * *

Nico carries me through the snow to our cabin, and I bury my face in his chest to hide from the wind.

"We're about to cross the threshold, Mrs. Van Asten," he says softly. Nico turns me to the side so that he can use his right hand to open the cabin door. There's a fire burning in the fireplace and rose petals make a path from the front door to the big brass bed with a rose petal heart in the center.

"This is so romantic," I whisper.

Nico's bowtie hangs on either side of his partially open tux shirt. His hair escaped the control of the product he applied before the wedding and is undone in a sexy way. He sets me on my feet and pushes the hood from my forehead before he unties the bow that secures my cape.

"You absolutely have to wear this on stage," he says. "It's very rock-n-roll, but more importantly, it will always remind me of the fantastic sex we had on our wedding night."

I laugh wickedly as Nico tosses the cape across a cozy stuffed chair. I open a few more of the buttons on his shirt and place my hands flat against his cold chest. "Aren't you freezing?"

"I don't know," he says. Nico places his hand behind my neck and kisses me. "Try to melt me."

I laugh as Nico nuzzles my neck and finds the zipper on my dress. "You looked like the cover of a bridal magazine today, Wife."

"It was the most magical day of my life, Handsome Husband."

Nico opens my dress and slowly frees my shoulders, kissing as he goes. I slide my arms free and drape them around his neck as my dress falls to the floor revealing the outfit I imagined earlier.

Nico notices the new lingerie immediately and growls. "Those boots are staying on."

The fireplace crackles and dances, making the light flicker. Nico picks my dress up and hangs it in the closet, alongside his tux jacket and pants. Then he pulls the comforter from the bed and lays it on the floor in front of the fireplace. He tosses some pillows on top of it and lifts me off my feet again. This time I wrap my legs around his waist, boots and all. Nico takes a knee and gently lays me on top of the fluffy comforter. "Cold?"

"No."

Nico places a pillow under my head, and I touch his face with my hands. "I love you."

"Oh, Maris, there isn't a word for how I feel about you. You're everything."

Nico lays on his side and I coax the tuxedo shirt from his body. I trace the muscles in his shoulder and run my fingertips down his triceps and across his forearm. These are my husband's arms, where I am always safe. Nico kisses my forehead, then my eyelids, and then the tip of my nose. When I open my eyes again, he's admiring me with a content smile on his face. He winks and me and then smirks before he kisses my collarbone and works his way down to the lacy French bra. He nuzzles the flesh underneath and runs his strong hand up the inside of my thigh. My fingers skim across the familiar terrain of Nico's muscular back, up his neck, and into his hair. I tousle his dark blond strands with my fingers. My bra loosens and Nico tosses it onto the stuffed chair.

"God gave you all the things," he says with a chuckle in his voice.

"That's what you said the first time we were together."

"I think it every time. I only say it on special occasions," he teases.

Nico gently pulls my panties aside and grabs my hips in his hands. I brace myself for what's coming next, but when I feel his tongue moving between my legs, I have no defenses, no composure. I'm quick. Too quick.

"It's going to be an early and often kind of night," Nico remarks.

Amid aftershocks, I can't help laughing. "We'll see if you can last longer, Big Man."

Nico makes sure that I experience all the pleasure possible from my first orgasm of the night before he enters me. I anticipated turning the tables on him, but he wants to be inside me. He keeps me on my back and kisses me as we sync into a rhythm that starts slow but becomes frantic. I suck Nico's tongue deeply into my mouth, the same way I would orally please him, and I feel him twitch inside me, so I constrict more tightly around him. "Early and often," I tease him as he thrusts deeper. Then I'm drawing out his orgasm to sustain the feeling for minutes rather than seconds.

"Who won round 1?" I ask when he relaxes on top of me.

"I think it was a tie."

The fireplace crackles some more and Nico lifts himself onto straight arms so that his weight is off me, and then he kisses me, slowly and passionately. I smell his Dolce Gabbana cologne mixed with his own essence, which stirs me. His kisses deliver a hint of whisky, and his touch sends shockwaves through my body. I'll never get enough of his voice in my ear, seeing his gorgeous face, or hearing him play guitar. I'll always want to play music with him, sing with him, make love with him, and be with him in the best of times and on our worst days. This is love.

FIVE YEARS LATER

THEO

PEOPLE WARN YOU ABOUT THE terrible twos, but, at three years and two months, Pearl hasn't hit a stage I'd call terrible yet. Like Ava, our daughter is super girly. The Van Asten boys, and Max's son Harry, treat her like a princess. The kids are accustomed to life on the road, and they're an adorable little tribe.

The kids share a green room at the American Airlines Arena in Miami, and it's the hub for the band and our spouses as well. Dressing rooms are only for dressing these days. We eat with the kids, warm-up with the kids, and do our Funkengroovin' pre-show prayer and hype circle with the kids.

Ava opens the door for one of the tour nannies who carries two shopping bags from Whole Foods. "Dinner is here!"

"Come and get it, little groovers," Sarah says with affection.

Vince and Vaughn get to the table first and, despite there being four open seats, they both aim for the same chair and *call it.* I love ragging on Nico over the twins' names. Vince Lombardi and Stevie Ray Vaughn were the inspirations, but I pretend Nico's a superfan of the actor Vince Vaughn. He hates that I'm the first person who realized the alternate assumption. Also, that I won't let it go.

"Gentlemen, you're forgetting your manners," Nico says. He's on the couch across from mine changing his strings. He looks at me and shakes his head as I warm up my wrists on my drum pad.

"Oh, yeah!" Vaughn pulls out a chair for Pearl.

"I would have done it, Pearl, but I was already seated," Vince says.

Nico and I chuckle.

"Can I sit by you, Vince?" Max's son, Harry, asks.

"Of course, my man," Vince says slapping the chair next to his.

"Thank you, Vaughn." Pearl takes her seat and Vaughn pushes her chair under the table. Like everything the Van Asten boys do, he does it with too much gusto, and she has to scoot herself back a few inches after he walks away.

"Hey, everybody!" Maris's team does her hair and make-up super early so she can have dinner with the kids. "What's for dinner?"

"Macaroni and cheese, and chicken, and soup, and crackers ..." Vince names each item that Sarah pulls from the bag.

"Essentially the same things they asked for in Tampa, and in Atlanta, in spite of my best attempts to diversify," Sarah says.

"Hey, if it works, it works," Ava says.

"I second that emotion." Maris helps Sarah and Ava distribute the food, napkins and utensils.

When the band's catering shows up, I text Max and tell him soup's on.

"How does everyone feel about the last night of the tour?" Ava asks.

"Booooooooo!" Vaughn starts the outburst and the rest of the kids, Nico, and I join in.

Ava and Maris laugh and roll their eyes.

"Can Harry and Pearl sleep over at our house tomorrow, Mommy?" Vince asks.

"I bet they want to sleep in their own beds for a few nights, but they can sleep over any time they want to." Maris sits on an adult sized chair by the tiny table and holds her dinner with one hand while eating with the other.

"I'm pretty excited to sleep in my own bed tonight," Max says, catching the tail end of the conversation as he comes through the door.

"Daddy!" Harry is a few months older than Pearl and he lives with Max full-time. They're relationship is hilariously adorable. It's almost like they're peers because Harry is such a little man.

"My dude," Max says, bending over to blow a raspberry against Harry's cheek, which makes the little Castellano laugh.

"Aunt Maris says we can sleep over whenever we want to," Harry tells Max.

"Cool! We'll definitely take that invitation, but Mommy and I want to spend time with you too, so we'll work it out."

Harry turns to Vince. "Yeah, I have to make sure I see my mom too, but I'll make time for you guys."

Vince nods and answers through a bite of chicken nugget, "Fair."

"These kids have been on the road forever," Ava says. "How do you think they'll adjust to having time off?"

"The same way we will, I suspect," I say, "Poorly."

"Oh, it's going to be nice to have some time off to write," Maris says. "Remember the old days when we would wake up, eat, write, eat, swim, eat ..." she laughs.

"Notice my wife doesn't even fantasize about sleep?" Nico points to the boys. "There's no sleeping at our house. Ever."

I finish my warm-up and grab some food. "That's what screens are for brother. Start a movie and you get another ninety-minutes."

Ava scoffs. "That has literally never worked and yet he tries it every morning."

I shrug. "Just haven't found the right movie … yet."

"Movies are boring," Pearl says. "Playing is more fun."

"Yeah, playing is more fun," Harry agrees.

"When you guys sleep over, we can play first thing in the morning," Vaughn promises.

Nico finishes tuning his guitar and starts playing a song the kids like to sing along to. They belt out the first verse of *Coming Around* and the four of us make eye contact with one another. It's incredible to watch these tiny versions of us. After the first chorus, Nico says, "Okay, back to dinner. Sarah made a special trip to get your favorites, so I don't want it to get cold."

"Thank you, Sarah," the kids say in unison.

"You're welcome little groovers," she says with a wink.

"Are going to change up the set list for tonight?" Max asks, sitting in an adult sized chair next to Maris.

"Nico and I put one together for you guys to check out. We have two encores in mind." I claim the adult sized chair behind Ava who's crouched beside Pearl, helping her cut up her chicken. "Should be in your shared notes."

"You look exceptionally gorgeous tonight, Love," Nico kisses Maris before he grabs his food, and again after he sits down next to her.

"They do that all the time," Vince tells Harry.

"Oh, I know," Harry says judgmentally.

"My mommy and daddy are kissy crazy too," Pearl tells the table.

"You can tell them not to do that in front of you," Harry says.

"Mommies and daddies kiss because they love each other. The same reason we kiss you little monsters. It's an expression of love," Nico tells the kids.

Vaughn pushes back his chair and runs to Pearl, then kisses her cheek. Nico looks at me with a worried expression, and I show him my fist.

"Not in front of the kids," Nico says with a smirk. "And let's be honest, she could do worse."

"I'm going to be the husband, not you, Vaughn," Harry says.

"Oh, shit, not again," Max says.

"Language!" All the kids yell in unison.

"Put a ten in the sweat jar, Uncle Max," Vince says.

"It's gonna be an IOU, my guy. I don't have cash on me."

"We'll accept an IOU, Uncle Max," Vaughn says. "You're good for it."

My phone alerts and I read the text out loud. "Phil is confirming the interview with Rolling Stone at my house at one o'clock tomorrow."

Maris winks at me and Max nods with his mouth full.

"Come over early and we'll do brunch," Ava says.

"What can we bring?" Maris asks.

"Brunch," I say, like the answer is painfully obvious.

"Daphne is flying in tonight," Max says. "She and Harry have a zoo day planned tomorrow, don't you, buddy?"

"Meerkats!" Harry says excitedly.

"How long will she be in town?" I ask Max. "Will we get to see her?"

"I hope so. She just delivered a contract photo package to Vanity Fair, so she's planning to be in Miami for a couple weeks. Selfishly, I hope a gig doesn't pop up. She worries about turning down jobs while she's in demand, you know?"

"Yeah, that's tricky," Maris says. "But if Daphne gets a shoot in Paris next week, her men can go with her since the tour is over."

"Very true," Max says. "We'd go to Paris with mommy, wouldn't we, Harry?"

Harry gives an enthusiastic thumbs up.

"You guys have done a great job making your relationship work even when it's been long distance, and Harry always has one of you. It's only going to get easier once we're off the road," I tell Max.

Four phone alarms go off simultaneously.

"Fifteen minutes!" The kids yell.

"Huddle up, Playas," Nico says. Once the four of us, Ava, Sarah, and the kids are in the huddle, Maris speaks.

"Dear Lord, thank you for the experiences we've had on this tour. Thank you for making a path for our music to reach people. Thank you for keeping us healthy and safe as we've traveled all over your beautiful creation. Bless our performances tonight so that we may share our gifts to the best of our abilities. May our music be a blessing to those who hear it, and may it inspire goodness and love. We are grateful for your abundant blessings. Amen."

I start the chant and the kids join in as they make their own huddle beneath our taller one. "Funkengroovin', Funkengroovin' …"

The kids end the chant with "Break legs!"

And then it's the four of us in the hallway behind the stage at the American Airlines Arena.

"I love that we're ending the tour at home," Max says.

"It feels sweet, doesn't it?" Maris asks.

Nico smirks at me and I know that means this audience is about to get a hell of a show.

The announcer's voice booms through the arena, "*Ladies, gentlemen, and groovers, please welcome FUNKENGROOVIN'!*"

We take the stage, and the audience continues the warm welcome after Maris yells, "What's good, Miami? It's great to be home!"

I count us into the first song and settle in behind my kit. The sound is typically fantastic and the separation in my ears allows me to hear exactly what I need to keep the train speeding above the rails. My foot is a little heavier tonight due to the excitement I feel to be playing in my hometown arena where I've seen so many of my musical idols perform.

Maris is already halfway down the runway that allows her and Nico to interact more closely with the crowd who paid good money to see us. She and Nico make sure to connect with every corner of the auditorium. Watching her on the big screen on the side of the stage brings a huge smile to my face. She's as beautiful as ever, probably more so, because she's happy. Maris has grown more than any of us over the last few years. She takes her role as a wife seriously, and when she became a mom, she grew two more hearts and found stamina I can't come close to matching. The evolution of her musicality, amid all the rest of it, is what makes me respect her most. Her playing and writing have become nuanced to the point where her techniques are being copied by other bass players. I love that for her. And she still rocks cut-off denim shorts like a supermodel even after carrying Van Asten twins.

Nico holds the neck of his guitar higher than usual. He's looking for hits, so I land a succession of off time stops and starts with him as Max and Maris follow along. We all laugh like the geeks we are, but we're still having fun together on stage, and that's what matters most. It's been a long tour. We need a break, and our families do too, but I'll miss having a calendar full of stadium dates. In order to get back out here, we have to write another album, our third, and then go through all the steps it takes to promote it and put a full tour together. That's the hard part. Playing is the easy part.

I look over at Max who is grinning from ear to ear. I remember the shy, long-haired, skinny kid who joined our band and moved into our house hoping to meet girls. He's self-confident now. Even has his own brand of swagger. He was pretty torn up when Rachel broke things off. They tried to make the long-distance thing work, they really did. But in the end, it was too hard. Then, on a video shoot, Max met a still photographer named Daphne, and they fit. They were pregnant with Harry a year after they got together, and they're really great parents. They have no interest in getting married, or sharing a domicile, but they spend a lot of family time together and support each other's non-traditional careers. It's working, and everyone involved is happy, loved, and thriving.

Nico is taking another guitar solo on a song that he and Maris wrote a few years back. He didn't come to suck, so I lock in to listen to where he wants to take the song. God, he's good. His fans call themselves Nicophiles. Getting married somehow raised his Sexiest Man Alive status and becoming a father earned him universal adoration. He's exactly the same as when he was broke, and no one knew who he was. Relaxed, funny, protective, laser-focused on his music, and Maris's biggest fan. He's a doting father, but he gives the boys a lot of room to roam. He wants them to have the wild childhood he had, and the Van Astens are going to spend the summer in the cabin they own in the Northwoods of Wisconsin to facilitate that goal. Ava and I are going to have to go visit because Pearl won't know how to live without those boys. Probably Max and Harry too. We're going to have to plan that.

It's time for Silver Springs and the stage crew brings stools out for Maris and Nico. The video production team plays a clip from the YouTube video that put us on the map, followed by snippets from early concerts, and other notable milestones that brought us to this moment. The crowd loves it, and the four of us always make eye contact while the video plays. I feel myself getting choked up and have to hide my face behind my hand for a minute. Then Nico's behind me giving me a combination hug/headlock. Before I know it, Maris and Max are at the drum stand. The video is still playing, and we stand with our arms around one another to watch it. We're all crying happy tears. Part of me wants to go back and take this ride all over again. But the ride isn't over, and Ava and Pearl are on it with me now.

When the video ends, Maris talks to the crowd. "Miami, you were the first city to support us. You came to see our band when we played Club Fish—" the crowd cheers. "We're so happy to be home. Tonight is the final night of a tour that's dominated the last eighteen months of our lives." The audience whistles and cheers again. "We're going to take some time to write new music, but we won't forget you, so please don't forget us!" Cell phones light the arena. "This isn't good-bye, it's see ya soon. But we have a few more songs to do for you tonight and this will always be one of my favorite song to sing because it changed our lives, and I get to look into my sexy husband's eyes while I sing it." The crowd cheers as Max, Nico, and Maris take their places on stage again.

When I sing the background lyrics now, they don't hurt. I'm no longer upset that Maris didn't let me love her. Ava is the yang to my yin, and she was on her way to me back then, I just didn't know it. Ava knows that I loved Maris once, but she understands and says that she loves her, too, and sees how that could be confusing for a dude. We had a big church wedding. Nico was my best man, Maris was a bridesmaid alongside Ava's sisters, and Max played the music for the ceremony. It was the happiest day of my life. Until Pearl was born. Ava can work remotely most of the time, so my girls have been with me on tour. Pearl doesn't remember a time when she didn't have a lanyard. She's so smart and beautiful. She wants to learn to play piano, and bass, and guitar.

Anything but drums, which Nico thinks is hilarious. As much as I don't want this show to end, I'm looking forward to putting Pearl to sleep in her own bed tonight and doing everything I can to keep Ava from falling asleep in ours. She takes good care of me and Pearl, and I love the idea of having little else to focus on beyond taking care of her in the coming months. She carried a lot during the tour. Juggled a lot. Now it's my turn to take as much off shoulders as I can.

Silver Springs ends and we're on the last song of the night. My emotions are in my throat. Maris's voice is breaking up here and there as she sings, so Nico places his back against hers, literally propping her up. Max and I make eye contact and the heaviness of the moment registers. We will share this moment again, but it will take a couple years. The kids will be older, which might make things easier, but also might make things more complicated. We will need tutors on the next tour. I chuckle to myself as I imagine the kids doing school while we rehearse, travel, and perform. We finish the song with a huge build-up, the way Nico likes to end. The stage lights go out and the audience starts chanting, "FUNKENGROOVIN', FUNKENGROOVIN'!" I hear Maris chanting along into her mic and the crowd goes nuts. Nico, Max, and I join in, and we're sharing our pre-performance hype chant with twenty-thousand people. That's when little feet start running across the stage. Pearl jumps into my lap, Vince goes for Maris while Vaughn beelines for Nico, and Harry clings to Max's leg.

Nico takes to the mic. "There's always someone younger and more handsome trying to take my job," he jokes. "Groovers, welcome our littles, this is Vaughn, Vince, Harry, and Pearl!" The kids giggle and clap along as the audience cheers. "This crew can dance, so keep your eyes on them as we do one more song before we tuck these minis into bed for the night. We love you, Miami. Thank you for taking this journey with us, and we will see you soon!"

I count us into the last song, and the kids gather center stage to dance. Vaughn notices that they're on the big screen and shows the others who smile, wave, and show off their moves. Nico smiles at me and I crack up at our little hams. Ava takes video from the wings, and I blow her a kiss. Maris and Nico dance with the kids while Max watches with amusement. I see Ava greet Daphne, and I get Max's attention to let him know she arrived. His face goes from happy to ecstatic. Daphne has a camera and begins shooting stills. The photos will show the tears streaming across my cheeks, but they will also show the smile of a humbled and grateful man. Nico raises his guitar neck and squares up with Maris. The kids jump into the air and land on the down beat. There's a deafening crescendo of appreciation and then … it's over. The stage goes dark, but the crew lights the wings. The kids run to greet Daphne and the four of us are alone. I step down from the drum riser and walk to center stage where Nico, Maris, and Max are standing. Without a word, we lock into a four-way hug. The four of us know what no one else could. There's so much love and gratitude in this circle. The photo that Daphne takes will become our next album cover, but we don't know that yet. In this moment, all we're aware of is the synergy of our four musical souls, and the lightening in a bottle we can only capture together.

LET'S KEEP IN TOUCH!

Website: www.marcisvoice.com
Instagram: marciviolagiebels_writes